PRAISE FOR THE NOVELS
OF KAREN WHITE

The Strangers on Montagu Street

"Hard to put down . . . a smorgasbord of literary enjoyment. [White's] characters are completely delicious and the Charleston locales add the seasoning." —The Huffington Post

"Charming and complex living characters, combined with unsettled ghosts that balance uncanny creepiness with very human motivations, keep this story warm, real, and exciting." —*Publishers Weekly*

"Her best book yet . . . spooky, sensual, suspenseful . . . simply put, this is a book you'll read and pass immediately to a friend because it's just too good not to share." —Southern Literary Review

"White's latest will keep you in its grip from first page to last." —*RT Book Reviews*

"White captures the true essence of Charleston by intertwining the sights and smells of the historic town with an enchanting story filled with ghostly spirits, love, and forgiveness . . . a once-in-a-lifetime series." —Fresh Fiction

The Girl on Legare Street

"Karen White delivers the thrills of perilous romance and the chills of ghostly suspense, all presented with Southern wit and charm." —*New York Times* bestselling author Kerrelyn Sparks

"If you have ever been fascinated by things that go bump in the night, then this is a bonus book for you . . . will have her faithful fans gasping." —The Huffington Post

"In *The Girl on Legare Street*, [White] embraces Charleston's mystical lore, its history, its architecture, its ambience, and its ghosts." —*Lowcountry Weekly* (SC)

"Elements of history, romance, and humor. I couldn't wait to see what was going to happen next." —BellaOnline

continued . . .

"Beautifully written, with interesting, intelligent characters and a touch of the paranormal. The story is . . . dark [and] ofttimes scary."

—Fresh Fiction

The House on Tradd Street

"Engaging . . . a fun and satisfying read."　　　—*Publishers Weekly*

"*The House on Tradd Street* has it all: mystery, romance, and the paranormal, including ghosts with quirky personalities."　　—BookLoons

Falling Home

"This sweet book is highly recommended."　　　　　　—*Booklist*

The Beach Trees

"[White] describes the land and location of the story in marvelous detail. . . . [This is what] makes White one of the best new writers on the scene today."　　　　　　　　　　　—The Huffington Post

"More than just a 'beach read.' It's a worthy novel to read any time of year—any time you wonder if it's possible to start anew, regardless of the past."　　　　　　　　　　　　　　—*The Herald-Sun* (NC)

The Memory of Water

"Beautifully written and as lyrical as the tides. *The Memory of Water* speaks directly to the heart and will linger in yours long after you've read the final page. I loved this book!"

—Susan Crandall, author of *Pitch Black*

"Karen White delivers a powerfully emotional blend of family secrets, Lowcountry lore, and love in *The Memory of Water*—who could ask for more?"　　　　　　　—Barbara Bretton, author of *Just Desserts*

Learning to Breathe

"White creates a heartfelt story full of vibrant characters and emotion that leaves the reader satisfied yet hungry for more from this talented author."　　　　　　　　　　　　　　　　—*Booklist*

"You savor every single word . . . a perfect 10."

—Romance Reviews Today

**More Praise for the Novels
of Karen White**

"The fresh voice of Karen White intrigues and delights."

—Sandra Chastain, contributor to *At Home in Mossy Creek*

"Warmly Southern and deeply moving."

—*New York Times* bestselling author Deborah Smith

"Karen White writes with passion and poignancy."

—Deb Stover, award-winning author of *Mulligan Magic*

"Karen White is one author you won't forget. . . . This is a masterpiece in the study of relationships. Brava!"   —Reader to Reader Reviews

"This is not only romance at its best—this is a fully realized view of life at its fullest."   —Readers & Writers Ink Reviews

"*After the Rain* is an elegantly enchanting Southern novel. . . . Fans will recognize the beauty of White's evocative prose."

—WordWeaving.com

"In the tradition of Catherine Anderson and Deborah Smith, Karen White's *After the Rain* is an incredibly poignant contemporary bursting with Southern charm."

—Patricia Rouse, Rouse's Romance Readers Groups

"Don't miss this book!"   —*Rendezvous*

Titles by Karen White

RETURN TO TRADD STREET

KAREN WHITE

Berkley
New York

BERKLEY
An imprint of Penguin Random House LLC
375 Hudson Street, New York, NY 10014

Copyright © 2014 by Karen White
Penguin Random House supports copyright. Copyright fuels creativity,
encourages diverse voices, promotes free speech, and creates a vibrant culture.
Thank you for buying an authorized edition of this book and for complying with
copyright laws by not reproducing, scanning, or distributing any part of it
in any form without permission. You are supporting writers and allowing
Penguin Random House to continue to publish books for every reader.

BERKLEY and the BERKLEY & B colophon are registered trademarks of
Penguin Random House LLC.

Library of Congress Cataloging-in-Publication Data

White, Karen (Karen S.)
Return to Tradd Street/Karen White.
pages cm
ISBN 978-0-451-24059-0 (pbk.)
1. Women real estate agents—Fiction. 2. Women psychics—Fiction. 3. Haunted
houses—Fiction. 4. Historic buildings—South Carolina—Charleston—Fiction.
5. Charleston (S.C.)—Fiction. I. Title.
PS3623.H5776R48 2014
813'.6—dc23 2013032459

New American Library trade paperback edition / January 2014
Berkley trade paperback edition / November 2018

Printed in India
9th Printing

Cover painting by Andrew Haines
Book design by Alissa Amell

This is a work of fiction. Names, characters, places, and incidents either are the product of
the author's imagination or are used fictitiously, and any resemblance to actual persons,
living or dead, business establishments, events, or locales is entirely coincidental.

To my readers, whose enthusiasm for Jack, Melanie, Nola, General Lee, and the rest of the characters encouraged me to continue their story

Acknowledgments

Thank you to the people of Charleston, South Carolina, for your warm hospitality and dedication to historical preservation, which allows people like me to appreciate the beauty and history of the Holy City. Thanks also to Lisa Estes of the Preservation Society of Charleston for your insight into the people and customs of your native city.

And thank you for the patience and assistance of my good friend Diane Wise, RN, MSN, CNM, for all the extremely helpful information regarding pregnancy and childbirth. Despite having gone through both twice, there's still so much I didn't know!

Greatest thanks to Martha and Bill Buckley for your help with Citadel customs and uniforms. I hope you don't mind my picking your brain for future books! You're too good of a resource to utilize just once.

A big hug goes to my dog, Quincy (the inspiration for General Lee), who patiently sits by my side as I type every word, and to my dear friends Susan Crandall and Wendy Wax, who unwearyingly read each word before it is published.

Thanks also to Tim, Meghan, and Connor, who have learned how to live with a writer and know better than to comment that dinner isn't on the table or that I've worn the same sweats for the past week when I'm on deadline. I love you!

RETURN TO
TRADD STREET

CHAPTER 1

My eyes flickered open in my Tradd Street bedroom, where splinters of light fed slowly into the room through the plantation shutters. The gossamer curtains that my mother had thought would add a touch of femininity to the otherwise masculine space moved softly from cool air being blown out the vent hidden in the wide baseboard. A wet nose and furry ear pressed against my cheek as General Lee's tail fanned my face. Yet none of these creature comforts eased the tightening in my chest that had seized me upon waking as the reality of my life once again came crashing down on my head like an avalanche with no impediments. Despite a lifetime of being in control of my destiny, and what I thought was a fulfilling life of purpose as a successful Realtor, I found myself in the most incomprehensible and extraordinary predicament: I was forty years old, single, and—most baffling of all—pregnant.

I glanced over at my bedside table to the small domed anniversary clock that had belonged to the home's previous owner, Nevin Vanderhorst. Like most everything else in the bedroom and the rest of the house, I'd kept it, although I wasn't altogether sure why. I liked to tell myself it was because the house would be easier to sell if I didn't put too much of a personal stamp on it. But sometimes, like now, I imagined I could hear Mr. Vanderhorst's voice telling me about the love he had for his family's ancestral home. *It's a piece of history you can hold in your hands.* I hadn't really understood what he'd meant at first, but now I was afraid I was beginning to.

I was wary of understanding that connection between history and family. Despite being a native Charlestonian with my own baggage of family trees and old houses, I'd done very well without it for nearly thirty-three years, after all. At least until my mother, who had abandoned me when I was six years old, decided it was time we reconciled.

I squinted at the round face of the clock, silently cursing my decision not to replace my electric clock with a similar one—except with even larger, brighter neon numbers I could read without my glasses. I fumbled in the bedside drawer before finding my glasses and sticking them on my nose. Seven thirty. I jerked up, mortified that I had once again slept in. Not that anyone ever got to Henderson House Realty before nine, but since I'd begun my employment there I'd been like Old Faithful, always at my desk by eight o'clock. It's what had put my name on the sales leaderboard in Mr. Henderson's office every single quarter since my first year. A record I'd kept until recently.

I'd begun to swing my legs to the side of the bed when the room tilted and the contents of my stomach left over from the night before began to jostle for attention. Groaning, I lay back down on the pillow, feeling no better despite a wet swipe from General Lee's tongue. A brief tapping on the door was followed by the appearance of Mrs. Houlihan, my housekeeper, entering the room carrying a plate of saltines.

"Seems I got here just in time. Your mama told me to have these on your bedside table each morning. You're supposed to eat a couple before you even raise your head off the pillow."

I'd inherited Mrs. Houlihan along with the dog and the house. Although I was still having doubts about the benefits of the latter two, Mrs. Houlihan was worth her weight in gold. And, after studying her broad chest and ample hips, I realized that would be a considerable amount, indeed.

"Thank you, Mrs. Houlihan," I said as I took a proffered cracker and stuck it on my dry tongue. I left it there to dissolve, afraid that if I moved my mouth too much my stomach would protest. I closed my eyes to keep the room from spinning and heard the sound again. It was what had awakened me, forgotten as soon as consciousness had claimed me.

"Did you hear that?" I asked, lying very still so I could both hear better and wouldn't throw up from any sudden movement.

"Hear what?" Her eyes met mine.

The sound was so small it would have been easy to ignore. Except that it was accompanied by a rush of frigid air, like the door to a tomb had just been opened.

"A baby crying," I said. As if he could hear it, too, General Lee jumped off the bed and ran out the door. I told myself it was because he was hungry and was searching for food in the kitchen.

She smiled and moved to the door. "No babies in this house—at least not yet. Maybe you're hearing a cat on the sidewalk. Or your ears are playing tricks on you to help you practice for what's to come." She stopped and faced me again, her bulk filling the doorway. "I'll make you some of that decaffeinated green tea Nola brought over for you. Just lay down and keep eating crackers until you feel like you can sit up." She pointed to the small handbell that my mother had placed next to the clock. "And just give me a ring if you need me."

A loud, grinding motor started under my window, making me jump. "What's that?" I asked, spitting saltine crumbs into the neck of my nightgown.

"That contractor Rich Kobylt is here doing the cleanup from the foundation work. He said he'd told you last week so you'd know to park your car on the street so he could have access to the rear garden."

Through a haze of nausea, I allowed my glance to fall on my Black-Berry and new iPhone—neither of which I'd turned on since yesterday, when I'd struggled in from work and fallen into bed around six p.m. I vaguely recalled a conversation with Mr. Kobylt, even remembered that I'd successfully avoided a full view of his rear cleavage from his ubiquitous drooping pants. I might even have put a note on my various calendars, none of which were any good to me with their power buttons in the off position. My desk calendar at the office was filled with doodles of He-Who-Would-Not-Be-Mentioned, showing him in crudely drawn vignettes in various medieval-type death throes, instead of carefully penned-in appointments. I closed my eyes and groaned.

"Don't you worry. Your daddy came by earlier and moved your car so you could sleep a little longer. Take your time, and just holler at me if you need something. I'll go feed General Lee."

As if he'd heard his name, a sharp bark came from downstairs. Before my pregnancy-induced morning sickness, he and I had shared a biological need to be fed at specific times throughout the day. Anybody could have set their clocks on either his barks or my increased whinniness. Now the thought of food completely unnerved me. I hurled myself out of bed and barely made it to the bathroom in time.

An hour and a half later, I struggled downstairs. After rewashing the ends of my hair and replacing my makeup three times from subsequent trips to relieve my stomach of all its contents and then some, I'd given up. I'd swiped my hair back into a ponytail and put a little powder on my nose. I didn't bother with my glasses, as I was truly uninterested in seeing the results of my toilette.

Two slices of dry toast—gluten free, wheat free, and taste free—sat on a plate on the table next to the steaming cup of promised decaffeinated green tea. Across the table sat my mother, former opera diva Ginnette Prioleau—looking as if she'd just stepped out of an ad for Gwynn's department store. Although in her sixties, she could have easily passed for somebody at least a decade younger, or even a brunette version of Dolly Parton, without the accent and with a slightly smaller bust. My only consolation with this whole pregnancy thing was that for the first time in my life I had a reason to be wearing an undergarment that didn't resemble a training bra.

I sat down in front of the toast and tried not to picture a chocolate doughnut. "Good morning, Mother. What brings you here so early?"

She took a short sip from her cup. "Do I need a reason? You're my only child, about to give birth to my first grandchild—isn't that enough?"

I eyed her warily. "Nola called you, didn't she?"

Nola, the teenage daughter of He-Who-Would-Not-Be-Mentioned, and I had formed a bond after her arrival in Charleston earlier that year following the death of her mother, Bonnie, in California. She'd been living with my mother and me in my mother's house on Legare Street until recently, when my home was deemed fit to live in again after an enormous—and bank account–emptying— foundation repair. She was quirky, funny, musically gifted, and smart, and if it hadn't been for her unfortunate choice of fathers, she would have been the perfect teenager.

"She's worried about you. She hasn't heard from you since you moved back here, and Jack won't talk to her about you, either."

I glared up at her. "You know we don't mention that name around here."

I felt Mrs. Houlihan behind me and pictured her raising her eyebrows at my mother.

"Melanie, darling. You and Jack are going to be parents to the same baby. Sooner or later you're going to have to talk to him. And the ball's in your court, you know. He *did* ask you to marry him, and you said no. I think you at least owe him an explanation." Her look of expectation made it clear that she believed that Jack wasn't the only one to whom an explanation was owed.

With exaggerated patience, I said, "I told him no for the same reason Bonnie didn't tell him about Nola—because she knew that as a gentleman he would offer to do the right thing. Well, I don't want to be the 'right thing.' He's already made it clear that he doesn't love me, and I don't want to marry for any other reason." I felt those infernal tears welling again. "And I'm certainly not going to waste my time chasing after him to make him change his mind."

"But he *does* love you, Mellie. I know he does."

I tried to snort, but it came out as a half sob. "Right. Then why did he respond with, 'I'm sorry,' when I told him that I loved him?" I picked up a piece of toast and bit into it, if only to hide the telltale quivering of my lip. Pregnancy hormones coupled with a rejected declaration of love and a marriage proposal based on pity had wreaked havoc on my self-confidence and backbone. I wasn't sure whether I could ever recover. Besides, I'd lived my life on the premise that if you pretended something wasn't there it would eventually go away. At least, it usually worked where dead spirits were concerned.

"It's all not going to go away, you know, if you ignore it." My mother, apparently a mind reader as well as a psychic, arched one eyebrow at me.

I focused on my tea and toast, careless of the crumbs that fell on my navy blue skirt and jacket. The skirt was being held together with a rubber band and paper clips, the jacket buttoned strategically over it to disguise my handiwork. Unfortunately, the straining button was attached to the jacket with only thread and a prayer.

I felt my mother's gaze on me and slowly raised my eyes.

"I also had a dream," she said quietly.

The room fell silent except for the sound of Mrs. Houlihan washing something in the sink and General Lee slurping up his food. My mother didn't have normal dreams, and we both knew it. She had "visions." The last vision had brought her back into my life to save it. For her to be having another could be no less monumental.

"What was it about?" I asked as I swallowed dry toast with my tea.

"A crying baby."

The food stuck in my throat. "A crying baby?"

Her eyes narrowed. "You've heard it, too, then."

I rolled my eyes, realizing too late that I probably looked like Nola. "Can't I have any secrets from you?"

She smiled softly. "Not really, no." Pushing her cup away, she said, "It might not be related to you and your pregnancy, though."

I stared back at her.

"I felt something when I heard the crying. Something powerful, and not necessarily good. But it felt detached, like it wasn't connected to me exactly, but wanted to announce its presence." She paused—a pause that, in another situation, I would have called a pregnant one. She continued. "And maybe ask for help."

I shivered as my mother watched me closely. I already had too many complications in my life and I wasn't eager to introduce one more. I'd been telling myself I'd imagined the sound, that it had nothing to do with me. That one more person, living or dead, wasn't asking something of me that I wasn't prepared to give.

I looked down at my empty plate. The ability to communicate with the dead was something my mother and I shared. Our ability was something she referred to as a gift but that I'd always considered a goiter on my neck. Although I'd been unaware of it at the time, it was what had torn us apart when I was a child, but was also what had brought us together again. I was thankful for that, and thankful that we'd been able to send a few troubled spirits into the light without calling too much attention to ourselves. But my own spirit was too troubled to concern itself with things that went bump in the night. Or cried out in the early-morning hours.

With forced conviction, I said, "I've owned this house long enough to know its ghosts. We sent Louisa Vanderhorst and Joseph Longo to their just rewards and I haven't seen them or Nevin Vanderhorst since. There are a few contented spirits lingering and we are mutually happy to leave one another alone. There's definitely no baby, or reason for a baby to be here."

"That we know of," my mother added.

I was about to argue when there was a knock on the door, and my mother and I locked gazes, feeling the same knot of dread in the place where the heart meets the soul.

Mrs. Houlihan went to the door and let in my plumber/contractor, Rich Kobylt. Since I'd originally inherited the house on Tradd Street, Rich had become as much a fixture here as the falling plaster and cracked foundation. I often wondered whether I should keep a room for him and charge him rent. Anything to help support the never-ending restoration work on the house.

He stepped into the kitchen, then hitched up his drooping pants before he spoke, and I shrank back. That was always a sign that he had bad news for me, and was always accompanied by the imaginary sound in my head of a cash register *cha-ching*ing as more money was sucked out of my bank account.

"Mornin', Miz Middleton, Miz Prioleau." He nodded to both of us. Mrs. Houlihan brought him a large mug of coffee, two sugars and one dollop of creamer, and placed it in his hands. I should charge him for that, too, I thought. I didn't ask him to sit down, mistakenly believing that the less time he spent in my presence, the less money I'd be forced to spend. Once again, the image of a parking lot on this particular spot on Tradd Street loomed in my head in an enticing way.

"What's wrong?" I asked, speaking the two words that always followed my greeting to him.

He held the steaming mug but didn't drink from it, and I noticed that he was paler than usual under his hat. I'd realized shortly after he'd begun to work on the restoration of the house that he was sensitive to restless spirits and that they sometimes made their presence known to him in disconcerting ways. I still couldn't tell whether he was in denial or if he really didn't realize that when paint cans kept emptying themselves, there was more to it than just pranksters or his inability to remember using up all the paint.

He looked at me apologetically, and I let all the air in my lungs expel in a long wheeze. "It's not another foundation problem, if that's what you're thinking," he said.

"That's a relief." I kept my gaze on his face, trying to determine whether he was telling me the truth. "So what is it?"

He jacked up his pants again, as if stalling for time, and it seemed that he was as reluctant to tell me as I was to hear. "Well, you know we've been making a big pile of mess in your back garden as we excavated the old foundation and replaced it. We didn't really pay much attention to the stuff we yanked out, because we knew we couldn't use it again. Well, today I've got a dump truck and a loader to clear all that stuff away, and in the middle of the second load that's when we saw it."

If possible, his face went a bit paler.

My mother stood, and I saw that her hand was shaking slightly. She reached for me and touched my fingers, an electric current seeming to jolt between us. I grasped her hand in mine, remembering our shared mantra as we'd faced our most adversarial spirits: *We are stronger than you.*

"Saw what?" I asked, my voice surprisingly normal.

He glanced behind him, as if he were afraid that whatever he'd unearthed had snuck up behind him. A shiver went through me and I half suspected that he might be right.

"Bones. In a small wooden box. Definitely human." His hand shook a little, sloshing coffee over the side of his mug. "A baby."

My mother grasped my hand harder as our gazes met, the weight of the world pressing down on me as the thought ricocheted through my brain and rained down on my already ruined life: *Here we go again.*

CHAPTER 2

I sat on the sofa in the front parlor with my mother on one side and my father on the other. I hadn't asked either one of them to be there, but I'd almost wept with gratitude when they'd selected their spots on the sofa. I was getting a little too familiar with police lights, yellow crime-scene tape, and dead bodies hidden on my property, but it was still a shock. I'd just barely recovered from finding the remains of Louisa Vanderhorst and Joseph Longo in the fountain less than two years before, and now apparently there was another body bricked into the foundation of the house. I was beginning to take it personally.

We faced Detective Thomas Riley, whose large frame was folded into one of two matching Chippendale chairs. He had light brown hair bleached blond on the ends, as if he spent a lot of time outdoors, and warm brown eyes set in a face of hard lines and angles that could have been the model for G.I. Joe. Maybe it was my raging pregnancy hormones, but I couldn't stop staring at him. There was something about Charleston men. Perhaps it was the pluff mud of Charleston's surrounding marshes or the summer heat that baked the soles of your shoes if you left them on the pavement too long that seeped into the bloodstreams of soon-to-be mamas pregnant with boys. Even if one chose to include He-Who-Would-Not-Be-Mentioned in that estimation.

"Are you from Charleston?" I asked before I was even aware that I'd opened my mouth.

He looked at me in surprise and I realized that while I'd been day-dreaming about how well his biceps filled his shirt and how big his feet had to be to fit in those large shoes, he'd probably been discussing the human remains found in the foundation of my house.

"Yes, I am. My mother's actually from Ireland, but my father was born and raised here. Both he and my grandfather were with the Charleston Police Department, but I'm the first detective in the family." He grinned, making my hormones dance a little jig, but I still couldn't shake the feeling that no matter how nice the smile, it would always pale in comparison to another smile on another handsome face, a face that still haunted my dreams at night.

Disconcerted, I sat back. My mother, apparently trying to answer the detective's question that had been directed at me, said, "Melanie's only owned the house for about two years. I'm afraid she doesn't know much about the house's history except that it belonged to the Vanderhorst family since it was built in 1848. She inherited it from Nevin Vanderhorst."

"Is he a family relation?"

I sat up, knowing where his line of questioning was headed. "No. I met him when I was called here to see about listing his house for sale. But then he died suddenly, and he left the house to me."

Detective Riley's pen paused over his notepad. "You only met Mr. Vanderhorst once, yet he left this house to you?"

"Trust me, I was pretty surprised, too. My grandfather and his father were best friends, so that must have been enough of a family connection for him." I decided to leave out the part about how I could see the ghost of Louisa Vanderhorst, Nevin's mother, in the garden, and how he'd been under the impression that she approved of me. That approval, coupled with the fact that he had no known next of kin, was enough for him to make me the very reluctant heiress to his crumbling house and all of its ghosts. Not to mention a dog and housekeeper, too.

He raised his eyebrows. "You must have some serious powers of persuasion."

I blushed. "There was no persuasion going on, believe me. I hate old houses."

Technically, this was said more from rote than from any lingering convictions, but I didn't want him to think—as many people did—that I had coerced Mr. Vanderhorst in any way. At the time, I'd seen this house as a great, gaping money pit with the potential to be a revenue-producing parking lot. I didn't completely believe that anymore, but I couldn't in all honesty say that thoughts of dousing the foundation with gasoline and striking a match didn't occur to me from time to time. Especially following a conversation with Rich Kobylt in which I'd been told that something else major and expensive needed to be fixed.

"But isn't your specialty historic Charleston real estate?"

I smiled patiently. "Yes, but that's because I can view the properties without bias. Generally speaking, though, old houses and I don't get along."

He leaned back and put his pen down, as if indicating that what he was about to ask me was off the record. "Why is that?"

I nodded. "I have several reasons." I shot a glance toward my mother. "But mostly because the cost of upkeep and restoration seem to be at odds with any kind of retirement plan. They're sort of like adult children who never leave home and expect you to support them forever."

A corner of his mouth quirked upward. "I see," he said, once again putting pen to paper. His warm brown eyes met mine. "Apparently I'm going to have to dig into the Vanderhorst family history to get a better idea of who the remains might belong to. There were a few other items found along with the remains that also might offer up a clue or two."

I didn't ask what those might be. I was happy to dump the whole problem on him so that my foundation work could be completed and I could begin to rebuild my life. Wanting this whole thing to be over as soon as possible, I said, "You might want to contact Dr. Sophie Wallen-Arasi. She's a professor at the College of Charleston in the historical preservation department and for some reason is completely fascinated with this house. She knows a lot about the house's history and would love to tell you all about it. Just make sure that you have a couple of hours to listen." Sophie was my best friend, a pairing that might be considered one of the wonders of the world. She was tofu to my hamburger, Birkenstocks to my Tory Burch flats, and Goodwill thrift shop to my King Street boutiques. But I loved her like a sister— most of the time—and couldn't imagine life without her.

I continued. "She and her new husband, Chad Arasi, took a month-long honeymoon to Angola to teach green farming techniques to local farmers, but they'll be back next Thursday."

He raised his eyebrows at me again, but I didn't elaborate. There were many things even a best friend couldn't explain.

Mrs. Houlihan had placed several pastries on a plate when she'd brought in our coffee. As my parents chatted with Detective Riley, I nonchalantly scooted to the edge of the sofa to make it easier to reach the plate without anybody noticing. I was still hungry, and too thrilled to be showing signs of an appetite to restrict myself. My hand was halfway to the plate when the pulling at my midsection suddenly eased and the single button on my jacket gave up and shot from the broken thread like a bullet, ricocheting off the silver coffee urn and hitting Detective Riley squarely in the middle of his forehead.

"Ouch," he said, half standing from his seated position, his move toward his gun halted midway when he spotted the offending object on the coffee table.

Mrs. Houlihan, standing in the doorway, saw the bright red mark on the detective's forehead and began a hasty retreat. "I'll go get some ice for that."

"I am so sorry," I said, mortified.

Detective Riley's gaze settled on my midsection with a questioning look in his eyes.

"She's expecting," my mother said in a conciliatory tone similar to the one she'd used to talk me into wearing the low-cut red gown for my fortieth birthday party that had gotten me in this predicament to begin with. "And she hasn't had a chance to shop for maternity clothes yet."

"Oh," he said, a confused look passing over his face. "I didn't re-alize you were married. . . ."

"She's not," my parents said in unison.

I cringed, trying to disappear inside the upholstery.

The detective actually looked flustered. "I'm sorry; of course I know better than to make assumptions." He smiled and, apparently calling on the charm that was inbred in all Charleston boys, he added, "I guess I just always assume that all the beautiful women are already taken."

"Oh, she's definitely available." We all turned to find Jack approaching us from the foyer, followed by Mrs. Houlihan holding a bag of frozen peas and a dish towel. She hastily wrapped the bag in the towel and handed it to Detective Riley.

"Mother!" I shot her an accusatory glance. There was only one reason Jack had landed on my doorstep.

Jack laid a package from Blue Bicycle Books on the coffee table, then greeted my parents, shaking my father's hand and kissing my mother on her cheek. He slowly straightened, a decidedly frosty blue gaze directed at me. "Hello, Mellie. It's been a while."

Granted, he had every reason to be angry with me. When one's marriage proposal is rejected, the object of the proposal should expect some sort of animosity. But in the month since, he hadn't called, or sent a message, or even sent Nola over to reason with me. Or to ask me why. Not that any of it would have changed my mind. But it was as if I, and our baby, had simply ceased to exist for him. For a while I'd made myself believe that that's how I wanted it. Now, after seeing him and experiencing that little bump in blood pressure he always caused, I wondered how I'd even managed to get out of bed each day. Still, he looked way too good to be a jilted lover, and that just made me angrier.

"Hello, Jack." I was proud of how neutral I kept my tone. "Are you lost? The erectile dysfunction clinic is on Broad Street. This is Tradd."

My mother shot me a warning look. "I called Jack because he's always been so good at this mystery-solving thing that I thought he could be of some help."

"Jack? Jack Trenholm the writer?" Detective Riley stood, still clutching his frozen peas and towel in his left hand. The mark on his head was beginning to swell and darken, leaving me to wonder what he would tell people. I sank down lower in the sofa, all thoughts of pastries gone from my mind at the same speed as the flying button.

Jack eyed the detective warily, sizing him up. "Yes, I am. And you are . . . ?"

"Detective Thomas Riley of the Charleston Police Department." He stuck out his hand and the two men shook. "I'm a huge fan. My parents and sisters and I have been waiting for your next book. We don't recall having ever had to wait this long between books from you."

A dark shadow passed over Jack's face. His nemesis and my onetime suitor, businessman Marc Longo, had somehow managed to scoop Jack's last story, a story centered around the disappearance of Louisa Vanderhorst. Although Jack had been given another story to write by the late Julia Manigault about her own family, losing to Marc Longo was not something from which he'd easily recover. Or that he'd forgive.

Jack smiled tightly. "Yes, well, there were unexpected delays. But I'm hoping to have another book out sometime next year."

Jack looked at the bag of peas in the detective's hand, then up to his forehead, as if noticing the growing knot for the first time. "Did Mellie hit you?"

"Not exactly." Thomas looked between Jack and me as if trying to figure something out, his eyes widening in apparent understanding. "Why? Has she hit you before?"

I stood. "Now, wait just a minute . . ." I began, looking at my parents for moral support, but they were both busy studying the thread count of the Aubusson rug.

Jack interrupted. "Only figuratively."

I slowly sank back onto the sofa, unable to argue, because even underneath all of my own self-pity and righteousness, I knew that he was right. Trying to salvage the conversation, I turned my attention to the detective. "So what do we do next?"

"Nothing, really. We'll have to leave your back garden a mess, I'm afraid, until the crime-scene people have had a chance to sift through everything, so I'll need your patience. And I'll contact Dr. Wallen-Arasi when she returns from her honeymoon and see if she can shed any light on the identity of the remains and why they might be hidden in your foundation."

The ethereal sound of a mewling baby drifted around us like a wisp of smoke, so soft that I would have thought I was imagining it except for my mother's shaking hand as she placed her teacup on its saucer.

My mother's voice was a lot calmer than she appeared to be. "You said you found something else with the remains. Can you tell us what that was?"

I found myself shaking my head, although I already had a feeling that any efforts to hide from lost spirits were gone from the first moment I'd awakened to the sound of a crying baby.

"It looks to be an old lace gown and bonnet, like the kind a baby would wear when being christened. Which, at first glance, tells us that the baby wasn't simply discarded. The fact that the child was buried in the gown tells us that he or she was either baptized before burial, or the child was important enough to be buried in it."

The wailing grew loud enough that I thought that the others might hear it, but I'd learned long ago that this blessing or curse or whatever you wanted to call it was reserved for very few.

My mother stood, and everyone else stood, too. "Well, then, we don't want to take up more of your time." She took the detective's arm and began to lead him to the foyer and the front door. "Please don't hesitate to call if you have any further questions."

I was about to ask her what the hurry was, but could suddenly feel the chill blowing softly on the back of my neck, as if an unseen pair of eyes rested on it.

My father and Jack wore identical looks of concern as my mother practically threw the detective out onto the front piazza, then shut the door in his face after a perfunctory good-bye. Her chest rose and fell with exertion, her hand pressed against her heart before reaching for me.

"Do you see anybody?" she asked, my father and Jack understanding that her question hadn't been meant for them.

I shook my head without really looking, the chill on the back of my neck still intense. My mother squeezed my hand. "Mellie, have you heard the baby before today?"

"No," I whispered, knowing where she was headed.

"There's a reason why it's been silent until now. Most likely it's because of the remains being unearthed." She paused, and I tried to pull away. "Or it could also be because of your pregnancy."

Panic and denial rose in me as I struggled to find words to extricate myself.

Jack stepped toward my mother. "Is the baby in danger?"

Hormones, my swollen body and ill-fitting clothes, the cold breath on my neck, and the ghostly crying all conspired against my resolve to keep my emotions in check. I turned on Jack, the closest available candidate for my pent-up frustrations—the least being that despite all that had happened between Jack and me, I still loved him with every part of my heart that was capable of loving another person.

"You're going to start caring now? I haven't heard one word from you in a month—any concern about me or the baby—and here you are trying to interfere and pretend that this baby means anything to you." I gulped back tears and rage and impotence.

My father cleared his throat. "Actually, Mellie—"

I cut him off as I faced Jack. "What my mother is trying to say is that whoever was found in that box under the house, or whoever it was who had been missing whoever it was, thinks they've found a kindred spirit in me because I'm pregnant."

My father tried to speak again. "Mellie, Jack and your mother and I . . ."

I held up my hand, not wanting to be distracted from my tirade directed at Jack. "And apparently my mother thinks it's a duty to guide all lost souls to the light, and she probably wants my help with this one even though I can't imagine adding one more thing to my plate right now. But she and I can handle it alone, without your help. Just like this baby."

Of all the expressions I'd seen pass over Jack's face—sarcasm, humor, anger, desire—I'd never seen this one, and it scared me. His eyes, darker than ever before, widened slightly, giving him the look of someone who'd been punched unexpectedly in the gut.

Just as quickly his expression changed, like a magician whipping away his cape to display a hidden bouquet of flowers when a sword was expected. His trademark grin that graced the back covers of his bestselling novels and had slain countless women since he was out of diapers crossed his face. I braced myself.

"If my memory serves me correctly, Mellie, you didn't make that baby by yourself."

He let the words sink in, and I was acutely aware of my parents' presence and how they were both looking at everything else except Jack and me. I might have actually squirmed. I was also aware of every hair on my head standing on end, and how the cold that had started on the back of my neck now enveloped my entire body.

My brain was busy formulating a response when suddenly Jack looked up toward the Venetian glass chandelier that lit the small vestibule area inside the front door.

"Mellie!" he shouted, and before I could tell him to stop calling me Mellie, he dived for me, tackling me to the floor. He'd managed to cushion me by landing on his back with me on top of him, sprawled halfway into the main foyer and far enough away to escape the falling chandelier as it crashed onto the exact spot where I'd been standing.

I was so shocked I couldn't move for a moment, and I remained lying on top of Jack, our bodies pressed together from chest to toe.

He was breathing hard, but his eyes held their old light as they looked into mine, making me aware of just how much of him was touching me and vice versa. "Just like old times, huh, Mellie?"

With my cheeks flaming, I scrambled off of him, wishing I still had my jacket button to aim at him. Carefully avoiding the broken glass, I stepped toward my mother and father, whose focus was split between me and the ruined chandelier.

"What was that all about?" my father asked, his military career leaving him wholly unprepared for explaining the unexplainable. It had been one of the reasons why my mother had left him all those years ago.

My mother's gaze held mine, and a weary sense of resignation settled on me as we turned to face my father and Jack. I took a deep breath, remembering for that one brief second a moment when my life had been my own, when I'd been content to let the restless dead flitter unnoticed along the periphery.

"They're back," I said, the words whipped back in my face by a strong, cold breeze.

CHAPTER 3

I stepped out onto the sidewalk, letting the door to Ruth's Bakery jingle shut behind me, feeling no better than when I'd entered five minutes before. In the past, Ruth had had my bag of doughnuts and extra-cream latte ready to grab and go on the way to my office. However, my mother and soon-to-be ex–best friend, Sophie, had paid Ruth a visit in an apparent attempt to ruin my life. Clutched in my hands was a bag of two organic bran-and-broccoli muffins, as well as a tall cup of green tea without sugar. I couldn't say for certain, but judging from my first and only bite I was pretty sure that the first two ingredients on the muffin recipe were cardboard and dirt.

I walked down the sidewalk on Broad toward Henderson House Realty, ditching the bag of muffins in the first trash receptacle that I passed. I'd had such high hopes when actual hunger pangs had gripped me after the early-morning nausea, and the thought of hidden candy bars in my office lightened my step so that I was almost skipping by the time I reached my building.

I pushed open the door, pausing midstride as I made my way across the reception area. Our golf-addicted receptionist, Nancy Flaherty— apparently fully recovered from a golf-ball injury to the head—sat in her usual seat behind the desk, golf-tee earrings swinging as she greeted me. She wore her ubiquitous golf visor with the Masters logo on the brim—a souvenir from a trip to the mecca of golf, Augusta,

Georgia—and held a ball of yarn and two flashing metal knitting needles that were moving in and out of something pink and small.

Sitting next to Nancy was a slightly older woman wearing a bright yellow cardigan with golfers embroidered all over it. She, too, was knitting, but with a blue ball of yarn. I stopped in front of them with a questioning look at Nancy. "Knitting?" I asked.

"Sure am." She grinned broadly, the knitting needles not slowing. "This here's Joyce Challis," she said, indicating the woman next to her. "She and I are going to be job-sharing. After my life-threatening injury, I realized that life is too short not to spend most of it on a golf course, so I talked to Mr. Henderson, and he said if I could find and train somebody, I could job-share. As a bonus, she's teaching me how to knit."

"Where's Charlene?" I asked, recalling the petite blond yoga enthusiast who'd covered for Nancy while she was recuperating from her head injury.

Joyce and Nancy looked at each other and rolled their eyes simultaneously. "She's decided to move to California and become a movie star. I think playing an extra in that Demi Moore film kind of went to her head."

"Isn't she a grandmother?" I asked, wondering whether there was an age cutoff for moving to Hollywood to make it big.

Joyce and Nancy nodded in unison.

"It's nice to meet you, Miss Middleton," Joyce said, her blue eyes smiling. "I've heard all about you from Nancy here," she said, pointing a knitting needle at her companion. "And Jack." She made a show of fanning her face with her hand.

I frowned. "I don't expect him to be darkening our door anytime soon, so may I suggest watching a few soap operas for your daily dose of drama instead." I forced my lips into a smile. "It's nice to meet you, Joyce. I'm sure if Nancy's training you, you won't have anything to worry about."

Facing Nancy, I said, "Are there any messages for me?" Even I was surprised at how unenthusiastic my voice sounded. It was bad enough that all I wanted to do was sleep, but it was worse that everybody else could tell, too.

Joyce put down her knitting and reached for a pink slip of paper on the corner of the receptionist's desk. With a gleam in her eyes that could be described only as mischievous, she said, "Just one. From Jack Trenholm. He said he's tried your cell but he must have the wrong number, because it keeps going to voice mail, and on the recording it's a deeper voice than yours and with a slight accent."

Both Joyce and Nancy blinked innocently at me as I tried not to blush at the memory of recording the message right after Jack had left the house the previous day following the chandelier-smashing incident. Before he left, he'd kissed my mother's cheek, shaken my father's hand, then looked at my ankles and suggested I stay away from salt, closing the door a little more firmly than necessary. My mother said my hormones were making me overly sensitive to criticism, but his words had been all I'd needed to convince myself that I could handle the pregnancy and upcoming motherhood fine on my own. If only the thought didn't leave me so dark and empty—a place more terrifying than any ghostly encounter.

The pink and blue yarn suddenly registered in my brain. I peered over the desk. "What are you making?"

Nancy's needles didn't pause. "Baby blankets. Since we don't know if it's a girl or boy, we're doing one of each."

Staring at the soft-colored yarn, I felt a rumble of panic—something that was happening more and more these days but whose source I couldn't yet pinpoint. I forced myself to start thinking of spreadsheets and feeding schedules and a birthing plan that included epidurals and anesthesia and I began to calm down a little.

"I hope it's a girl," I said, the words springing from my mouth before I could call them back. Both sets of knitting needles paused. "I mean, I really just hope for a healthy child." I crumpled my lone phone message and left it on the counter. "I guess I'd better get to work."

I turned and began walking toward my office, trying to imagine a baby boy with eyes as blue as his father's, and how in the world I could find the mental and physical stamina to raise a mini Jack. Yes, I wanted a healthy child, but, dear heavens, *don't let it be a boy.*

I opened my office door and shuffled inside. The office had been rearranged back to its pre–feng shui status—something Charlene Rose had felt necessary but I had not—and I felt a little of my old self return. Even the fish in their bowl—the "water feature," as Charlene had called it—were gone, I was thankful to note. I didn't want to think about the fate of the two fish, since the thought made me teary eyed again.

I dropped my purse and briefcase unceremoniously in the middle of my office and lurched toward my credenza, where I'd stashed a bag of Halloween candy I'd found on sale at Tellis Pharmacy, before they'd closed for good, to find support hose for my ever-burgeoning ankles. I pulled open the first drawer, and then the second and the third, and then the cabinets underneath in a growing panicked frenzy. I knew I was being irrational, but I'd never been this long without processed sugar or chocolate and I was desperate.

"Is this what you're looking for? Sophie told me where to look."

I swung around to see Jack perched casually in one of the chairs facing my desk, holding up the plastic bag of miniature candy bars. His face held an expression of mild curiosity and amusement.

I swallowed heavily, torn between giving in to my sugar craving and diving at the bag, and self-preservation. The latter won. I hastily turned back to the credenza and picked up a pencil sharpener that hadn't been used in about five years. "Oh, here it is."

I sat down at my desk and pulled out a pencil from the top drawer and began to sharpen it. "I don't remember you having an appointment this morning, Jack, and I'm afraid my schedule is jam-packed—"

He interrupted, "I don't think mechanical pencils need sharpening, Mellie."

A wave of heat started somewhere in my chest, then crept up to swamp my face. I stopped grinding the hapless pencil and looked up at Jack, who was openly grinning now.

"Pregnancy hasn't changed you a bit."

"Is it supposed to?"

"I'd hoped." He held up his hand—not the one with the bag of candy—to stop me from saying more. "I didn't come here to argue. I wanted to talk with you. See how you're doing."

"I'm fine," I said quickly. *As long as I'm not thinking about you, because that makes my heart hurt and sometimes I can't even remember to breathe.* I slapped the palms of my hands against the desk as if to magically make my lie into truth, and maybe even to shake loose those thoughts.

"Why are you so mad at me? You're the one who rejected my marriage proposal." His words were quiet but intense.

I couldn't meet his eyes. "You haven't called. Or asked about the baby. I assumed you didn't care."

There was a pause before Jack spoke. "I was kind of waiting to hear from you, considering how we left it. But I've been checking in with your mother and father every day to see how you were doing. To see if you needed anything and if everything was okay with the baby."

I remembered my dad trying to interrupt me the previous day in the middle of my rant directed at Jack, and I felt the heat creeping back into my cheeks.

Jack continued. "And I've been asking all of my friends who are parents for advice on the best pregnancy books. I brought *What to Expect When You're Expecting* and a few other books over yesterday, but you didn't give me a chance to give them to you."

I resisted the impulse to crawl under my desk in utter shame and instead raised my gaze to meet his while trying to form a sentence that would be both an apology and a reproach.

He was resting his elbows against the arms of his chair and regarding me with those intense blue eyes. "You're still beautiful, you know. Maybe even more so."

My half-formed sentence flew from my head. He'd always had a knack for chiseling my defenses away one pebble at a time. But his words had been more like a wrecking ball against my castle walls. I started to smile, but then I remembered my reflection in the bathroom mirror as I'd dressed that morning—the bloated face and body, the lanky hair, and the zit on my chin. I hadn't kept Clearasil in my bathroom cabinet since I was about sixteen, and I'd dabbed on a spot of whitening toothpaste instead—an old home remedy I'd probably read in *Seventeen* magazine—and belatedly wondered whether I'd remembered to wipe it off before heading to the office.

I sat back in my chair, my stomach grumbling as I tried not to think too hard about the bag of candy in his hands. "What do you want, Jack? I'm very busy. . . ."

As if I hadn't spoken, he said, "Your eyes are brighter than I ever remember seeing them, and your face looks good with a little padding." He paused, leaning forward, his voice lowering a notch. "And your body—it's like ripening fruit." His eyes dipped for a moment to my chest, where I knew the buttons on my blouse were straining to keep it closed. His eyes rose to meet mine. "Pregnancy definitely suits you."

My hands loosened their death grip on the edge of the desk, and I looked down into my lap. "Jack, please. Don't."

"Don't shut me out. Not now."

I hadn't heard him leave his chair or come squat beside me, but he was there now, touching my cheek and wiping away a tear that I had no memory of shedding. I couldn't speak, afraid I'd start bawling like a little girl who'd fallen and scraped her knee.

Jack took my hands in his, the jolt from his touch doing wild things to my heart rhythm, and I focused on breathing in and out. He continued. "Mellie, regardless of what has gone on between the two of us or where we stand now, there's a third person we need to consider. It's no longer just about you and me. We *do* work nicely as a team—and there's no reason why we can't put our feelings aside and work together to bring this baby safely into the world, and to give him or her the best life that we can. You won't marry me, but that doesn't mean I can't be a father to our baby. Don't you agree?"

His thumb was rubbing my knuckles, threatening to interfere with my brain waves. Since the first time I'd met him, I'd found it impossible to think clearly when he was anywhere near me. That—and the infamous red dress—were mostly to blame for my current predicament.

I nodded, unable to speak any words that might be interpreted as, "You're right."

He took my hands and brought them to his mouth before kissing the back of each one. I must have suffered a ministroke, because I didn't recall him standing or pulling me up with him, his hands on my shoulders.

He was smiling widely. "You're making the right decision, Mellie. There's no reason we can't act like responsible adults for the sake of our baby." His hands were rubbing my shoulders, and it was all I could do not to melt at his feet.

Jack continued. "I'll coordinate with you regarding all your pre-natal appointments, because I don't want to miss a single one. And of course we'll want to sign up for Lamaze classes. . . ."

I woke from my daze. "Lamaze?"

"Yes, and breast-feeding classes, and we'll need to go shopping for a crib. . . ."

I sank down into my chair. "A crib?"

Jack regarded me warily. "Yeah, a crib. You don't want our baby sleeping in General Lee's crate, do you? Maybe we can convert your dressing room into a nursery, and then one of the bedrooms down the hall when the baby gets older. . . ."

I felt like a bird hurtling toward a glass window. I was going to have a *baby*. One day, that little person inside of me would want to come out and would probably even need a place to stay. And even clothes to wear. The source of my panic was starting to form a clearer picture in my mind. I blinked rapidly at Jack and he stopped talking.

"Are you all right, Mellie?"

I nodded, not completely convinced myself. But I felt buffered from the impact of whatever it was I was hurtling toward; the knowledge that Jack and I were in this together had given me a cushion from the inevitable collision.

"And that's the other reason why I came to see you today. I'm going to need a bigger place to live—with Nola and the baby it's going to be crowded in my condo."

I continued to blink and stare.

"Is something in your eye?"

I shook my head, trying to collect myself. "No. I'm just . . . surprised. Your condo is so . . . you." I wanted to say "bachelor," and "elegant," or even "holds a lot of memories—especially the couch," but I clamped my mouth shut.

"Exactly. But it's just not going to function in my life anymore, as a dad of a teenager and a baby. Time to grow up." He grinned and I was made to believe that he wasn't thinking that growing up was such a bad idea. He *was* a good father to Nola, and when I pictured him now with a tiny baby in his arms, something inside my chest thawed just a little.

I straightened in my chair, his words finally making sense to the ordered and logical part of my brain. "And you want me to help you find the perfect house for your new family?"

"Pretty much. You're always telling me you're the best Realtor in town. I won't even ask for the friends-and-family discount."

I was shaking my head before he'd stopped speaking. "This isn't a good idea, Jack. I agree that we need to find a way to parent our child, but I don't think working together to find a house is a good idea." *Because every time I look at you I relive the humiliation of saying those three little words and how you could only say, "I'm sorry."*

"But who else knows what I need more than you do? Our son or daughter will be living at least half the time with me and you'll want him or her to be in a great environment." As if that were the end of the argument, he continued. "I'd like something big—something with lots of entertaining spaces so I can throw huge birthday parties for Nola and the baby. And a big garden that has space for a little swing set—maybe even a spot for a small lap pool for Nola. Definitely something older, even historical, with lots of architectural elements and loads of character that you can't find in today's cookie-cutter McMansions. I think all the bedrooms should be on one floor—preferably upstairs—so if the baby cries at night I can be right there. . . ." He paused. "Don't you need to write this down?"

"I haven't agreed to work with you."

"But you will."

I frowned. "How would you know?"

He grinned *that* grin and I braced myself. "Because that's how it always works with us. I say something, you say no, I keep going as if you hadn't said anything, and then eventually you say yes." His gaze traveled down to my swollen belly. "Sometimes the results are unexpected, but you can't say the journey wasn't fun."

I felt my cheeks heat. "Jack . . ."

He reached across the desk and took my hand. His voice turned serious. "Please, Mellie. There's nobody else I'd trust to do this. You know Nola, and you know me. More important, you'll have control over our baby's environment. And we both know how much you enjoy controlling things." He smiled gently, taking the sting from his words.

Our eyes met and I was momentarily transported back in time. *Marry me, Mellie.* It was the first and only time he'd ever taken no for an answer from me. But we'd both moved too far beyond that point to go back and analyze or question. At least without losing a part of ourselves. Like two dogs fighting over a single bone, Jack and I had a knack for tenaciously clinging to things we didn't know how to share.

Realizing that arguing with him would be a waste of energy, I sighed. "Fine. I suppose you do need a new home, and I'd probably be perturbed if you chose another Realtor." I felt a thrill of excitement course through me at the thought of not only being back in the real estate saddle again, but also at knowing that I'd be seeing Jack on a regular basis. The latter reassured me and terrified me at the same time.

I sighed again. "When would you like to get started?"

"As soon as possible. I'm in the middle of the Manigault book, so I'm at home working most days and my schedule's flexible. I'm assuming you still have my cell number on speed dial?"

He knew me so well. "Of course. If Nola ever needed you while she was with me, I would need to get hold of you."

"Uh-huh." He stood, then moved toward the door, clutching the bag of candy. It took all my willpower not to look at the bag or beg for just a single piece. "I'll look forward to hearing from you soon." He opened the door, then looked back at me. "If you want to go maternity-clothes shopping, I'd be happy to go with you."

Straightening in my chair, I protested, "I'm barely three months pregnant. I probably won't start showing for another few months."

He didn't say anything for a moment, his smile frozen in place. "Sure. Well, good-bye then." He let himself out of the door and had almost closed it behind him before he jerked it back open. "Mellie?"

I perked up. He was going to give me a piece of candy without my asking! "Yes?"

"You really are beautiful pregnant, you know."

Before I could respond, he'd closed the door, leaving me with a mouth that kept opening and closing like a sucker-punched boxer's. I felt a cool spot on my chest, and I looked down at my blouse that I had carefully buttoned that morning and found myself wondering how long I'd sat there talking to Jack with the gaping hole where the buttons had sprung open, revealing my utilitarian—and too small—white lace bra and a wide expanse of skin.

I pressed my forehead against the top of my desk, relishing the cool feel of the wood, and considered at what moment my once carefully ordered life had suddenly veered so permanently off course, and why the thought of returning to that life filled me with so much panic.

CHAPTER 4

A few days later, I was sitting in the front parlor of my house with my feet up on the recently recovered eighteenth-century Chippendale ottoman, trying to focus on my laptop. I was in the middle of preparing a portfolio of possible homes to show Jack—not too close to Tradd Street but not too far, either—but I kept getting distracted at the sight of my slightly swollen ankles that managed to make mini muffin tops over the edges of my thick socks.

Mrs. Houlihan had already gone home and the house was silent except for the ticking of the antique grandfather clock and the sound of General Lee licking himself. I hadn't heard the crying baby since Jack's visit; nor had I heard anything from Detective Riley. I knew better than to believe that I'd heard the end of the story of the remains and why they were in my foundation, but my favorite pastime was denial, and while I sat in the quiet of my old house, I was content to think that maybe this time I was right.

General Lee's head perked up, his attention focused expectantly on the foyer. I had no idea how old he was, having inherited him, but his ears were sharper than mine. I followed his gaze toward the darkened vestibule. I was eager to replace the broken light fixture, but I'd made the mistake of mentioning it to Sophie in an e-mail and she was adamant that I wait until she returned from her honeymoon so that she could help me find a historically accurate replacement. Which actually meant overpriced and damaged in some way that would require extensive and expensive restoration—two words I had become overly familiar with since moving to 55 Tradd Street.

General Lee stood and moved toward the foyer, his plumed tail motionless where it fell over his back. I closed my laptop and listened carefully. The dog gave a soft woof at the light footfall on the outside piazza, and then a much louder woof when the doorbell rang. Relief poured through me. The dead rarely rang the doorbell to announce their presence.

I shuffled to the vestibule, not wanting to slip in my socks, and peered through the sidelight before opening the door.

"Nola!" I said, my welcome completely overwhelmed by General Lee's, who threw himself at the teenager and liberally washed her face with his tongue when she knelt down to pet him.

She laughed, craning her neck to avoid the doggy kisses aimed at her mouth.

"He's not the only one who's missed you," I said, trying to keep the reproach out of my voice.

She nuzzled her face into the dog's fluffy neck, her dark hair gleaming in the porch lights. I had to force myself not to look away when she glanced up with Jack's eyes. Nola looked like the fourteen-year-old she was supposed to be instead of the black-eyeliner-wearing waif with the combat boots and heavy attitude who'd shown up on my doorstep less than a year before.

I blinked as if needing to clear my vision as I realized what she was actually wearing: a purple-and-ivory plaid skirt and gray blazer, and black kneesocks—albeit socks to which peace-sign pins had been attached in a row on one side. I'd have to ask Sophie who'd given Nola the idea. "You've started school already?"

She grinned her father's smile and my heart seemed to slam against the wall of my chest. I almost opened my mouth to recommend she start wearing heavy makeup again so she'd stop reminding me so much of her unfortunate paternity.

Leaning down, she placed General Lee on the ground, where he stayed so he could gaze up at her adoringly. "Yeah. For a few weeks now." She crossed her arms over her chest and tried to suppress the excitement I could read on her face. "It doesn't suck too much. Well, except for math, anyway. But Alston and I are in the same French and math class, which makes it bearable." She paused. "And I'm taking piano and voice. My teacher says I should audition for the school musical." She shrugged as if she were barely able to find the energy to even talk about it. "I guess I could if I'm not doing something else."

"That's wonderful!" I opened the door wider. "Come on in. Mrs. Houlihan made some brownies that I'm not supposed to know about—presumably for my dad or Jack or anybody who's not me—and I have about three dozen bran-and-broccoli muffins from Ruth's Bakery that I haven't thrown away yet, if you'd prefer those."

She glanced over her shoulder once before stepping inside and stopping abruptly. I followed her gaze upward, where the hanging chain from the shattered light fixture still swung from the ceiling. Before she could make a comment, she caught sight of my straining blouse buttons and waterlogged ankles. "You should travel to all the area high schools as a sort of warning against pregnancy, you know? Kind of like those pictures they show kids of the blackened lungs of smokers, or the rotting teeth of meth addicts."

"Thank you, Nola," I said, starting to walk toward the kitchen. "If I decide to switch careers, I'll keep that in mind." I pushed open the kitchen door and flipped on the lights. From what Mrs. Houlihan told me, it was a chef's dream—all granite and stainless steel. As I was still happily ignorant as to what the appliances besides the dishwasher and microwave were really used for, I had to take her word for it.

When I caught sight of Nola in the better light of the kitchen, I noticed the small stripe of green hair on the side of her head that could probably be fully hidden by a well-placed barrette. I smiled to myself, glad to see that even though she was wearing a school uniform, Nola—aka Emmaline Amelia Pettigrew—was still the same teenage girl I'd grown to love.

I pulled out one of the unopened bags from Ruth's Bakery—which I still went to every morning in the hopes Ruth would take pity on me and throw in just one doughnut—then leaned down into the warming oven. I pulled out the Tupperware container of brownies that

Mrs. Houlihan had attempted to hide under a roasting pan. Apparently she hadn't been working for me long enough to know that I had the sense of smell of a bloodhound and that my pregnancy had only made it stronger.

I motioned for Nola to sit down, then placed plates and napkins on the table along with the brownies and a paper bag full of the inedible muffins. I took a brownie and placed it on my plate while sliding the bag of muffins in Nola's direction. "Enjoy."

"Do you have any organic soy milk?" she asked, her face neutral.

I stood and filled two glasses—my search for normal milk having ended in disappointment—and when I returned I noticed that the bag of muffins remained untouched, but there was a suspicious-looking brownie crumb stuck to the corner of Nola's mouth. I reached over and handed her a napkin, giving the crumb a pointed stare.

"I'm glad to hear Ashley Hall is working out for you. I don't think your grandmother or my mother could have handled the disappointment." I played with my milk glass, wondering how to word my next question. "How's . . . everything else?"

"Dad's fine."

I opened my mouth to let her know that I hadn't been asking about Jack, but immediately closed it. She would have known I was lying.

Nola took a sip of her milk. "He's still a bit shell-shocked from you turning him down, but he's surviving. He's working a lot on his book, but when he's not, he's spending an awful lot of time watching all those stupid baby shows on TLC. He even takes notes." She rolled her eyes. "It's not like you'd ever allow a natural childbirth, so why he's even bothering I have no idea."

She paused, as if waiting for me to make a rebuttal, but I remained silent.

"But he's real excited about finding a family home. I guess I wouldn't mind having a little more privacy. Last week, Alston brought over her older brother, Cooper—he's a first-year at the Citadel—to meet me. Dad spent about fifteen minutes grilling him on the intercom and checking him out on the closed-circuit TV before letting him into the building. It was embarrassing."

It was a struggle to keep my face straight as I imagined Jack's new role as guardian of his daughter's virtue, knowing full well that he'd been the object of the same sort of scrutiny when he was a teenager. And with good reason.

I eyed a stray crumb that had fallen on the table, wondering whether I could snatch it without Nola noticing. "He's certainly looking for something with more living space—with lots of entertaining rooms and a big garden. And he definitely wants something older, with tons of character—which is just another way to say money sucking—with all the bedrooms on one floor, preferably upstairs." I sighed. "He's being so specific that I'm not sure I can find everything he wants in a single house, so he's going to have to compromise. . . ."

Nola was looking at me strangely.

"What?"

She slowly shook her head. "You're the expert, Mellie, so I'll let you handle it. But I'm sure you'll be able to find at least one house that meets all of his criteria. Just give me enough room so that Dad's not breathing down my back every second." She gave me a bright smile. "I'd like a bedroom on the first floor, or if it has to be on the second then maybe a room with a nearby tree or soft hedges beneath the window."

It was my turn to roll my eyes.

"Oh, and I figured I should warn you that Dad's researching Lamaze classes, too."

I took a bite out of the brownie and closed my eyes at the joy of actually eating something with taste, and not feeling the urge to vomit. At least this way I'd actually have something to throw up when I awoke in the morning.

"I have absolutely no intention of going to Lamaze classes. Not to worry—I'll set him straight." I took another bite of my brownie and chewed slowly, studying the teenager across from me. Maybe it was her resemblance to her father, but I couldn't help but think her visit had ulterior motives. I narrowed my eyes. "It's not like I'm not happy to see you—I am—but I'm just wondering why you came here tonight. Is everything really all right?" I paused. "Is your mother back?"

Nola's mother, Bonnie, had killed herself in California, where they'd been living, precipitating Nola's unexpected appearance in Charleston and her father's life. But unfinished business had kept Bonnie at Nola's side until my mother and I had been able to send her into the light.

She shook her head. "No. I mean, not really. I always feel her with me. Here." She pressed a fist against her heart and I felt the ever-present tears sting my eyes. "But I don't see her anymore, and nobody's moving my furniture or stuff. It's just . . ."

I waited for her to speak, holding my breath.

She took a deep breath. "Remember when Julia Manigault died?"

Julia's dead father's spirit had tried to kill me. It wasn't something one easily forgot. "Yes," I said slowly, trying not to hold my breath.

"She left me her piano."

Relief pricked at my skin. "Oh. That's wonderful. One of the last things she said to me was to make sure you kept practicing. This will make it so much easier for you."

She smiled, but she still seemed tense, as if she had more to say.

I leaned forward. "And . . . ?"

"There isn't any room in Dad's condo for a grand piano."

She continued to smile at me, and I wondered whether we were both thinking of the front room in my house. I had recently donated all the furniture—including the grand piano—that I'd inherited with the house to the Charleston Museum, with the dream of making the room into my new home office. I'd even already started working with Amelia Trenholm on the design and had asked her to start looking for furniture.

I was shaking my head when a brief tapping sounded on the glass of the kitchen door. We turned to see Jack standing on the back stoop, the porch light making his dark hair gleam.

"I'll get it," Nola said, sliding back her chair before unlatching the door to let Jack inside. General Lee, who'd followed us into the kitchen, gave an enthusiastic yip and threw himself at Jack with the same gusto he'd shown for Nola.

Jack bent down to scratch the dog on the tummy that General Lee had graciously rolled over to reveal. "At least one member of this family knows how to greet me."

I stayed where I was, stealthily sliding my napkin to hide the crumbs on my plate. "I'm surprised you didn't just use your key and barge in like you usually do."

Without being asked, he moved to the kitchen table and took a seat. "For some reason my key didn't fit in the lock on the front door."

I was confused for a moment before I remembered that in a fit of spite after the first week of his not calling me I'd changed all the locks. I took a sip of my milk so I wouldn't have to respond.

"I'm not going to ask why you're here, because I'm too happy to see Nola to question who brought her. But you could have waited out in the car. Spent some time working on your smile in the rearview mirror."

Ignoring me, he turned to his daughter. "Did you ask her yet?"

"About the piano? Not yet, but I could see where she was heading," I said. "I'm, um, not so sure—"

Nola interrupted. "It wouldn't be for long—just until you find a house for Dad and me. I really want to have a piano I can play anytime I want, and I don't want to go to the Montagu Street house because it creeps me out. And who knows who the new owners are going to be? They might even say that the piano belongs to the house and won't let me take it." Her expression of woe and destitution was an Oscar-worthy performance.

I quickly switched my gaze to Jack, not able to look at Nola's pathetic face anymore.

"And you've heard Nola play," Jack interjected. "She's really good, so it wouldn't be a hardship listening to her practice. You can give her a key to the house so she can come and go without bothering you."

I eyed the brownies, wishing I could have one more. "I just got rid of a good piano. Nobody played it, and the museum wanted it. And I really need a home office. It's very hard to work in the parlor without a desk. If I spread out my papers on the sofa and chairs, General Lee ends up either sleeping on them or using them for a snack."

I looked at them, expecting to see sympathy. Instead, all I saw were two sets of matching blue eyes and dimples. It was a look guaranteed to coerce, and multiplied by two, it made it nearly impossible to say no.

"Maybe I can think about it?" I asked hopefully.

Their expressions didn't change.

I stared at them for a long moment, weighing the pros and cons in my mind. It would be good to see Nola on a regular basis, and the sound of music in the house would be nice. When she'd lived with my mother and me at my mother's house for the first few months after she arrived in Charleston, she'd entertained us with her guitar and singing—although not intentionally. When she'd moved back in with Jack, I'd at first reveled in the peace and quiet, and the way I didn't have to shout to be heard over her stereo. But I'd missed the sound of her voice and guitar.

Quietly, Nola said, "I'm working on a new song, and Jimmy Gordon is very excited about it and wants to hear the whole thing as soon as I'm done." Her basset-hound face reappeared. "But I'll never get it done without easy access to a piano."

Nola and her mother had written a song together, "My Daughter's Eyes," that had been sold to pop star Jimmy Gordon for his latest album and was now being played on every radio station. It was the sort of success that Bonnie had dreamed of when she'd moved out to California, yet never managed to realize.

I sat up straighter. "How do you know Julia left you the piano? I know she left something for me, too, but I haven't heard a word from the executors of the estate."

Jack's smile brightened. "I happen to have an 'in' with Dee Davenport—Miss Julia's house manager. She's the one who's been so generous with the Manigault family papers for my book."

I frowned. "The large blond lady who makes the Santa Clauses? That Dee Davenport?"

His smile didn't dim. "The very same. She likes me."

I looked up at the ceiling, praying once more that I was going to have a daughter. I couldn't imagine raising a mini Jack who was able to woo women of all ages, shapes, and hair color.

He continued. "Dee found the new will behind the hall mirror, along with Miss Julia's instructions to allow me access to the family papers for my book. She told me about the piano."

"Did she mention what Miss Julia left for me?"

Jack and Nola shared a look. After a brief pause, Jack said, "A cradle. One that's been in her family for generations."

"A cradle? But how would she have known . . ." I stopped, my eyes widening as I realized that she would have known about the pregnancy the same supernatural way I had known about the will behind the hall mirror to tell Dee. But a phone call from the dead wasn't something I liked talking about. I shivered, remembering the last thing Miss Julia said to me before the line had gone silent. *You are stronger than you think. You'll have cause soon to remember that.*

I leaned back in my chair, grateful the bequest was just a cradle and not the whole dilapidated house. I couldn't help but think that it would look much better as a parking garage. And be more useful, too. "That's too bad. I already have a cradle—I saw it in the attic when I was up there with the animal-control guy about the pigeons. It's practically buried under furniture and old clothes, and is probably filthy, but it's there if I should want an antique cradle—which I doubt. What about the house? What poor soul has to deal with that albatross?"

Nola piped up. "She left it to Ashley Hall—but it's up to them to decide whether they're going to sell it or use it for some school purpose. It's pretty far from campus, so who knows? Which is why I want to make sure that my piano is safe with me."

They were both looking at me again, aware that I'd tried to steer the conversation away from the piano issue. As if reading my mind, Jack took a brownie out of the Tupperware and placed it on my plate before sliding it closer to me. "It would just be until you found us a house, which I'm sure you've already started working on."

I took a bite out of the brownie and pretended to think while I chewed, but it was probably already as apparent to them as it was to me that I wouldn't be able to say no. I washed it down with soy milk before I spoke. "All right. I suppose my home office can wait a little bit longer. Just let me know when you schedule the movers so I can put it on the calendar."

Jack cleared his throat. "Actually, they're delivering it here at eight o'clock tomorrow morning."

Nola slid her chair back and glanced at her empty wrist, where I'd never seen a watch. "Wow, look at the time. I'd better get to my English homework."

Jack stretched and faked a yawn. "And I'm exhausted. I've been writing all day and it just makes my brain fuzzy."

Always the gentleman, Jack bent down and kissed my cheek. "Don't bother standing. We'll let ourselves out. See you at eight o'clock tomorrow."

As they began to beat a hasty retreat toward the kitchen door, Nola said, "Don't forget to rearrange the brownies so Mrs. Houlihan doesn't notice any are missing."

I opened my mouth to retort but was stopped by the sound of a loud crash from somewhere upstairs. General Lee whimpered and ran to his dog bed, where he promptly hid his snout in the soft cushion.

"Stay here," Jack commanded Nola and me, but he'd barely made it through the kitchen door before both of us were following him through the foyer and up the stairs. We all stopped in the upstairs hallway at the sight of the attic door gaping open like a yawning mouth. I always kept it locked, and it couldn't be unlocked from the inside.

We looked at one another, seeing our frosty breaths as if we were standing outside on a January morning instead of inside the house at the end of summer. Together we inched forward to peer up the attic stairs.

We stopped, and I blinked several times to make sure I was seeing what I thought I was seeing. At the top of the steps, somehow pulled out from under a heap of old furniture and junk, was an ancient cradle, outlined in the fading light of early evening from the window behind it.

"Cool," Nola whispered, her deep blue eyes showing no fear.

Then from somewhere behind us came the sound of a baby crying, the mewling echoing against the plaster walls and tall ceilings of the old house, and sending a chill deep down into my womb, where my own baby lay, protected.

Jack reached out and put a hand on my abdomen, touching our child for the first time. Our eyes met in a mixture of fear and anticipation, as if we were both realizing that we were in this together, and that we were up against more than we'd bargained for.

CHAPTER 5

I opened my eyes as soon as I felt the car stop. My mother's slow and erratic driving was too hard to take with both eyes open. I would have gladly driven myself or walked to Hominy Grill to meet Sophie for lunch, but my mother, having missed most of my childhood and growing-up years, had begun to treat me like a glass doll incapable of doing anything on her own.

"I wonder if they have valet," my mother said, idling the engine. She'd found curbside parking on a side street only two blocks away from the restaurant on Rutledge Avenue.

"I'm sure I can walk without breaking."

Reluctantly, she turned off the ignition. "You really shouldn't be walking anywhere in heels in your condition. You know, your ankles wouldn't be so swollen if you didn't insist on wearing those shoes in this heat. And I found that bag of potato chips buried in the kitchen garbage can. All that sodium isn't helping, either."

I unbuckled my seat belt. "I only have small windows of not feeling nauseous, and I refuse to waste them on foods that taste like tree bark." I opened my door and climbed out so I wouldn't have to hear her response.

My mother caught up to me on the sidewalk. "And I think that General Lee is having a sympathy pregnancy. He's looking a little portly."

"He is not. He's just fluffy. And big boned. But if he has gained a few it's because I haven't been able to walk him—it's way too hot. And my feet hurt all the time."

She looked pointedly at my shoes but self-preservation made her keep quiet.

We had just reached the front entrance of the iconic red clapboard barbershop-turned-restaurant when I heard my name called.

I turned to see my best friend rushing toward me with both arms outstretched. Regardless of how many times I'd seen Dr. Sophie Wallen, her outfits never ceased to make me pause and wonder how she could be my best friend. Her dark hair was unbraided for a change, the curls bouncing around her face and shoulders, with wide light brown sun streaks framing her cheeks. She wore head-to-toe tie-dye, including leggings, but excluding the plaid scarf she'd draped around her neck like a necklace. Her ubiquitous Birkenstocks graced her feet, where I was happy to see that at least her toenails were tie-dye-free.

"Melanie!" she screeched, catching me up in a bear hug that suddenly made me feel much, much better, reminding me once again why Sophie and I were the very best of friends.

She held me at arm's length, looking at me closely, her smile fading as she narrowed her eyes at me. "You don't look so great. Are you feeling all right?"

My mother stepped forward. "She has horrible morning sickness, and she's retaining water like a watermelon." Sophie released me so my mother could kiss her on both cheeks. "And her skin is breaking out like a teenager's."

"I can hear you, you know," I said, glaring at my mother and now ex–best friend.

They both turned to look at me with matching expressions of pity. Ignoring them, I opened the door to the restaurant. "I'm hungry," I called over my shoulder, not caring whether they followed me.

We were seated quickly at a wooden table in the front window, the bottom half of which was covered in a lace curtain. I was starving, but not because I hadn't eaten breakfast. After I'd swallowed enough saltines so I could raise my head from the pillow, I'd actually felt hungry and had allowed Mrs. Houlihan to heat up one of the broccoli muffins for me with about a drop of butter on it. It had lasted in my stomach for almost three minutes.

I studied the menu with the hunger of an Olympic swimmer, and after ordering the sweet tea, she-crab soup, the fried chicken small plate, a side of corn bread, and the low-country purloo, I had to explain to the stunned waiter that I wasn't ordering for the whole table. Sophie ordered the vegetable plate—all locally grown—and a large glass of water with lemon. My mother ordered the soup and salad, and neither one would return my belligerent gaze.

Eager to divert the subject from my dietary habits, I turned to Sophie. "So, how's married life? How was the honeymoon? I hope you brought pictures."

Sophie shyly tucked her hair behind her ear, ignoring how it sprang back immediately. "The honeymoon was pretty awesome, and I highly recommend married life." She blushed a little and I looked at her closely, wondering what, besides the sun-streaked hair, seemed so different. Her eyes sparkled, and her skin practically glowed. If it had been anybody but Sophie Wallen, I would have suspected that she'd just had a chemical peel and facial—two things I knew with all certainty that she had never subjected her skin to.

"You look absolutely beautiful," my mother said, echoing my thoughts and obviously overlooking the outfit. "Married life definitely agrees with you." She sent a pointed glance in my direction.

"Seriously," I said. "What are you using on your skin these days? I've seen babies with skin that doesn't look that good."

My mother sat up straighter and, with a small gasp, pressed her hands against her mouth.

Obviously not catching on, I looked from Sophie to my mother, then back again. "What is it? What am I missing?"

"I'm pregnant!" Sophie almost shouted.

"You're pregnant?" I shouted back, making other diners turn their heads in our direction.

She nodded, her skin glowing pink like a ripened peach.

"But how . . . ?" I gestured with my hands to indicate her radiant face, narrow waist, and trim ankles.

"The usual way, I suspect, Mellie," my mother said, frowning.

"I meant how can you look like . . . that, and be pregnant?"

Their smiles dimmed slightly as they contemplated me, strategically keeping their gazes on my eyes and not my blotchy face, my cankles, or my skirt that was stretched uncomfortably across my lap.

My mother placed her hand on top of mine. "All pregnancies are different, Mellie. I was sicker than a dog throughout my entire pregnancy with you, which meant that I didn't gain much weight. But I looked green most of the time and my bustline was simply unmanageable. But a few years later, when Amelia was pregnant with Jack, she looked fabulous—she simply glowed, and you could only tell she was pregnant by a little baby bump in front."

"Is that supposed to make me feel better, Mother? Because not only did you remind me that Jack is younger, but you also let me know that I might feel and look this way for the entire nine months." I bit back a sob, realizing my hormones could probably be seen arcing their way across the table like a rainbow-colored fountain.

Our waiter approached with a pitcher of water but quickly reversed direction when he spotted me in midbreakdown.

Sophie took my other hand and squeezed it. "I'm sure when your hormones calm down you'll feel much better, and when you feel better you'll look better." She smiled and I noticed that even her teeth looked whiter. "And don't forget how important nutrition is, not just for the baby but for you, too. Has your doctor given you any literature yet on what you should be eating?"

I studied my white cloth napkin in my lap as if it were suddenly the most important thing in my life.

"Mellie?" my mother prompted.

"I'm starving," I said, looking for our waiter. "I hope they bring my soup fast."

"Mellie?" she said again, her voice rising a notch and prompting the waiter to retreat again. "Have you not seen a doctor yet? It's never too early to see a doctor, especially since you're at a certain age now."

I slapped my hands on the table. "Thanks, Mother. Maybe you can help me find a doctor who specializes in geriatric obstetrics."

"Mellie, be reasonable. . . ."

Sophie held up her hand. "You're what—almost three months along?"

I stared at her. "I, um, I haven't really, uh, thought about it."

"Surely you have an idea of when you conceived?" Sophie prodded.

"Excuse me for a moment, will you? I need to go powder my nose." My mother sent us a gracious smile before standing and heading for the restroom. We both stared after her.

"She probably doesn't want to know the specifics," Sophie said. "Sort of like you not wanting to acknowledge that your father is practically living at her house on Legare."

"Ew," I said, feeling a little of the morning's nausea return.

"Exactly." She pulled her chair up a little closer to the table. "So, I'm assuming you conceived the night of your birthday party." She began counting on her fingers, starting with her thumb—something I'd always found odd but also endearing. "That would make you about two and a half months pregnant. I'd say it's the perfect time to find an ob-gyn. I've got a list from a colleague of all the doctors in the area who work with midwives and favor drug-free home births. I'd be happy to share. . . ."

"No," I said, not needing to hear any more. "I agree that I should look for a doctor who can delivery my baby, and I'm a little embarrassed to say that this is the first time it's occurred to me that I might need some help—mostly because I can't give myself an epidural, which is what I'll be requiring sometime in the third trimester. But I'm not doing a home birth, and I'm most definitely not doing it drug-free."

She blinked at me in silence for a few moments. "Well, then. I'll keep my list to myself. But I think you should at least consider alternative—"

"No," I said, my voice firm. "But thanks," I added to soften my response. "I fainted when I got my ears pierced, remember. I want to be unconscious from about eight months to when the baby starts sleeping through the night."

A secretive smile danced across Sophie's face. "I think you might surprise yourself."

I started to argue but was interrupted by my mother's return to the table. The waiter finally became confident enough to approach with more water and a bread basket. As I buttered my corn bread, ignoring the looks sent to me by both of my tablemates, I turned to Sophie.

"I wanted to give you a heads-up that a Detective Thomas Riley will be calling you about the history of my Tradd Street house and the Vanderhorsts. I told him you were the expert."

Her brows puckered. "That's fine, but why?"

I took a drink of sweet tea before answering. "It appears the foundation work has revealed more than just old bricks and mortar."

Sophie leaned forward, her eyes wide, like those of a prospector who'd just struck gold. "What?" she asked, her tone reverential.

"The remains of an infant. And what looks like a christening gown and matching bonnet—haven't heard back on anything definitive about that yet."

My mother leaned forward so she could whisper, "Mellie's been hearing a crying baby, and a not-so-nice spirit has been making its presence known."

"Joseph Longo?" Sophie hissed.

I shook my head. "No. He's definitely gone. This was . . . somebody else. Somebody who was awakened when the baby's remains were found."

"So they're related," Sophie said, almost to herself.

"That's what we figured, too," my mother added, dabbing at the corners of her mouth with a napkin.

"And then yesterday, when Jack and Nola were over, there was a little incident in the attic."

"An incident?" they said in unison.

"A cradle that I know was buried under a lot of heavy furniture and boxes was moved to the top of the stairs."

"A cradle?" Sophie asked, her eyes narrowing. "Was it made of black ash with twisted spindles and rockers shaped like egrets?"

I stared at her. "Yes—exactly. How did you know?"

"Because I was at the Charleston Museum at the end of last semester with a bunch of my students and I saw it there. It was labeled

'Vanderhorst family cradle.' There are so many Vanderhorsts in the city that I couldn't be sure if it was from *your* Vanderhorsts."

"They're not *mine*," I corrected. "But it does sound like the same cradle. Maybe there was a two-for-one special when they bought them," I said, buttering another piece of bread. I'd felt a cold lump of dread settle in the back of my throat when Sophie had mentioned the second cradle, and I needed to lighten the mood so my appetite wouldn't go away.

"There could be lots of reasons for there being two of them," Sophie said. "We should probably do a field trip to check it out. It might tell us something."

"Is it behind glass?" my mother asked.

I looked at my mother with surprise. "You wouldn't touch it, would you?" She was what people referred to as a "sensitive"— someone who could touch an object to communicate with the spirits of those who'd once owned it. But the last two times she'd done it had nearly killed her.

"I could if it might help. I'd like to at least see it."

"You and Sophie can go. You know I don't do museums."

She and Sophie nodded in understanding, knowing that my aversion to museums had nothing to do with a dislike of history but more to do with the insistent spirits of people who didn't know when to let go of a favorite armoire. Or cradle.

The waiter brought our food, and as I was tucking into my plate of purloo I turned to Sophie again. "Anyway, I told Detective Riley that you were the expert on the Vanderhorsts and my house, but I told him he needed to wait until you got back from your honeymoon. If there was any foul play, my guess would be that the perpetrators got away with it and there won't be any pending arrests."

"Undoubtedly." Sophie paused over her vegetable plate, her brow wrinkled as she appeared deep in thought. "Do they have any idea of how long the remains were there?"

"No," I said. "They're trying to determine that now. Why?"

"I need to go dig into my files, but I know that there was some kind of renovation done to the house in the mid–eighteen hundreds.

If I were going to hide something I didn't want anybody to find, bricking something up in the foundation of a house would be the perfect way to do it."

I looked at Sophie with growing unease. It's not that I'd ever thought that the presence of the baby in my foundation could have been an *accident*, but the certain knowledge that somebody had deliberately, and perhaps maliciously, hidden it there brought a cold chill to the edges of my skin.

She took a long sip of her water. "I'll look into it and let you know." She paused for a moment, thinking. "Why would somebody want to hide the body of an infant?"

We were all silent as we considered the possibilities, none of them uplifting.

My mother's voice was quiet when she spoke. "And what are they willing to do to keep their secret?"

I stared at my plate, my appetite completely deserting me. Almost whispering, I said, "Why can't the dead just stay dead?"

My mother put her hand on mine. "Because they need your help."

I could almost hear the high-pitched wail of a crying infant as I thought of the falling light fixture and the force required to move the cradle to the top of the stairs. I looked up and met my mother's eyes, realizing that our thoughts were moving in tandem, and I was suddenly very, very afraid.

CHAPTER 6

On my way out the door two days later, I paused to grab my car keys off the hall table, accidentally catching my reflection in the nineteenth-century Venetian mirror over it. I'd learned by now that all the effort of actually getting out of bed and making it to the mirror wouldn't be rewarded regardless of how much makeup I used. Unless a makeup had been developed for puffy, blotchy skin, I was better off remaining ignorant, and simply swiped on mascara, lipstick, and powder while sitting on my bed, far away from any offending reflective surfaces.

I stared at my reflection and tugged at the top of my jacket, hoping to hide a little more of my newly rounded cleavage. I was meeting Jack for our first house showings, and while I hadn't wanted to go overboard with paying too much attention to what I looked like, I didn't want Jack to run off screaming into the nearest woods, either. I'd put on my favorite jacket that zipped up the front, thinking it would be easier to hold everything in without those pesky buttons that liked to pop like a cork from a champagne bottle when one least expected it.

I was leaning forward to examine what couldn't possibly be another pimple on my chin when the distinct sound of a piano key being hit with force jerked me around. My eyes scanned the foyer and the adjoining rooms, then swept up the stairs as I looked for a patch of shimmering air. I saw nothing more than the hand-painted Chinese wallpaper that had cost me an entire commission check to restore and the cracked plaster medallion that attached the Baccarat chandelier to the ceiling. Luckily Sophie hadn't yet noticed the crack or I'd be out another commission check.

I relaxed a bit, thinking I'd only imagined the sound, when it came again, only this time it was another note, slightly higher. Very slowly, I walked toward the room that was supposed to be my study, stopping at the threshold. The black grand piano looked much as it had when at Julia Manigault's house. But when I drew in a breath and my lungs froze, I knew I was no longer alone.

I am stronger than you, I said to myself, repeating the mantra that my mother had taught me and that we'd put to good use in the last year. I felt the familiar urge to hum an ABBA tune to block out anything the spirit might want to tell me so that whoever it was would give up and leave me alone. I hesitated, thinking of my mother, who held the belief that she and I had been given our "gifts" to help lost spirits move into the light, and a part of me had even begun to agree. But now, standing alone in my house with a spirit who would not allow itself to be seen and who dropped chandeliers on people, I didn't feel so sure.

"Hello?" I said, my frosty breath reaching out into the room. I wanted whoever it was to go away, *needed* it to go away. I had far too many complications in my life already. "I know you're there. You're hiding, but I can tell." I took a deep breath, ignoring everything my mother had taught me, in the distant hope that perhaps *this* spirit would be easy to eradicate. I'd seen this technique work on one of those haunting shows Nola liked to watch, so it had to be valid. I cleared my throat. "This is my house, and I want you to leave. Look for the light and follow it."

I listened carefully, hearing only the ticking of the grandfather clock across the hall. I imagined I could feel the temperature returning to normal and was about to give myself a fist pump when another key from the piano was pressed by an unseen hand, followed by a burst of icy cold air on my face that formed itself into a single word: *Mine.*

I screamed, then turned to run toward the front door and found myself enveloped by a pair of large, muscled arms. I stopped screaming and didn't struggle, my mind and body knowing immediately that I was safe, that it was Jack, and that I didn't need to be afraid anymore. The cold air had completely dissipated and I'd suddenly gone warm all over.

"What happened?" he asked, his lips very close to my ear.

I kept my head pressed against his chest, too comfortable to pull away. "Somebody—some*thing*—was playing the piano."

"Were they any good?"

I jerked back and pulled away. "I'm glad you find this amusing, Jack, but it was a little unnerving—even for me. It's like my house has been invaded, and I don't like the intrusion."

"You've had ghosts here before, if you'll recall."

I blinked up at him. Of course, he was right, and for a moment I wasn't even sure why it was different. "I guess it's because I think of the house now as mine—my *home*. And before, well . . ."

"It was more like a boil on your backside."

"Always so eloquent, Jack."

"I'd thank you, except those aren't my words. I'm actually quoting you verbatim."

Instead of arguing with him—mostly because I was afraid he might be right, that those had been my words—I put my hands on my hips and stared up at him. "How did you get in here?" I looked down at his feet, where General Lee was happily sitting. I wagged my finger at him. "And what kind of a guard dog are you? You're supposed to let me know when there's an intruder."

"Perhaps because he feels like I belong here," Jack said, holding up a brand-new house key. "Nola lent me her key. She wanted me to stop by after our house showings and pick up some of her music she left in the piano bench, but since I was driving right by here . . ." He shrugged and sent me his killer grin.

I responded with my "I'm immune" grin—which wasn't completely accurate—and said, "Next time please use the doorbell."

"I did, actually. I guess it's not working again."

I groaned, but didn't stamp my feet. I'd already spent the equivalent of a small nation's GNP trying to keep it working consistently, but something about the salt air and humidity in Charleston seemed to conspire against old doorbells. It was a well-known fact among most of my South of Broad neighbors that if nobody answered the doorbell, they could knock once and let themselves in.

I looked at my watch. "Let me just call the office to let them know that we're heading out from here." I tossed him my keys. "Go on out to the car and start the air-conditioning. I have to go search for my purse and phone."

He stopped me. "Actually, I was hoping I could drive. I've got a new car."

"A new car? Did you sell your pickup truck?"

"I'm never selling my truck, except to get a new one. I believe I've told you that it might be illegal for a South Carolina boy not to own one."

I lowered my voice to a tone of hushed reverence. "You sold your *Porsche*?"

"Sure did," he said, his killer grin back on his face.

"What did you get?" I asked, moving out onto the piazza. I scanned the street, looking for something red and Italian.

"Go get your stuff and I'll take you to it. But you have to keep your eyes closed. It's a surprise."

Too curious to be suspicious, I did as he asked, then allowed him to lead me, with my eyes closed, off the piazza and down the front walkway to the sidewalk, his hand warm around mine.

"You can open your eyes now," he said, dropping my hand as my eyes popped open.

I looked up and down Tradd Street for something low-slung and foreign, but didn't see anything. "Where is it?"

He patted the driver's-side door of a vehicle parked directly in front of me with the dealer's sticker still in the rear side window. "It's this little beauty right here."

I blinked several times. It was foreign—Japanese—and it was definitely red. But it was far from being low-slung. "It's a minivan," I said.

"Sure is. Can't fit a baby seat in a Porsche, and my truck doesn't have all the safety features I'd want if I'm going to be driving a baby around."

He pulled the door lever, and the whole side panel opened slowly. "It's got pinch-proof doors that won't close if something's in the way, and all the seats are leather—easier to clean off apple juice spills. There's a built-in booster seat, too, for when the baby graduates from the car seat." His eyes were shining, and he was talking so fast that one would have thought him a teenager with his first copy of *Playboy*.

"And check this out." He leaned into the backseat and pushed a button. "It's a DVD player so Jack Junior can be entertained while on our way to golf tournaments—Nancy Flaherty has promised us free lessons—and Carolina football games. Only educational programs, of course. No violence or foul language or anything not age appropriate."

I wondered for a moment whether I'd accidentally stepped into some alternate universe. But all I could think to say was, "Jack Junior?"

"Well, it's just a thought. We have some time to think about it. It sure would be cute if we shortened it to JJ."

I was distracted from my focus on the bright red minivan for a moment. "She could be a girl, you know."

My heart squeezed as I watched his animated face and saw that the excitement didn't wane. "Well, sure. And I'd be happy to have another daughter. But I figured it would be nice to have one of each, too."

I crossed my arms. "And have you thought of a name for her?"

"I was thinking we could name her after your grandmother, since she was so special to you. Sarah's a good, strong name. Like for the CEO of a company, or president of the country." He grinned, and my knees softened just a bit.

"Is Jack Junior a presidential enough name?"

Jack shrugged. "It could be. But he won't have to be president or control a company. He'll be able to have enough power and influence just from his charm. Runs in the family, you know." He winked.

I shook my head, trying to clear it, then surreptitiously slid a glance down the street, looking for television cameras or Ashton Kutcher to tell me that I was being punked. I turned back to Jack. "You traded in your Porsche for a minivan. And you've already named the baby." I felt a little tug of what I could only call jealousy. My thought processes had barely made it to the point where I was thinking it might be time to buy maternity clothes. Jack had probably already started booking college tours.

He took my hand, and the spark that shot up my arm brought me back to reality. "Come on and get in. It's a really sweet ride."

He opened the passenger door for me and helped me inside before walking around to the driver's seat, a decided swagger in his stride. He closed his door and began extolling all the wonderful features of the van. I could listen with only half an ear, as I was too mesmerized watching him. I hadn't seen his face as animated since . . . well, since the night the baby was conceived. I would never admit it, but I was finding this whole new side of Jack rather hot. I closed my eyes and shook my head, wondering whether the pregnancy hormones would affect my thinking for the entire nine months.

I started, realizing he'd asked me a question. "I'm sorry, what?"

"You should also look into getting a new car. If it's more than three years old, it doesn't have all the latest safety features. I actually did a little car hunting for you—if you'll look inside the glove box, you'll see a few brochures."

More amused than annoyed, I opened the glove box and pulled out a brochure. I stared at the photo on the cover. "You want me to drive a station wagon."

"Not just a station wagon—a Volvo station wagon. So it's stylish, yet safe. And it has plenty of room for a car seat as well as for your clients." He grinned, making my heart do that swishy thing again.

"So, you don't think I should have a minivan, too?" I was only half joking.

"I figured one was enough for this family, don't you?"

Family. The word caught me off guard, thickening my throat so that I couldn't speak. I distracted myself by glancing down at my BlackBerry, scrolling for any missed messages or calls.

"Where are we going?" he asked.

I looked up, disoriented for a moment as I tried to remember why we were both sitting in a red minivan in front of my house. "I'On. In Mount Pleasant. It's a mixed-use New Urbanist TND community."

"'TND'?" Jack asked.

"Traditional Neighborhood Development," I explained. "Lots of sidewalks and front porches and shops and restaurants all within walking distance. I know it's not South of Broad, but the houses are beautiful and replicas of many of the historical houses here, except they're new. There are a few available with beautiful lake and creek views, and they all have nice-size yards. You did mention having a swing set and a pool—not something one finds in Charleston." I neglected to add that I'On was close enough to me, but not too close.

He was frowning. "I really wanted something old, and even something that needed a little work, so I could put my own personal stamp on it. I wouldn't even mind a ghost or two."

Our eyes met for a moment before he returned his gaze to the road. "Be careful what you wish for," I muttered.

"Isn't there anything around Tradd Street that we could look at first?"

I struggled to keep my voice from sounding too strangled. "Do you really think that's a good idea, Jack? Every time we get too close, it ends up in a disaster."

He glanced down at my belly for a moment before meeting my eyes. "Not always."

I blushed, and looked away. "Let's just go see the two houses in I'On. All I ask is that you keep an open mind."

My iPhone buzzed and I looked at the screen before answering. "Hello. This is Melanie Middleton."

"Hello, Miss Middleton. This is Detective Riley. I hope I'm not catching you at a bad time." His voice was low, deep, and Southern, and not at all hard on the ears.

I glanced over at Jack. "No, not at all. What can I help you with?"

"Actually, I was calling you with some news. Seems like the lab has some preliminary results back on the remains we found at your place."

"Wow—that was quick. The last time we found remains it took a lot longer to get results."

"The last time?"

"Well, I didn't personally find the remains. They were on a boat that had belonged to my family that sank in the harbor during the

Charleston earthquake. Old story. Same with the two bodies found buried beneath my fountain."

"I see," he said. "So you're just a magnet for old remains."

If you only knew the half of it. "You should probably keep me on a retainer for all of your cold cases."

"I just might." He paused. "Look, why don't I tell you the news in person? I'm in your neck of the woods right now. Maybe over coffee?"

I glanced over at Jack, whose fingers were gripping the steering wheel of the minivan so tightly that his knuckles were white. I wasn't sure he could hear every word of my conversation in the enclosed space, but he could at least tell that the caller was male.

"Actually," I said, facing the side window so my back was to Jack. "I'm with a client right now and I'm expecting to be occupied with showings for most of the day." I hesitated. I liked Thomas Riley, could even admit that I found him attractive. And he, by some aberration of nature, apparently found something attractive in me, too. But he wasn't Jack. But he also wasn't the man who'd said, "I'm sorry," in response to my declaration of love, or who'd asked me to marry him only because I was pregnant.

I cleared my throat. I had to move on from that pathetic person I had become, even if it meant leaving Jack behind. "How about dinner?"

I could hear the surprise in the detective's voice. "I'd love that. Do you like Italian?"

"Love it, actually."

"Great—I know a terrific restaurant on King Street, if that's all right with you. Can I pick you up at six?"

"Perfect. But, Detective Riley . . ."

"Please, call me Thomas."

"All right. Thomas, you've got to give me some clue as to what they found. I don't think I can wait until tonight to hear everything."

He laughed softly, and I liked the sound. "The remains appear to be male, although with so little to go on, it's really inconclusive. The bones have been holed up there for over a century—maybe even closer to two. I've put a call in to your friend Dr. Wallen-Arasi to help pinpoint a time when construction might have been happening on the house. And from what can be determined, the baby was most likely a newborn. Unfortunately, it will be nearly impossible to determine a cause of death."

I swallowed. "So it could have been a stillborn, or died naturally shortly after birth."

"Of course. Or not." He paused, allowing me to fill in the missing parts. "Usually natural deaths aren't hidden in the foundations of houses."

"Good point. Anything more on the gown and bonnet?"

"Yes. They're made of a very delicate linen, so most of it has disintegrated. The clothing seems to be much older than the remains. But the collar of the dress, which was made of a different material, is pretty much intact. Lucky for us, because somebody using silk embroidery thread conveniently left a name. Susan Bivens."

"Any idea who that is?"

"No, but I was hoping you or Dr. Wallen-Arasi might."

I glanced over at Jack, who was still squeezing the steering wheel in a death grip as he navigated the entrance ramp onto the Arthur Ravenel Bridge that connected Charleston with Mount Pleasant. "We, uh, I have a friend who works in the historical archives. I can ask her to look."

"Great." He drew a deep breath. "It seems I've told you pretty much everything. Are you still on for dinner with me anyway?"

I could almost feel Jack's eyes boring holes into the back of my head. "Of course. I'm looking forward to it."

"See you at six, then. I know the address."

We said good-bye and I tucked my phone back into my purse.

"So what do we need to go see Yvonne about?"

We. I'd noticed the word the same way I'd noticed the tightness in his voice. "The christening gown they found with the infant's remains appears to be older than the actual remains, and has a name embroidered in the collar—Susan Bivens. Ring a bell?"

He shook his head. "No, but I bet Yvonne could tell us. I can call her right now and ask for an appointment. When are you available?"

I thought of my recent conviction that separating myself from Jack was best for all concerned. But then I thought of him selling his Porsche and buying a minivan, and how we'd made such a great team in solving mysteries together, and I hesitated. And then he looked at me with those blue eyes and I was lost, already forgetting that he didn't love me, and that he'd probably break my heart again if I wasn't careful. But like a lemming throwing itself off a cliff, I couldn't seem to stop myself.

"Thursday's pretty open," I said, trying not to squirm at the recollection of my nearly empty calendar. "Anytime—just not first thing. I need time for my stomach to settle first."

He smiled the smile that told me he knew he'd won, then pressed a button on his steering wheel to dial the call.

I stared out over the Cooper River as we passed over the middle of the giant cable-stayed bridge. A tall-masted ship with full, billowing sails meandered toward us, an American flag with not nearly enough stars on it flapping at the top like a nervous bird. I sat up and stared, aware that the top mast was too tall to slip under the bridge unscathed. Just as I was about to shout something, the ship, with all of its people, sails, and flags, disintegrated, disappearing back into the mist of time from where it had come.

"Is everything all right?" Jack asked.

I nodded, not able to put a voice to the lie, to smile and say that seeing dead people on a regular basis and believing that Jack and I could just be friends was a reasonable existence.

I turned my head toward my side window, then closed my eyes so I wouldn't have to lie anymore.

CHAPTER 7

I stood in my quiet Charleston garden with my back to the Louisa roses and the fountain that sat beneath the protection of the long limbs of the old oak. A rope swing still hung from the ancient branches like something lingering in one's peripheral vision. Despite my sure knowledge that Mr. Vanderhorst was gone, I couldn't help myself from straining to hear the sound of the rope against bark as a lonely little boy waited there for his lost mother.

I studied the bruised foundation of my house, crisscrossed with neon yellow caution tape, and the piles of debris where the box of remains had been found. The house was littered with spirits who were content to remain and leave me alone, and we gave one another a wide berth. But the spirit who'd been awakened with the discovery of the remains was not one of those. I shivered, thinking of the word blown icy cold into my ear. *Mine.*

What had she meant? Although I'd not seen her, I'd felt, along with that frigid chill, that it had been the spirit of a female. For some reason that had made it worse, making it too easy for me to connect the angry woman and the infant's remains.

I closed my eyes, my thoughts in a whirlwind. In my resurrected diligence, I'd started purchasing and reading every pregnancy and early childhood book that I could find—including the ones Jack had given me. Among all the "breast-feeding is best" and "natural child-birth" admonitions, there was more than enough literature on the physical changes after birth, sex after a baby (I easily skipped over those chapters), leaking breasts, and postpartum depression.

My mother assured me that she hadn't had any issues with the latter, and that comforted me. But when I thought of the dead infant, and the angry spirit of the woman, I couldn't help but wonder.

I turned away, my early-morning nausea threatening a reappearance. My gaze wandered toward the groomed bushes and paths of my father's parterre garden. Although it had originally been designed by the famous landscape architect Loutrel Briggs, my father had resurrected the garden as his housewarming gift to me while also giving him a purpose and focus while attending AA meetings.

Narrowing my eyes, I examined the large corner lot and gardens with my Realtor's eyes, realizing that there was room for a small lap pool and swing set—just like what Jack was looking for. We'd seen several such lots the previous day in I'On, but the houses had been too "new" for Jack. I made a mental note to look for more corner lots in Charleston's many historic neighborhoods—all except South of Broad.

"Mellie?"

I swung around and saw Nola standing outside the kitchen door.

"Hi, Nola," I said, walking toward her with a smile. It was Saturday, so instead of wearing her school uniform, she wore an eclectic combination of leggings, purple high-tops, a denim skirt, Ashley Hall T-shirt with hand-stitched peace-sign appliqués, and a rainbow-colored scarf—eerily reminiscent of one I'd seen Sophie wear—draped artfully around her neck. She and Sophie might shop at the same stores, but Nola had an element of style that Sophie, very contentedly, lacked.

"Nice outfit," she said.

I looked down at my oversize T-shirt that I'd swiped from my father's drawer, and the baggy white capris with the loosely knotted drawstring Mrs. Houlihan had given me out of pity. She said they had belonged to her daughter, but I had the horrible suspicion that they had actually belonged to the robust Mrs. Houlihan herself.

"Thanks," I said. "I haven't had a chance to go shopping yet for maternity clothes."

"Been busy showing houses to my dad?" Her blue eyes narrowed as she examined the garden, and I wondered whether she was thinking the same thing I had.

"Pretty much. And doing lots of reading about pregnancy and child-birth. I like to be informed." I left out the fact that I'd also started preparing a spreadsheet with the projected changes to my body and the baby's on a week-by-week basis. I definitely didn't tell her that my projected weight at the end of the nine months—assuming I gained at the same rate as the first two—would double my prepregnancy body weight.

"Cool. Now I can get all the gross pregnancy stuff from both you and my dad. You know, I think I could live my whole life very happily without ever hearing the words 'placenta' or 'afterbirth.' Well, unless I get unlucky enough to actually fall in love and get married and then have a kid of my own. Not necessarily in that order," she said, her gaze flicking over me.

I walked into the kitchen, enjoying the cool blast of air-conditioning. Eager to change the subject, I said, "Have you had breakfast?" I stood inside the pantry door, my hand hovering over the box of glazed doughnuts I had surreptitiously put there after Mrs. Houlihan left for the weekend.

"Yeah. I just came over to see if I could practice the piano for an hour or so."

My gaze settled on the box of organic cardboard cornflakes Sophie had given me, along with a recipe book for homemade baby food—neither of which I had any intention of actually using. "Sure. As soon as I'm done with breakfast, I'll be in the front parlor with my laptop catching up on some work. I enjoy listening to you play, so you won't be disturbing me at all."

"Cool." Instead of leaving, she sat down in one of the kitchen chairs and folded her hands in front of her.

With an inward sigh and a last lingering look at the doughnuts, I picked up the box of cereal and set it on the table.

Smiling up at me, she said, "By the way, I think we need to have the piano tuned. Three notes are sticking and it's a real pain. It must have been from the move, because the piano worked perfectly when it was at Miss Manigault's house."

"All right. I'll find a tuner as soon as possible." I thought of the doughnuts in the pantry and looked at her hopefully. "Will you be able to practice today?"

"Yeah. They only stick sometimes."

Holding back a sigh, I retrieved a bowl and spoon and reluctantly dragged out the carton of soy milk.

When my back was to her, she asked, "So, how was your date with Detective Riley?"

I turned to her, startled. "It wasn't a date. We were just talking business. And how would you know about Detective Riley, anyway?"

She shrugged and began picking at her black nail polish. "I may have overheard Dad talking on the phone with Grandmother." She looked up at me with Jack's eyes. "He didn't seem too happy."

I sat down across from her and poured my cereal. I desperately wanted to know more, but I also knew with the same certainty that what Nola was trying to tell me had nothing to do with me at all. Focusing on my bowl, I said, "You do know that regardless of my relationship with your father, you are always welcome here. You're like a daughter to me, and that will never change, okay? I'll always be here for you."

She looked up at the ceiling as if in mid–eye roll, but I'd seen the moisture there. "Whatevs," she said before pushing back her chair and standing.

The phone rang and I ignored it as I always did, while I poured the milk over my cereal and stuck my spoon in the bowl, mentally preparing myself.

"Aren't you going to answer that?"

I looked at Nola, confused for a moment before I realized what she was talking about. "The phone? No. I never answer my landline, since it's always telemarketers. Anybody I want to hear from knows my cell number."

"Then why do you still have it?"

I looked at her, my spoon held halfway to my mouth. "That's a good question. I'll have to think about that."

This time she completed her eye roll. "Later," she said, exiting the kitchen with Jack's swaying walk.

I'd just settled into my favorite armchair in the parlor with my cup of decaf coffee (my stash of the real stuff having apparently been discovered and disposed of) when the doorbell rang. I groaned. It seemed the doorbell worked only when it wanted to. Nola was busy practicing her scales and hadn't heard it, so I hoisted myself from my chair and made my way to the door. The shimmer of pink through the Tiffany glass told me who it was, and I was about to quietly back away and hide, but General Lee had other plans. He began to throw his small, furry body against the door and started whimpering.

"Melanie? It's Rebecca. Are you in there? I can't tell if your doorbell is working or not."

I looked down at Mrs. Houlihan's capris and my father's T-shirt and I knew this wouldn't end well. Resigned to my fate, I unlocked the door and opened it.

My cousin, Rebecca Edgerton, stood in a vision of pink—pink sundress and pink cotton sweater tossed elegantly over her shoulders, with white pearls at her throat highlighting a delicate tan. And at her feet, attached to Rebecca by a thin strip of pink leather leash, sat a miniature version of General Lee, albeit a version who wore things like a rhinestone-studded pink collar and tiny pink bows attached to both ears. General Lee immediately shot over to the small dog and the two began a frenzy of nose touching and butt sniffing.

Rebecca tugged on the leash, an expression of disgust marring her perfect features. "Pucci—bad girl. That is not showing nice manners."

"Poochie?" I repeated, hoping that's not what I'd actually heard.

"Spelled P-U-C-C-I—like the Italian designer. Since General Lee loves me so much, I thought I should get a dog of my own. And see? General Lee likes having a sister."

I eyed my dog, thinking that a sister relationship wasn't exactly what he was thinking about. Then I trained my gaze on my cousin— albeit a distant one—realizing that getting a dog was the closest a person ever got to picking one's own relatives.

Without waiting to be asked, Rebecca brushed past me and into the vestibule, Pucci prancing faithfully behind her in a movement that

I was sure was meant to entice my dog. I picked up General Lee and patted his head just to let him know that all females weren't bitches.

"Is there something you need?" I asked, closing the door behind me. Ever since my huge blowup with Jack when he'd confronted me about my knowledge of why his book had lost its publisher—and which Rebecca had witnessed—I'd been avoiding her, wanting to block the whole scene from my memory. Apparently she had no such qualms.

Her gaze slowly took in my fuzzy slippers, baggy capris, and giant T-shirt, ending at my face with an expression that said, *Oh, how the mighty have fallen.*

"I'm assuming all pregnancies don't look like that, or the human race would have ended long ago." She shook her head slowly. "You know, if you want Jack back, you're going to have to try a little harder. He likes his women fit and groomed." She smiled brightly, as if personifying the perfect Jack-woman, and I wondered whether I could blame pregnancy hormones for any physical acts of violence enacted upon another person.

"Thank you, Rebecca, as always, for your keen insight. Now, if you only came over to say hello, then let's get it over with. I've got work to do."

"How can you think over that racket?" she asked, her head indicating the music room.

"Nola's practicing, and she's quite good. I actually enjoy listening to her."

Rebecca raised her eyebrow just like Scarlett O'Hara had in the scene at Ashley's surprise party. I wondered momentarily whether my cousin was one of those adolescents who'd practiced the look in the mirror. Or knew that she'd be left with a permanent wrinkle there when she was older. I decided to let her figure that out on her own.

She turned and began walking down the hallway toward the rear of the house. "Let's go to the kitchen—Pucci needs some water. And we need to talk."

Rebecca's "gift"—or whatever you wanted to call it—involved her dreams, in which she saw the future being played out in living color. I was about to ask her what she'd seen when my attention was caught by the flash of light from her left hand as she tugged on the leash.

I followed her into the kitchen before grabbing her left hand. "What's this?"

She splayed her fingers out in front of me so I could better see the rock she wore in a platinum setting on her third finger. "From Marc. We're getting married."

I felt my cereal stir in my stomach. It wasn't that I regretted that I had let Marc Longo go—I didn't even particularly like him, especially after his slick deal to steal Jack's story. It wasn't even that I was jealous of Rebecca, who was younger, prettier, slimmer—and now engaged. I could be wearing Jack's ring on my finger. He'd asked, after all. It was just that her life was so . . . settled. And mine was up in the air like a juggler's pins. At least—and I couldn't believe I was even thinking this—I had my house. It was the one constant in my life that was guaranteed to never stop needing me. The thought brought me enough comfort to smile.

"Congratulations," I said, leaning forward to kiss her cheek. "When's the big day?"

"We're still working out the details, but the date's set for March twenty-second. No church decided on yet, but we already booked Alhambra Hall for the reception—you have no idea how hard it is to get a reservation there! And I'd like you to be a bridesmaid." She beamed as if just announcing that I'd been canonized.

"I, um, the baby might be due around then. . . ."

"Oh, you'll look just adorable all round and pregnant up there at the altar. So I'll take that as a yes."

I blinked at her, wondering whether being engaged affected women the same way pregnancy did and had deleted a few of her brain cells. "But what if—"

I was cut off by her screech. "Pucci! You are not that kind of girl!"

I turned around to see General Lee trying to climb up the smaller dog's back, and she didn't seem to be protesting overly much.

Rebecca gathered her tiny dog up in her arms. "Can't a girl get a drink without getting molested? I hope General Lee has at least been neutered."

"I have no idea. I inherited him, remember."

"You mean you've never looked?"

"Of course not. Besides, I figure he's too old to, um, perform."

Rebecca pursed her lips and took a deep breath. "May I have some water, Melanie? I'm parched."

I sat down at the table. "Of course. And would you please get me one, too, while you're at it?"

With a malevolent glare, she dumped Pucci into my lap and took two glasses from the cabinet. She left the dog in my lap when she returned with the water.

She sat down, her spine straight as if she wore a corset, and I couldn't help but wonder whether she did. It wouldn't have surprised me at all.

"Do you ever answer your phone, Melanie?"

"Only my cell phone. I know, I should get rid of the landline. I've already had this conversation today."

"What about phone messages at the office? Do you ever return those?"

I considered that for a moment. "If it's a potential or existing client, always. If it's on my list of people I don't want to speak with, the receptionist knows not to bother taking a message. I've trained Nancy Flaherty very well." And she pretty much went by the rules except where Jack was concerned. I always got his messages, whether or not I wanted them.

She took a sip of her water. "Does your list include reporters?"

"Top of the list. Right under insurance salesmen and people wanting a séance."

"Well, that explains a lot. One of my colleagues, Suzy Dorf, has been trying to get ahold of you."

"I never speak with reporters, remember? I only speak to you because you're a relative."

She raised her eyebrow again and I was happy to see the crease in her skin remain even after she lowered it. "Well, I'm glad I came. She's writing the featured story in this Sunday's edition of the *Post and Courier*. It's about Mr. Vanderhorst."

"Mr. Vanderhorst? My Mr. Vanderhorst?"

"The very same. All Suzy needed to know is what you'd decided to do about the house. The will stipulated that you needed to live in it a year before you could sell it. It's been well over a year."

I stared at her. How could I have forgotten? From the first moment I'd read the stipulations in Mr. Vanderhorst's will, I'd been counting the days until I could lift this albatross from my neck and be free of it for good. But somewhere along the way, in the middle of refinishing floors, replacing fixtures, replastering walls, and shoring up a sagging foundation, I'd lost track. Because tucked into those projects, nearly hidden by the daily anxieties of money and more repairs, were my beautiful garden, the growth chart of a small boy scratched into the parlor wall, the comforting smell of beeswax, and the sighs of all the people who'd lived and loved in this house who couldn't quite say good-bye.

"I, um, don't know. I've had other things to worry about." I smoothed my hands over my stomach. "It's not like I *had* to sell it after a year. I can sell it at any time. I just haven't figured it out yet."

She sent me a knowing look. "I don't know, Melanie. You look pretty entrenched, if you ask me. This house is so, well, *you*. It's sort of quirky and idiosyncratic, and despite its age can still look good with a little work."

I wondered fleetingly whether a jury of twelve pregnant women of a certain age would ever convict me. Pucci looked up at me from my lap, her round brown eyes full of alarm.

I unclenched my fists. "Is that all, Rebecca? I really do need to get back to work."

She stood and gathered her little dog into her arms. "Almost. I'll be sure to pass on what you told me to Suzy just in case she needs it for the article."

"Fine, whatever. What else?" I stood and headed back toward the kitchen door.

"I had a dream."

I paused. "About what?"

"A cradle. Two, actually. And there was a woman, but her back was to me. I didn't think it was you, though—she was very petite. But I got the impression that she was really pissed about something. I was wondering if you had any idea what it meant."

I took a deep breath, my skin tightening over my bones. With a light tone, I said, "Everybody seems to be into cradles these days. We have an old Vanderhorst one in the attic, and apparently Julia Manigault left one for me in her will."

Rebecca's eyes narrowed, her brow furrowing. It wasn't an attractive expression, and I saw that the lines between her brows didn't completely go away when she spoke, either. *Good.* "Interesting," she said. "I'll let you know if I have any more dreams."

"You do that," I said as I opened the front door. General Lee yipped, and I picked him up so he could say good-bye to his new friend.

"What's that smell?" Rebecca asked.

I looked at General Lee, but his face was blank. "I don't smell anything."

"It's like roses. You don't smell that? It's really strong."

"It could be from the garden—the Louisa roses are still blooming."

She gave me a speculative glance. "You know, they say that pregnancy hormones can dull or even sometimes completely eradicate certain supernatural gifts in some people. Maybe that's why you're not smelling it."

"Maybe." I said good-bye, then closed the door. I put a whimpering General Lee on the floor with a pat of assurance that he'd see Pucci again, then straightened as I breathed in deeply without catching the scent of roses.

I walked slowly toward the parlor, where I'd left my laptop and now cold coffee, and sat down. I stayed there for a long while just listening to Nola playing the piano, wondering whether what Rebecca had said was true, about my sixth sense taking a pregnancy hiatus, and trying to decide whether I was happy about it. A cold chill brushed my neck and I closed my eyes, thinking that I might be.

CHAPTER 8

My mother held up what appeared to be a red knit muumuu in one gloved hand and an identical blue one in the other. "These would look beautiful on you, Mellie. I think you should try them."

"Right. And when I'm done with them, I can let Mrs. Houlihan wear them, because they'd probably fit her."

My mother closed her eyes as if trying to summon strength. "Darling, if you'd just give these a try. Look." She stuck the red one closer to me. "See the deep scoop neckline? It will show off your décolleté to advantage, drawing the eye upward instead of around your middle. You can wear it bare or with a great necklace, or even a bright scarf."

I stared at the expanse of knit, actually seeing what she wanted me to, but still resisting the idea that my new size was closer to Mrs. Houlihan's than the clothes that hung in my own closet. And expanding daily.

She continued. "And you know how much Jack likes you in red." Her eyes sparkled.

"I'll try the blue one on, but you can hang up the red one."

"Nonsense," she said. "It's not like he can get you pregnant again right now, so you might as well." Hanging on to both tops, she moved to the next rack and started flipping through the hangers. "So, how's Detective Riley?"

I pretended to study the fabric of a nursing bra—a contraption I couldn't quite figure out. "Except for the small indentation in his forehead from my flying button, he seemed to be well."

"So it was a nice date?"

I rolled my eyes. "It wasn't a date. We just went to dinner to talk about the investigation. Then he told me a little bit about his child-hood and I told him a little bit about mine, and then he drove me home. Not even an attempt at a kiss good night, so definitely not a date. How did you hear about it?"

"Amelia. She's heartbroken about you and Jack but refuses to in-terfere. By the way, she has some beautiful furniture that just came into the store, which would be perfect in a nursery, and she wants you to come look at it. She has it on hold, because she knows it will be swept up very quickly."

"Mother, you know I don't do antique furniture. Remember what happened with the dollhouse."

Our eyes met as we both recalled the antique dollhouse Amelia had given to Nola, the dollhouse that, unbeknownst to us at the time, harbored an entire family of restless spirits.

"Actually, it's brand-new. She went to an estate sale, and an entire nursery of furniture—the tags still on it—was included. It's really high-end, and all mahogany, so it would look beautiful in your house. Or Jack's," she added as an afterthought, managing to slide in a note of disapproval.

Ignoring it, I said, "I guess I can go look at it. As long as it's not an antique cradle. I've already got one more than I need."

She looked at me oddly.

"What?"

"Nothing, it's just . . ."

"Mother, have you been talking with Rebecca? She's already told me about her dream about the two cradles and the angry woman, if that's what you're not wanting to tell me."

She seemed startled. "Actually, no. But thanks for telling me. What else did she have to say?"

"That's pretty much it. And that the woman definitely wasn't me, because she was petite."

My mother nodded as she turned back to the rack, but I could tell that she was no longer focused on maternity clothes.

I stepped closer to her. "Then what is it?"

Her mouth tightened. "I spoke with your grandmother."

We were both silent for a moment as we considered that only the two of us, and perhaps Rebecca, would think a conversation about receiving a phone call from beyond the grave was normal.

"She said she's been calling you, but you haven't been answering the phone."

I shook my head, not wanting to have the same conversation again. "What did she want?"

"She says you need to be careful. And to not be afraid to ask for help—from all sources."

She gave me a meaningful glance, and I remembered how Rebecca had smelled roses in my house and I hadn't.

"Do spirits come out of retirement when they feel they're needed?" I asked.

"What do you mean?"

I began flipping through a rack of what seemed to be more brightly colored muumuus and giant tent-shaped dresses and pants with pouches. "Remember how I always could tell Louisa Vanderhorst was about to make an appearance because I smelled roses? Rebecca smelled roses when she was at my house, so I was wondering if maybe Louisa might think I needed her. The baby was found in her house, too, after all."

"It's possible, I suppose. But why didn't you smell the roses?"

"I don't know. Rebecca says that sometimes pregnancy can mask certain gifts. Is that true?"

My mother regarded me for a long moment, then placed her gloved hand on my arm. "Yes. With me, anyway. When I was pregnant with you, I didn't need to wear gloves—at least from the second trimester on. I could still sense things when I touched certain objects, but there was a kind of filter between them and me. Maybe it's Mother Nature's way of protecting the baby from stress."

"But it came back after I was born."

"Pretty much the same day. I took a pen from a nurse to sign my release papers from the hospital, and I could see her mother in the cancer ward on the third floor. Except her mother was at home and healthy at the time, as far as she knew."

"Was it nice? Not having to deal with it for a few months?"

Her eyes were grave. "No. I thought it might be, but instead it was like having a missing limb. Or being separated from my child."

I studied my mother, still the beautiful woman I remembered from my childhood, and knew we were both recalling the thirty-three years she'd been absent from my life. My hand fell to my abdomen, my heart seeming to expand and contract as I thought about my baby being separated from me. Was this what motherhood felt like? Like having a part of you walking around outside of your body? I was no longer sure I wanted to find out.

I looked away. "Sometimes I think it would be nice to be able to walk into an antique store and not be greeted by a crowd of dead people, or to be able to look into a mirror without wondering who's standing behind me. Or to answer the phone and know for sure that it's a living, breathing person on the other end."

She moved to a table where various items of lingerie were displayed and began looking through them, her brow furrowed, and I knew she wasn't finished. Without turning around, she said, "Have you made any decision about staying in your house? You know you're always welcome to move in with me on Legare Street. It's a big enough house that we'd each have our own privacy." She blushed and I thought of the clandestine visits my father made that they didn't think I knew about.

"Are you sure you haven't been talking with Rebecca? Because she just asked me the same thing. As I told her, I don't think there's any rush. I'll figure it out—eventually."

She raised her eyes to meet mine. "I haven't seen Rebecca. It was your grandmother. She wanted you to know that you need to decide sooner rather than later what you want. And then be ready to fight for it."

I felt a small tremor in the pit of my stomach. "Fight for the house?"

"If that's what you decide you want."

I opened my mouth to tell her that I hated old houses, that I had since the moment I'd found out that she'd sold our family home after telling me for years that it would one day be mine. And I hated them because they always came with spirits who wanted my help. But I couldn't say it. Because, I was beginning to admit, it might no longer be true.

She put down what looked like a pair of enormous granny panties and forced a large smile onto her face. "You do need new bras. Let's try these dresses on and then we can go over to Bits of Lace and get you fitted properly for a bra in your new size. You'll want to be prepared the next time a button decides to fly off your jacket."

I wanted to make a retort, but she'd already turned her back to me and was heading toward the fitting rooms. *You need to decide sooner rather than later what you want. And then be ready to fight for it.* I stared after her and shivered, wondering what it was my grandmother thought I needed to fight for, too afraid to think about all the things I didn't want to lose.

My mother dropped me off in front of my house despite her offer to help me inside with my packages. I'd declined. I was bone tired and could think only of dumping all the packages in the front vestibule before passing out on the first sofa I found.

I pushed open the door to the piazza and paused. Sophie sat in a lotus position in the middle of the piazza floor, her eyes closed, the middle fingers and thumbs of each hand forming a circle. She wore a flowing muumuu-like top—not dissimilar to the ones my mother had just bought for me—but hers was filled with psychedelic colors in a tie-dyed pattern that almost brought up my lunch. Her Birkenstocks were parked under one of the rocking chairs, her bare feet tucked under her purple-legging-covered knees. There was no purple in the tie-dye—thank goodness—but at least they matched the purple elastic bands that pulled Sophie's hair back from her face in about a dozen places around her head.

Her eyes popped open before she moved lithely to a standing position, making it easier for me to see her outfit. It was the first time I realized that Sophie could probably continue wearing her same wardrobe throughout her pregnancy. The thought did not cheer me.

"Sorry! Mrs. Houlihan said you'd be home soon, so I asked her if I could meditate out here while I waited."

She must have seen my shoulders sag, because she walked toward me and took some of the shopping bags. "You've been shopping—good for you. You must be exhausted."

"You have no idea," I said, sticking my key in the front door lock. "It's not that I'm not happy to see you—but did we have plans? My memory is so fuzzy lately."

Sophie moved into the foyer and stacked the bags at the foot of the staircase. "No. But I've been doing some research on Mr. Vanderhorst's family and I found something really interesting that I wanted to tell you in person." She straightened. "Oh, and there was a package at your front door—I put it in the rocking chair. Hang on a minute."

She returned wearing her Birkenstocks and carrying a brown paper-wrapped package. The paper looked soft and had small creases radiating across the surface like a topographical map. It appeared to have gotten wet or was very old. Or both. The package was criss-crossed with knotted twine, the way packages used to be wrapped before modern shipping machines made the practice obsolete.

I kicked off my heels, leaving them in the middle of the floor along with the shopping bags I'd been holding, and reached for the package. "Who's it from?"

"It doesn't say. It only has the address—fifty-five Tradd Street, Charleston. No zip code or name—like it was hand-delivered. I have to say, though, that this looks really old. Like it was sent in the last century, before zip codes and parcel post delivery, then stuck in a time warp for a hundred years before being dropped here. Or . . ." She paused, holding her chin, which she did when in heavy thought and her hair was pulled back so she couldn't twist it.

"Or what?"

"Or somebody decided this is something you needed to see now."

Our eyes met in silent understanding that in my life, what she suggested was entirely possible.

I stared at the front of the package, at the elegant cursive—the careful penmanship so different from the way people wrote today—and felt a familiar tingle at the base of my neck. I wished my mother were there to touch it, to let me know whether I should open it. But I couldn't ask her, regardless of how much I wanted to be warned.

I forced a brightness to my voice that I didn't feel. "I've been receiving random gifts ever since my mother found out I was pregnant. She mentioned it to her former agent and I guess the news spread. I've got all the loot in a room upstairs, and you're welcome to go shop through the piles. I have no idea what half of the stuff is." I began to walk toward the back of the house, where I heard Mrs. Houlihan singing in the kitchen to General Lee. "Come on. I need some caffeine, if I can find any—just a smidge; I promise—and I'm sure Nola's left some of her flavorless green tea in there somewhere that you can have. We'll open the package and you can tell me what you've discovered."

I didn't need to turn around to see Sophie's frown of disapproval at my mention of caffeine.

Mrs. Houlihan, with her purse over her arm, was on her way out the back door when we entered. She poked her head back into the room. "Hello, Miss Melanie. I've got a meatless multigrain pot pie—from that cookbook on prenatal nutrition Miss Sophie gave me—warming in the oven, and a salad in the refrigerator for your supper. And there was something else." She paused to think for a moment. "Yes. If you need to leave, make sure the television in here is set on Animal Planet—I just discovered General Lee likes watching that, and if he's entertained, he won't chew on the welcome mat. Have a good evening, ladies, and I'll see you tomorrow morning."

The door began to close behind her before she opened it again. "Oh, and one more thing—an Irene Gilbert called twice and a Mr. Drayton called once. They both said it was very important that you call them back as soon as possible. I didn't give them your cell number but told them I'd let you know that they'd called. Neither one would leave a message, but I left their numbers on the pad by the phone."

She waved her fingers at us before shutting the door behind her.

"Mr. Drayton?" Sophie asked. "Wasn't he Mr. Vanderhorst's lawyer?"

"Yes," I said slowly, the tingling at the base of my neck growing stronger. "I wonder what he could want. I haven't spoken with him since Mr. Vanderhorst's estate was settled. And I have no idea who Irene Gilbert is."

Sophie placed the package on one of the kitchen table chairs, then pulled out another before bringing over the phone and message pad. "Why don't you sit down and return the calls while I make us both a nice cup of green tea?"

Both sounded equally unappealing, enough so that I contemplated making a run for my bedroom and locking the door. Unfortunately, I lacked the energy, and Sophie would have me cornered before I'd even reached the other side of the table.

I'd already decided I would wait for Irene Gilbert to call me back, since I didn't know who she was. Mr. Drayton had left both his office and his cell numbers and, squinting to see the numbers, I dialed the first one. After several rings the office answering machine picked up, which, seeing as how it was after five o'clock, didn't surprise me. I glanced at the cell phone number for a second before placing my phone facedown on the table.

"No luck?" Sophie asked from the sink, where she was filling a kettle with water.

I shook my head. "No. I'll try again tomorrow." I flipped the pad over, my head now practically ringing from the tremor that had exploded from the base of my skull like a kudzu vine. I was the queen of avoidance. Dealing with spirits since childhood had taught me that if I ignored them long enough, they would—most of the time— eventually go away. I'd expanded this theory to all unpleasant things that I didn't want to deal with. I'd only just begun to understand that some things, when ignored, could only get worse. Which didn't make me stop testing my theory again and again.

Sophie turned off the tap but continued to stare straight ahead through the large windows that held a view of my beautiful Charleston garden. "When the kitchen was updated, did you replace the windows?"

I sat up straighter. "No, why?"

She moved to the stove and turned on one of the gas burners. "Well, I can feel the heat pouring in, which means you might as well be throwing money out the windows every time you use the air conditioner. And there's a little dark spot near the sill that might be mildew from moisture getting trapped between the window and the wall."

"Don't," I said, spearing her with the look I usually reserved for a broker intent on making a lowball offer.

Sophie paused with a tea bag suspended in each hand. "Don't what?"

"I can't take another thing right now or my head will explode. I don't want to know what replacing windows in this house would cost, or removing mildew, but I'm sure it's more than I can afford unless it involves selling my baby. Which I'm not prepared to do."

"But you can't just pretend—"

I cut her off. "Yes, I can. Just watch me."

The teakettle whistled, and she took her time pouring the hot water into two mugs. She set one on the table in front of me before sitting in a chair opposite with the other mug. She took a sip from her mug. "How did your house hunting with Jack go?"

"Not so good. Every house I showed him looked good on paper—checked off just about every box on his wish list—the number of bedrooms, the size, the yard, and easy commute to Ashley Hall. But he nitpicked them to death. He keeps insisting he wants old with lots of history, with fixer-upper projects, and a garden big enough for a small pool and swing set. He even said he wouldn't mind a few ghosts." I rolled my eyes. "Where am I supposed to find him a house like that?"

She looked at me oddly for a moment. "Where, indeed?" she said as she took another sip from her mug, her gaze falling on the package she'd placed in a chair. "Aren't you going to open that?"

No! I wanted to shout, but didn't. Sophie Wallen-Arasi wasn't the kind of person to take no for an answer, and would have simply found a pair of scissors and opened it herself. Besides, I had a strong suspicion that I'd wake up and find the package in bed next to me, demanding to be opened. The only choice I had was to delay opening it as long as I could.

"So, what is it you wanted to tell me?" I asked, eager to redirect the conversation.

"Oh, yes—something very intriguing, but I'm not even sure if it will mean anything."

"Jack and I have an appointment with Yvonne Craig next Monday, so give me what you have and I'll share it with her. The woman is a genius at putting puzzle pieces together."

Sophie sat up straighter, wrapping her hand with their short, unvarnished fingernails around her mug. "Good, because she'll have more extensive family trees than I have to see if this means anything. And I'm still looking through the archives about foundation repairs that were made to the house. That might be able to help us pinpoint when the body was placed there. I'll keep you posted." She puffed out her breath, as if trying to contain news so that it would simply burst forth and amaze me.

"And?" I prompted.

"Mr. Vanderhorst's great-grandfather John Nevin Vanderhorst was a twin."

I couldn't see anything, but I imagined I heard the air ping. I considered her words for a moment. "Wasn't John Vanderhorst the naval officer who hid the Confederate diamonds in the grandfather clock?"

"Bingo. Same guy."

"But I thought Nevin Vanderhorst came from a long line of only children and had no living relatives to leave his estate."

"Which is true. The twin died when he was three—possibly of yellow fever."

"So why is that so interesting?"

"Well, having fraternal twins can be an inherited trait. Mostly it's carried down the female line, since it's the female who will have the tendency to hyperovulate. Which, technically, might not be as clearcut with the Vanderhorsts, since they typically married cousins—meaning the inherited trait might still be passed on through the family on the father's side.

"I was thinking of the two Vanderhorst cradles—the one in your attic and the one at the Charleston Museum—and I couldn't help but wonder if twins ran in the Vanderhorst family."

"But surely just one incident doesn't mean that it's an inherited trait."

"True—but I only had the family tree go back as far as the great-grandfather. Maybe Yvonne can go back further."

"So what are you suggesting? That one set of parents didn't like the idea of twins, so they bricked one up in the foundation?" I shook my head. "I don't see how that would have any connection."

Sophie stared into her mug for a long moment, giving me a full view of her purple hair ties, and I had a sudden vision of her with a daughter with a matching hairstyle. I stifled a shudder.

"Not exactly. I was thinking more along the lines of how easy it would have been to hide the death of one of the twins. Back then, determining a multiple birth wasn't exactly a science—and sometimes a doctor wouldn't know until the mother went into labor that she was having more than one baby."

She waited a moment, giving me time to digest what she'd just said. Sophie continued. "Or maybe the mother dropped a baby and it died, or for whatever reason the parents decided to keep the death hush-hush, which would have been easy to do, because nobody knew there'd even been a second baby."

The temperature in the room plummeted, and the air shifted around me, like a wave in a storm changing directions. My gaze darted from one corner of the kitchen to another, and although I saw nothing, an icy breath crossed my cheek and I felt more than heard the single word: *Mine*.

"Wow," I said, nearly choking. "I'll definitely mention that to Yvonne." My gaze seemed drawn to the package, and to the air surrounding it that seemed to shimmer and glow. Sophie merely sipped her tea, blissfully unaware of whatever else was in the room with us.

"I think I should open the package now," I said, moving across the room to the utility drawer where Mrs. Houlihan kept the scissors before returning to the table. For the first time I noticed that some of the twine appeared to be knotted together, as if the package had been opened and then resealed. I began to snip each band of twine, the air seeming to pop and sizzle with each closing of the blades. When the twine had been completely removed, I realized there was no adhesive holding the package together. I tipped the package over and shook it, staring in surprise at the wad of newspaper that slid out onto the table.

"Newspaper?" I asked as Sophie reached for it.

"Very old newspaper," she replied, smoothing the top of one of the pages. "From the *New York Times*. It's from July 1898."

My eyes slid from Sophie's face back down to the wad of newspaper. "I think there's something wrapped inside." I'd started to shiver from the cold, and I noticed that Sophie had goose bumps on her arms, too. I very carefully unwrapped the old paper, knowing Sophie would have a fit if I followed my instincts and frantically tore at it, eager to end the suspense and find out what I was so afraid of.

When the newspaper wrapping finally parted, we froze, our hands suspended over the gossamer layers of yellowed linen and lace.

Carefully I lifted the tiny garment, seeing now the small pearl buttons, the neck opening, and two impossibly little armholes. Remembering what Thomas Riley had told me about what they'd found in the box with the remains, I brought the neck opening closer to my face. Inside the linen collar, embroidered in small, careful stitches, was the name Susan Bivens. I shook the paper, wondering whether there might be a bonnet, too, but it hung flat and empty.

"It's beautiful enough to be a family heirloom," she said, her voice almost reverential. "For a family with lots of twins in the family tree, it makes sense that there would be two sets—this one and the one in the foundation."

My eyes met Sophie's again as puffs of our breath mingled in the chilly air before rising toward the ceiling. Sophie caught my arm just as I collapsed into my chair, the sound of a crying infant coming up through the floors of the old house and echoing in my heart.

CHAPTER 9

The following morning, I flipped on Animal Planet, then kissed General Lee good-bye, leaving a note for Mrs. Houlihan reminding her that I didn't want her giving out my cell phone number to anybody, no matter how hard they begged. I had my hand on the doorknob before I forced myself to return to the notepad and tear off the phone messages from the previous day and shove the page into my purse. Maybe today would be the day that I finally acknowledged that facing a problem head-on might be easier than being blindsided. Maybe.

Rich Kobylt, my contractor, was standing in the back garden with his hands on his hips—not, unfortunately, holding up his pants, which sagged dangerously low in the back—and staring at the piles of bricks and debris with yellow police tape still encircling them.

"Mornin', Miz Middleton."

"Good morning, Rich. I wasn't expecting to see you today. Did I forget an appointment?"

He shook his head. "No, ma'am. I was just wondering when I might be able to come back and finish the job. I don't feel like the job's complete without having everything put right."

I frowned. "I don't see why this is still roped off, but I'll check with Detective Riley to be sure and I'll let you know. But go ahead and submit the bill to my dad, and I'll tell him to pay it."

He scratched the back of his head. "Well, see, Miz Middleton, that's just it. I already submitted the bill, but when it didn't get paid I sort of figured you were waiting until the job got finished. 'Cause usually your daddy pays the bills the same week I submit them."

The sun seemed to be a little stronger on my shoulders as pinpricks of sweat erupted on my forehead. "Maybe it got misplaced or something. I'll check with my dad and make sure it gets paid ASAP."

"I sure appreciate that. My boy Brian started at Clemson last month and that tuition bill sure has made things a little tight for us at home."

"I completely understand, and I'll make sure it's all taken care of."

"Thank you, Miz Middleton. You have a nice day now, you hear?"

"You, too, Rich." I started to leave, but I hesitated. He hadn't moved, but was now staring at the piles of rubble with a heavy frown.

"Is there something else?" I asked.

I thought for a moment that he hadn't heard me, but instead he turned toward me, a peculiar expression on his face. "Do you ever hear a baby crying sometimes when you're out here?"

It was as if a vacuum had suddenly sucked all of the moisture from my throat. I swallowed. "Out here? No. I haven't. Why?"

He scratched the back of his head again with thick, blunt fingers. "Well, ever since we found that box with those bones in it, I've been hearing it." He stared silently at me for a moment, as if willing me to say something. When I didn't, he said, "My wife says it's probably a cat. I ain't never seen one out here—just your General Lee and a few palmetto bugs that are just as big as a cat, but I ain't never seen one. I'm just hoping I'm not going crazy or nothin'."

I smiled at him. "You're not going crazy, Rich. Old houses always have creaks and groans—it's like their voices. You get used to it after a while."

He hesitated for a moment before responding. "I guess," he said, his false smile matching my own. "Thank you."

"You're welcome. I'll make sure your bill's taken care of right away."

He tipped his Clemson baseball hat to me and I left the garden that still seemed as full of secrets as it had been the first time I'd seen it.

I met Jack halfway down the drive as he was walking toward the house. It was always awkward greeting him. Did we shake hands? Kiss on the cheek? Embrace? Kiss on the lips? None seemed appropriate. Which was odd, really, seeing as how we'd somehow managed to create a baby.

Being the mature adult I was, I opened my purse and pretended to search for a lipstick that I'd spotted the moment I'd opened it. I managed to "find" it right after I'd passed Jack. I held it up like I'd never seen it before. "Sorry to be a few minutes late. I had to speak with Rich Kobylt about the foundation repair."

"You're still ten minutes earlier than the time I said I'd meet you. I'm learning, but there are so many Mellie-isms that I slip up sometimes." He hurried past me and opened the passenger-side door of the van before helping me inside. He even reached over to buckle my seat belt.

"Really, Jack? I'm not an invalid. But you might be if you don't stop treating me like one."

He flashed his smile at full wattage before patting my belly. "Precious cargo." His smile didn't dim as he shut my door, then climbed into the driver's seat. "Do you know how to get there?"

I pulled out my iPhone and a folded piece of paper. "I Googled Dr. Wise's office last night and plugged the address into my phone's GPS, and also made a MapQuest printout just in case."

"Of course you did," Jack said, taking the paper from me and glancing at it. "And you're sure Dr. Wise is the best?"

I tried very hard not to roll my eyes. "My regular gynecologist recommended her because she specializes in high-risk pregnancies."

He turned to me with alarm. "High-risk?"

This time I gave in to the eye roll. "Only because I'm over forty and it's my first pregnancy. She gave me a checkup and said everything looked fine so far, and that Dr. Wise will probably do an ultrasound today."

"Will we be able to tell if it's a girl or boy?"

I shook my head. "It's too early. Besides, I'm not sure if I want to know ahead of time."

"But that would give us time to argue about the baby's name."

"You mean it's not already decided? You seemed pretty sure about Jack Junior and Sarah." I couldn't resist a smile.

"Oh, those are just at the top of my list. But I was wondering if we should keep to the pattern Nola started."

"The pattern?"

He grinned. "Well, Nola means New Orleans, Louisiana, which—as she likes to announce to strangers—is where she was conceived. I was thinking we could continue on the same theme."

I looked at him in horror, not sure whether he was joking. "What, and call the baby Charles or Charlotte?"

His grin widened. "Or we could be more creative. Like Redress. Or Couch. Or Granite—Granitia if she's a girl."

Despite myself, a small snort of laughter escaped from my nose. I elbowed him in the arm. "Just drive, please. We're going to be late, and I hate being late."

"Yes, ma'am," he said as he put the van in gear and pulled away from the curb.

At the doctor's office, I expected that Jack would sit down in the waiting room while I approached the registration desk, but after guiding me through the door he tucked my hand neatly into the crook of his arm so that we reached the desk together.

The woman sitting behind the desk was in her late twenties, with bright blond hair and big blue eyes that widened even farther after she caught sight of Jack. She gave me a fleeting glance before refocusing her attention on him.

"May I help you?" She actually batted her lashes.

"Yes," I said, moving to stand between Jack and the desk. "I have an appointment with Dr. Wise at nine o'clock."

She looked disappointed as she turned her attention to me. "Your name?"

"Melanie Middleton."

After a glance at a list on a clipboard, she crossed out a line, then handed me another clipboard. "Fill out the fronts and backs of all three sheets, and don't forget to sign the back of the third one."

I had almost made it to my seat when she called me back. "Mrs. Middleton? I'll need your insurance card."

I returned to the desk and slid my card toward her. "And it's Miss Middleton."

A light erupted in her eyes that could only be called a glimmer of hope. The words seemed to rush out of her mouth before she could call them back. "You're not married?" She at least had the audacity to look embarrassed.

"No," I said.

"Not yet," Jack said simultaneously.

I glared at him while her gaze moved from me, then to Jack, then back to me. "I'll let you know when the doctor is ready to see you."

I was almost through filling out the forms when my phone buzzed. Blondie looked at me with annoyance before pointing a finger at one of the many PLEASE TURN OFF YOUR CELL PHONE signs.

I glanced down at the screen and saw it was my mother. Making a mental note to call her back, I turned off my phone and stuck it in my purse, noticing the scrap of paper with Mr. Drayton's phone numbers on it. I'd return his call after I talked with my mother.

"Mrs. Middleton?" a matronly-looking nurse with graying curls called out from a doorway at the side of the desk.

"It's Miss," the blonde said with a note of satisfaction.

"Right," the nurse said as she marked something on the chart she held, her smile not wavering. "Would you come with me, please?"

I stood and Jack stood, too. "You don't have to come with me, Jack. I'll be fine."

He blanched a bit, but hid it by smiling. Pressing his hand against the small of my back and leading me forward, he said, "It's my baby, too, Mellie. I missed all of this with Nola, and I'm not going to miss it again."

I wasn't sure whether it was his touch or his words that made my knees forget how to work, but he was there to gently support me when I stumbled.

We were led to a giant scale and I stopped, staring at it as if I were an antelope in a circle of hungry lions. "I'm sure that's not necessary," I said.

The nurse—Peggy, according to the name tag on her cheerful pink-heart-covered scrub top—just smiled. "I get that a lot. But it's very necessary to track your weight throughout the pregnancy. You can take off your shoes if you like."

"I promise I won't look," Jack said, staring up at the ceiling.

I took off my shoes, my watch, my bracelet, my necklace, and my earrings and handed them along with my purse to Jack, then stepped onto the scale. "Don't say anything out loud, okay?"

Nurse Peggy nodded as she began moving the weights.

"And don't look," I reminded Jack.

He held up three fingers. "Scout's honor."

"You were a Boy Scout?"

"I made it to Cub Scouts but was asked to leave when I put a *Playboy* pinup picture on my Pinewood Derby car."

I narrowed my eyes at him. "Just don't look, okay?"

Peggy finished adjusting the weights in front of my field of vision, and I closed my eyes.

I heard a loud wolf whistle behind me. I jumped off the scale. "Jack! You weren't supposed to look."

He smiled so that his dimple appeared. "I'm just kidding. Besides, you're beautiful to me no matter what you weigh."

I waited for Peggy to say, *I've heard that one before, too*, but when she didn't, I turned to her, only to see her gazing dreamily at Jack.

"He's a keeper," she said to me in a loud whisper.

I took my belongings back from Jack without looking at him, unable to talk past the thickness in my throat to let her know that he wasn't even mine to keep.

After I supplied a urine sample, we were led into the examining room, where Peggy took my blood pressure, then began rolling up my sleeve to draw blood. Being a naturally squeamish person, I turned my head away while Jack took hold of my other hand without asking and squeezed it gently until Peggy told us she was finished.

Peggy beamed at us, making me disengage our hands. "I just need to ask you a few questions." She pulled up a pair of reading glasses hanging on a chain around her neck and placed them on her nose. "Let's see. What is the date of your last menstrual period?" She held her pen poised over my patient folder.

I blinked. "Excuse me?"

"When was your last menstrual period?"

I blinked again. "I don't have a clue. I've never been regular, and I've never had a reason to keep track."

It was her turn to blink back at me. "So you have no idea when you last had your period? It's a real help when pinpointing your due date."

Jack cleared his throat. "Maybe I can help. We conceived on June twenty-sixth—her fortieth birthday."

I closed my eyes, wondering whether being forty should have left me immune to this kind of embarrassment.

"It's better than nothing." Peggy put down the chart and then picked up what looked like a color wheel for choosing wall colors, with two round pieces of cardboard attached in the middle so that they could slide in both directions.

"Let's see," she said, her voice low, as if she were talking to herself. "This isn't an exact science, but let's just say you ovulated here." She turned one of the wheels, and paused a moment to read something. Then she looked up at me and smiled. "And that would make your estimated due date March twenty-third."

I felt something like panic squeeze my stomach. *March twenty-third.* "But that's so . . . soon." It wasn't that I didn't know a pregnancy was nine months. It was just that bringing my—our—son or daughter into the world was something I'd relegated to the distant future. Something I'd deal with when I could. Something I could postpone. Not March twenty-third.

Peggy gave me an encouraging smile. "At least you won't be heavily pregnant during the worst of a Charleston summer."

I barely heard her. *March twenty-third.* Jack took my hand and I let him.

The nurse placed my folder on a small table and began walking toward the door. "I'm going to get Dr. Wise now."

A glimmer of my old self, the one who craved control and order—two things that had been conspicuously absent from my life in the last few months—shimmied to the surface and I began to think again in the comforting patterns of spreadsheets and calendars.

"When do I do my birth plan?" It was something I'd read about in one of the books Jack had bought for me, and after listening to Sophie talk about natural childbirth, getting my plan down on paper had suddenly become very important. I didn't want to risk running out of time, especially now that I realized there was so little of it. "I want to make sure that I get an epidural as early as possible. Maybe even as early as the eighth month."

I could tell that Peggy had heard that a lot, too, by the battle-weary look on her face. "I'm sure Dr. Wise will go over all of that with you. You still have plenty of time."

"And I'd like to be unconscious during the delivery, if they still do that."

Peggy's smile was thinning. "You can go over all of your concerns with Dr. Wise. Right now, I need you to get into this gown—opening in the front, all of your clothing off—and push this button when you're ready." She indicated a square button mounted on the wall next to the examining table.

As the nurse moved toward the door, I looked at Jack. "You can wait outside while I change."

"Really, Mellie? It's not like I've never seen you without your clothes on."

My face flamed as Nurse Peggy suppressed a giggle before leaving the room, the door smacking shut behind her.

I made Jack turn his back while I put on the aqua gown, then assumed the position on the examining table with the blanket draped modestly in place. I pressed the button and after only a few minutes a statuesque woman with dark blond hair pulled back into a chic chignon entered the room. She wore a stethoscope and a lab coat; otherwise I might have mistaken her for a model who'd lost her way to a photo shoot. I was embarrassed to admit how relieved I was that Jack hardly seemed to notice.

She held out her hand to me and smiled, her teeth perfect. "I'm Dr. Diane Wise."

Jack and I introduced ourselves, then shook hands with the doctor while I tried very hard to suck in my stomach so I wouldn't appear too troll-like next to Wonder Woman, especially with Jack in the same room.

"So," she said, clasping her hands together as she approached the examining table. "Let's take a look and see what we have here."

I glanced at Jack, thinking that now would be an appropriate time for him to leave. Instead he was sitting in a chair and leaning forward, looking like a medical student at his first autopsy.

Accepting my fate, I stared up at the ceiling while Dr. Wise examined me, starting with my breasts, then moving down to my abdomen. She pressed gently on the slight mound of my stomach, moving her hands to various points, then seemed to be doing some sort of measurement with three of her fingers. She straightened, then glanced at my chart with a small frown.

"You're looking a little large for just twelve weeks. We'll have to see what the ultrasound says." She smiled reassuringly at both Jack and me, and I smiled back only because I'd become immune to people telling me that I was large.

When she'd completed the physical exam, she said, "I'm going to use a fetal heart monitor now to hear the baby's heartbeat." She set up a small machine that looked like a transistor radio and flipped it on, then lubricated my belly with a warmed gel. Using a wandlike device, she began running it over my abdomen, stopping it when a muffled *thud-thud* emanated from the speaker.

Jack stood next to me, his hand somehow holding mine again, and we were both grinning stupidly at the doctor. "Is that the baby?" Jack asked, his voice hushed.

"It is." Dr. Wise moved the wand back and forth, the *thud-thudding* sound getting quieter, then louder. A small pucker formed again at the bridge of her nose as she moved the wand around, back and forth, pausing it in the same two spots again and again.

"Is there something wrong?" I asked, my voice higher than normal. Jack squeezed my hand.

The doctor gave us both another reassuring smile, and I wondered whether she had to practice that in the mirror. "The baby sounds healthy. Let's see what the ultrasound tells us." She walked toward the corner of the room, where a mobile ultrasound machine stood, and wheeled it next to the examining table. It had a keyboard and a screen that Dr. Wise kept facing her, and a wand that was larger than the one used to check the fetal heart rate. After adding more warm lubricant, she began sliding the wand across my abdomen, focusing on the same spots she'd focused on before.

She didn't say anything for a few minutes, moving the wand and then typing something on the keyboard. I found myself holding my breath, wondering whether she'd start frowning again, and thinking about how unprepared I was for any of this. I held on to Jack's hand as if he alone were keeping me earthbound, something I found alarmingly reassuring.

"Do you want to see your baby?" she asked, turning the screen toward us.

Jack and I leaned forward as a unit. The baby was so small, yet so incredibly human, with a beating heart and recognizable arms and legs. It was *our* baby. Mine and Jack's. My heart seemed to expand, dimming memories and creating a fog around previously made convictions.

"That's my boy," Jack said, a wide grin on his face. "And he already takes after his daddy."

His words broke through the fog, shining a bright light into my delirium. I blinked at Jack, seeing again the handsome charmer who'd broken my heart once and who seemed destined to do it again.

"That's actually a leg, Mr. Trenholm. It's too early to determine the sex of the child," Dr. Wise said gently, while turning the screen back so only she could see it as she began to move the wand to the other side of my abdomen.

"What are you doing?" I asked, watching as the little pucker again formed between the doctor's brows.

"I thought I heard something while listening to the heartbeat, and I just wanted to make sure."

"Sure of what?" I asked, my skin suddenly cold under the lubricant, my chest rippling like a sudden freeze had solidified everything inside.

She didn't say anything right away, but continued to move the wand up and down over my abdomen. Suddenly she stopped, then typed some more on the keyboard. "Well," she said, the word drawn out into two syllables.

"Well what?" Jack asked, his tone unfamiliar to me, recalling the fact that he'd once been a soldier who'd been taught how to deal with a crisis and obliterate the enemy. I closed my eyes, waiting for the doctor to speak, knowing that I could handle it because Jack was there with me.

"Well," she said again. "It looks like there's another baby in here." She turned the screen while Jack and I stared at another small, perfectly formed baby, its heart beating in its liquid world inside me.

"What do you mean?" Jack and I demanded in unison.

Dr. Wise beamed at us. "Congratulations. You're having twins."

CHAPTER 10

Jack and I sat in the van, staring out the windshield. He'd started the engine so the air conditioner was blowing full blast in our faces, but he hadn't made a move to actually put the car in gear and drive somewhere. It was as if neither one of us knew what needed to happen next.

"I'm glad I bought the van," Jack said finally, his smile a little shaky.

I nodded, my head already making calculations where everything was multiplied by two: two cribs, two high chairs, two car seats. Two college tuitions. I fought past the knot in my throat. "What are we going to do?"

"What we were planning on doing before. Just twice as much."

"I know. That's what scares me. I was still struggling with the idea of having just one baby and wondering how I was going to manage *that*."

He reached across the console with the large cup holders and took my hand. "You're not alone in this, remember. I'm here. We'll just have to think like an army sergeant—divide and conquer."

Despite myself, I laughed. "Who would have thought that being a soldier and being a parent had so many similarities?" I withdrew my hand and placed it on my lap, unable to control my anxiety over the fact that I was going to have *two* babies, mixed with the flood of emotions that threatened to overtake me every time Jack touched me. I closed my eyes, feeling the beginnings of a headache. They popped open as I remembered my mother's phone call while I'd been in the waiting room.

I turned on my phone and was startled to see that I had five phone calls from my mother and one voice mail. I held the phone to my ear and listened. Her voice was strained, as if she were forcing herself to sound calm, which of course sent the first alarms of panic through me.

"Mellie, dear. Please call me as soon as you get this message. I'm at your house, and you need to come home as soon as possible. It's . . ." She paused, and I pictured her turning toward someone else, because when she spoke again, I could actually hear her brittle smile. "It's rather urgent."

I hit redial and turned to Jack. "Head toward Tradd Street. My mother says I need to meet her there and it's urgent."

He put the van in gear and started to drive, neither of us speaking, as if we were both afraid of voicing our fear that we could only hope that my mother's news wasn't as life-altering as our own.

My mother picked up on the first ring, as if she'd been holding the phone, waiting for my call. "Mellie, thank goodness. Are you on your way?" She was whispering, and I thought I heard voices in the background.

"Yes. We're in Mount Pleasant about to go over the bridge. What's going on, and who's there?"

She began speaking in a whisper so low that I couldn't hear her.

"Mother, you need to speak louder."

After the second attempt I finally interrupted her. "Look, why don't you text me? Nola showed you how, remember?"

There was complete silence for a moment. "You know I can't."

I sighed. Fat thumbs and an abhorrence to small letters were inherited traits in my family—just like a fast metabolism and talking to dead people. My own efforts at texting had ended up—thanks to Nola—on an obnoxious Web site called whenparentstext.com.

"Never mind. I'll be there in fifteen to twenty minutes. Can you tell me who's there?"

After a brief pause, she said, "Mr. Drayton. And a Mr. and Mrs. Gilbert. They're here to look at the house."

I felt my stomach shift, as if analyzing my breakfast and finding it wanting. "What? Why would they think it's okay to tour my house?"

My mother whispered more unintelligible words into the phone as my stomach continued its protest against breakfast, the news that we were expecting twins, and the fact that complete strangers and Mr. Vanderhorst's lawyer were currently traipsing through my house.

"Never mind. We're on our way."

I dropped my phone into my purse and plastered both hands over my mouth. We were in the middle of the bridge with no place to pull off. I looked around me desperately at the new leather seats, the pristine carpet, the gleaming buttons on the dash.

"Are you all right?" Jack asked, sparing a look at me from the road. "Not that it's not a good color for you, but your face is a bit green."

I eyed one of the large cup holders by the armrest and, with a mental apology to the engineers and factory workers who designed and built the van—and to Jack—I leaned over and threw up into the perfectly round hole.

"Poor Mellie." I felt Jack's hand gently pulling my hair away from my face as I emptied the contents of my stomach in his brand-new vehicle, and I think I might have fallen in love with him all over again. "I'll pull over as soon as we get off the bridge."

My stomach was empty and I was already leaning against the back of my seat, a cold sweat enveloping my body as I used a tissue from my purse to wipe my mouth. "No. I need to get home. My mother said that Mr. Drayton and some couple are there and it's urgent I get home as soon as possible. I can enter through the kitchen and clean up there. The cup holder is removable, and I'll rinse it out with the garden hose before disinfecting it with Lysol or Febreze. Or maybe both." I dropped the tissue on top of the mess to hide it from view.

He patted my leg. "I'll take care of it. I have a feeling this won't be the last time I'll have to clean vomit out of the van."

I sent him a weak grin as he aimed the van toward our exit from the bridge.

As he pulled into the end of the driveway at my house, he said, "I'll come in with you."

If it had been a question, I would have said no. Which was probably the reason it wasn't. Considering the circumstances, I found it remarkable how sometimes we reminded me of an old married couple.

A large Mercedes sedan, presumably Mr. Drayton's, sat at the curb in front of my house directly in front of an older-model baby blue minivan with New York plates. After Jack helped me out, I walked toward the other van while Jack did what he needed to do with the contents of his cup holder.

I peered into the van's windows, seeing a box of Kleenex on the front dash, various stains on the cloth seats, two baseball gloves on the rear seat, and what could have been dog snot from a very large dog covering most of the side windows. I was suddenly grateful that General Lee wasn't large enough to reach one of the windows, much less leave reminders that he'd even been there. Besides, he had a car seat that I kept in the middle of my backseat so that he wouldn't be tempted to drool on my windows even if he could.

I glanced across the street, noticing Sophie's new Prius for the first time. She'd either just arrived for what I was beginning to think of as an intervention or my mother had forgotten to mention that she was there. Either way, if she'd been pulled from her classes in the middle of the day to come to my house, it couldn't be good.

The street darkened as heavy clouds elbowed their way in front of the sun, a thick breeze full of moisture stirring up the dead leaves from the sidewalk. It reminded me of the first time I'd seen this house, right before I'd knocked on the front door and met Nevin Vanderhorst. My gaze strayed to the old oak tree, and I almost expected to see Louisa Vanderhorst, Nevin's mother, pushing the empty swing.

The swing swayed gently, from the storm-scented wind or from an unseen hand, I couldn't tell. If Louisa was there, I could no longer see her, or smell her roses. But I imagined I could *feel* her. Feel her maternal presence watching over me like the tall limbs of the oak tree watched over my house and garden.

"Are you ready?" Jack stood nearby, holding out his hand.

I nodded, touching my fingers to his, and allowed him to lead me through the garden gate toward the kitchen door at the back of the house.

"Any idea why those people are here?" Jack asked.

I shook my head, then dropped his hand as I continued walking up the path. I didn't know why those people were in my house, but I knew with certainty that it couldn't be good news.

Jack didn't press me further, but when we reached the kitchen door he turned me to face him. "I'm here, okay? Whatever this is all about, I'm on your side. Don't forget that."

I looked into his vivid blue eyes, my pregnancy hormones firing on all cylinders, and was oddly grateful for the fact that I had just thrown up in his car. Otherwise I would have been tempted to press him up against the door and allow the hormones to take over.

"Thank you," I said, ignoring the light in his eyes and the curve of a smile that made me think that he'd just read my mind.

He opened the door and we quietly entered the empty kitchen. I looked for General Lee, sure my mother would have put him there if strangers were in the house. It took him a while to warm up to new people, and he liked to greet visitors with incessant barking unless I was there to calm him down. I assumed my mother was holding him, keeping him calm until I arrived.

I opened my purse and pulled out a travel-size toothpaste, tooth-brush, and a bottle of mouthwash, then moved to the sink.

"You carry all that in your purse?" Jack couldn't hide the amuse-ment in his voice.

"It doesn't hurt to be prepared." I almost said that I should have added condoms to my emergency kit, but after seeing our babies and their heartbeats on the ultrasound monitor, I couldn't wish them out of existence. They might be the only permanent tie to Jack that I could ever claim.

When I was finished cleaning up, I put on fresh lipstick, blotted it with a paper towel, then headed toward the kitchen door and stopped, not really sure why.

"Remember—I'm right behind you," Jack said quietly.

I wasn't strong enough to look up at him, but I was strong enough to nod at the closed door. He opened it for me, allowing me to go first. Sophie's voice came from the upstairs hallway, trickling down the grand staircase.

"As you can see, Melanie has spent an absurd amount of money, time, and energy on restoring the house, but it's been like spitting in the ocean—a bottomless ocean, actually. The windows are an energy nightmare—some with cracks between the sills, and windows so large that palmetto bugs don't even need to duck to get inside." I heard her whistle. "And boy howdy, you sure don't want those critters in your house."

Jack and I looked at each other with raised eyebrows, wondering why Sophie was all of a sudden sounding as if she were one of the characters on the reality show *Gator Boys*.

She continued. "Might be an improvement, though. Maybe they could eat through all the mildew and rotten plaster that's all over the house. Can you smell that? Pee-eww! Just about makes me want to toss my grits every time I walk in here. Poor Melanie, being saddled with this pile of lumber. She's always been one for lost causes, though. Bless her heart."

I walked through the foyer to stop at the bottom of the stairs, wanting to see who this person was who sounded exactly like my best friend. I looked up to see a group of five people clustered around the newel post at the top of the stairs. According to Sophie, it had been hand-carved by renowned Charleston cabinetmaker John Bonner. During the Civil War it had apparently suffered more than one saber wound, slicing off bits of the pineapple finial and making it look more like a kumquat. I'd wanted to cut the rest of it off, but Sophie had started swooning at the mere mention.

Sophie—and it was definitely her, because I recognized the hair with the twenty or so different pigtails held back with plastic pink bows—faced away from me and continued talking. She pointed to the finial. "As you can see, repairs have been delayed or postponed indefinitely because of the prohibitive costs associated with restoration. I've told her more than once that it would be an act of mercy if she'd just douse the whole house with gasoline and set a match to it, but she can't forget her promise to dear Mr. Vanderhorst, rest his soul. Even if it kills her trying."

"Sophie?" Jack and I said in unison.

She looked down at us over the railing. Without skipping a beat, she said, "Here's the poor girl now. You can see on her face the toll restoring this house has taken."

I opened my mouth to protest, but stopped when I saw the two strangers standing behind her. They were a middle-aged couple, both pleasantly plump, with curly brown hair. The man wore a Yankees T-shirt with jeans and sneakers, the woman dressed almost identically except for a floral blouse instead of a T-shirt. Both were peering at me quizzically through large round glasses, as if I were the unwelcome visitor.

My instincts told me to be wary, but the couple appeared to be trying out for roles as sitcom parents. They looked perfect for their parts playing the loving yet goofy mom and dad of a brood of active and raucous children. It was no stretch of the imagination to assume the baby blue van outside was theirs, and I quickly quashed the thought that Jack and I would look just like that after a few years of raising our children. We already had the van, after all.

And then I noticed my dog. The same dog who, despite his lack of stature, tried to verbally assert his authority and protect his territory from strangers was nestled comfortably in the woman's arms, his eyes mere slits, as if I had interrupted him from a nap.

We seemed to be in a standoff or a staring match, with nobody knowing what to say or where to start. We were spared from standing there for the rest of the day by Mr. Drayton, who stepped out from behind my mother. He was tall and thin and wore a dark suit that contrasted with his silver-gray hair. If I hadn't known who he was, I would have mistaken him for an undertaker.

"Why don't we all go downstairs so I can make proper introductions?" He smiled and indicated for the rest of the group to precede him down the stairs.

Once we were assembled in the foyer, my mother and Sophie moved to stand on either side of Jack and me, the couple and my dog standing opposite. Mr. Drayton stood between us like a referee.

Clearing his throat, he said, "Melanie Middleton, I'd like you to meet Irene and George Gilbert. Mr. and Mrs. Gilbert, this is Miss Middleton."

At the mention of the word "Miss," I saw Irene's gaze dart to my stomach and then over to Jack before returning to my face. She kept her expression neutral.

"And this is . . ." Mr. Drayton paused, looking pointedly at Jack.

"Jack Trenholm," he said, offering his hand to Mr. Drayton.

"The writer?" Irene almost squealed, her eyes sparkling behind her glasses as she allowed her gaze to travel up and down Jack.

"Yes, that's right. I'm also—"

Sophie cut him off. "The baby daddy." She patted her still flat belly, but one she seemed to be trying to make larger under her tentlike dress. "Yep—something about this house seems to encourage getting knocked up. I hope you're not thinking you're through having kids yet!"

My mother looked up at the ceiling while Jack and I stared at Sophie, wondering whether she'd suddenly become possessed or if her pregnancy hormones were just affecting her in a different way.

To break the awkward pause, I moved to extend my hand to shake when I again spotted my dog snuggling up in this stranger's arms, and I froze. Maybe it was because of the news I'd just received at the doctor's office, or maybe it was because I just wanted to collapse on the floor in a fit of fatigue and despair but couldn't because these people were in my house, but I snapped.

I reached for General Lee—who had the audacity to let out a low growl—and pried him from the woman's arms. "Okay, enough with the pleasantries. Who the hell are you and why are you here?"

My mother put a calming arm around my shoulder and I noticed that she wasn't wearing her gloves.

Irene spoke first. "If you ever answered your phone or returned any phone calls, you'd know. We don't mean to ambush you, but you left us with few options. We were hoping that the newspaper reporter would have given you a copy of her article before it appeared in this Sunday's paper so you'd be prepared, but even she's had a difficult time reaching you."

"The reporter?" I vaguely recalled Rebecca telling me about some reporter who was doing a story about Mr. Vanderhorst. "What does the reporter or the article have to do with me?"

My mother tightened her hold on my shoulder. "It's a little complicated, Mellie; why don't we all go sit down in the parlor. . . ."

"No. I think we've waited long enough." Irene squared her shoulders. "My husband is the only living legitimate descendant of John Vanderhorst, Nevin Vanderhorst's great-grandfather. That means that Nevin Vanderhorst's estate is rightfully ours, and we're here to contest his will."

My ears started ringing as I realized why Sophie had suddenly developed a split personality. She'd been trying to defend me. *They want my house.* The thought scared and enraged me, two strong emotions I wasn't used to feeling at the same time. The last time it had happened I'd been in a cemetery with an evil spirit who'd been trying to kill me.

I stared at the woman with her jeans and sneakers and thick New York accent, and then over to her husband, and knew they couldn't have been genetically farther from Nevin Vanderhorst than if they'd been another species.

I was shaking my head before I'd begun to speak. "No. That's not possible. Mr. Vanderhorst made it clear that he had no living relatives."

George moved to stand next to his wife. "He was mistaken. We have proof of our claim."

"What proof?" I asked. Spots had begun to form in front of my eyes, and I realized that what little I'd eaten at breakfast had been left in the van's cup holder. I blinked hard, needing to keep focused.

We watched as Irene Gilbert opened her large purse and pulled out something wrapped in tissue. Very gently, as if holding a baby, she reached inside and pulled out a yellowed linen bonnet. The kind of bonnet that was usually worn with a matching christening gown.

I heard Sophie's intake of air as we both recognized the embroidery along the edges of the visor. I hadn't yet shown the gown to my mother, but she could tell from our reaction that the bonnet was something important.

Very slowly, I reached over and took the bonnet from Irene and flipped it inside out. And there, in carefully stitched letters, was the name Susan Bivens.

My mother reached for the bonnet, her bare fingers touching it just as I closed my hand over hers to stop her. Frigid air pushed at us in viscous waves as an unseen hand pressed against my throat, choking the air from my lungs. I called for Jack, but the words died, fading like the light. Just as everything went dark, I saw an angry woman standing next to two empty cradles, while invisible fingers played the same three notes over and over on the piano.

CHAPTER 11

I blinked several times, registering only a dimly lit room, soft sheets, and a warm hand holding mine. Then something fuzzy and wet nuzzled my neck, making me press my face into a vaguely familiar scent. "Jack?" I murmured.

"Actually, no. I'm over here."

Both eyes jerked open and I found myself staring into a pair of soft brown eyes and a very black, wet nose. General Lee barked once in greeting before Jack lifted him off the bed and set him on the floor. "That's enough of that. Who would have thought that my competition would have more hair on his chest than I do?"

My smile faded as I remembered the angry woman and the fingers pressed against my throat. I quickly sat up, and then just as quickly regretted my decision as my head tried to spin off my shoulders.

"Slow down, Mellie. You've been through a lot today and you need to take it easy. For all three of you." He grinned, but I saw the worry in his eyes. "Luckily, Mrs. Gilbert is a registered nurse and was able to reassure us that you'd only fainted and that your vitals were all strong. She suspected you might be a little dehydrated, which is probably right, since I had firsthand knowledge that your stomach had been recently emptied and I hadn't seen you drink anything to replenish your fluids. Just in case, I called Dr. Wise, and she thought it would be a good idea to bring you in. But I left out this part, because I didn't think she could help with that." He lifted the hair off of my neck.

Raw welts rippled under my fingers when I touched where the icy hand had been. I swallowed, my throat feeling thick and bruised. "I'm fine. Really. I allowed myself to be vulnerable and unprepared. I won't be next time."

He didn't look convinced. "Next time? If you think there's a good chance of a 'next time,' then maybe I should move in, just to be sure."

Right. Like that would help me sleep at night. "No, Jack. I can handle this. I know how. And if I need help, I'll call my mother." I frowned, having a vague memory of her screaming as the lights went out. I straightened, all grogginess gone. "How's my mother? She touched the bonnet without her gloves."

Jack released my hand and rubbed the stubble on his cheek. "She's fine. Your father came and took her home. Quite the spectacle to see both of you fainting at the same time. If that didn't freak out the Gilberts, then hopefully Sophie's tales of doom and gloom and unending battles with mildew will make them run screaming all the way back to New York."

"Do you really believe that?"

He paused, considering. "No." He sat down on the edge of the bed again, and I held myself still, straining against my body's need to curl up against him. "Remember what Mr. Vanderhorst said to you? About this house being more than bricks and mortar, but a piece of history you can hold in your hand? I think the Gilberts get that. I don't think they're here for the money. I think they're here because it's Mr. Gilbert's birthright, his connection to a family he never knew existed."

"But all they have is a bonnet. How can that be proof?"

"That's all they showed us. They didn't have time to tell us any more, because you fainted. But I think the article in this Sunday's paper might be illuminating. I don't think Mr. Drayton would be with them if he didn't think they had enough evidence to make a case."

I glared at him. "So you're taking their side?"

His eyes darkened. "I'm always on your side, Mellie, and I wish you didn't make me jump through hoops to show it." He held up his hand to stem the flow of words threatening to tumble from my mouth.

"But if we can push aside all the emotions, I'm sure you'll have to agree that we need to find the truth. Obviously the bonnet and christening gown are connected. We'll go visit Yvonne and see what we can discover and then go from there. I don't know what the Gilberts have in their arsenal, but I don't think it'll be long before we find out. And I think you should get a lawyer."

"A lawyer? Can't we just get to the bottom of this and find out that they're wrong, and then they'll go away?"

"But what if they're not wrong?"

I regarded him steadily as worry and fear spread up from my feet like a vine, winding themselves around my heart before squeezing tightly. "Then I could lose my house."

"'*My* house,' Mellie? So it's no longer 'that pile of termite-infested lumber'? Or the 'goiter' on your neck?"

He was right, of course. My eyes burned with anger, tears, or frustration—maybe all three. Or maybe I could blame it on the pregnancy hormones. They had become a good catchall for everything that seemed to be ailing me.

Softening his voice, Jack said, "Have you considered that the discovery of the bones in the foundation happened now for a reason? That somebody thought that the house was ready to give up its last secret?"

My eyes met his as I struggled to find my voice. "That's what's worrying me. That it's not just the Gilberts who think I have no claim to this house."

I couldn't find the strength to hold back my tears and they fell down my cheeks, wetting my blouse. Jack pulled me into his arms, which released even more tears, as if a plug had been pulled on a drain that had been blocked for a very long time.

"I–it's the hormones," I managed to stutter, my words muffled by his warm, solid chest.

"I know, Mellie. I know," he said as he patted my back.

I continued to cry, hounded by my grandmother's words about finding out what I wanted and being ready to fight for it. But what if there were *two* its? And what if I'd already lost both because I'd been too stupid to know what I had when they were mine?

I dragged myself through the door of Henderson House Realty the following morning, sweating more than the early-morning temperature warranted. I felt as if I'd already run a marathon instead of having simply gone through the effort of putting on panty hose while nibbling saltines to stem the tide of nausea.

I paused at the front desk as Nancy Flaherty and her receptionist-in-training, Joyce Challis, looked up at me.

"Wow," said Nancy.

"Wow?" I repeated.

Nancy and Joyce exchanged a look before Nancy turned back to me. "Were you planning on doing your hair and makeup once you got here?"

I raised my hand to my hair, and then my lips, then stared back at Nancy in horror. I'd been so proud of getting myself showered and dressed and making it out the door without throwing up that I'd simply forgotten to brush my hair or put on makeup.

Nancy stood, clutching a sizable cosmetics bag in a green argyle pattern with a large embroidered golf ball on the side. "Not to worry—I always come prepared."

As she walked out from behind the desk I noticed that they'd both been knitting again. I looked down at the little half-finished knitted golf visors—one in blue and one in pink. "You finished with the blankets?"

Nancy nodded. "I already promised Jack that I'd teach the baby how to golf, so I figured he or she should be prepared."

I hoped, at least for Nancy's sake, that the twins would be one of each. Otherwise she'd have more knitting to do. "It's twins," I said, my voice cracking. We hadn't even told our parents yet—not after the fiasco of the day before with the Gilberts' visit.

They both smiled. "Twins! How exciting!" they said in unison.

My own smile wobbled. "Yes, it is. It's just taking some getting used to, that's all."

"Any pregnancy will do that," said Nancy, taking my arm.

I paused. "Before I forget." I pulled out the memo pad I always kept in my purse along with my oral care items. "Please take note of the names of people I do not wish to speak with. Anybody with the last name of Gilbert, Rebecca Edgerton, or Suzy Dorf. If Mr. Drayton calls, or one of my parents, I'll take it. Same goes for Detective Riley with the Charleston PD."

Joyce busily scribbled down the names. "What about Mr. Trenholm? Which list is he on this week?"

I shot a glance at Nancy, who shrugged. "I'm teaching her everything I know."

With as much dignity as I could manage, I said, "He has my cell number, but if he calls the office, I'll take the call."

"But ask again tomorrow," Nancy threw over her shoulder as she led me back to my office.

After fifteen minutes with Nancy and her makeup bag, I was looking almost human again. She gave me a thumbs-up, then left to go back to knitting, working on her chip shot, and occasionally answering the phone.

I turned on my computer and stared desultorily at my mostly empty calendar. I'd been studiously avoiding the leaderboard posted outside Mr. Henderson's office, because I knew I was no longer number one. I had a feeling that I wasn't even in the top ten. Even though the knowledge didn't ignite a fire in me the way it used to, I still found it mildly irritating.

I had a prospect list and a few phone messages to return. I flipped through them several times and was about to stick them on the corner of my desk to deal with later when I heard Dr. Wise's words echoing in my head, reminding me why it was important that I actually earn money. *Congratulations. You're having twins.* If I was planning on being a single mother and supporting my children, I needed to get busy.

With as much enthusiasm as I could muster, I made my phone calls, and even managed to put a few appointments on my calendar to view a house, show a house, and list a house. It wasn't my usual amount of activity, but I felt better knowing that I was diving back into the world of earning an income. I might have to buy a house to live in, in the

not-so-distant future; moving in with my mother was not an option I
wanted to seriously consider. Being single, pregnant, and over forty
was hard enough to deal with. Living with my mother would send me
over the cliff into the world of patheticness. It was gratifying to know
that after everything that had happened, I at least still had my pride.

When I was finished, I returned to my computer to search out new
listings for houses to show Jack. Finding the perfect house had proven
to be a lot harder than I'd anticipated, his checklist of wants impossible
to find in a single house. If the house was old enough, it didn't have
the space. If the house had the right amount of yard space and garden,
it wasn't old enough.

I was jotting down notes about possibilities when Nancy's voice
came over the intercom. "There's a Detective Riley here to see you,
Miss Middleton. He says it's business."

I sat up, ridiculously glad that I'd allowed Nancy to fix my hair and
makeup. "Please send him back."

I stood and walked around to the front of my desk, smoothing my
hair and feeling relieved that I hadn't worn the same suit with the
recently replaced button that I'd worn the first time I'd met Thomas.
Instead I was wearing the red maternity dress my mother had picked
out for me. Despite my reluctance to buy it, I knew it was a good color
for me and didn't cling to my new bumps and bulges, giving an illusion
of my old slim figure.

I leaned against my desk, wanting to appear casual, then wondered
whether that made it look like I was trying too hard. I straightened,
thinking I should be on my phone and looking busy instead of just
standing around waiting. I picked up my iPhone from my desk and
immediately dropped it on the floor. By the time Nancy had escorted
Detective Riley back to my office, I was on my hands and knees under
my desk.

"Need some help?" he asked, humor in his voice.

Not wanting anybody besides General Lee to witness me rolling
to a stand—the easiest way I'd found to go from prone to standing—I
nodded. "If you wouldn't mind."

Despite being so large, he was surprisingly gentle, placing his hands beneath my arms and pulling me to my feet. With delicate precision, he removed several strands of my hair stuck to my lipstick, then bent to pick up my errant phone.

I immediately held it to my face and spoke into it. "I'll call you back later."

I placed it on my desk, realizing too late that it was faceup with the locked screen plainly visible. Jack would have made a comment to let me know I'd been caught, but Thomas was too much of a gentleman. I felt a flicker of disappointment and then it was gone.

As gracefully as I could, I moved to my desk chair, indicating one of the chairs opposite. "It's good to see you, Thomas. What can I do for you?"

He placed his elbows on his knees and leaned forward, his hands clasped. "This is actually a courtesy call. There have been a few developments."

"Developments? As in you have the final lab reports on the remains?"

"Not exactly." I expected him to rub his chin like Jack, but instead his hands remained folded and still. "It's going to take some time. But I wanted to give you a heads-up on what could be a related matter."

I arched one eyebrow, then quickly lowered it, remembering how it had left a crease on Rebecca's forehead.

"I'm sure you've already read the article on Mr. Vanderhorst."

I looked up at the ceiling. "I'm beginning to think that I might be the only one in Charleston who hasn't. I, uh, missed a few phone calls from the reporter, so I guess I'll have to wait until Sunday to read it."

"Luckily I have an 'in' at the paper." He reached into his jacket pocket and pulled out an iPhone. "Hang on a second and I'll forward it to you. What's your e-mail address?"

I almost gave him my personal e-mail address—ABBA#1FAN— but thought better of it and gave him my business one instead. My phone beeped and I picked it up, thumbed over to my e-mails, and opened it.

I stared at it for a long moment, blinking several times and wondering whether there would be a way to sneak my reading glasses out of my desk drawer without him seeing me, then distract him long enough so he wouldn't notice me putting them on.

"Do you need to borrow my reading glasses?" He was already reaching into his pocket.

"No, that's all right. I think I might have some here." I opened the drawer and pretended to root around for a moment. "Oh, here they are."

The article must have been copied and pasted into the e-mail, since there wasn't any formatting except for paragraphs. But the headline was big and bold, just as I imagined it would appear in Sunday's paper:

The Vanderhorsts of Tradd Street

**The last in the family line, or secret interloper?
New evidence demands a verdict.**

My eyes stung as if I'd been peeling onions, but I couldn't stop. I read the opening lines:

Nevin Vanderhorst lived in his ancestral family home at 55 Tradd Street his entire life, and when he died without heirs, he was the last in a long line of an old Charleston family. With no known relatives, he bequeathed his venerable house to Realtor Melanie Middleton, whom Mr. Vanderhorst had met only once in his life just a few days before he died.

Enter New Yorkers Irene and George Gilbert. Spurred on by the inheritance of an old steamer trunk following the death of Mr. Gilbert's father, Irene began dissecting her husband's family tree, and what a tangled vine it has turned out to be.

I scrolled down past a picture of the house—*my* house—and then a photograph of the Gilberts, presumably with their two teenage sons. I glanced up at Thomas, then returned to the article, feeling like a motorist gawking at a train wreck. Except I was the one who seemed to be pinned in the wreckage.

Inside the trunk Mrs. Gilbert found a lace-and-linen baby's bonnet, as well as an apparent deathbed confession from a Bridget Monahan Gilbert dated 1898. Miss Monahan had been in service at 55 Tradd Street before moving to New York, and what she claimed she was asked to do by the family she worked for sent Mrs. Gilbert on the hunt for clues in a mystery taken right out of a Jack Trenholm book.

I tried to scroll down farther but there was nothing else. "Where's the rest of the article?" I asked, my voice high with panic.

Thomas looked at me apologetically. "I'm afraid that's it for this week's installment. I don't think the next one is even written yet—Ms. Dorf is waiting to see how things develop. They're apparently making it into a serial over several weeks—or longer, depending on my investigation and what we turn up. And what happens with the ownership of the house. Apparently, the whole series is about old Charleston families and their houses—so the story could take years if it needs to, and she can just fill in the weeks where there's nothing going on with the case with stories of other families."

I reached up to the scarf around my neck to loosen it, only to realize that I wasn't wearing one. "So I have to wait for who knows how long while my name is dragged through the muck. She's making it seem like I was the instigator here, strong-arming Mr. Vanderhorst into leaving me his house."

"I suggest you call her and give her your side of the story so it won't sound so biased. I would also get a lawyer."

"That's what Jack said, too."

"Then we both have your best interests at heart."

"I'm not sure I need one. I'd like to think we could just talk it out like reasonable adults."

He didn't say anything right away and a shiver of apprehension tightened my skin. "I think you need to get a lawyer now, because the Gilberts are requesting a court order to exhume Mr. Vanderhorst to extract DNA."

I sat up, indignant. "What will that prove?"

Again, he paused. "Perhaps nothing. But they want to compare the DNA with Mr. Gilbert's to prove that they're related."

"And I need a lawyer to block them?"

"You probably won't be able to do that. But a lawyer will know how to stall them—at least until you know where you stand and can build your own defense."

I slumped back in my chair. "Maybe he can help me claim bankruptcy. I can't imagine that article will send sellers flocking to me."

Thomas smiled softly. It was a Jack smile, but without the zing that always left my heart singed. "You'd be amazed how people react to things. I bet buyers will be ringing your phone off the hook come Monday. You're obviously a Realtor who gets results."

"I used to be, anyway," I said, rubbing my belly as it let out a loud growl.

"Hungry?" Thomas asked.

I nodded. "I couldn't face more than saltines this morning."

"Can you handle eggs? Sometimes pregnant women can't stand the thought of them."

"I could eat about a dozen right now. Preferably with bacon, biscuits, and gravy." I tilted my head. "How do you know so much about pregnant women?"

"I have three sisters, with twelve kids between them. I know so much about pregnancy and child development that I feel as if I've been pregnant myself."

I laughed, the article momentarily forgotten, and I eyed him gratefully. "So where can I get some eggs?"

He stood and walked behind my chair. "I happen to make a mean omelet, and my condo is right over on Bay Street, if you don't mind my bachelor mess."

I hesitated, eyeing my computer and notepad. "I really need to work. . . ."

"But you're hungry, and you're eating for two."

"Three, actually."

His eyes widened in comprehension. "Wow. Congratulations." He even looked as if he meant it. And he didn't run screaming from the room.

"Why are you being so nice to me?" I asked, suddenly suspicious.

"Because I like you. You're . . . different."

"Quirky?" I asked, not sure how I wanted him to answer.

"Yeah. In a good way. And I'd like to get to know you better."

"Even though I'm pregnant?"

He chuckled. "What can I say? I love kids. Ask my nieces and nephews who their favorite uncle is. So how about those eggs?"

My stomach growled again as he pulled back my chair and I stood. "Only if you don't mind cooking."

"I love to cook. My mother and my sisters made sure I knew how, so that some poor woman would want to marry me one day."

My smile matched his as I thought of his sisters teaching their gorgeous brother how to cook—as if he'd need a skill to attract women. He put his hand on the small of my back and led me to the door of my office, then paused.

"So you and Jack . . ."

"We're not a couple."

He seemed relieved. "But . . ." His gaze traveled to my belly.

"Yes, he's the father. And he will want to be very involved in his children's lives." I thought of Jack buying the minivan and I had to suppress a wistful smile. "But beyond that, there's no attachment."

Thomas drew his head back. "So he didn't offer to marry you when he found out you were pregnant?"

I sighed and leaned against the door. "He did. But I turned him down. He was only doing it because he thought it was the right thing to do. He doesn't love me, and I didn't want duty to be the only reason he'd marry me. So I said no."

He was regarding me very closely, like I imagined he would examine a crime scene to make sure no evidence was overlooked. "How do you know he doesn't love you?"

My smile faltered. "Because when I told him that I loved him, all he said was that he was sorry."

"Ouch," he said. His gaze met mine. "Do you still love him?"

Yes, I wanted to shout. But then I looked into Thomas's hopeful face and knew that if I was serious about moving on, I couldn't tell him the truth. "I don't know," I said instead.

"Good," he said, opening the door and allowing me to go first. "So at least I have a chance."

I led the way out of my office, thinking about chances and wondering why his words had suddenly made me feel so sad.

CHAPTER 12

I walked down the garden path of my mother's Legare Street house and passed the blooming crape myrtles and boxwoods, the scent of the tea olive trees flitting through the leaves and blooms like a ghost. This had been my grandmother's house, the only place as a child where I'd felt as if I were truly at home. Grandmother Sarah had been dead since I was a little girl, but her presence here was as palpable as the humidity that permeated the city for much of the year. Grandmother had once told me that if I stayed out of the sun I'd have good skin, since the humidity would always keep it moist. I was almost glad that she couldn't see me now. Or was at least keeping quiet on the subject.

"It's twins, isn't it?" my mother asked before I'd even reached her where she sat at the wrought-iron table near the hummingbird feeder my father had given her for Christmas.

I sighed. It was impossible to keep anything a secret from my mother. As much as I'd missed her during my childhood, I also realized that having a psychic mother during one's teenage years could have been a distinct disadvantage.

I slipped my purse from my shoulder and set it on one of the chairs. "Jack and I are hosting a barbecue at my house on Saturday with his parents. We were planning on telling you all then. Can you at least pretend to be surprised?"

"I'll do my best," she said with a smile.

I sat down, noticing a small packing box on the ground, strips of old masking tape pulled up and curling around the edges. "What's that?"

"Your baby clothes."

I stared at the box, surprised at its very existence. My mother had disappeared from my life when I was six, and my nomadic life with my army father meant that we traveled light, leaving little room for anything as sentimental as baby clothes.

"Where did you find them?" I asked.

"Wherever I've called home, I kept the box in my closet so that I'd know where it was. In case you ever needed proof that I hadn't forgotten you."

I blinked, hoping the sting in my eyes was from something in the air. "So why now?"

"I figured you didn't need any more proof. But I thought you might want to go through it and see if there's anything you'd like for the babies. There are blankets and bonnets, and a couple of smocked dresses that your grandmother made for me when I was a little girl. I've always thought that old clothes are a lot like old houses; they bring the past and present together."

My eyes met hers, and I could see that hers were damp, too.

She continued, her voice soft. "For a long time I didn't wash them, wanting to be able to smell you whenever I pressed my face into one of the blankets. But then I realized that they'd be better off if I had them cleaned properly before storing them. They all look to be in perfect condition."

I rubbed my eyes, wishing the sting would go away. "Have you gone through it all?" I bent to pick up the box, but my mother stopped me with her gloved hand.

"I'll do that. You shouldn't do any lifting, even if you don't think it's heavy."

"Mother . . ."

She gave me a look that brooked no argument. I wondered whether I'd be learning how to imitate it in the very near future, or if it was a natural gift given to all mothers.

She lifted the box and set it on the table. After opening the lid, she took out several layers of tissue paper, then began gently placing articles of baby clothing on top—dresses and other outfits in soft pinks and pastels, cushiony blankets, a tiny bathing suit with bright polka dots and a large bow, and a bag full of plastic barrettes and other hair accessories.

I held up the bag. "Were these mine or Sophie's?"

"Definitely yours. You were as bald as a bowling ball until you were well past three years old. Even when you wore pink dresses, people thought you were a boy. So I improvised. Sadly, what hair you had was so fine that most of the barrettes and headbands just slid from your scalp. I will admit to using tape to affix a bow on a couple of picture-taking occasions." She sighed. "I just didn't want you to feel less about yourself because of what a stranger or photographer might say in a careless comment. I knew that you would grow into your looks. And I was right."

My eyes continued to sting as I stared at the bag, not remembering the little girl my mother spoke about. Not remembering a mother who wanted to protect her child. I cleared my throat. "Hopefully at least one of the babies is a girl. But maybe she'll get Jack's hair. Don't tell him I said so, but he's got the most gorgeous head of hair I've ever seen on anybody."

My mother smiled gently. "Your secret is safe with me. But if the children look like their mother, it wouldn't be such a bad thing, either."

Embarrassed, I dug into the bottom of the box and pulled out a large, hard-sided book with a spiral binding. A pink bunny with bows on its ears and chewing a carrot decorated the front cover. "What's this?"

"Well, it started as your baby book, but after I left, it became more like a scrapbook of all of your accomplishments."

I opened up the front cover and found tucked inside a piece of cardboard with two impossibly small footprints stamped in the middle. "Mine?" I asked, forcing the single word past my tight throat.

"Yes." She reached over and turned the page, where a small curl of hair, held together with a tiny pink bow, was taped to the paper. "And this is hair from your first haircut. You were four and a half and didn't really need it, but all of your friends were getting theirs cut and I didn't want you to think that you were being left out."

I touched the curl gently with my index finger, marveling at how fine it was, and how light. "So I was a blonde."

"Most babies are. Jack wasn't. He was born with a head full of thick, dark hair."

"Of course he was. And he probably smiled at the nurse and dimpled, and she brought him extra milk."

My mother laughed quietly as I turned another page, this one full of pictures of me in this very garden and house, sitting on a swing or a bench, and one in the middle of the fountain, completely naked. These were photos I'd never seen, had never known even existed—photos with my grandmother and parents, and with little friends whose names I could no longer remember.

I pulled the album closer, examining a scene at the beach. I appeared to be about five or six, and there was a younger, dark-haired little boy sitting in the middle of a sand castle—or what remained of one—while the younger version of me had her hands on her ruffled hips and looked as if she were trying very hard not to cry. Behind me, lying on the sand, was a collection of sand-castle building tools, all placed in a deliberate, neatly spaced row.

"Some things never change, do they?" my mother said, leaning over to look at the photo.

"That's Jack?" I asked, already knowing the answer.

"Of course. Look how much enjoyment he's getting from sitting in the middle of your sand castle."

I shook my head. "When I met him a few years ago, I didn't remember knowing him when we were children."

"Despite Amelia and me being such close friends, our lives were so different that we didn't have a lot of time to spend together once we had children. And then I left. . . ." She took a deep breath. "Amelia's parents had a house on Edisto, and we took you and Jack a couple of times. We didn't do it a lot, because the two of you seemed to enjoy tormenting each other. Made the experience more trying than relaxing."

Some things never change, do they? I wasn't sure whether I should be appalled or amused.

The photographs ended when I was about six years old, and the last pages of the book were filled with old newspaper clippings from my high school and college graduations, and then from my real estate ads. "You collected these?"

"I had friends clip them and send them to me." Leaning forward, my mother pointed at my picture from one of the more recent ads. "I'm glad you're not wearing your hair like that anymore, Mellie. It wasn't a good choice."

She was right, of course. I'd only wished she'd been there to tell me *before* I'd gotten the haircut.

"Mother?"

She looked at me, her eyes glowing. "Yes?"

"I'm glad you're here now. I have no idea what I'm doing, and no idea how to be a mom. So I wanted you to know that I'm thankful beyond all reason that you are here to show me the way."

Putting her arms around me, she said, "I'm trying to make up for all the years I wasn't here for you. I didn't expect you to give me twin grandchildren to give me the opportunity, but I'm glad just the same."

She hugged me tightly, and I was tempted to remain there for a very long time, at least until all of my fears and anxieties about encroaching motherhood had dissipated to a manageable level. But that could take years.

Slowly she pulled away. "Did you bring the christening gown?"

I nodded. "Against my better judgment."

"Mellie, we have to figure out the truth before the Gilberts do. We have access to this gown and they don't. Let me help. Please."

"If this is from some misplaced sense of guilt—"

She cut me off. "It's not misplaced. Besides, I'm your mother. Let me help." She started putting the baby clothes back into the box. "Let's clear off the table first."

I hesitated, then began folding the little dresses and sweaters. When we were finished, I reached into my purse and pulled out the gown, now wrapped in a clean pillowcase.

"I really don't think this is a good idea. We're meeting with Yvonne tomorrow and can find out who Susan Bivens is. . . ."

"And that's all well and good," my mother said. "But she can't tell you who sent it to you. Or who it belongs to."

I carefully placed the pillowcase on the table and began to unroll it, revealing the old linen gown little by little. We stared down at the small garment for a long moment.

"Have you shown this to anybody else yet? Detective Riley?"

I shook my head. "Only Sophie's seen it. But I told Jack about it. We were going over questions to ask Yvonne and he mentioned the bonnet. I thought it was important that he know that both were made by the same seamstress."

"Good. This is our secret weapon for now, so the fewer people who know about it, the better."

She sat down, then indicated the chair next to her. I sat, too, then held out my hand.

She shook her head. "I don't want to take any chances with the babies. If I'm mentally prepared—and I am now—and I focus on the message instead of the surprise, I can handle it. Having you nearby will help, too, as well as being here in your grandmother's garden. Together *we* are stronger than any spirit."

"Are you very, very sure?" She had been back in my life only a short while, and I was unwilling to let her go again so soon. I leaned closer to her, realizing with a bit of a shock that she actually looked even better than usual. Her eyes sparkled, and her skin gleamed. Even her cheeks appeared rosier. Despite the outward appearances, I had to make sure for myself. "Jack told me that Dad had to bring you home last night after you touched the Gilberts' bonnet."

The color in her cheeks deepened, and I recalled what Sophie had said about my father now practically living in this house. Even though they had once been married long enough to have a child together, the thought was still a bit unsettling. They were my *parents*.

I sat back in my seat. "Yes, well. You do seem completely recovered. So if you're really, really sure . . ."

"I'm sure," she said before taking off the pair of gardening gloves she'd been wearing.

I took out my cell phone and placed it on the table. In answer to my mother's questioning look, I explained, "In case I need to call nine-one-one."

"That won't be necessary. . . ."

"Humor me, okay?"

She nodded, then focused her attention on the gown lying on the pillowcase in the middle of the garden table. She moved her head to the side. "Do you smell that?"

"Smell what?" I asked slowly.

"Roses. So strong it's like I'm at a wedding. Or a funeral."

I drew in a deep breath through my nose, smelling only the boxwoods and the scent of old newspapers that still clung to the linen of the christening gown. I took another deep breath just to be sure before shaking my head once. "No. I don't smell roses at all." Before she could ask her next question, I added, "And I don't see anyone, either."

"I think it's Louisa Vanderhorst."

"But she went away after we discovered her remains beneath the fountain and solved the mystery of her disappearance. Why would she be back?"

"Perhaps to return a favor—from one mother to another."

We looked at each other in silent understanding, and I imagined a cool hand brushed my cheek.

My mother returned her attention to the christening gown and, after a deep breath, leaned forward before placing both hands palm-down on the yellowed linen.

I kept my phone in one hand as I watched my mother's body go rigid, her chest rising and falling. Her hands shook but she did not lift them off of the gown. Her lips moved, forming words I could not hear; nor were they meant for me. I watched in horror and fascination as the gown beneath her fingers began to writhe, as if a living child were inside of it, the two small sleeves reaching up toward her.

The metal of my chair and the table beneath my hands pricked at my skin as if covered with frost, but I was too transfixed by what was happening in front of me to move. My mother's eyes opened abruptly, two blackened charcoal eyes that I did not recognize gazing back at me. I tried to push back my chair, to create a distance between us, but something—some*one*—held me back.

Those unrecognizable eyes stared at me with rage and hatred. This wasn't my mother. This wasn't anybody I knew. I could only sit and stare, transfixed, and pray for my mother to return.

The table began to shake beneath her hands, the gown twitching and twisting, the chairs rattling. An unearthly groan oozed between my mother's slightly open lips, and my own mouth dropped open in surprise and abject fear. She jerked to her feet and leaned across the table, her face close, and I smelled damp, dark earth.

I wanted to shut my eyes, but something was holding them open, making me watch.

Her mouth opened wide, and with a loud howling wind that brought with it the scent of moist dirt and rotting leaves, the word formed around me: *Mine*.

My mother slept on the couch in the front parlor, the old stained-glass window behind her covering her with a blanket of colors. I sat in the chair next to her, still trembling and watching, listening to her breathe.

As soon as that one word had rolled from my mother's lips, she'd collapsed into her chair; whatever had possessed her had gone along with the smell of death. She hadn't fainted, but she'd been too fatigued to do anything but allow me to walk her to the sofa and help her lie down. She'd been asleep before I'd taken off her shoes.

I heard the key turn in the latch of the front door, followed by the sound of someone whistling the tune to the song "Fever," and heavy footsteps that moved into the middle of the foyer and then stopped.

"Ginny? It's your stud muffin. Where are you?"

Too stunned to say anything, I remained silent.

"Are you in bed? That certainly makes things easier."

Footsteps approached the stairs, but as they crossed the entry to the parlor, I called out. "Dad?"

His footsteps stopped, then retraced themselves. "Melanie?"

I wasn't sure who was more embarrassed, but I would have bet that the scarlet shade of his cheeks probably matched my own.

He held a bouquet of red amaryllis, and I could smell a light scent of lemon cologne. *Stud muffin?* I felt the morning's nausea return.

"Hello, Melanie. I didn't expect to see you here. . . ." His voice died as he spotted my mother on the sofa. He walked quickly across the room and knelt by her side. "Is she all right?"

"I think so." Knowing how my father felt about my mother's gift in particular, and the paranormal in general, I wasn't sure how much I could tell him. "She was very tired and needed to lie down. I had a few questions to ask her, so I thought I'd wait until she woke up."

He looked at me oddly, realizing there was a lot I was leaving out, but knowing better than to ask. After placing the flowers on the coffee table, he pulled up the blanket I'd placed over my mother, then sat down next to me.

With a lowered voice, he said, "How are you? You look . . ." Not one who was comfortable with lying, he stopped.

"Pregnant? I know. Hopefully this is only a first-trimester thing."

He didn't look convinced. "Your mother bounced back right after you were born, so I wouldn't worry." He beamed a glance at my mother, whose breathing was still deep and even. "And look at her now."

If only I could get past the fact that they were my parents, I might have actually thought this whole senior love affair was cute.

I looked at him for a moment, trying to remember something I kept forgetting to ask. And then I recalled my conversation with Rich Kobylt in the garden, about the bill that he'd submitted but that hadn't yet been paid. "Dad, can I ask you something?"

"Of course, sweetie. Anything."

"Is there any money left in the trust to continue to fund the restoration of my house?"

His eyes shifted away from mine for a moment and I felt something curdle in the place where my heart was. "Sure, we have money. We did have a lot more invested at one time, but I had to liquefy some of the assets to pay for more immediate needs, like the roof and foundation repairs. Those couldn't wait for another commission check, if you remember." He reached over and patted my leg like he used to when I was little and asked him whether he was going to stop drinking. "Why are you asking?"

"Because I had a conversation with Rich Kobylt about a bill he submitted for the foundation repair. He said he hadn't received a payment, which was unusual, because you always pay his bills on time."

He scratched his chin. "I'll look into it. I'm sure it's just a mistake. Probably got lost in the mail or something. Don't you worry about it." He smiled, but it failed to reassure me.

My mother moaned, and we turned to see her opening her eyes. Her gaze rested on my father before traveling to my face. "Are you all right?" she asked with concern.

"I'm fine, Mother. How are you feeling? You almost passed out again."

"What?" my father demanded.

I picked up the amaryllis from the coffee table and handed them to him. "Dad, why don't you go find a vase in the kitchen to put these in?"

With a reassuring nod from my mother, he left the room, looking back only twice.

I helped her sit up, rearranging the blanket over her shoulders. It was warm in the room, but I could see the chill bumps on her arms, as if whatever she'd experienced hadn't completely left her.

"What happened?" I asked. "What did you see?"

Her eyes were haunted as she looked back at me. "I saw the woman again, and the two cradles."

"Were they both empty?"

She nodded. "And the cradles matched—they were black, and they had these unusual rockers in the shapes of egrets."

Tiny feet pricked their way up the back of my neck at her description, which matched not only the cradle in my attic, but also the one in the Charleston Museum that Sophie had seen. The Vanderhorst cradle.

"Who is she?" I asked, my throat suddenly parched.

"I don't know." She shook her head. "I'm sorry I couldn't get more helpful information. But I had the strangest feeling. . . ."

She leaned forward, her elbows on her knees and her head in her hands.

"What do you mean?"

"I'm not sure." She dropped her hands and her eyes met mine. "I don't know her name, or who she is, but I got the distinct impression that she is the wronged party."

"The wronged party?"

Her long fingers began plucking at the blanket. "She's angry because the cradles are empty, and they shouldn't be." She swallowed heavily. "She's looking for her babies, because she doesn't know where they are."

I stared at her in silence for a moment, trying to make sense of what she'd just told me. "You said a word before you collapsed—you said, 'Mine.' That's the same thing I heard when the piano keys were playing by themselves. I'm thinking she must be the same woman who tried to drop the light fixture on me and tried to choke me when we were standing in the foyer with the Gilberts." My gaze held my mother's. "She obviously doesn't like me, but what does she think I have that belongs to her?"

I watched as my mother's eyes traveled down to my belly and then back to my face. Instinctively I placed my hands on my abdomen, as if that would protect the babies from something even I didn't understand.

"We're stronger than she is. Remember that. We'll figure out who she is and what she wants and send her on her way."

We heard my father's whistling as he walked toward us from the kitchen.

With a sense of growing panic, I said, "But what if I don't want to give her what she wants?" I stood abruptly, feeling as if I needed to run as far away as I could.

"Then we will find another way." Her gaze was fierce, like that of a mama alligator guarding her nest.

"There's my girls," my father said as he appeared in the doorway holding a vase with the flowers, unaware of the dark currents flooding the room.

I forced a smile, still thinking of my mother's words, desperate to believe she was right, but deathly afraid that she was not.

CHAPTER 13

Late Monday morning, as I passed the front desk on my way to meet Jack for our appointment with Yvonne Craig, Nancy Flaherty handed me a thick stack of pink message slips. I'd been on the phone all morning with prospective clients, and apparently there were even more waiting to speak with me.

"Really?" I asked, hesitating before I took the pink bundle. "One stupid article in the paper and the phone starts ringing. I'd say it was better than paid advertising, but apparently there are a lot of wackos out there wanting to waste my time."

Out of the twelve phone calls I'd already taken, ten had turned out to be people just wanting advice on how to convince their own elderly relatives to include them in their wills. By the seventh call, I'd run out of patience trying to explain that my job as a Realtor had nothing to do with coercing the elderly, and I'd simply hung up. The only upside was that I'd had two solid prospects, both home owners who'd known Nevin Vanderhorst and figured that if he trusted me enough to leave his entire estate to me (one of them simply mentioned the dog), then that was the only reference they needed. I had appointments with both in the upcoming week.

Jack was just pulling up outside as I left the building. His hair was still a little wet from a recent shower, the collar of his striped oxford-cloth shirt slightly damp, looking nothing less than gorgeous. As he stood with the door open, grinning at me, I couldn't help but think how much he still resembled the little boy sitting in the middle of my sand castle, in more ways than just the grin. *Some things never change.*

"You don't always have to be so early, Mellie. Try being a few minutes late for a change. With two babies to feed and dress in the near future, you might want to start practicing now."

I gave him a disdainful look. "My children will be on a strict schedule, so that there will be enough time for feeding and dressing before we have to be anywhere." I buckled my seat belt, waiting for him to close the door. But when I looked up at him, he appeared to be vastly amused.

"Babies don't always listen to logic or reason, Mellie. I'm not quite sure a spreadsheet or schedule will work in this case."

Luckily, he closed the door before I'd had the chance to tell him that I'd already started making one of each.

We headed toward the Fireproof Building on Meeting Street, where the library for the South Carolina Historical Society was located. I was happy to notice that the cup holder in the van had been cleaned and was now filled with a new bottle of water.

Jack saw me eyeing the bottle. "That's for you. I've been doing a lot of reading and I learned that you should be drinking lots of water. You need to keep extra hydrated, especially now, when it's so hot. It will help with the swelling, too."

I pulled my ankles back from view. "I've been doing a lot of reading, too. Sophie gave me a book about child birthing around the world."

He sent me a wary look. "Why am I not surprised?"

"Did you know there's a tribe somewhere in West Africa where, when a woman is in labor, they have the man lie down next to her on the floor, and they tie a string around his balls so that whenever she has a labor pain she can pull on the string? That way they both can share the experience of labor."

His face visibly paled. "Wow. Can't wait to read the rest. But I still think you should drink more water."

I knew he was right—I'd read the same thing in the pregnancy book he'd bought me. I just wasn't going to give him the satisfaction of drinking it in front of him. Wanting to change the subject, I said, "Did you hear that Rebecca and Marc Longo are getting married?"

He sent me a sidelong glance. "Yeah. I heard."

I kept looking at him. "Are you upset?"

He made a choking sound in the back of his throat before shaking his head. "I can't believe that you asked. No. I'm not upset. Rebecca was only a . . ."

"Distraction?" I prompted.

"A substitution."

I squirmed in my seat, pleased and dismayed at the same time.

"What about you?" Jack asked. "Sad that Marc is now taken?"

"Me? No. Of course not." I almost told him that Marc had also probably been a substitution, too, but I wasn't going to toss another match onto that particular fire. We rode the rest of the way without talking, the air heavy with all the things that were best left unsaid.

If I'd been driving, I would have circled the vicinity for more than half an hour before finding a spot to park. Jack found a space within thirty seconds, only a block from the Fireproof Building, on cobblestoned Chalmers Street. He helped me out, then kept his hand at my elbow as we climbed the flight of stairs to the front door of the beautiful Palladian-style building with its graceful Doric columns, and then again as we climbed a circular set of stairs to get to the reading room, where Yvonne waited for us. I wanted to protest, but I enjoyed his touch too much to ask him to stop, or at least inform him that I was only two and a half years older than he and not yet an invalid.

Yvonne walked toward us, her low-heeled pumps clicking across the long room. Her white hair was pulled back from her face in a low bun, accentuating her high cheekbones that wore just a hint of blush. Rhinestone clip earrings sparkled on her ears, and a matching brooch decorated the lapel of her navy blue suit. I couldn't help but wonder whether she put extra thought into getting dressed on the days she saw Jack. It would have been nice to know that I wasn't the only one.

Jack enveloped her in a bear hug, then kissed both of her cheeks with a loud smack, making Yvonne giggle like a young girl. She swatted at his sleeve. "Jack Trenholm, how dare you manhandle me that way? What will people say?"

"That I'm one lucky man," Jack said with a wink that made Yvonne's cheeks turn even pinker.

I gave her a more sedate kiss on her cheek. "It's so good to see you again, Yvonne. You look wonderful, as always. I really need to find out what kinds of vitamins you're taking."

Yvonne was looking at me oddly, her arms crossed over her chest as she studied me. "There's something different about you. Something . . ."

"Pregnant?" I interjected.

Her eyes widened in surprise. "So you two finally figured out you were crazy about each other and got married! I hope it was an elopement, or else I'll be upset that I didn't get an invitation to the wedding."

"Not at all," I said.

"Almost," Jack said at the same time, his grin still strong.

I sent him a look of exasperation before turning back to Yvonne to try to explain. "We're not married. Nor do we have any plans to be."

Yvonne kept her expression carefully neutral. "So, you married someone else?"

I looked around me, grateful there were only two other people in the room and they were sitting at a far table, their attention on the books they were reading. "I'm, uh, not married."

Yvonne blinked once, and then again as her gaze moved from me and then to Jack and back again. "Is Jack the father?"

"Definitely," I said.

"I hope so," Jack said simultaneously

Yvonne turned on him. "And you won't marry her? Jack Trenholm. I'm surprised at you. I realize that this is the twenty-first century and things are done a little differently now than when I was younger, but I happen to know that you were raised better than that."

Jack's voice held no humor. "I asked. And she said no." His blue eyes bored into mine with the same intensity they'd had right after he'd asked me to marry him. It was a rare glimpse into Jack's real feelings, an ocean's depth of feelings he usually kept carefully hidden behind a beguiling smile and easy quips. They belonged to the Jack I'd fallen in love with.

Yvonne was waiting for me to respond, her eyes kind and sympathetic. I took a deep breath to give me a moment to think. "It's complicated. That's all I can say. But I know that we'll both do our best to be the parents we can be for the children."

"Children?"

I smiled. "Don't tell anybody—we haven't officially announced it to our parents yet—but we're having twins."

"Twins?" She smiled broadly. "How wonderful. But . . ." A frown furrowed her brow and she became suddenly serious.

Jack stepped toward her. "What's wrong?"

"Let me show you something." She began to lead us to the back of the room, past the glass-topped cases that held rare manuscripts and books, to what I'd begun to refer to as "our" table. We'd spent enough time in the archives with Yvonne Craig to warrant ownership.

She moved to one side of the table and opened up a folder. If we'd been from the same generation, I would have long suspected that she and I were separated at birth. She was so organized that I always felt compelled to study her techniques.

Yvonne began flipping through several sheets of paper. "You know, if I hadn't read that article about the Vanderhorsts in Sunday's paper, I might not have noticed this. And it might even just be a huge coincidence, but I found this very interesting."

My gaze met Jack's and I knew we were both thinking of his oft-repeated phrase, *There's no such thing as coincidences*. We moved to stand on either side of Yvonne.

"You'd asked me to pull the Vanderhorst family tree, which I did. And as far as I could tell, Nevin Vanderhorst was the last in his line." She slid a legal-size page from the folder and laid it on top before pulling up her reading glasses that hung from a chain around her neck.

"As you can see, Nevin was born in 1922. His parents were Louisa and Robert. Robert Vanderhorst was an only child, born in 1896. His father, William—Nevin's grandfather—was born in 1860 and was also an only child."

She looked at us over the top of her glasses. "As you can see, having several generations of only children is a great way for your line to die out completely. Since Nevin never married, it made it even easier. But here's where it gets interesting."

Her neatly manicured index finger slid to a line on the chart, two lines higher than Nevin's. "Great-grandfather John was a twin. There's no documentation about a brother, because the twin died at age three."

"Assumed to be from yellow fever," I said, disappointed that I already knew about the great-grandfather. "Sophie told me about John, so it's not really a surprise. But I'm not sure what I'm supposed to get all excited about."

Yvonne's eyes twinkled as her finger moved higher on the chart. "Because as you'll see here, every generation that we have a record of shows twins—most likely fraternal twins, since that runs in families on the mother's side."

Jack continued. "And since the practice back then was to marry cousins to keep property and wealth contained in a family, that would explain why the trait was passed down along with the Vanderhorst name."

"Exactly," Yvonne said, beaming at Jack as if he were her genius protégé. "But if you'll notice, twins stopped at William."

I stared at the photocopied image of the Vanderhorst family tree, all the lines with names like so many leaves, ending with just a single name at the bottom. It seemed as if the tree had grown in reverse order, diminished to a lone seed.

"But what does this mean?" I asked. "Besides its being a very odd coincidence that I would be having twins."

Jack leaned on the desk, studying the family chart. "Well, it could explain why the Gilberts think they have a claim to the estate. What if one of the twins on the family tree didn't die young, or did have surviving progeny that aren't recorded on the family tree?"

"Or was bricked up in the foundation of a house?" I added quietly.

Jack touched the small of my back, a gesture of comfort that only made my skin tingle and my blood gallop through my veins. I stepped forward, ostensibly to look more closely at the chart. "But a dead child wouldn't explain the Gilberts' claim," I added.

"No, it wouldn't," Jack agreed. "As soon as you have your lawyer, we'll need to meet with the Gilberts and find out exactly what's in that deathbed confession from the maid."

"Which reminds me," Yvonne said as she tugged the folder out from beneath the family tree. "You'd asked me about the name Susan Bivens. I couldn't find anything in the property records or census—which doesn't surprise me, considering the hurricanes, floods, and wars this city has seen in the last three hundred years. But I did find this." She slid a photocopied page out of the folder and placed it in front of Jack and me.

It was a page from the *Daily Advertiser* dated February 23, 1800. It consisted mostly of advertisements for various medical tinctures, hair pomades, and local business establishments. And tucked in the middle of the page near the bottom was an ad for a shop on Broad Street: *Susan Bivens Fine Linens and Embroidery. Best prices for quality work.*

I looked at the date again. "Eighteen hundred. That sounds right for the Vanderhorsts to have acquired a christening gown and bonnet—or two, considering their habit of having twins. The house wasn't built yet, but the family was most likely already living in the city by then."

Jack turned to Yvonne. "Have you found out anything else about the shop—any invoices or receipts? I'd be interested to know exactly what the Vanderhorsts bought from Susan Bivens, and when."

"That's next on my list. I had a whole busload of genealogists from Atlanta last week, so I'm a little behind. I promise to let you know whatever I turn up."

I was still studying the chart, my interest piqued by a small detail. "Poor Great-grandfather John. His wife died the year after William was born. In 1861."

Jack stood behind me, looking over my shoulder. "Doesn't look like he grieved for very long. He married his second wife the following year." He tapped the page. "No children from that marriage—most likely due to John's being killed in the war in 1863."

"Still," I said. "To lose a wife so young."

Yvonne nodded. "It happened a lot back then. Would you like me to see if I can find out more?"

Jack nodded. "Yes, if you wouldn't mind. I don't know what the Gilberts have in their arsenal, but it wouldn't hurt for us to have more information. And see if you can find where John's twin is buried. I'd hate to think he's the one walled up in the foundation."

Yvonne winked. "I'll do my best."

Jack leaned over and kissed her on the cheek. "You're the best. You have my cell—and Mellie's. Call when you find anything."

I said good-bye to Yvonne, and Jack and I left the old building, blinking at the bright sunshine. I squinted up at him. "Thanks, Jack, for your help. I don't know what I'd do without it."

He stood very close to me, the sun in my eyes so that I couldn't read his expression. "This could be good material for another book." He removed his sunglasses from the neck of his shirt, then slid them onto his nose. "Besides, I need another excuse to spend time with you."

He began walking down the steps toward the sidewalk. I ran after him. "What do you mean? You don't need an excuse. . . ."

He stopped and turned around to face me. "Remember, Mellie. I wasn't the one who said no."

I stared after him for a moment, watching as he walked down the sidewalk toward the van, understanding what he was telling me yet unable to put my rebuttal into words that would make sense to him. Or to me.

I was distracted as a line of ragged and sweaty men connected by chains on their feet, their hands roped together behind their backs, marched past me heading toward Broad Street in the direction of the Old Exchange and dungeon. They were hazy, like a station on an old television that was set between two channels, letting me know that I was definitely losing my sixth sense. I watched as they flickered, then completely vanished into a line of stopped traffic. Even after they'd disappeared from view, I could still hear their chains clanking together.

Turning my head, I caught sight of Jack holding my door open, his expression unreadable with his eyes hidden behind the sunglasses. As I walked toward him, I imagined I could still hear the sound of rattling chains, giving me the odd sensation that they belonged to me.

CHAPTER 14

The old grandfather clock chimed eleven times, reminding me that I'd been standing beside it for half an hour, my gaze drifting from the rain-soaked street outside to the growth chart etched into the wall almost one hundred years before. *MBG*. My Best Guy. That was the nickname Louisa Vanderhorst had given to her beloved son, Nevin, as she'd marked his height on the wall of their home. I'd had it covered with a sheet of Plexiglas to preserve it so that it would remain a part of the house for as long as I owned it. Which, I reminded myself, might not be as long as I'd once thought.

The sound of tires on wet pavement brought my attention back to the window. I watched in surprise as Jack's red minivan pulled up to the curb, the passenger door shooting open before the vehicle had even stopped. Nola bolted out of the van, her guitar, backpack, and over-stuffed duffel banging against her legs as she marched toward my front gate and threw it open.

General Lee was already waiting by the front door by the time I reached it and pulled it open before Nola had a chance to ring the bell. Without pausing to say hello, Nola marched past the dog and me, dumping everything she'd been holding in the middle of the vestibule.

"He's impossible, and if I have to spend another minute in his presence, I'm going to go postal."

"Not if I beat you to it. Living with a hormonal teenager isn't exactly a walk in the park, either, you know," Jack said from the doorway.

General Lee and I turned to see Jack, looking as if he'd just been dragged through a swamp backward. His hair stuck up in every direction, and he was wearing only an undershirt, khaki pants without a belt, and his loafers without socks. It appeared as if his departure from his condo had been a quick one.

I stepped back, opening the door farther. "Please do come in. Welcome to my home."

Jack frowned at me as he walked past me to stand in front of his daughter. If I hadn't understood how delicate a teenage girl's feelings were, I might have laughed as the two of them faced each other with almost identical profiles—including the indignant jutted-out chins.

Nola turned toward me, her blue eyes damp, but I could tell she was trying very hard not to cry. Years of parenting her own mother had taught her to be strong. But she was still learning how to let go.

"I can't live with him. You have no idea. He's overbearing and overprotective, and acts like I'm three years old."

"No three-year-old would hide in a closet to talk on the phone to a *boy*." He emphasized this last word as if he were saying the word *Satan*.

"Because whenever I try to speak with Cooper, you stand next to me like you need to censor my conversation." Her voice rose a notch. "And let's not forget that time when you actually took the phone away from me and spoke to him yourself!"

I turned to Jack. "You really did that?"

He had the good sense to look abashed. "I might have. Just once, though. And it was because I didn't like the direction their conversation was heading."

"We were talking about a *movie*, Dad. Not our real lives. Like I would throw myself in front of a train. Like I'd even know where to *find* a train."

I thought for a moment. "You were talking to a boy about *Anna Karenina*? You actually know a boy who's seen the movie?"

Nola nodded. "Cooper took Alston and me to see it. She didn't think it was so great except for all the cool dresses and jewelry, but Cooper and I really liked it. We've both read the book, so we had a lot to talk about."

I crossed my arms over my chest and faced her father. "Really, Jack?

I think there are a lot worse things your teenage daughter could be discussing with a boy, but maybe that's just me. And he's Alston's brother. I know her and her mother, so I can only imagine what kind of a Tolstoy-reading badass Cooper must be."

"But she took the phone into a closet when she was supposed to be in bed, and they were making plans to see each other. That's as good as lying, in my book."

I took a deep breath, unwilling to put myself in the middle of it when they most likely needed only a bit of a time-out. I eyed Nola's belongings spilling across my floor, remembering the state of her room when she'd stayed with me before, and the loud music that made the windows rattle. "You're welcome to stay here for a few days until you've both calmed down enough to speak rationally."

"I told you she'd say yes," Nola directed at her father. She turned to me. "We thought you'd be asleep, so I was just going to use my key. I figured you could say yes in the morning."

"You know you're always welcome here." I looked behind her to where General Lee was already halfway up the stairs, waiting for her. "And I guess I'm losing my sleeping buddy tonight."

Jack bent down to pick up her duffel, but Nola yanked it out of his hands. "I'll do it myself, thanks." With a grunt, she hoisted it onto her shoulder before grabbing the backpack and guitar, then began her staggering walk toward the stairs.

Jack moved to go after her, but I held him back. After a moment, he gave in. Under his breath, he said, "Please find us a house as quickly as possible. We really need more space."

I neglected to mention Nola's request of soft bushes beneath her window or a first-floor bedroom for the new house, thinking this wouldn't be the appropriate time. Instead I said, "You know, the kind of space Nola needs isn't going to be fixed by square footage."

He looked at me as if I'd begun speaking in a language he wasn't familiar with.

With a sigh, I said, "I'll find you a home. Your list is a little long, so it will take a bit of time, but we'll find it."

"Thanks, Mellie." His dimple made an appearance. Glancing down at my abdomen, he said, "If one of those is a girl, maybe we can consider boarding schools for high school."

"And if one of these is a boy, I'm sure there will be lots of fathers just like you forbidding their daughters to speak with him on the phone."

He was thoughtful for a moment. "There's really no easy way to parent, is there?"

"Nope. Not that I'm an expert by any means, but it seems to me that we just have to muddle through as best we can. Luckily we both have terrific mothers who can guide us."

"Do you think they'll agree to raise them until they're twenty-one?" Jack asked hopefully.

"We could ask."

He smiled, but a filter of doubt marred its effect. I touched his arm. "It'll be okay. She's a good kid, Jack. It's just part of growing up."

He surprised me by taking my hand and holding it in his. "I bet you had a lot of growing pains, didn't you?"

I wanted to snatch back my hand, but it felt too good where it was. "I might have," I admitted. "Not that anybody would have noticed."

He took a step closer while I held my ground. "My poor Mellie. I guess that explains a lot, doesn't it?"

I frowned. "What do you mean, it expl—"

He put his finger on my lips, silencing me. "Don't frown. It'll give you wrinkles. You don't want people to think you're the children's grandmother instead of their mother, right?"

I tried to say something, but his finger was still pressed against my lips, and he was standing so close that I forgot how to form words. He slid his finger from my mouth and then to my chin, gently tracing the curve of my throat. I tilted my head back, my eyes closing as my lips parted, waiting for his kiss.

"Mellie?"

I jerked my eyes open.

"I think you have toothpaste in your hair."

I stared at him, trying to think of what he was really saying, and why he was talking instead of kissing me.

He ran his finger and thumb through my hair by my temples,

coming away with a chunk of dried blue paste. "I just thought you'd want to know."

I felt like a tire that had hit a pothole, and my body sagged as the air slowly leaked out. I managed to force my knees to work and turned abruptly toward the door. "Thanks, Jack. I usually like to leave a chunk of toothpaste in my hair in case General Lee wakes up hungry in the middle of the night."

Jack sauntered past me, standing between me and the door in the darkened vestibule, where the chain from the broken light still hung. "Thanks for letting Nola stay for a few days. It means a lot to both of us knowing that she can always come here."

"Good," I said. "And I want her to feel free to come and go as much as she wants. But I think . . ." I stopped and looked at the floor, noticing I had a hole in the toe of one of my fuzzy socks.

"But what?" he asked softly.

I couldn't meet his eyes, so I focused on his chin instead. "I think it's best that you try to keep your visits to times when I'm not here. It'll be easier in the long run. For both of us."

He didn't say anything. Instead, he turned around and opened the door, allowing in a burst of humid, heavy air. He paused on the piazza, and when he spoke his voice was cool and detached. "Are the Gilberts still in town?"

I tried to match his tone, and tried not to remember that just a minute before I'd wanted him to kiss me. "For a couple more days. They're waiting to see if they can get the exhumation order taken care of before they leave."

"Did you hire a lawyer yet?"

I nodded. "Sterling Zerbe. He's an old army buddy of my dad's. He's trying to stall the process as much as he can. To give us time to figure things out."

"Good. I was thinking that maybe you should invite the Gilberts to the barbecue tomorrow."

"Why would I do that?" I frowned, wondering at Jack's lack of judgment. It didn't happen often, but when it did, it was huge. Like his little fling with Rebecca.

He raised an eyebrow. "Because maybe we'll get lucky and the spirits in this house won't like them. The Gilberts might not have been here long enough last time to rile anybody up."

I held back on my urge to throw my arms around him with gratitude, knowing that to touch him would be my undoing. Instead, I simply grinned. "Great idea. I hope it works."

"Me, too," he said, regarding me with intensity for a moment before turning away again. He shoved his hands in his pockets, then began walking down the piazza. Before he disappeared through the door, he called back, "I think that was almost-kiss number eight. Not that you're counting."

I pressed my palms against my warm cheeks, embarrassed to have actually thought that he hadn't realized I'd tilted my head and parted my lips for him.

I closed the front door and stepped into the foyer, catching sight of Nola sitting in the middle of the stairs and holding a very contented General Lee. "So did he say I could live here?"

"Um, we agreed you can stay here for a few days. But he is your father, Nola, and he does love you. He's just learning how to be a dad."

"Isn't there some senior-citizen college course he can take instead of torturing me? He doesn't have a clue."

I sat down on the steps in front of her and reached up to scratch General Lee behind his ears. "Probably not. But he does love you, Nola. Don't ever forget that."

She fixed me with a hard blue stare that reminded me so much of Jack that I had to look away. "Did he tell you what we were fighting about tonight?"

I shook my head. "No. Does it matter?"

"Obvi."

I stared at her, not understanding.

"Ob-vi-ous-ly," she said, speaking slowly, as if I were hard of hearing, very old, or very stupid. Or all three.

"I still don't get it. Why would it matter?"

Her eyes rolled. I was glad eye rolling didn't leave wrinkles, be-

RETURN TO TRADD STREET   139

cause by the age of twenty she'd look like an octogenarian. "Because," she said, emphasizing the second syllable, "it was about you."

"Me? Why would you be arguing about me?"

She sighed as if she didn't have the energy for another eye roll. "Because it's stupid that you're both trying to pretend that you're not totally obsessed with each other. I mean, everybody knows you hooked up." Her eyes drifted to my abdomen. "But, like, you'd have to be blind not to see it's more than that."

She leaned back against the step behind her and threw her arm across her forehead with a dramatic sweep. "I'm flippin' exhausted listening to you both give me reasons why you're not together. You both need to grow up and admit you're wrong, say, 'I love you,' get married or whatevs, and give the rest of us some peace."

When I didn't say anything right away, she lifted her head. "What-e-ver. Do I need to get you an urban dictionary or something so we can have future conversations?"

I took a deep breath, having no idea how I was supposed to re-spond. It was hard to remember that she was only fourteen, although her first thirteen years had taught her more about life than most people learned in forty. "Nola, I think maybe you're misinterpreting your father's feelings. . . ."

She lifted both hands in the air as if appealing to a large audience. "Seriously, Mellie? He sold his Porsche. For a minivan. Need I say more?"

Both Nola and General Lee settled their gazes on me, as if I were the only one who wasn't seeing the light. "Yes, well, I appreciate your trying to fix things for your father and me, but I'm afraid our reasons are very complicated. It's not as simple as our just apologizing."

She lifted her head again and narrowed her eyes at me. "Have either one of you actually tried it?"

"Of course . . ." I started to say, before stopping as it occurred to me that I might be lying.

She sat up again. "Growing up with a single parent is tough. Be-lieve me, I know. And even if you and Jack are partners in this whole thing, it won't be the same. I'm not saying you should get together just because you're pregnant, but it seems to me that you should be able to figure something out. I mean, you're both getting pretty old. You might not get another chance."

I was about to ask her what she meant when the distinct sound of a piano key striking drifted up from the music room.

Nola looked at me with surprise. "Is there somebody else here?"

"Sort of," I said.

Her eyes widened. "You mean like a ghost?"

"Obvi."

Nola smirked while we both stood, waiting. General Lee whimpered, then ran back up the stairs, disappearing into Nola's room.

Another note struck, louder this time, as if the key were being hit with force. Slowly, we began to walk down the stairs, the temperature dropping several degrees with each step. Before we'd reached the doorway to the unoccupied music room, a third note sounded, louder than the first two.

"Those are the same three notes that always stick when I play." Nola's words came out with billows of frosty air. "Do you see anything?" she whispered.

I peered into the room, hoping I'd see the ghost almost as much as I hoped I wouldn't. I shook my head and whispered back, "No. But there's definitely somebody in here."

Nola sucked in a large gulp of air. With a tone of surprise, she said, "It's E, C, and A." She turned to me, her eyes wide. "I think your ghost might be trying to tell us something."

Before her words had completely registered in my mind, the prop holding up the top board of the piano shot out as if hit by an unseen hand, sending the lid crashing down onto the piano in a cacophony of rattling keys accompanied by the unmistakable mewling cry of a newborn baby.

Grabbing Nola's arm, I said, "I think you might be right."

CHAPTER 15

I sat in the rope swing beneath the branches of the old oak, swaying from side to side, my thoughts mimicking the action. I watched with some detachment as a small group of family members and friends milled around the tables of food prepared by Mrs. Houlihan and Sophie—the edible and inedible, as I defined them.

My parents stood near the sweet-tea pitchers putting ice in glasses, their heads bent together. My dad said something in my mother's ear, making her giggle. Jack stood on one side of the food tables with his hands on his hips, facing Nola and Alston and Alston's brother, Cooper, as the latter selected a flaxseed-and-carob-chip cookie that Nola had contributed to Sophie's table. To a stranger, it would appear that Jack was smiling, but to me it was definitely more like a glower.

Cooper was exactly as I'd pictured him, tall and slender like Alston, with a close-cropped cadet haircut, impeccable manners, an easy smile, and a firm handshake. And he read Tolstoy. He looked smart in his cadet summer-leave uniform of gray trousers, white short-sleeved shirt with shoulder boards, and white hat, and neither Nola nor I could find any fault in his appearance. He was three years older than Nola, but from what I could tell, they were just friends with common interests. Which made it even more fun for me to watch Jack react.

Sophie's husband, Chad—wearing Birkenstocks with socks—was chatting with Jack's mother, Amelia, while Jack's dad, John, sat in the shade next to her wearing a seersucker suit and straw hat, the consum-

mate Charleston gentleman. I could never decide whether Jack got his
charm from his father or his mother. But when I caught sight of John
Trenholm smiling, I couldn't help but think it was probably both,
maybe leaning a little heavily toward the Trenholm side. Judging by
the grandparents on both sides, I was fairly confident that the twins
had a good chance of ending up charming, smart, good-looking, or
all three. They might also be able to see dead people, but I wasn't
prepared to go there yet.

Sophie stood on the edge of the garden near the flagstone path that
led from the kitchen door to the front of the house. She looked as if
she were part of the garden, with her garish floral A-line dress, paisley
scarf tossed carelessly around her neck, and lime green Birkenstocks. I
wanted to ask her whether the latter had been custom ordered, but
then decided that I really didn't want to know.

She was pretending to follow the conversation between Nola,
Alston, and Cooper while she sipped at a tall glass of water with organic lemon, but she was keeping an eye on the curb in front of my
house like a cat at a mouse hole.

I continued to sway on the swing, too hot and tired to eat or do
more than say hello to my guests. The main goal of the whole gathering was to tell everyone about the twins. Despite the new awkwardness
between Jack and me caused by my words the previous evening, I was
looking forward to the announcement.

The only other fly in the proverbial ointment was the Gilberts. Mr.
Drayton said they had accepted my invitation and would be stopping
by the barbecue. Despite Jack's plans to frighten them off, I couldn't
easily dismiss their claims, as much as I wanted to, at least without
knowing what other ammunition they had besides the baby bonnet.
And I had a horrible feeling that I was about to find out. Even worse,
the person I'd want to turn to with my disappointment was the one
person I couldn't.

The sound of the fountain made me want to go to the bathroom
again, and I was about to stand and move inside when Sophie perked
up like a hunting dog on the scent of a fox. Our eyes met, and she
didn't need to tell me that the Gilberts had arrived.

Sophie greeted them warmly as I approached, the chatter of the already assembled group diminishing somewhat behind me. The Gilberts appeared pretty much as they had when I'd first met them, wearing jeans and T-shirts, Irene's face freshly scrubbed and makeup-free.

I could almost feel my mother's finger prodding me in my back as I struggled to find a cordial greeting. I held out my hand to George, and then Irene. "We're happy that you were able to make it today, at the very least so I'd have a chance to thank you for your nursing care when I fainted the other day."

Irene smiled, her brown eyes warm behind her glasses. "Thank you for having us, and I'm glad you're feeling better."

I really wanted to dislike her, but there was nothing frightening or menacing about either her or her husband. They were the soccer parents always on the front row, constantly driving somewhere for some kind of game or activity, or in the drive-through line at Starbucks or McDonald's in their minivan. They probably went to Disney World in the spring and the beach in the fall, because that was what families like the Gilberts did. They were the kind of people you wanted to live next door to you, because instead of giving you the cup of flour you needed to borrow, they'd give you the whole bag, just in case you needed more. The only thing wrong with them was that they believed they were the rightful owners of my house.

"I am, thank you. It was just a pregnancy thing," I acknowledged.

Irene laughed. "Oh, don't I know a thing or two about that!"

I was about to ask her something about her children when I noticed Mr. Drayton walking up the path toward the house. I'd invited him only because I'd needed him to communicate with the Gilberts for me. I hadn't actually thought he'd come. Apparently neither had he. He wore a dark, three-piece suit and starched white shirt—with a matching white pocket square in his jacket pocket. He looked like a black candle already lit by a flame and getting ready to melt.

Jack appeared by my side to greet the old lawyer before dragging him away toward the food table. The look he shot over at Sophie said that he was clearing the decks so that she and I could do what needed to be done.

As if on cue, Sophie allowed her shoulders to hunch. "We are so pleased you could make it. And I apologize that it's all outdoors, since you're from up north and probably not used to our summers here. I mean, here it is, almost October, and it's hotter than Hades! But the air-conditioning has been pretty flaky lately, and we can't seem to cool down the first floor. At least out here we have a little bit of a breeze. We just hope and pray it's not caused by the movement of wings by a flock of those palmetto bugs. That's a sight you should see! Maybe we'll get lucky and you can experience it firsthand tonight."

Irene and George took a noticeable step closer to each other, each darting a wary glance up at the bright blue sky.

"They're really that big?" George asked as Sophie began escorting them toward the rest of the party.

Sophie gave a self-deprecating chuckle. "Well, I might be exaggerating a *little* bit," she said, holding up her thumb and forefinger about an inch apart. "But let's just say you wouldn't want one of those little buggers getting sucked into your plane's engine."

Sophie and I took the couple around the garden and introduced them to everyone, and my estimation of them increased when they filled their plates with fried chicken, barbecued shrimp, and pork ribs instead of the soy burgers and Tofurky hot dogs.

Chad joined us as we sat down at one of the cloth-covered tables, clapping his hands loudly around and beneath the table after he'd set down his plate of food. Before I could ask Sophie whether he'd been hit in the head or was just feeling the pressure of impending fatherhood, she turned to the Gilberts.

"Palmetto bugs don't like loud sounds. When I'm visiting Melanie, I always make sure to stomp or clap really loudly before entering any room."

The couple stared at her, their bespectacled eyes blinking in unison.

"What's going on with the yellow tape?" George asked.

I glanced over at my dad, who decided at that moment that he needed to analyze the carob-chip cookies as if they might be hiding something valuable. He'd told me he'd already spoken with Rich Kobylt and the tape and debris were supposed to have been removed before the party. In my distracted state, I hadn't even noticed that nothing had been touched.

"Wellll," Sophie said, drawing out the word. "You already know about the dead body discovered in the foundation. One of three dead bodies found on the property, just in case you weren't already aware. We can only hope and pray there aren't any more!" She smiled widely. "But if the house hadn't been on the verge of collapse, we wouldn't have found this last one." She took a bite of her Tofurky burger and chewed thoughtfully as the Gilberts exchanged glances.

Irene Gilbert coughed. "Three dead bodies?"

Chad waved his hand at them. "Oh, don't worry about them. Two were dug up last year and buried. That's why the fountain's working again."

I saw Mr. Drayton listening intently to the conversation and looking like he was about to intervene, when Jack accidentally spilled his glass of water on the lawyer's pants. My mother immediately went into action, escorting Mr. Drayton to the kitchen and dry towels.

"Well, that's good, I suppose," Irene said. "But what did you mean by 'on the verge of collapse'?"

She directed her question at me, so I had no choice to answer honestly, since I hadn't been prepped like everybody else seemed to have been. "Um, not exactly. It was just that the foundation had cracked, which isn't good, but it was far from being on the 'verge of collapse.' I mean, I guess it could have been if we hadn't had it repaired."

"At great expense," Sophie interjected. "You know what they call old houses around here, don't you?"

My eyes widened as I prepared to hear Sophie repeat my own words. "They're like a boil on your behind. They're always there, claiming your undivided attention whenever you want to sit down and rest."

Jack approached, apparently satisfied that Alston was sitting on one of the garden benches between Cooper and Nola, all eating off of plates in their laps. It hadn't escaped my notice that Cooper had helped himself from both food tables and seemed to be enjoying dipping Amelia's gourmet cheese straws into Sophie's homemade hummus.

Jack stood at the opposite end of the table behind Sophie, his eyes trained on me. "Did Mellie tell you what happened to the antique lighting fixture in the vestibule?"

All heads turned in my direction. I quickly swallowed my bite of fried chicken. "It fell." I watched as General Lee removed himself from under the shade of the table and planted himself on top of Irene's feet. He bent his head, tilting it from side to side, as if unseen hands were scratching him behind his ears.

In that one movement, I knew with all certainty that Jack's plan wasn't going to work.

There was something not right about how calm the air was, how warm the breeze on my skin. For the first time in my life, I wished I could see the spirit who was here. Maybe then I could understand why it was making its presence known by petting my dog, and making these two strangers feel at home. *Because they* are *home,* the voice inside my head whispered.

Jack's voice refocused my attention. "Melanie thinks it was a ghost. It certainly wouldn't be the first time something unexplainable happened. I know I won't look in any of the mirrors inside the house. I'm always afraid I might see something standing behind me."

After a dramatic pause in which it seemed he was waiting for something to happen, he smiled, but his face retained a sinister cast, something I hadn't seen since the day I'd told him that I loved him. He turned to me, his eyebrows lifting in silent appeal, and it wasn't hard for me to figure out what he wanted me to do next. As if I could conjure spirits; as if by raising my hands a whirlwind of brittle leaves and foggy air would magically appear as the dead eased themselves from the earth. But that happened only in movies. Just like happy endings.

I stood, hitting the side of my glass with a spoon to get everyone's attention. "I . . . um, Jack and I have an announcement to make." Jack moved to my side as the conversations ceased and the small gathering focused on us. I kept waiting for Jack to touch me, to take my hand or put his arm around me, but he didn't. Just like I thought I wanted.

He leaned toward me to whisper in my ear, "Where's the angry ghost? The one who was playing the piano last night for you and Nola?"

"She's here," I whispered back. "But I'm afraid it's not the Gilberts she's angry with."

He sucked in a quick breath. "Don't give up too quickly, Mellie."

"I'm not a quitter," I hissed.

"Really? You could have fooled me."

I wanted to ask him what he meant, but we both looked up as my mother came forward and handed me a small yellow gift bag with yellow and green tissue paper billowing from the top. My hands shook with anger as I dug into the bag and pulled out two pairs of yellow knitted booties from Nancy and Joyce. I made myself smile, the fact that I was having twins at the age of forty now firmly in the realm of the least of my worries.

"We're having twins," I said as I held up the two pairs of booties, my gaze sliding to my mother to make sure her feigned surprise was real enough.

There were screeches from Amelia, Alston, and Nola, and then a belated one from my mother as all four women approached me with a hug and the men patted Jack on the back, as if twins were some evidence of masculinity. As if he were doing all the heavy lifting.

Irene surprised me with a warm and genuine smile. "Congratulations. Two is better than one, in my opinion. They'll always have a friend."

"Thanks," I said, feeling very awkward. If she had her way, my twins would never play in this garden, or learn to walk on the old wood floors that still bore the marks of those who'd trodden on them for more than one hundred and fifty years.

"Congratulations again, Melanie."

I looked up at the masculine voice and spotted Detective Riley. He greeted my parents, then kissed me on both cheeks. "I'm sorry to interrupt. I didn't know you were having a party. I rang the doorbell, but when nobody answered I figured I'd check out back here."

"The doorbell doesn't always work," I said stupidly, feeling Jack's gaze burning a hole in the middle of my back.

He nodded. "Twins are great. My oldest sister has a set—both boys. They're thirteen now—both football players. When she was pregnant, we could tell that they would probably be linebackers—she got as big as a monster truck and was always hungry. And they haven't stopped eating since the moment they were born."

He stopped talking when he noticed my smile dipping. "Maybe you'll have girls," he said with a look of encouragement.

Jack approached, and the two men shook hands, each regarding the other with a wariness usually reserved for a gazelle at a jungle watering hole. "Good to see you, Tommy. I'm hoping you have breaking news in the case to make it worth interrupting our little party."

I glared at Jack, but Thomas didn't seem to be bothered by Jack's posturing.

"Actually, Jack, Tommy's my dad. Friends and family call me Thomas. Everybody else calls me Detective or sir."

The two men were of similar builds and height, which would have made them excellent sparring partners in a boxing ring. Or in a back garden. I stepped between them. "You're always welcome, Thomas, so I'm glad you're here, whether it's a social call or not." Tugging on his elbow, I turned him to face the Gilberts and introduced them and Mr. Drayton as the lawyer joined us. The older man pressed his handkerchief against his forehead and cheeks, doing little to stop the constant drip of perspiration. I wanted to suggest that he take off his jacket, but I didn't want him to be too comfortable.

Thomas seemed surprised to see the Gilberts, but I didn't try to explain, because even I was no longer sure why I'd invited them. "Well, I guess it's good you're all here, as it will save me some time. I just learned that there's been a delay in the exhumation order. A lawyer representing Mr. Vanderhorst's heir has filed paperwork to deny the order."

All eyes were on me again. I nodded. "Yes, I hired a lawyer, but not only because of what you're all thinking. I knew Mr. Vanderhorst. Granted, I only met him once, but I think I can say that I knew him well enough to know that he deserves to rest in peace unless there's a very good reason to disturb him. All you have is a bonnet and, accord-

ing to a newspaper article, a deathbed confession by a Bridget Monahan Gilbert. I don't know yet who she is, but she died in 1898—before
Mr. Vanderhorst was even born. My lawyer simply needs more information."

The Gilberts looked at each other before Irene—apparently the
spokesperson for the couple—turned to me. "You can wait for this
Sunday's installment in the paper, or I could show you now. Either
way, your lawyer will have to agree it's worth investigating."

Without waiting for my reply, she reached into her purse and pulled
out a piece of white paper that had been folded into quarters. I opened
it to find a photocopied letter in a beautiful script, with elegant flour-
ishes of the letters at the beginning of each sentence. With both Jack
and Thomas looking on behind either shoulder, I began to read.

October 10, 1898

*The following is inscribed by Elizabeth Ferguson at the request of
Bridget Monahan Gilbert, who is too ill to put pen to paper, and whose
own writing abilities, by her own admission, are limited. With only
grammatical corrections, these words are not mine, but hers.*

To Whom It May Concern,

*I am near my time to be called to meet my Maker, where I will have
to face my sins. But I know I will not rest unless the truth is known
here on earth, where old wrongs might still be put right.*

*I swear on the holy Bible that the following is what actually hap-
pened on the 22nd day of March, 1860.*

*I was then employed as a housemaid at a house in Charleston,
South Carolina, on Tradd Street by Mr. and Mrs. John Vanderhorst.
On that day, Mrs. Vanderhorst gave birth to twin sons. The birth was
attended to by a doctor and his nurse, with Mr. Vanderhorst waiting
outside the door. I know this, as I was the one sent to fetch water and
towels and anything else they might need by the doctor and his nurse.*

*The first child, whom they called William, was born into this world
fat and with a lusty cry, and we were all relieved that Mrs. Vanderhorst
had been delivered of a healthy son. But that was until Mrs. Vander-*

horst began having more birthing pains and delivered William's brother twenty minutes later. He was blue, and still, and we all thought he was dead.

The doctor gave him a sound slap to his backside so that he sucked in a breath and began to cry, but it was soon believed by Mr. Vanderhorst and the doctor that the child should have been left to sleep, and to return to the good Lord. His cries were louder than his brother's, but his limbs on one side of his body were horribly deformed. I overheard Mr. Vanderhorst saying he would only be good for a circus show.

After some discussion, which I did not hear, the doctor's daughter, acting as his nurse, wrapped the child in a blanket before handing him to me. She said it was a blessing that his mother had fainted from the pain and was not awake to see the horror. She then instructed me to take the child somewhere far away, and leave it on a church doorstep, where he could not bring shame on the family. Mr. Vanderhorst gave me a lot of money for my trouble and for my silence, and enough to get me started in a new life. I was poor, with no immediate family of my own, and so I took the money and left with the baby.

I went north, where I had distant relations, intending to leave the child somewhere in between Charleston and New York. But the baby had the most beautiful face, and was so sweet that I had fallen in love with him before we had even reached Virginia. He became my own flesh and blood on that train, and I could not leave him. It was then that I decided to call him Cornelius, as his father had given him to me without naming him.

When I arrived at the home of cousins, I told them that I was a widow and Cornelius was mine, and they accepted us without question. Despite his physical deformities, my son was strong and smart, and he grew up to know nothing but love. For that, I am not sorry for what I did.

I married Thaddeus Gilbert, who adopted Cornelius and gave him his name. Yet even when Cornelius married and had a child of his own, I kept our secret. Although we had never been rich, we have shared an abundance of love, and I have never desired to ruin the happiness that Cornelius has found so far from the family who threw him out like trash. I do not think he wishes for another life, but maybe it will be different for his children or children's children.

So now, at the end of my life, I must try to set things right. Cor-
nelius was given to me with a christening gown and bonnet by the nurse
who helped bring him into the world. I am keeping the bonnet with this
letter, but I am mailing the gown to the Vanderhorsts' home in Charles-
ton as a reminder to them that their loss has been my gain, and that a
child they believed worth nothing is alive and well, shining his special
light in the dark corners of this world. And that if they wish to set right
a wrong, they will come forward with open arms.

God forgive me, but God forgive those who read this and do not
seek justice for the sins of the past.

The signature at the end of the letter sprawled across the page,
as if the signer were in a hurry to get it in ink. *Bridget Monahan*
Gilbert.

I looked at the people crowded around me, seeing only the christening gown that had been left at my front door, the writing on the
outside faded with age. A package that had been mailed nearly one
hundred years before, in 1898. The same year Bridget Monahan Gilbert had written her deathbed confession and mailed a package containing a baby's gown.

"Thank you for showing this to me," I said, handing it back to
Irene, my fingers eager to release the paper and the words that seemed
to weigh it down. "William was Nevin Vanderhorst's grandfather. I
saw the family tree yesterday in the historical archives. William was
listed as an only child."

Irene nodded. "Which makes sense, since his twin brother was
taken from the house before anybody knew of his existence. Including
his mother. It's all in the letter."

"But it's not proof," Jack added gently.

Irene regarded him calmly. "No, I suppose it's not. But Mr. Drayton believes it's enough to get the exhumation."

Mr. Drayton cleared his throat and stared at us somberly. Irene
settled her purse on her shoulder as her husband took her hand in his.
"Thank you so much for the food—it was all very wonderful. We'll
be heading back to New York tomorrow, but we're prepared to wait

as long as it takes. Your lawyer is stalling things, but he can't stall for-ever. And I think we both want to know the truth."

Jack stood behind me, not touching, but near enough that it felt as if he were. I just nodded, my throat too tight for me to speak.

The wind picked up, blowing rose petals around the Gilberts' feet as we watched them walk down the path with Mr. Drayton, George stomping his feet and clapping loudly every few steps.

The familiar feeling of hot and cold on the back of my neck alerted me that I was being watched, but when I lifted my head to the win-dows at the rear of the house, I saw only darkened glass and a bruised foundation where a baby's remains had been found.

I felt dizzy, the many pieces of the puzzle spinning around my head like debris in a hurricane. I turned back to the pile of rubble where the remains of a baby and a christening gown and bonnet had been found, trying to make sense of Bridget Gilbert's letter and the package that had ended up on my doorstep more than one hundred years after it had been mailed. Glancing up, I saw Jack and Thomas watching me intently.

"Are you all right?" Thomas asked. "You look like you've just seen a ghost."

The fried chicken I'd consumed only twenty minutes before de-cided at that moment to make a return visit. I began running toward the kitchen, Jack close behind, as eager to throw up in private as I was to hide the hysterical laughter that was threatening to spill out and never, ever stop.

CHAPTER 16

I stood in front of the reception desk at the Charleston Place hotel, looking out the glass doors at the parking horseshoe, where Sophie was locking up her bike. Her flowing dress had been knotted around her legs with what appeared to be twist ties, and her hair—never the tamest part of her—was sticking up in all directions from under the protection of a tie-dyed bike helmet. As she reached up to remove the helmet, I headed toward the door, ready to tell her that it was probably better if she left it on, but I stopped. In all the years I had known her, she had yet to take any of my fashion advice.

Leaving the helmet dangling on the handlebars, she shouldered her backpack and headed toward the doors, where a uniformed doorman greeted her with a smile and didn't even glance at her outfit. She hugged me with her usual enthusiasm, as if she hadn't seen me in years, instead of just days ago at the barbecue. Holding me at arm's length, she regarded me carefully. "Are you getting enough sleep, Melanie? You look tired."

Before I could respond, she began untying the wire ties that held her dress up above her knees. "I think it kind of looks cute this way, but I don't want to hear you complaining."

"I wouldn't complain. . . ."

Her look silenced me. "Come on; let's go get something to eat. I'm starving. The steamed edamame I had as a snack an hour ago didn't keep both of us satisfied for long." She smiled and rubbed her belly as we moved in front of the hostess stand at the hotel's Palmetto Cafe.

"Neither did the stale glazed doughnut I found in the back of my pantry," I said.

"Really, Melanie?"

"But I washed it down with a banana and a glass of vanilla soy milk," I said indignantly. "Did you know a bunch of those organic bananas you made me buy are almost twice as much as the regular kind?"

She looked at me and took a deep breath. "Has anybody ever told you that you're resistant to change?"

"Maybe." I crossed my arms and waited as the hostess approached us.

After we were seated outside in the courtyard surrounded by greenery and a burbling fountain, I was able to examine my friend more closely. Her skin still glowed as if lit from within, and although there seemed to be a little softening around her middle, she looked like just a better version of her old self. Except for her clothes. Gone were my hopes that she'd soon get too big to wear any of her old things and I'd force her to go maternity-clothes shopping with me.

We placed our orders, and I ordered the same menu items as Sophie—lean grilled chicken, salad, and fruit—but only because I hoped it meant she'd let me order dessert when we were finished.

She looked at me suspiciously as the waiter left with our orders. I just smoothed my napkin in my lap and looked at her eagerly. "Well? You said you had news."

"I do. I'm just not sure where it all fits." She shifted in her seat, as if trying to get her thoughts in a more comfortable order. "I've done a lot of research into the history of your house over the years—even before you owned it. It's such a great specimen of Charleston architecture that has been owned by the same family since it was built. So when you told me that a baby's remains were discovered in the house's foundation, it rang a bell. I remembered reading about something being changed, something that altered the original footprint of the house at some point in the home's history. But my brain's so foggy these days that I couldn't pinpoint an approximate time period to go back and dig into the archives."

The waiter returned with our glasses of water and fresh lemon. I was on the verge of asking for a sweet tea but caught Sophie's "teacher eye"—what I called her expression that looked like she'd just caught a pair of students passing notes in class. For such a small and unassuming woman, she could sure pack a lot of punch in just one look. It would probably make her a very good mother.

"And?" I said after the waiter left.

"It wasn't until I was chatting with Detective Riley at the barbecue and he started asking me about some of the house's history that I remembered what it was. We'd spoken before, but it was his interest in the provenance of some of the house's furniture that made me remember. Did you know he likes to collect antiques?"

"No, I didn't. But go on. What is it that you're thinking I should know even though you haven't yet told me?"

With an exasperated sigh, she said, "I remembered the dining table." She leaned back in her chair, a smug expression on her face.

"The dining table?"

"Yes. John and his wife—Nevin's great-grandparents—bought a new dining table in Italy during their yearlong honeymoon in Europe. The problem was that it was six feet longer than the dining room table that was originally in the room, and which the room was designed around."

I still wasn't getting it. Granted, the pregnancy hormones had slowed my brain down to the speed of giant sea turtles racing in wet sand, but I still didn't think that there could be a logical connection between a dining room table and a body buried in a house's foundation.

After a look of exasperation, she continued. "So it didn't fit in the dining room! But they'd already had the table shipped all the way over from Italy and paid a small fortune for it." She spoke slowly, just like Nola did when she was trying to explain something to me.

My eyes widened with understanding, and with relief that I'd figured it out without being told. "So they had to enlarge the dining room at the back of the house so it would fit."

"Bingo!" she said, loudly enough that our fellow diners looked over in our direction. "But that's not all. Guess when they enlarged the dining room?"

I frowned, wondering when her questions were going to get easier. "Well, if they got the table on their honeymoon, that should be easy to figure out. When were they married?"

"September 1858. And they were on their honeymoon for a year."

She nodded, her eyes expectant.

I slapped my hands on the table, making the glasses and silverware rattle and the couple at the next table glance in our direction again. "Which would have brought them back to Charleston sometime in the fall of 1859."

Sophie was nodding. "Exactly. And just in time to give birth the following March."

"And that would have been March 1860." I was silent for a moment, thinking, as the waiter placed our food in front of us. After he'd left, I leaned across the table. "So it's possible that work on the house—which included extending the foundation—could have been going on when William and Cornelius were born."

"Exactly what I was thinking." Sophie took a sip from her water.

I stared down at my plate, unable to focus on the food or to even feel the hunger pangs that had been dogging me since breakfast. I imagined instead that I was driving at night through fog, my headlights picking out only vague shapes in the distance. "But that doesn't make sense. If twin boys were born—and one was given away and the other raised as an only child, then who is the baby buried in the foundation during the same year they were born?"

Sophie was eating with relish, as if all this talk about history, old bones, and even older houses was fueling her appetite. "Well, there could have been triplets. But the one eyewitness report—Bridget Gilbert—states that there were only two babies. And if they were willing to go to the trouble of making one disappear because of physical deformities, then it wouldn't make sense that they'd hide the death of another. Why not just bury the baby in a proper cemetery?" She shook her head. "I agree. None of this is making sense."

We ate in silence for a few moments before Sophie spoke again. "You know, there might be a way to figure some of this out, but you might not like it."

"Why am I afraid to hear this?"

"Because you don't like change. And what I'm suggesting could be a game changer."

I didn't bother arguing. Instead, I placed my knife and fork on my plate and leaned back. "Go ahead. I'm ready."

"Well, the police are examining the baby's body for clues. Granted, it's an old case, so they're not trying to beat any land-speed records to get to the bottom of what really happened. I know like every other police department in this country they're short-staffed and need to put their efforts on more current cases."

"But . . . ?" I prompted.

"I was going to suggest that if they can pull any DNA from the bones of the baby's remains, they should compare them to George Gilbert's. I figure that if he's willing to dig up Nevin Vanderhorst and compare his DNA, then why not compare it to the bones discovered in the foundation of the house he claims is rightfully his?"

"But what would that prove?"

She didn't answer right away. "Maybe nothing, if there's no match. But if there is, then it would mean that there's a legitimate reason for exhuming Nevin."

I could feel the pulse in my temples, making it impossible to concentrate. "I'm not following. If the remains match George Gilbert's, why would that give us a reason to dig up Nevin?"

"Well, because no match between the remains and George *could* mean that one of the three isn't related to the Vanderhorsts at all. And that's when the real fun begins."

I stared down at my partially eaten lunch. "I think I'll just wait to see what happens with the existing exhumation order. Sterling Zerbe, my lawyer, says it could take a while. Then we can figure out what to do next. Although I have a feeling that the Gilberts are probably going to figure out that it would be in their best interests if they compare George's DNA with the remains. If I suggest it now, it might speed things up."

Sophie regarded me for a moment. "All right. But you do realize that ignoring something doesn't make it go away, right? Kind of like a pregnancy."

I took a bite and chewed slowly, not tasting anything and having no idea what I'd just put in my mouth. "Yeah, I'm aware. But I'm not ignoring this. I just need more time to try to figure everything out." I took a sip from my water as something else she'd said niggled at my brain. "So how did you know about the dining room table?"

She practically beamed. "Remember—I've got the college's fabulous archives to help me. When I was digging through old records from fifty-five Tradd, there was a cross-reference to a postcard written by Mrs. John Vanderhorst to her mother in Charleston while on her honeymoon in Florence. The letter was in the historical society archives, so I put a phone call in to your Yvonne Craig, who was happy to help once I explained that I was a friend of yours and Jack's. She made a copy of it and stuck it in your file for the next time you visit the archives."

I stopped chewing and frowned.

Sophie stopped eating, too, and stared back at me. "What? What's wrong? Yvonne can be my friend, too, you know."

I almost laughed, which had probably been her intent. "It's not that. It's just how she ropes Jack and me together, as if we're a couple."

"Well, you kind of are. I mean, you're going to be parents together." She leaned closer to me, clutching her fork, and I noticed her unvarnished and neatly trimmed nails, something I found oddly comforting. Sort of like tomato soup and a grilled cheese sandwich on a cold day.

She continued. "Melanie, I probably know you better than most, and I love you like a sister, which is the only reason I'm going to say this. But I know that you love Jack, and even though he hasn't said anything to me, it's obvious that he loves you. You both need to get over all the past hurts, forgive yourselves and each other, and decide to be happy."

I rolled my eyes upward, startled to find blue sky through the fronds of a palm tree. "If it were only that easy."

"Have you ever considered the thought that maybe it is?"

I sat up as I watched the waiter approach with dessert menus. "You sound like Nola. Please stop. I have an aversion to having my heart steamrolled again. It hurt enough the first time."

The waiter stopped by our table, a Cheshire-cat grin on his face at the prospect of offering sweets to two pregnant women. "Can I interest you ladies in some dessert this afternoon?"

My smile diminished when I turned to Sophie, who was already reaching into her purse and shaking her head. "Not today, thank you. Just the bill, please."

I allowed her to pay the bill, then walked outside with her in front of the hotel. "Do you want to take a pedicab to the museum or have them call us a taxi?"

She looked at me as if I'd just suggested she should cut her hair or wear high heels. "We can walk. It's less than a mile."

"But it's hot out," I complained. "And I'm wearing heels."

She reached into her large backpack and pulled out the lime green Birkenstocks she'd worn to the barbecue. "Wear these. We're the same shoe size and they're very comfortable to walk in."

I stared at them without comment, wondering what the best way was to end a friendship. But then I realized that I couldn't possibly look any worse, and took them from her. "Whatevs," I said, mimicking Nola. "But you'll have to carry my heels in your backpack."

With a look of smug satisfaction, she stowed my heels, then led the way toward Meeting Street and the Charleston Museum. Sophie walked quickly, with a spritely gait, barely breaking a sweat. After just a block, I was panting beside her, so she adjusted her pace.

"You should really be exercising, Melanie. You'll have a much better delivery if you're fit and your muscles are toned. I know you've never had to exercise before, but pregnancy is different. I'm taking this fabulous yoga class for expectant moms that you would just love. I'm doing a prenatal swim class, too. It's to get me comfortable with water, just in case I decide to go for a water birth."

I stumbled on a crack in the sidewalk. "A what?"

"A water birth. It's where you get into a large tub, or even a kiddie pool, and give birth underwater. We want a home birth, so we can set up the pool in the living room and have all of our friends around us, sharing the experience. You're invited, of course."

I stared at her in horror, almost running into a lamppost, but she didn't seem to notice.

She continued. "Water births really make sense, if you think about it. The baby's been swimming for nine months in amniotic fluid, so coming out into the world from the womb isn't such a big shock if they're expelled into warm water."

I shuddered. "Please don't use the words 'amniotic fluid' so soon after I eat, okay? And I think I'll skip the water yoga and water birthing. I plan to be unconscious for the birth, and I don't want to drown."

She sent me a sidelong glance. "Yes, well, you should still start exercising. It will help your stamina both during labor and afterward."

"I'll think about it," I said. My mother and Amelia power-walked three mornings a week and had been asking me to join them. As long as I didn't have to wear ugly trainers or—even worse—Birkenstocks, I might agree for a trial run.

"So," she said in that tone of voice that warned me that I probably didn't want to hear what followed.

I kept silent, hoping her pregnancy had messed with her memory as much as mine had, and that she'd forget what she'd been about to say.

"What's with this Detective Riley? The way he was looking at you at the barbecue made me wonder if there was something up with that."

I was close to being out of breath, so I kept my answer short. "We're . . . friends. For now. Keeping my options . . . open."

"Has he asked you out?"

"Dinner. Breakfast."

She raised both eyebrows.

"Late breakfast. He cooked."

Her eyebrows remained raised.

"Picked me up at my office. Not . . . sleepover."

We were silent for a few moments, the sound of my heavy breathing filling the conversational lull. "Good," she said eventually.

"Good?"

She nodded. "Good for you. And good for Jack. Maybe a third party will help you both come to your senses."

By the time we reached the Charleston Museum after walking for fifteen minutes, I was perspiring heavily, feeling my makeup pooling along my jawline, and my hair sticking to my scalp. Sophie had only a dewy glow about her face, her hair slightly more curled than usual. I wished I could hate her.

I paused in front of the modern brick building, the back of my neck already prickling in response to all the sets of unseen eyes that sensed my presence. I hated museums like I hated hospitals; hated the way the volume of voices in my head always paralyzed me with fear. I began humming "Dancing Queen" in preparation.

"I already got our tickets, so we don't have to make your visit here any longer than it has to be—just long enough for you to look at the cradle to see if it's the same one in your attic and read the label to see if it rings any bells. There's an exhibit of the Charleston militia and the Civil War that we'll have to pass to get to the permanent exhibit where the cradle is. I'll just grab your elbow and propel you along and you can sing ABBA as loudly as you want. I don't embarrass easily."

I studied her frizzy hair and plastic barrettes, her garish dress and Birkenstocks, and decided that she was probably right.

The hum of voices began as soon as we pushed through the glass doors. Sophie showed our tickets, then grabbed my arm. She hurriedly tugged me through a textiles exhibit, where I heard the babble of women's voices as if they were in the process of quilt making, and then past the Civil War militia exhibit, where, although I couldn't smell the gunpowder or the tang of blood, I heard the shouts of men's voices carrying over those of the women. But I could not see a single specter. It was more frightening, almost, to simply hear them surrounding me, to sense the cold air, but not see the eyes that bored into me like bullets seeking their target.

We ended up in one of the larger exhibit rooms, where the permanent displays of Charleston's history through the years were kept. So-phie led me past a collection of Edgefield pottery, with their faces of exaggerated mouths and eyes, then stopped in front of a wide glass case.

"Is that it?" Sophie asked.

She didn't need to point to the item we'd come to see. The black ash-wood cradle, with its twisted spindles and egret-shaped rockers, sat empty behind the glass, and I wondered whether it was my imag-ination that saw it move. "Yes," I whispered. The woman's voice was loud in my ear, blocking out all other sounds. *Mine.*

I stepped back, but Sophie held on to my arm. "Are you all right?"

I didn't answer as my eyes moved from the cradle to the plaque beside it. VANDERHORST FAMILY CRADLE. In smaller letters underneath were the words DONATED IN 1922 BY L. VANDERHORST. Something clawed at the back of my neck, and I jerked out of Sophie's grasp and started running for the exit.

She caught up with me outside, where I was gasping for breath on the sidewalk, my hands on my knees. "What happened?"

I shook my head. "That woman—the spirit in my house that keeps saying the word 'mine'—was in there. With the cradle. She scratched me." I lifted my hair, where the salt from my sweat was making the skin sting.

"Oh, Melanie—I'm so sorry I brought you. I didn't think . . ."

"Neither did I. But I'm glad I came. Because that woman is really starting to piss me off. Wronged party or not, she's got to go." I straightened, my anger feeding my indignation and bringing back a little of my former self.

A small smile lifted a corner of her mouth. "And that's good, right?"

"It might be. I just need to figure out who she is so I can get her where it hurts." I paused for a moment, catching my breath while my brain slowly chugged into action.

"You know, Melanie, that might be the answer to all of your cur-rent problems."

I scowled at her. "What do you mean?"

"Figuring out what you want and then going for it. You'll never get what you want until you admit to yourself what that is."

I pressed a clean tissue against the back of my neck, but I still felt the sting of Sophie's words. Without responding, I said, "I'm taking a pedicab back to the office. I'd be happy to give you a lift to your bike."

"No, thanks," she said. "I think you'd rather be alone. I'll call you later." She dug in her backpack for my heels, and we exchanged shoes. Then, with a wave of her hand, she turned and began making her way back up Meeting Street.

I snagged a pedicab waiting at the museum, then sat in silence as the driver pedaled me back to Broad Street as my grandmother's words reverberated inside my skull. *You need to decide sooner rather than later what you want. And then be ready to fight for it.* When I'd first heard them, I'd thought that the hardest part would be the fighting. But I was quickly figuring out that it was not.

CHAPTER 17

By the middle of October, I was no closer to finding any of the answers I was seeking. The whole world seemed to be dragging its feet in sympathy: The exhumation request was still bogged down in paperwork, the final DNA results on the remains had not yet been completed, and the identity of my tormentor and the crying baby remained as elusive as ever.

Even the regular newspaper serials about the Vanderhorst house and the "interloper" had paused, moving on to other venerable Charleston families and their homes, just with a lot less salacious stories to tell. I imagined the reporter Suzy Dorf waiting like an alligator on a creek bed for the next tidbit to be thrown her way so she could write the next installment.

Nola remained with me, despite Jack's best efforts to get her to reconsider, and I found myself enjoying the presence of a living, breathing person in the house—usually three, since Alston and Cooper Ravenel were frequent visitors. Nola saw Jack a lot, but true to his word, he avoided visiting her when I was home. Still, I'd taken him to see approximately one hundred and thirty houses in the Charleston area, as well as to my frequent doctor's appointments. He was courteous and solicitous, but kept himself aloof and distant. Just as I'd asked.

From Nola I'd learned that he was making good progress on the Manigault murder book, and had found a new literary agent, who had big hopes that Jack would have a contract soon. I told myself that this explained Jack's preoccupation when he was with me. Just in case, I asked Nola, who confirmed that there was no new female in his life. Not that it mattered to me, of course.

As I passed into my second trimester, my nausea subsided, as did most—although not all—of my skin woes. My hair became thick and shiny for the first time in my life, and my appetite returned with a vengeance. I'd started power-walking with Amelia and my mother, but even that didn't offset the alarming amount of weight I seemed to be gaining by simple osmosis. I'd begun to regard appointments with Dr. Wise as being sent to the principal's office.

The inertia of my earlier pregnancy also seemed to fade, spurring me into mommy nesting mode. It was as if my subconscious realized my earlier resolve to figure out what I wanted and fight for it had stagnated due to all the proverbial brick walls I kept hitting my head against. I needed to find something else to strategize, organize, and put on a spreadsheet. At least it would keep me too occupied to dwell on my complete failure to move forward in any aspect of my life.

As I pushed open my front door, notes from the piano danced out onto the piazza. I quietly let myself in, placing my shopping bags—acquired on a trip with Amelia and my mother to accessorize the nursery—in the vestibule before easing my swollen feet out of my heels and tiptoeing across the hall to the music room.

I'd heard a part of the melody before, but this version was richer, with fuller chords and detailed lyrics. I stayed in the entranceway listening to Nola, her voice and the music easing away all of the day's tensions. She stopped abruptly, slamming her hands down on the keyboard and making me jerk upright.

"Stop it!" she shouted. "You're distracting me!"

"I'm sorry, Nola. I didn't think you knew I was here."

She looked startled to see me, then shook her head impatiently. "Not you. *Her.* Can't you smell the roses?"

I sniffed, smelling nothing but furniture polish and whatever vegan meal Mrs. Houlihan had in the oven. "No. But you can?"

She nodded. "At least it's the roses ghost. The other one is more annoying. She keeps making those same three notes stick."

I leaned against the doorway, trying to cross my arms, but giving up because my breasts were in the way. "I'm sorry they're bothering you. I'd make them go away if I could. But it's hard when I can't communicate with them, and harder still when I have no idea who they are or why they're here."

She let out an exaggerated sigh. "I know. It's just that I'll never get this song finished for Jimmy Gordon at this rate. My agent—and I still can't believe I have an agent, but Dad said I needed one—gave me a deadline, which I'm not sure I like, but I guess I'll have to deal with it. It's just really hard to get anything done with distractions like dueling ghosts."

"Welcome to my world," I muttered as I entered the room. "I'm glad they don't frighten you."

Nola shrugged, her fingers tapping lightly on the keyboard. "It's kind of hard to frighten me. I mean, my mom came back, and she didn't scare me. It's like if you're a nice person when you're alive, chances are you'll still be nice when you're dead."

"I think you're right, mostly. At least, that's been my experience." I thought for a moment. Lowering my voice, I said, "Except for the ghost who seems to be connected to the baby's remains. My mother seems to think that she's been wronged in some way and that's why she's angry—not that she's a mean person."

She nodded, then stopped, tilting her head to the side. "Do you smell the roses now? It's even stronger. It's like I've been tossed face-first into a rosebush."

"Ouch," I said, trying to lighten the oppressive atmosphere that had started to gather in the small room like dark clouds on the horizon. I sniffed deeply. "Still no roses."

Nola narrowed her eyes. "Do you miss it? Seeing dead people and stuff?"

I remembered asking my mother the same question, and how easily I'd dismissed her response. "I'm not sure. Maybe if I'd never had the ability, I wouldn't know to miss it. And now sometimes I think how nice it is that I can't see things at all anymore—not even hazy images that I did in the first part of my pregnancy. I can actually look in a mirror and not be prepared to see somebody standing behind me. But a part of me . . ." I shrugged, unsure of what I'd wanted to say.

"Yeah. I get it. Like living with my dad. It's like I miss him when we're not together, but when we *are* together he drives me nuts."

"Your dad has that effect on a lot of people."

She gave me a heart-stopping dimpled grin, and then we both sighed, making us laugh. She dropped her gaze back to the keyboard, her expression becoming serious. Gently stroking one of the white keys, she said, "I'm playing Mary in the school Christmas play, so I was thinking that maybe you'd like to come. Like, if you weren't already doing anything that night with that detective guy who's always around. It's December sixth."

"Congratulations! That's pretty amazing, considering you're only a freshman." I held up my phone and began typing into the calendar. "There. Done. And even if I did have plans, you come first."

"Just don't bring the detective guy, okay?"

"I thought you liked Thomas."

Which, I considered, was my problem. I liked Thomas. A lot. We had shared meals, events, movies, picnics, boating expeditions, and even a niece's first communion. Yet I still only liked him. He hadn't tried to kiss me yet, either because of my growing girth or because he suspected that every time I looked at him, I wanted to see Jack.

"He's nice and all; it's just . . ."

"It's just what?"

"Well, all of my friends have a mom and dad, and they'll all be at the play. I was just thinking that since you're the closest thing I have to a mom, you and Dad can sort of be like my mom and dad for the night."

Jell-O seemed to have replaced my heart, but if I'd learned anything from dealing with teenagers, it was that I had to remain neutral despite my initial urge to throw my arms around her and squeeze as tightly as I could.

"I'd be honored to, Nola. You're the closest thing I have to a daughter, so it looks like a win-win."

Her cheeks lifted in a smile as her fingers began a delicate descent on the keyboard, the sound stopping as she hit certain notes. "Look, she's doing it now."

I stepped closer, peering inside the piano, the sudden chilliness in the air stinging my cheeks. "Play them again."

She began playing each note slowly, starting in the lowest register of the keyboard and working her way up to the higher notes. I watched as the strings vibrated on most of the keys, but when particular ones were pressed, it appeared as if an invisible finger were pressing on the string.

"I thought you said it was only three keys," I said.

"It is. A, C, and E. But it's in every register—not just in the middle of the piano. She's definitely trying to tell us something."

"A-C-E?"

"Or C-A-E or E-A-C or whatever combination. The letters only mean something if you know where you're supposed to start." She moved her lips into the shape of an O and blew out, her breath creating little clouds.

I watched as they dissipated, the three letters A, C, and E somersaulting over one another in my brain. "Hang on a minute," I said as I left the room with my cell phone and moved into the front parlor. I'd learned from experience that modern technology didn't always work when other currents were flitting around the same space.

I flicked to my contacts, then hit the call button for Yvonne Craig, thinking as it rang that I should probably add her number to my favorites for quick dialing. She picked up on the third ring.

"Hello, Yvonne. This is Melanie Middleton. Can you talk?"

"I'm taking a break and sitting outside watching the latest season of *Downton Abbey* on my iPad, but I'll be happy to put Lord Grantham and his family on pause for you."

I smiled at the mental image of Yvonne with her iPad. "Thanks. I appreciate it. I left the folder you made for me with all of the photocopies in it at my office, but I had a quick question about the Vanderhorst family tree that I was hoping you could answer without too much trouble."

"Oh, that's too easy. I just pulled all of the books out for Jack, and they're still on the table upstairs."

"For Jack?"

"Oh, dear. I don't know if I was supposed to tell you that."

"Tell me what? That he's helping me? He already said he'd help—I just assumed we'd be working together."

There was a long pause before she spoke again. "Yes, I know. It's just . . ."

"Yes?"

"It's just that I think he was looking for an excuse to call you or to see you."

I stared at my phone, ready to argue that I saw Jack regularly, because I was helping him find a new house, but even that had become sporadic lately as the pool of homes that matched his specifications had dwindled.

"Oh," I said, feeling like a high school girl who'd just been told that the guy she had a crush on liked her, too. When we'd left our last visit with Yvonne, I thought he'd been joking about trying to find an excuse to see me. It made me feel awkward, and excited, and sad, too, stretching my emotions to their limit like a rubber band. I could only wait for it to snap back and hit me.

"Well, do you remember what he was asking about?"

"Certainly. When you were here, you remarked that John's wife died the year after William was born and that John remarried soon afterward. I wanted to find out anything about those events that looking at a family tree just can't tell me. Unfortunately I haven't had the time, but it's on my list. That's why I pulled the books out again, hoping I might have time later this afternoon."

"Well, later on, if you have time, could you please take a peek at the family tree again? I'm looking for any name of any family member around the year 1860 that would have the letters E, A, and C in it. If that year doesn't work, we'll look at other generations, but since 1860 is the year the foundation was altered, I thought that would be a good place to start."

An exaggerated sigh came through the phone. "Really, Melanie. You'll need to try harder to stump me. There are two names that popped into my head immediately—I most likely remember them because they're the same names as my mother and mother-in-law. I'll certainly double-check to confirm, but I believe the names you're looking for are Camille and Charlotte."

"Camille and Charlotte," I said slowly, as if tasting every letter. "Yes! Those work!" I shouted in my excitement, hoping I hadn't deafened the poor woman. "Who were they?"

Nola came into the room, her eyebrows raised in question. In response, I gave her a thumbs-up.

"Camille was John's first wife, and William's mother. Charlotte was John's second wife."

An electrical hum zipped through my phone, ending the call. I tried to turn it back on, but it was completely dead despite having had a nearly full battery charge when I'd started my phone call. I turned to Nola to ask her whether I could borrow her phone, but I stopped in midsentence when I saw her face.

Her usually pale skin was now bleached of all color, her black hair sticking up in all directions as if she'd just pulled a thick woolly sweater over it, her eyes wide enough that I saw mostly white. And she was staring at something directly behind me.

I turned around in time to see the front windows undulating as if they were still liquid, pulling in and bulging out, groaning and snapping like a ship in a storm. I heard the crack of one of the window mullions, watched it fall to the floor as if in slow motion. Before I even realized what I was doing, I dived for Nola, crashing us both to the floor just as both windows exploded, covering us and the room with a million shards of glass.

CHAPTER 18

I quietly closed Nola's bedroom door, then stepped back into the hallway, my index finger over my lips as I passed Jack. He looked rumpled and tired, but much better-looking than he had a right to be after receiving panicked phone calls from both Nola and me right after the windows had decided to act like angry toddlers instead of inanimate objects. He'd been in the middle of a run and had just kept running until he'd reached us. Not that I would admit it, but it hadn't even occurred to me to call anybody else.

I walked down the hall toward my bedroom before speaking. "She's asleep, although it's hard to imagine how. I can't believe we didn't get anything more than a few scratches and bruises—and that was mostly from me tackling her. I almost wish I could say she was scared, but she was angry more than anything. You should have heard her screaming right after it happened—calling the ghost a coward for picking on a pregnant lady and a helpless little kid."

"A helpless little kid?" Jack asked.

"Her words, not mine. But it seemed to work. Everything just sort of stopped."

He rubbed his hands over my arms. "Were you scared?"

"Out of my mind. You know, I thought it would be easier not seeing them. It's not." The central heat flicked on, shooting a blast of warm air from a baseboard vent. "The scariest thing will be telling

Sophie that her original windows are broken, and then her telling me
how much it's going to cost to replace them."

Our gazes moved to the pile of sheets, blankets, and a pillow on
the floor outside my door. "You can sleep in the other guest room,
Jack. Or the nursery. You don't have to sleep on the floor."

"Boarding up windows is hard work—I think I could fall asleep
anywhere."

"But you don't have to. The floor in the nursery is carpeted, and
there's a twin bed with a really old mattress in the guest room. And
don't forget the sofa in the upstairs drawing room. I believe that's an
old favorite of yours."

"As tempting as those options are, I'd rather keep an eye on you.
That's why I'm here, remember?"

I felt suddenly warm, and was suddenly glad that I had a protruding
abdomen between us. "Thanks, Jack. I appreciate your coming and
agreeing to stay for a bit. We both do."

"You know, you're welcome to come stay with me, too. At least
until we get those windows replaced."

"Absolutely not. Whoever it is can't be allowed to think even for a
minute that she's won."

He tilted his head to the side and rubbed his jaw. "Oh, Mellie. You
are one stubborn woman."

"Thank you," I said, glad I sounded more indignant than insulted.

He looked past my shoulder and into my room. "What's that?"

I tried to stop him, but he was already in my room before I could
pull him back. With a heavy tread, I followed him to the easel I had
set up, with my work-in-progress clipped on top.

"It's a spreadsheet," I said, hoping he'd lose interest before he
looked too closely.

He didn't. Leaning closer, he read the title, " 'Nine Months and
Counting.' " His head bobbed up and down as he followed the two
line graphs I'd hand-drawn over the computer printout of the babies'
month-to-month expected size and development.

"What's the graph all about?" he asked.

I mumbled my answer.

"I'm sorry; I couldn't hear you."

I was sure he had, but I shouted it out anyway. "My weight. The green is what I should be and the red is where I am."

He had the decency to express neither horror nor disgust nor even surprise. "I see," he said, his attention shifting to the calendar I'd tacked up next to the spreadsheet. He zeroed in on the square I'd highlighted in red, March 23. With a bold Sharpie pen, I'd written in large letters, *GIVE BIRTH.*

He tapped on the paper calendar square. "What does this mean— 'give birth'?"

I frowned at him. Jack was usually pretty bright. "It's my due date, so that's when I'm planning on going into labor."

"You're planning on going into labor?"

I tried once again—and failed—to cross my arms over my recently expanded chest. "Are you having problems with your native tongue? Yes, my due date is when I'm planning on giving birth. That's normally how it works."

His eyes sparkled as if he were holding in something that was vastly amusing but that he didn't feel like sharing with me. "Um, you do know that your due date is just a prediction, right? That it could come before or after—and that with twins it could come much earlier."

I waved my hand. "Oh, I know. We're both reading the same book, apparently. But I've found that sometimes it just takes mind over matter to harness chaos and uncertainty into something more manageable. I'm planning on giving birth on my due date, so I've got all of the preplanning activities already marked on the calendar so that everything is ready by the time I get to the hospital."

"I see," he said, stroking his chin. He looked back at the calendar. "You have 'mani-pedi/haircut' written on the twenty-fourth."

I tried to put my hands on my hips, but when I couldn't locate them I made do with resting my flattened palms against my sides. "I want to look nice for visitors." I thought for a moment. "Unless you think I should do it the same day?"

I watched him swallow—twice—before he spoke. "You know, Mellie, you might not be up to it right after giving birth. Besides, if you have a C-section, you could be in the hospital for more than just a couple of hours, like you're obviously planning. Perhaps you should work in a little more wiggle room."

Expelling a deep, exasperated breath, I reached for the Sharpie I'd attached to a string from the top of the easel. "Reading a few books does not make you an expert on childbirth, Jack, but if it makes you happy, I'll change my nail appointment to the twenty-sixth." Using a ruler I kept at the bottom of the easel, I lined through the original appointment reminder and rewrote it on the new date.

Stepping back to admire my handiwork, I caught Jack watching me with an expression I couldn't decipher, although it seemed to match the one he used when watching episodes of his favorite show, *Lizard Lick Towing.*

His voice seemed very tight when he spoke. "I'm surprised you haven't already put the twins' feeding and sleeping schedules on a spreadsheet."

"Oh, but I have." I flipped up the pregnancy spreadsheet and folded it over the back of the easel. "See? Feed every four hours starting when they wake up at eight o'clock in the morning; then it's playtime for an hour before they go back to sleep and wake up in time for their next feeding at noon. . . ."

I turned around at the gasping, choking sound I heard coming from Jack's throat.

"Are you all right?" I asked, pounding him on the back.

"I'm fine," he said, although I thought I caught the trace of tears in his eyes. "I'm just really tired. I should go get ready for bed."

"All right. I can show you the rest another time. There're clean towels and a washcloth in the hall bathroom for you, as well as a new toothbrush, toothpaste, and disposable razors in the medicine cabinet. And extra soap and shampoo under the sink."

"Expecting overnight guests, Mellie?"

Glossing over his innuendo, I said, "I like to be prepared. And see? It was a good thing I was."

"I can't imagine that the world knows how to revolve without you."

Ignoring him, I said, "I found the pair of pajamas I bought for you at Berlin's when you stayed with me before." I gave him an accusatory glance. "They still had the tags on them, but I took them off and gave them to Mrs. Houlihan to wash. I hung them behind the bathroom door just in case you needed them."

"I don't wear pajamas."

I blushed at the memory. "I know. But I figured with your daughter in the house, you might not want to be sleeping naked in the hallway."

"Or outside your door," he said with a wicked grin.

I squelched the seed of excitement that tried to take root deep in my belly. "I think I might be able to resist you, Jack."

He arched his right eyebrow, giving him a piratical look. "It wasn't your restraint I was worried about."

Despite the little rush of heat that coursed through me, I gave an exaggerated roll of my eyes. "Really, Jack?" I indicated my curvy body and the baby bump that Hollywood starlets always managed to look cute with but that on me looked like I was trying to hide a John Deere tractor. "I really don't think I need to worry."

"Don't be so sure," he said with a grin as he headed down the hall toward the bathroom.

I quickly closed my door, pressing my hand against my chest, where I felt my heart thudding in a schoolgirl sort of way. I looked over at my bed, where General Lee was already waiting for me, his expression one of perplexity.

"He's not sleeping in here," I said, as I discarded my robe before pulling down the sheets and sliding between the covers. With a sigh, the little dog climbed to the top of my pillow to settle in his regular spot while I arranged and then rearranged the fifteen or so smaller pillows around my body until I found a comfortable sleeping position.

I listened to the sound of running water in the old pipes and then the click of the bathroom door latch opening before the padding of Jack's bare feet on the carpet runner in the hallway approached my door. I stared at the fuzzy face on my bedside clock as Jack spent the better part of an hour rustling into his bedding in the hallway, and I was still staring and listening long past the time when General Lee started snoring.

I lay awake so long that my previously comfortable position that I'd spent so much time constructing no longer seemed as comfortable. I tried to shift, only to find that one of the pillows was now a lump wedged into the middle of my back instead of supporting my hip.

Biting back a groan of frustration, I stared up at the ceiling as if expecting an answer, but the only response I heard was another restless turn from the outside hallway and an increase in volume from my dog, who was now sleeping with all four paws in the air. Mrs. Houlihan had told me that dogs who slept like that were secure in their environment and knew they were loved. I didn't ask her what a person who slept in a tightly curled fetal position meant.

I began rolling from side to side, creating enough momentum so that I could launch myself out of the high bed. I landed with a thud, but before I'd completely turned the switch on the lamp, Jack was standing in the doorway, ready to pounce.

"Jack! What are you doing, besides trying to give me a heart attack?"

"I heard a noise and had to come investigate. That's what I'm here for, remember?"

I expelled a deep breath. "Sorry. I guess I landed too heavily on the floor. I couldn't get comfortable."

"Me neither," he said, looking behind me toward the bed, where the pillows now lay thick like marshmallows on hot chocolate. "Were you and General Lee having a pillow fight?"

"I wish. At least that would have been more productive than trying to sleep while listening to you toss and turn. Are you sure you wouldn't prefer the guest room?"

"Positive." He looked behind me again at my large four-poster bed with the thick mattress. "So what are all those pillows for?"

"To help support all the suddenly bumpy, heavy parts of my body so I can sleep comfortably. It takes a bit of setting up, but usually it does the trick."

"But not tonight?"

I shook my head, my gaze darting back to his face at the change of tone in his voice. My nerve endings suddenly began to stretch and open their bleary eyes.

"You know . . ." he began.

"I know what you're going to say, Jack, and I don't think it's a good idea. I mean, what would Nola think?"

"That you can't get pregnant again? Or that two consenting adults could sleep together without *sleeping* together?"

"Jack—be serious. She's almost fifteen, but she's still a kid. Shouldn't we try to keep her that way as long as possible?"

"She's almost fifteen going on thirty-five. I don't think there's a lot that she hasn't already seen in her life." He held up his hand. "But I see what you're saying. I could always set my alarm to get up before her. Because if I sleep on that floor I'll need to walk with a cane tomorrow." To emphasize his point, he twisted to the side, making his back crack in several different places, and then gave me a pitiful expression he must have learned from General Lee when he begged for food at the table.

With a small groan showing an exasperation I didn't really feel, I said, "Oh, whatever. But only for one night. I'll call your mother tomorrow morning to see about a new bed for the guest room. . . ."

The words were barely past my lips before Jack was at the bed, tossing all of the extra pillows onto the floor.

"What are you doing?" I asked, horrified at the thought of sleeping without the padding.

"I've got a better solution." He pulled down the sheets on the other side of the bed and crawled in. General Lee looked up, then slid into the space between Jack's pillow and mine, as if Jack's presence were the most natural thing in the world. Patting my side of the bed, Jack said, "Come get in and I'll show you what I mean."

My previously dormant nerve endings were now jumping up and down and shouting, *Pick me! Pick me!*

Moving slowly, I closed the door, then flipped off the bedside lamp before pausing at the side of the bed. "I'm still not sure this is a good idea."

"Mellie, I promise to be a gentleman. The prospect of not being crippled for a few days is strong enough for me to keep my hands to myself."

I snorted. "Like you'd be tempted with the way I look right now."

He didn't say anything right away, and I thought I could see his head shaking in the dim light coming through the curtains. "There's not a lot you could do to yourself that would make me not want you. And the fact that you're pregnant with my babies makes you even more beautiful to me." I heard him patting the bed again. "Now hurry up and climb on in so we can both get some sleep."

I was glad I was standing so near the bed, as I wasn't sure my knees would have supported me much longer. Thankful for the darkness that hid my awkward movements, I used momentum to drop and roll onto the bed, ending up pressed against Jack.

"Have you gotten to the chapter in the book yet about comfortable sleeping positions?"

His voice was close to my face, his breath warm on my cheek. I sighed, then refocused so I could answer his question. "No. I've been sidetracked with all of Sophie's pregnancy and early childhood books. It's not like I'm ever going to use any of the advice in them, but it's fascinating reading."

"Well, here," he said, reaching over and rolling me to my side. "Side sleeping is best. Then all we need to do is put this here." I felt a pillow being nudged between my knees. "And then this here," he said as he stuck one of the smaller pillows under my hip. "Lastly, this." He moved up behind me, spoon position, and placed his arm around me, his hand resting on my belly. "How is that?"

Like I never want to move out of this bed. "I'm comfortable," I said. "Thank you." General Lee let out the contented sigh I wanted to.

"Good night, Mellie," Jack whispered in my ear.

"Good night, Jack."

I closed my eyes, feeling myself drifting into a comfortable and contented sleep despite my body being aware of every inch that was in contact with him.

"Mellie?"

"Um-hm?"

"Thanks for calling me instead of your police guy."

"He's not mine," I muttered, already half-asleep.

There was a slight pause, then, "Good."

And as I fell asleep in the warm cocoon of Jack's arms, I imagined I felt the gentle pressure of his lips against the back of my head.

Amelia and I stood at the open front gate, supervising the unloading from a Trenholm's Antiques delivery truck of a queen-size bed to go into the guest room. She hadn't questioned me as to why I needed it so quickly, but when she'd seen the boarded-up windows and noted Jack's presence, I'm sure she figured it out. But hopefully not the part about him sleeping in my bed the previous night.

"This is from that estate sale where I got the first crib I was going to give you. Of course, that's not going to work now, because we're going to need two, but I have a little surprise in store for you and Jack."

"Please don't tell me you found two antique cradles. I've got enough of those. Or cribs. You know how I feel about antiques."

"I understand. Believe me, after that dollhouse I gave Nola, I think I've started to look at antiques a lot differently than I used to. And that's saying something, seeing as how my livelihood is based on selling them."

"Luckily for both of us, not every antique piece of furniture comes with accessories."

She smiled, but her attention was distracted by Sophie, who was marching up and down the piazza in front of the boarded-up windows, talking loudly on the phone, occasionally wiping at her eyes with a handkerchief. She said it was allergies, but I knew that she was really upset about the windows. They were original to the house, after all.

"Is she going to be all right?" Amelia asked, concern etched on her face.

"I'm not sure. Thank goodness it wasn't the Tiffany window in the front door. We might have had to have her committed."

Amelia nodded solemnly before turning her attention back to me.

"I'm so glad your mother and father were out of town for this. Your mother would be quite distraught."

"I know. Which is why I haven't mentioned it to her yet. I'll wait until they get back. They went to Flat Rock, North Carolina, of all places. It's up in the mountains with absolutely nothing to do. I hope they listened to me and brought a deck of cards and some good DVDs."

Amelia was looking at me strangely, as if somebody had just made a joke and I was the only one who didn't get the punch line. "Yes, well, you're probably right not to tell them. There's nothing they can do, and it would just worry and upset them."

Sophie pocketed her phone, then stormed down the piazza steps toward us. "Can you believe I had to find somebody in *Savannah* to replace these windows? Pu-lease! Charleston has the best record for historical preservation in the whole country, has been a *leader* in preservation since even before it was popular, yet I had to go to *Savannah* to find somebody who could hand-make the replacement glass so that it looks like the windows in the rest of the house."

"Hand-make?" Of Sophie's entire diatribe, those were the words that shouted out at me. "Um, isn't that more expensive than, say, going to Home Depot?"

She looked at me as if I'd just suggested putting General Lee on a spit and roasting him over an open fire. "I'll send the bill to your father first for approval, but I went ahead and sent the dimensions so they can get started. At least it's secure for now, and watertight—Jack did a great job."

"Yes, he did," I said, not really thinking about the windows.

"It should only take a month or so to get the replacements, so it's a good thing."

"A month or so?" Amelia and I said in unison.

Sophie shrugged. "They use all the old methods—no machines—so it takes a little bit of time. But it will be worth it." She moved toward the open front door and stood looking up at the vestibule ceiling and the hanging chain. "I'm still looking for a replacement for this. Maybe the people in Savannah can custom-make—"

"No," I said. "Amelia has been kind enough to be on the lookout for a similar one that won't send me to bankruptcy court. But thank you anyway."

Amelia passed us in the vestibule to follow the moving men, who'd been joined by Jack, moving the parts of the bed upstairs. I felt Sophie's eyes on me and turned to meet her gaze.

"So, what really happened?"

I'd given her and Amelia a G-rated version—leaving out the three notes on the keyboard and the apparent displeasure of a disgruntled spirit after I said the two women's names out loud—not wanting to worry them. I'd simply said that there must have been some sort of hairline cracks in the windows and that a strong wind had been all it took. They were very old, after all.

"Remember the three notes that were sticking on the piano and how Nola thought that was some kind of a clue? Well, when she was playing the piano last night, those same three notes stuck again."

"Which three?" Sophie asked.

I looked over my shoulder, as if I could still see any lurking spirits. Very quietly, I whispered, "C, E, and A. So I called Yvonne to see if there were any names on the Vanderhorst family tree around 1860—which is the year the foundation work was done—and there were. Two, to be exact."

She leaned forward. "Which ones?"

"I'm not saying them out loud again—at least, not until my mother is here. We work better as a team." I smiled, but the edges of it wobbled. I was more scared than I cared to admit. "They were John's wives."

She rested her hands over her small baby bump, hardly any bigger than it had been during the previous two months. "I think I know one of the names—she wrote the postcard to her mother about the dining room table." She frowned, thinking. Slowly, she said, "And I think I know the second one—but not from the family tree. It was in the postcard."

I looked at her, beginning to feel uneasy. "I'm trying to think of all the reasons why John's first wife would be writing about his second wife in a postcard home to her mother during her honeymoon. Or maybe the second wife and the first wife's friend could be two separate women with the same name."

Before I could speculate further, my phone buzzed. I looked at the screen, my previous uneasiness now pushed to full panic mode. "I've got to take this. It's my lawyer."

The conversation was brief. I quietly listened as Sterling Zerbe informed me of what was happening with the Gilberts and their court order and his plans for what to do next. I said good-bye and hung up, then found myself staring at the dangling chandelier chain, wondering whether I should even bother to replace it.

Sophie approached me with a look of concern. "What's wrong?"

"They've approved the exhumation. It'll probably happen in the next couple of weeks. He suggested I be there to show a sympathetic face to the press."

My phone buzzed again and I looked down at the screen before hitting the "ignore" button. "It says the *Post and Courier*, but I'm sure it's Suzy Dorf, the journalist. She's zeroing in for the kill. I'll bet she'll be at the exhumation, too. At least then I can ask where she got my cell number from, although I'm pretty sure it was Rebecca."

Sophie rubbed my arm. "It might not be such a bad thing, Melanie. Don't you want to know the truth?"

I looked back at her, not having the first clue as to how I was supposed to answer her. "I'll get back to you on that," I said as I walked quickly out the door, then through to the garden, where the oak tree still stood sentry over the old house. I pressed my forehead into its rough bark, remembering the first time I'd seen it, and how even then, I'd felt as if the garden already knew me. I forced myself to remember, too, how much I'd insisted I hated this house, and the fountain and the garden, and wondered whom I'd offended.

I gazed up toward the sky, past the space where the limb had been that had crashed into the fountain to reveal two graves, seeing the undersides of the tree's branches that seemed to offer a shady embrace under its matronly arms. I closed my eyes and whispered an apology, hoping that I wasn't too late.

CHAPTER 19

The following week, as I was packing up my briefcase for yet more house showings with Jack, my intercom buzzed on my desk. "Melanie? Are you speaking to Jack this week?" I heard the sound of clacking knitting needles behind Joyce's voice.

"For now. I'm meeting with him this morning for more showings, so tomorrow might be a different story."

"That doesn't sound very encouraging, Mellie."

I looked up to see Jack standing at my open office doorway with his most charming smile. My blood did its usual swishy thing, while all my nerve endings stood at attention. Keeping my voice steady, I said, "Really, Jack. You should let Joyce and Nancy do their jobs and screen the visitors. You shouldn't take advantage of the fact that they're apparently holding board positions on the Jack Trenholm fan club."

"I have a fan club?" He raised an eyebrow as if he really wanted an answer.

"Yes. All female, amazingly enough."

"Go figure." He dimpled his cheek.

I hoisted my briefcase off of my desk, but Jack held up his hand. "Hang on, Mellie. Why don't you show me the listings here so I can nix them without wasting our time. Yvonne called me, asking if we had time to come over this morning. She's found something she thinks might be of interest."

My shoulders slumped. "That's not really the best way to look for a house. Looking at a home on paper tells you only a small part of the story. Seeing it in person, and getting a feel for it, and imagining you and your family in it, is really what home buying is all about."

He took the briefcase from me and set it back on the desk. "I know this is what you do for a living, and you're very good at it. However, I'm guessing that I'm the one percent of the population who won't compromise on the perfect house and will wait until he finds it."

I clutched my belly with both hands to emphasize my point. "Yes, well, it's going to be very crowded in your two-bedroom condo if all of your kids are visiting at once. Perhaps you should learn how to lower your expectations so that the babies don't have to sleep in dresser drawers when they're at your place."

His smile never dimmed. "Oh, ye of little faith. I would have thought that you've known me long enough by now to know that I always get what I want, and that I will wait as long as it takes." The expression in his eyes hardened just enough to make me nervous.

"Always?" I asked, trying to sound flippant, but my voice rose a notch so that I practically squeaked the word.

He took a step forward and my nerve endings began twitching in earnest. But instead of reaching for me, Jack plucked the listings folder out of the top of my briefcase. "Let me just thumb through these and eliminate the ones that I know won't work."

Leaning on my desk, he opened the folder of one-page information sheets I'd compiled that synopsized each of the house's features, square footage, price, date built, neighborhood, and photographs. One by one he flipped through them, taking them out of the folder and placing them facedown on my desk as he eliminated them.

"Built in 1950." *Flip.* "Condo." *Flip.*

I picked up the sheet off the discard pile. "Yes, it's a condo," I protested. "But read the rest. It's got four bedrooms, five baths, a community pool—"

He cut me off, taking the sheet and replacing it on the upside-down pile. "It's a condo. I don't want a condo, even if it's the size of Buckingham Palace. I want my children to be raised in a house with a yard."

He continued. "Mount Pleasant." *Flip*. "Johns Island." *Flip*. "Beach-front." He paused, holding that listing in midair. "Really, Mellie?"

"Well, it's not a pool, but the ocean and the best sandbox a kid could hope for are right there. . . ."

Flip. "I'll consider a small beach house when they're a bit older, as a second home, but it's not really the safest choice when they're small. Plus there's the issue of hurricanes. I wouldn't want to lose all of their artwork that will be framed on the walls, or the photo albums. I don't have any of that for Nola, so it will be that much more important for the twins."

Despite my best efforts for it not to, my heart went all mushy again.

He picked up the last one, examining it for longer than all the rest combined. "This is a possibility," he said slowly. "Is it South of Broad?"

"No," I said, then quickly added, "It's just north—in Ansonbor-ough. It's a bit of a walk, but you can easily drive from my house to there fairly quickly."

He looked doubtful. "I suppose we can go look at it." He stuck the single listing back in the folder before replacing it in my briefcase. Smiling again, he said, "I guess that means we have time to see Yvonne. Want to do that first?"

With a wistful glance at the rejected listings that had taken me hours to compile, I said, "Whatevs." I reached for my briefcase but Jack beat me to it, hoisting it off the desk.

"Allow me."

We walked past Joyce and Nancy, their knitting needles clacking away, both of whom looked up only to say good-bye and stare dream-ily at Jack.

He winked at them, causing their knitting needles to pause momentarily.

"You're such a flirt," I said as he helped me into the van.

Before he could respond, his cell phone rang. "It's my agent. Ex-cuse me a moment while I take this." He closed my door, then stood outside for a few minutes to finish the call.

When he climbed in, he turned to me with an odd expression.

"Is everything okay?" I asked.

"Yes. And no. The good part is that my agent says we have two strong offers on the table for my book, which has also garnered some interest from at least one other publisher. It will probably go to auction."

"That's fabulous—congratulations," I said, understanding how important it was to him that this book sold well after the fiasco of his previous book. Without thinking, I leaned over to kiss his cheek, but he turned his face at the last moment so that our lips brushed instead. The jolt was electric, and I pulled away quickly, but not before I saw the look in his eyes that told me that if he hadn't done it on purpose, he was happy it had happened.

I cleared my throat. "What about the not-so-good part?"

"Marc Longo's agent called mine asking if I would give a promotional blurb to use on the cover of his book."

"Wow. What did you say?"

"Hell, no." He started the engine and pulled away from the curb. Sliding me a sidelong glance, he said, "You should have mentioned that Marc has bigger balls than I gave him credit for."

I refused to comment, and we rode the short distance in silence.

As usual, Jack greeted Yvonne warmly and enthusiastically, leaving the older woman with sparkling eyes and a glow to her skin. She turned to me and accepted my kiss to her cheek.

She took my hands and held them out, away from my body. "Well, my dear, you're looking just like a pregnant woman should. Expectant mothers shouldn't be skinny, and that's just the truth. And remember, the bigger the babies, the sooner they'll be sleeping through the night."

"I'll keep that in mind," I said, glad the cooler fall weather had given me a reason to wear pants that covered my ankles. Even Yvonne would have had to agree that they belonged in a zoo and not on any woman, pregnant or otherwise.

We followed her to our usual table, where a large metal file box rested next to a thick book filled with archived documents in plastic sleeves. Jack and I stood on either side of Yvonne as she removed a file folder from the box and placed it on the table in front of us.

"I've been looking and looking for anything about Susan Bivens or her shop, or any of her shop's records, and was getting quite frustrated that there seemed to be nothing that has survived. Considering that Susan Bivens Fine Linens and Embroidery was in business from 1800 until 1873, it's a bit surprising. I did find out that her daughter and granddaughter took over the store at some point, but that wouldn't help you. So on a hunch, I decided to look backward, starting with customers we knew purchased items from her shop and seeing if I could find an invoice or other paperwork that way."

She pulled out a thin piece of paper, securely placed inside a clear archival plastic folder. "And that's how I found this." She handed it to me, and I looked at what appeared to be a handwritten invoice dated March 1860. Written in an elegant script in the middle of the page were the words, *1 christening gown and bonnet, Belgian linen and lace, $10. Ordered by C. Vanderhorst.*

I held it up for Jack to see. He studied it for a moment before turning to Yvonne. "Where did you find this?"

She smiled a smile that made me think of the Dalai Lama and what he'd look like when asked about the meaning of life. "Well, you'd told me that the Vanderhorsts had items purchased from the store. As I believe I've mentioned before, the family kept pretty much all of their papers, and so the public historical archives are rather sparse regarding the Vanderhorsts." She tapped her temple with an index finger. "But I remember while doing research on something else, a listing of a donation of miscellaneous papers from a family member in the early twenties. And that's where I found it—in a box of what most people would call junk—receipts, theater tickets, handbills—all apparently donated to some historical society by Louisa Vanderhorst in 1922. She must have been cleaning out the attic and decided to donate rather than discard. Even back then, Charlestonians realized the importance of preservation."

"Louisa?" I asked, startled at the mention of a familiar name. "L. Vanderhorst—that's who donated the cradle to the museum." I looked at Jack. "In that pregnancy book you gave me, there's a whole section on nesting, and how so many expectant moms turn to spring cleaning before their babies are born. Nevin was born in 1922—I wonder if that was what Louisa was doing."

I felt giddy for some reason, as if the mental image of a pregnant Louisa had made her more real to me, more like a friend who understood what expecting a baby was like.

"That's certainly true," Yvonne said. "When I was pregnant with each of mine, I painted the interior of the house with the first, and then redecorated the entire bottom floor with the second. I couldn't seem to stop myself." She smiled, apparently still unrepentant.

I took the invoice back from Jack. "We know that two older christening sets exist. If Bridget Gilbert took one of the two original gowns and bonnets with Cornelius when she went to New York, and a second set was buried with the baby in the foundation, then why was this third set made? And where is it?"

We looked at each other, our minds spinning. "Maybe there really were triplets, and Bridget just didn't talk about the third baby in her deathbed confession," Jack said, his voice lacking conviction.

"I'd like to think that you're right, but whoever put that package with the christening gown at my front door did it for a reason. And my sixth sense tells me that it's more complicated than triplets."

Yvonne moved over to the folder with all of our photocopies inside and pulled out two sheets of paper. "I'm not sure if this will help you or confuse you more, but here's the other interesting tidbit I discovered." She slid the Vanderhorst family tree in front of us. "We already talked about Camille giving birth to William in 1860, and then dying the following year. And then her husband, John, married his second wife, Charlotte, in 1862. Again, not really the way we do things now, but back then it was expected for a child to be raised by two parents, and John would have wanted to find a mother for little William as soon as he could."

I tapped on the two women's names. "Camille and Charlotte. Those are the names," I said to Jack, emphasizing the word "names" so that he'd understand without my having to explain to Yvonne that they were the reason my two front parlor windows had blown themselves to smithereens.

He nodded. "I see." Turning back to Yvonne, he asked, "But what's the extra tidbit you found?"

Yvonne beamed like a star pupil about to impress her favorite teacher. "I found Camille's death certificate." She slid the other paper on top of the family tree. "She was young when she died—only twenty-one. But the really tragic part is where she died."

She tapped her finger on the paper. Before I could even squint, Yvonne handed her reading glasses to me, and I slipped them on my nose without comment. I followed the line where she indicated and read out loud. "'Place of death, South Carolina State Hospital, Columbia.'"

Jack took a quick breath. "That was a mental institution, wasn't it?"

Yvonne nodded. "At least, it was until the end of the Civil War, when they used it for a prisoner-of-war camp for Union officers. And then when that irritable redhead General Sherman came and burned Columbia, many of its residents took refuge there. But, yes, when Mrs. Camille Vanderhorst lived there, it was a lunatic asylum."

I turned back to the paper, my eyes scanning each line until I found what I was looking for. "'Cause of death, psychosis.'" I looked up at Yvonne. "Did that mean the same thing then as it does today?"

She shrugged. "Mental illness wasn't well understood back then, and they tended to lump all sorts of disorders under the one word. It could have been anything from postpartum depression to bipolar disorder. Unfortunately, we have no way of knowing."

"So she died at the age of twenty-one in a mental hospital, leaving behind a one-year-old son." As an afterthought, I added, "That would certainly be a reason to come back."

Yvonne looked at me oddly. "Except she'd be dead."

I just nodded, then returned to examining the death certificate. I read quickly over all the facts I already knew, her age, her name, her place of residence, all the way to the bottom of the page, where a physician, a Dr. Robert Pringle, had signed it to verify he'd been present at the time of death.

I slid the glasses off and handed them back before replacing the copy of the certificate in the folder. "Thanks so much, Yvonne. I know this will be useful; I'm just not sure how yet. I'll be sure to let you know."

We said our good-byes; then Jack and I left the building, both of us moving slowly, as if our brains were occupying all of our physical movements. A gust of cold wind tossed itself at us and Jack instinctively put his arm around my shoulders as we began our walk back to the van.

"The longer this goes on, the more complicated it gets, doesn't it?" I said.

"Are we still talking about the mysteries in your house?"

I stopped to look up at him, not sure what he was saying. "Of course. What else could I be discussing?"

His arm fell from my shoulder. Shoving his hands in his pockets, he began walking again. "You talk in your sleep, you know."

I had to jog to catch up to him, not an easy feat, considering. "I do? Did I say anything embarrassing?"

He lifted an eyebrow, but kept walking.

"Jack, come on! Don't say something like that and not elaborate. What did I say?"

We'd reached the van, so he had to stop and face me, his expression unreadable. "Do you really want to know?"

I hesitated for only a moment. "Of course."

"You said two words over and over—which I'd heard you use together before, except for the one time I actually needed to hear them."

I knew what he was going to say before the words came out, the heat rising in my chest, neck, and face like a thermometer suddenly thrust into boiling water. "Don't. . . ."

" 'Yes, Jack. Yes.' "

I stared at the door handle, willing the door to open on its own so it would force Jack backward and I could enter the van without actually looking at him.

"You wanted to know," he said quietly.

I took a step forward to open the door, but stopped midstride as an odd sensation of muscle twitching erupted on one half of my belly. "Whoa," I said, grasping my side.

Jack's hands were on my arms immediately, steadying me. "Are you all right?"

I nodded, holding still as the fluttering began again. "Yes. I'm fine. But I think one of the babies just kicked me."

Jack eyes went immediately to my middle. "Which one?"

"This one," I said, pointing to my right side.

"Can I feel?"

I unbuttoned my coat and pulled it aside. "He—or she—might not do it again, but put your hand here just in case."

I moved his flattened palm to where I'd felt the movement, then waited, my gaze finding Jack's. Despite everything that was unsettled between us, these babies were the one thing on which we were in perfect accord. We'd agreed about not finding out the sexes of the children, and that the two of us would be the primary caregivers. And that Granitia might not be the best name for one of the babies if it was a girl. Or boy.

When the movement came again, it was more like a tickle, as if somebody were running a finger down the inside of my skin. "Whoa!" Jack said, his hand jerking back before he quickly replaced it. "That was a baby?"

"I sure hope so. Nothing else should be moving in there."

"Obviously a future USC linebacker," he said, his eyes sparkling.

"Then I hope that's not a girl." I moved his hand to the other side, where the second baby seemed to still be sleeping. "This one could be a girl. Probably reading a book."

He threw his head back and laughed, then moved both hands around to me so that I was forced to step closer to him. I kept my eyes open, hoping I wouldn't embarrass myself again by beginning to imagine he would kiss me.

"Thank you, Mellie."

"For what?"

"For everything. For these babies. For the way you mother Nola. For the ways you make me laugh—intentionally and not." He gave me a quick kiss on the forehead before releasing me and helping me into the van.

He started the engine, then turned to me. "Do you want to eat lunch before we go see the house?"

Yes. I fiddled with my seat belt and then my gloves—anything to distract me so that I wouldn't have to look at his face. "That's probably not a good idea. The house isn't too far from here, so we should be done within the hour. Plenty of time for you to drop me back at the office and then go grab lunch. Separately," I added hastily.

Without a word, he pulled out onto the street and began driving, my head singing an accompaniment to the rhythm of the wheels against the pavement. *Yes, Jack. Yes.*

CHAPTER 20

Pewter skies spit out an icy drizzle as Detective Riley and I huddled together under a large black umbrella at Magnolia Cemetery, watching Nevin Vanderhorst's remains being removed from the family mausoleum where his mother had only recently been reinterred.

We'd already verified the marker inside the mausoleum identifying the final resting place for John's twin brother, Henry. All that meant was that it wasn't Henry bricked up in the foundation. Which raised the question, If it wasn't him, then who?

As much as I hated hospitals and museums, they could not compare to the torture of going right to the source of restless dead people. If Thomas had not been with me, I would have brought my iPod and stuck in the earbuds, hidden from the photographers by a warm knit cap. Instead, my ears were bare and nearly numb, and I was reduced to humming various ABBA tunes to drown out all the voices of the dead I could still hear, but could not see.

"Is that 'S.O.S.' you're humming?"

I turned to Thomas with pleasant surprise. "You know ABBA?"

He snorted. "Who doesn't? You know they've sold more albums than the Beatles?"

"I've heard that. But nobody believes me."

He was silent for a moment. "I saw *Mamma Mia* twice, and I bought the DVD for my mom so I could watch it without claiming ownership."

I laughed out loud, but the sound was quickly stifled by the growing whispers that were becoming clearer and louder. *I can't find my daughter. We were on the boat together, but now I don't see her. Can you help me find her? She's only four years old and she shouldn't be alone.* The voice came from behind me, close to my ear, high-pitched and carrying years of grief. I stepped forward, forcing Thomas to walk with me to keep the umbrella over us. I stopped when we reached one of the giant oaks with their drapes of moss that watched over the cemetery like sentinels, tall enough to see the sluggish Cooper River, whose banks created one of the cemetery's borders.

A small group of reporters and camera crews looked on, but were kept at a distance from the burial site by two police officers who'd arrived with Detective Riley. A truck from the Charleston County coroner's office was parked near the mausoleum, its rear doors open like welcoming arms.

"I think they've spotted you," Thomas said, bringing my attention back to the group of media personnel.

"Great," I muttered, surreptitiously watching three of them: a photographer, an assistant whose job seemed to be to hold an umbrella over the camera, and a petite woman who looked like she had to be a reporter. She wore penny loafers with tassels, the brown leather turned black from the rain, a beige Burberry trench coat with a signature Burberry plaid scarf thrown around her neck. She was already smiling by the time she was ten yards away, looking a lot like the Cheshire cat. I thought about hiding, but besides ducking behind the large tree trunk, I had nowhere to go

Thomas spoke quietly through his plastered smile. "Be nice. Remember that she can and will print everything you say. And keep reminding yourself that this is the kind of case that gets tried in the court of public opinion, and public opinion goes a long way in Charleston and with its judges. Think of it like eating your favorite doughnut that's been dropped on the floor. After the first few bites of dirt, it'll taste just like a doughnut."

I turned to him with new admiration. "Detective Riley, I think we speak the same language."

He slanted a meaningful gaze down at me. "That's what I've been trying to tell you."

"Miss Middleton?" The reporter was now within shouting distance, and I could see that we were about the same age, except she was about six inches shorter and fifty pounds lighter. Her dark brown hair, worn short in a nod back to the unfortunate Dorothy Hamill wedge hairdo of the seventies and early eighties—to which I'd also fallen victim—was smooth like a helmet despite the wind and rain. I knew my own hair probably closely resembled a Brillo pad, and I stared suspiciously at the camera, making sure it wasn't pointed at me.

"Yes," I said. "I'm Melanie Middleton."

The woman stopped, and she had to tilt her head back to talk to me. "You're a hard woman to get a hold of." She stuck her hand out and I shook it, and it felt like a child's. I wondered whether her desk at the newspaper had to be retrofitted to accommodate her small stature. I pictured her sitting on a stack of telephone books, and the corner of my mouth lifted involuntarily.

She continued. "You have really great gatekeepers at your office and residence."

"I know. It's how I'm able to do my job with the least possible distractions." I stared pointedly at her, but she didn't seem to take notice.

She turned and offered her hand to Thomas, whose hand swallowed hers up to the wrist. "Good to see you again, Detective Riley. My colleague Rebecca Edgerton mentioned you might be here. I understand you've been reading my columns prior to publication." She held up her hand. "I know your brother-in-law is my boss, so I'm not going to say anything. I will admit that I was hoping it would give me an 'in' to an interview Miss Middleton, since Rebecca couldn't seem to accomplish that for me. Not that it did, but things always have a way of working themselves out." She grinned broadly, showing tiny, perfect white teeth. I almost asked her whether she'd lost all of her baby teeth yet.

"So, here we are." She held up a small tape recorder. "Mind if I record our conversation?"

"On that?" I asked. Surely the newspaper could afford more modern equipment. Like pen and paper.

She giggled. "What can I say? I'm a big fan of the eighties—can't seem to get away from all the stuff that worked so well for me back then." I eyed her loafers, trench coat, and hair and saw that she was telling the truth. I imagined her jogging with a Walkman and using a car phone that came in a bag and required an antenna.

"Does this mean you're asking for an interview?"

"Believe me, this is more for your benefit than mine. I already have a copy of Bridget Monahan Gilbert's letter and pictures of the christening bonnet, and now we have the exhumation and eventually we'll have the results of that. That's more than enough to fill three more columns, at least. It would just look bad if the woman who inherited everything—from an old man she met just once—refused to talk to the media."

I looked at Thomas, who gave me an encouraging nod. "Fine, then. Although I really don't know if I have anything to add. Everything that has been reported so far is all new to me as well. All I know is that Mr. Vanderhorst's father and my grandfather were old friends, and he seemed to think that was enough of a connection to leave me his house."

"So this has nothing to do with the fact that Mr. Vanderhorst believed you could see ghosts and claimed to see the spirit of his mother in the garden?"

Oh. "Where did you hear that?"

She smiled smugly. "Marc Longo's book. Rebecca Edgerton gave me an advance reader copy."

I was about to ask how Marc would have known about Louisa's ghost, but stopped. *Rebecca.* The same woman who was now pestering me to go for a fitting for my bridesmaid's dress for her wedding. I wanted to shriek and stamp my feet at my cousin's subterfuge, but didn't want a report of my throwing a temper tantrum to find its way into Sunday's paper, so instead I smiled calmly.

"Mr. Vanderhorst was an old but very sweet man. That's the reason I'm here today—to pay my respects. At the time of our first and only meeting, I allowed him to believe what he wanted to, because I thought that made him happy."

"Or because you wanted him to feel an empathetic bond with you, which would make it an easy choice when he was trying to decide what to do with his estate upon his death."

"Stop putting words in my mouth. I was called to his home that day because of a cold call I'd made to him in which he agreed to a discussion about listing his house for sale. I told him then that I hated old houses. At no point in our discussion did I allow him to believe that I wanted his house."

"You hate old houses? Isn't that your specialty at Henderson House Realty?"

I felt Thomas's hand on my back, and I welcomed the solid support. "I disliked the idea of living in one myself due to events in my childhood that involved my grandmother's house on Legare." I swallowed thickly. "I don't believe I feel that way anymore."

"Will you fight the Gilberts if their claim holds water?"

Something nudged my shoulder, while unseen hands lifted my hair, as if someone were leaning close to whisper in my ear. *You need to decide sooner rather than later what you want. And then be ready to fight for it.*

I looked up suddenly, expecting to see my grandmother before realizing that the voice had been male. *It's like a piece of history you can hold in your hands.*

"Mr. Vanderhorst?" I'd spoken quietly, the words catching on an icy breeze before being scattered like seeds over the garden of stones.

"I didn't catch that. Could you repeat it, please, into the tape recorder?"

I cleared my throat and leaned forward toward the machine. "The Gilberts and I both want the truth. That's my only comment for now."

"Do you see dead people, Miss Middleton?"

I took a quick intake of breath. *Damn you, Rebecca!* "I don't think that has anything to do with our interview. So, if you don't have any more questions about Mr. Vanderhorst, I have a busy day." Leaning on Thomas's arm, I lifted my heels out of the sucking mud and began to walk away.

She called out to my retreating back, "Because if you do, maybe you should ask one of them for the answer to who the baby is in the foundation at fifty-five Tradd Street. And if Nevin knew he had a living cousin. It would save us all a lot of trouble."

Without turning around, I shouted, "This interview is over, Miss Dorf. And if you print anything out of context, you will be hearing from my lawyer."

Thomas kept a firm grip on my elbow as he led me past crumbling mausoleums and sun-bleached white obelisks. The whispers of the dead grew louder as I neared the gates, as if they were sensing that an opportunity had been lost.

I pressed my hands against my ears until Thomas and I were safely inside his car and driving away.

He kept his expression neutral and didn't say anything, which, I realized, was either because he'd grown up with sisters and knew when to stay silent, or because he was a detective and knew it was sometimes best to wait.

Finally, I broke the silence. "Aren't you going to ask me if it's true?"

"I figured if you wanted to tell me, you'd tell me in your own good time. I imagine it's not something you talk about with just anybody."

"No. Not really." I took a deep breath. "But it's true. It seems to be something I inherited from my mother. It's how I was able to figure out that Louisa Vanderhorst and Joseph Longo were buried in the fountain in my garden, the identity of the body found on a sailboat owned by my family, as well as the Manigault murders." I gave him a shaky smile. "I guess that means it's not all bad, right?"

He let out a low whistle. "I wouldn't say it's bad at all if you were able to help some people and solve a few cold cases. I think I mentioned this before, but maybe I should put you on staff." He didn't appear to be joking.

"The thing is, I can't see them anymore—because of the pregnancy. I used to think I'd be happy if it went away, but I miss it. Probably because I can still hear them—which almost makes it worse."

"Why would you be happy if it went away? I know it sounds corny, but I became a policeman because I wanted to help people. I wasn't crazy about the idea of spending so many years in school and I figured I couldn't be a doctor, so I picked the next-best thing. Seems to me you've been given a unique opportunity to help people—either by putting their minds at rest that their loved ones are at peace or sending lost souls to the light."

I looked at him suspiciously. "How do you know so much about it?"

"Oh, I watch all those shows—*Medium, Ghost Whisperer, Long Island Medium*. My old girlfriend was obsessed with them and it's kind of stuck."

"Well, you can't believe everything you see on TV," I said. "But some of it's true—like ending a haunting by sending a soul into the light. It is a good feeling— although I hate to admit that."

"Why?"

I was more surprised that he'd thought to ask the question than by the question itself.

"Because it was something I'd inherited from my mother, and until recently I didn't have a good relationship with her."

"And now?"

"And now? Well, I guess being in denial and hating it have sort of become second nature. Plus, I don't want to become some sort of freak show. I do have a reputation and a business I need to uphold."

He was thoughtful for a moment. "Yeah, I get that. But you could keep it anonymous. Like if a local police detective needed a little help on a cold case, maybe he could call you in. You'd get the satisfaction of helping out, and nobody would be the wiser." He winked at me before returning his attention to the road.

"Did you just offer me a job?"

"Just an offer of consulting now and again. Assuming it comes back."

"It should. My mother's sixth sense disappeared when she was pregnant with me and came back the moment she gave birth. But if it does, you're serious?"

"As a heart attack. I like to keep an open mind, and I think you could offer a new dimension to our detective work."

I felt what I could only describe as the warm-and-fuzzies, like putting on pajamas in the middle of the afternoon and curling up in front of a fire. It was the first time I truly felt as if my gift—or whatever I wanted to call it—had some value besides being a circus act or parlor trick.

"I'll think about it," I said.

"Take all the time you need. But thanks for considering it."

I was silent for a moment, my conscience nudging me. "You might change your mind after I tell you something. I haven't been completely forthcoming with you."

"You mean you're not really pregnant?"

His words surprised me so much that I barked out an unladylike laugh, then immediately slapped my hand across my mouth. "If I were faking this, that wouldn't say a lot about your abilities as a detective, would it?"

He just smiled, and I knew he was waiting, and would continue to wait for as long as it took for me to tell him.

"I, um, received a package on my front doorstep a while back— before I knew what was in Bridget Monahan Gilbert's deathbed confession."

"What kind of a package?"

"An old one. From 1898. There was no name on the package; it was just addressed to fifty-five Tradd Street. It looked like it had been opened before, because the twine that had been used to wrap it had been cut and knotted. Inside the package was a bunch of newspaper from the *New York Times*—that's how we guessed at how old the package was."

"We?"

"Sophie and me. She was with me when I opened it—which I did because she's one of only a handful of people who know about my 'gift' and doesn't freak out when something weird happens. And when I saw the package, I knew there wasn't anything normal about it. It's just a feeling, and I've learned that I need to pay attention to them."

"Were you right?"

"Oh, yes." We were both silent for a few moments as I searched for the courage to spill the rest of the story and he just waited. "It was a christening gown—without the bonnet. Made by Susan Bivens, just like the set you found with the remains. It looked very old—older than the mid–eighteen sixties."

There was a long pause, as if he were digesting the information. "And just like the bonnet Irene Gilbert has."

"Exactly. But I didn't get how strange it *really* was until I read Bridget Gilbert's confession, where she says she mailed the gown back to Charleston when she knew she was dying, but kept the bonnet. And she died in 1898."

He was nodding, as if slowly organizing all the pieces of information into a huge file cabinet in his brain. "So, if it is the same gown, where do you think it's been all this time?"

"If I knew that, it would help us figure out how I got it. Some part of me wants it to be a neighbor who was cleaning out his attic and happened to find this parcel with my address on it and so just dropped it off at the front door. But that's not usually how things happen in my life."

"Was there a postmark?" he asked, his expression giving nothing away.

I shook my head. "No. Sophie told me that parcel post didn't start in this country until 1913, so if the package was originally sent from New York in 1898, it would have been delivered by a private express company."

"But it just suddenly showed up on your doorstep."

"Yes. And I believe that it might have been delivered by . . . unconventional methods. I wouldn't be surprised. I mean, I have phone conversations with my grandmother, and she's been dead for years." I looked closely at him to read his expression, but he remained neutral.

"Don't you believe me?"

He took a deep breath. "Like I told you, I like to keep an open mind. I'll ask around the neighborhood and do my due diligence, see if anybody found it while cleaning the attic. Anything's possible." He paused for a moment. "I think I already know the answer to this, but why didn't you tell me this before?"

It wasn't an accusation, but I still hesitated before answering. "Because the most plausible explanation about how it ended up on my doorstep was one that I couldn't hope to explain to you. Before now, anyway." I looked at him as a thought occurred to me. "Does this mean I'm in trouble for withholding evidence?"

"No, because you're going to give it to me when we get to your house. We'll compare the gown and the Gilberts' bonnet, as well as the one found with the remains to see if there's a connection."

"Do you have any doubt?" I asked. "Because I don't. That's how my life works."

He was silent for a moment, then surprised me by laughing.

"What's so funny?"

"Remember how I once told you that I found you quirky? I just had no idea exactly how much."

"But quirky in a good way," I reminded him.

He reached over and took my hand. "In the best way."

I felt warm and tingly, but in the way a comfortable pair of slippers made me feel. Not the warm and tingly feelings Jack gave me, the kind of feelings that made me think of fireworks and sunsets over the Ashley River.

I smiled and squeezed his hand before removing mine to my lap, realizing that I had as much control over my heart as an old house did over the vagaries of time.

CHAPTER 21

I climbed the steps toward my mother's front door, trying not to pant as heavily as I wanted, General Lee still prancing energetically beside me. I'd decided to actually listen to all the advice people had been throwing at me for the last five months and had walked the three and a half blocks from my house. It was a sunny but windy November day and at the time it had seemed like a good idea, but it took all of my energy to stay upright and ring the doorbell instead of collapsing on the top step like a beached whale.

My mother opened the door, her expression showing her surprise. "Why are you ringing the bell, Mellie, dear? You know I gave you a key so you can come and go as you please. Besides, we were expecting you."

"I saw Dad's car, so I didn't want to come barging in."

I followed my mother inside before she bent to unlatch General Lee's leash and scratch behind his ears. "Don't be silly. Your father and I would never do anything that would embarrass you."

Too late, I thought, remembering my father referring to himself as her "stud muffin" when he didn't know I was within hearing distance. I followed her into the parlor, where she'd set up my grandmother's silver tea service, along with wheat-bread tea sandwiches with all the crusts still on, and what looked a lot like the flourless and tasteless cookies Sophie had brought to my house several times, and which I had avoided as a matter of self-preservation.

My dad put down his glass of iced tea and stood to hug me and greet my dog, then returned to his seat. I noticed that he wasn't really drinking, but using his glass to beat a steady rhythm with his fingers. If I didn't know my father as well as I did, I would almost guess him to be nervous.

My mother poured me a cup of green tea, then offered me the plate of cookies. "Nola brought these over yesterday. She said she found them in your pantry stuffed under a pile of reusable grocery bags." She stared pointedly at me, but I refrained from commenting.

"No, thank you," I said, reaching for one of the sandwiches instead. I bit into one and nearly gagged. "What's in these?"

She beamed. "Sophie's recipe. It's soy paste with chopped sprouts. I thought they were quite good."

I turned to my dad in desperation. "Is there any real food in this house? I'm starving." I mimicked General Lee's begging-puppy expression, then rubbed my belly for effect.

He made a move to stand, but my mother stopped him. "James, we both know that a healthy diet is best for her and the babies. It's called tough love."

With an apologetic look, he sat back down. "Sorry, sweetie, but your mother is right." He picked up a sandwich and began to chew, and even almost successfully hid his grimace. "And actually, this healthy food isn't so bad once you get used to it."

I watched him until he swallowed, so that he couldn't raise a napkin to his mouth and spit it out.

I picked up a glass of ice water with lemon off the tray and took a long sip. "So, did you have a nice vacation up in the mountains?"

My mother hesitated just a moment, giving me time to notice that both she and my father appeared to be sunburned, or windburned, or maybe both. Regardless, their enhanced coloring seemed to dip into the collars of their shirts, making me wonder where it ended.

"It was lovely, thank you. The weather was perfect—a little on the cool side, but the sun was out every day. We spent a lot of time outdoors, hiking, picnicking—that sort of thing." The flush in my mother's cheeks deepened, making me wonder exactly what "sort of things" she was referring to.

"Our cabin had a hot tub outside," my father added. "I never thought I'd enjoy such a thing, but it was nice."

Both my mother and I looked at him, and probably for the same reason. *TMI*, as Nola would say. I forced myself to stop wondering where the rosy blush to their skin had come from.

"Glad you enjoyed yourselves. I had a quiet week myself, except for Nevin Vanderhorst's exhumation. Detective Riley was with me, and that helped a lot. So was that annoying reporter Suzy Dorf. I allowed her to interview me, which means we need to buy up as many copies of the Sunday newspaper as we can find."

My mother sat down next to me, her pinkie extended as she took a sip from her china cup. "Why? Did you say anything you regret?"

"I don't think so. But she knows about my 'special gift'—thanks to Rebecca—and I know she's going to use the information any way she can."

My father stood, lifting General Lee, who'd been napping in his lap, with him. "I think that's my cue to take the dog for a walk." He looked pointedly at my mother. "I'll be back in twenty minutes."

I waited until we heard the front door close before I turned to my mother. "See what I mean? My own father thinks I'm making it up."

"Your father was in the army his whole life. He can only see in black-and-white, and what we do is so far beyond his comprehension that it pushes his limits. I won't give up on him—and I've already seen cracks—but I realize it's going to take time."

"But I don't want everybody in Charleston knowing about it."

She took another sip of tea, swallowing slowly. "Would that be so bad?"

I was about to reply, *Of course*, but stopped, no longer really sure what my answer should be. Instead, I said, "I'm just not sure how it will affect my business if people think I moonlight as one of those call-in psychics or something."

She placed her cup and saucer on the coffee table. "Mellie, this is the twenty-first century, where Kim Kardashian can tweet what she did in bed with her boyfriend the previous evening and garner more viewers for her reality show. Or Britney Spears can appear in public without underwear and still sell out concerts."

"Please, Mother. I'd like to think that I have more credibility than Kim Kardashian or Britney Spears. Besides, their fans aren't expecting them to sell their houses."

She took my hand in hers, and her skin was soft without her gloves. "What you can do isn't something you should be embarrassed about. Ever. People can make you feel less about yourself only if you allow them to. And if you think different, I take full responsibility. If I'd been around while you were growing up I would have taught you that, just as my mother taught me." She sat back. "I've never hidden my abilities, and it never hindered my career. It's just something you should think about."

I fiddled with my napkin in my lap for a moment. "Thomas said something along those lines—how it's a gift I could use to help people. He even asked if I'd want to help out from time to time on some of their cold cases."

"So you told him?"

"I didn't really have a choice, since Suzy Dorf had pretty much already spilled the proverbial beans. He took it in stride—probably because he's already seen so much in his line of work and it's hard to surprise him anymore."

"Good," she said, a small smile settling on her lips. "So you like Detective Riley?"

"I do. A lot. He's kind, and considerate, funny, and smart. And he's family-oriented and loves kids." I thought for a moment. "But what I like the most about him is that he's so easy to be with. We're even happy to just sit together on a park bench without saying anything, or worrying about what the other is thinking. It's kind of nice."

"Well, *there's* an adjective I don't use very often. A new pillow is nice, or finding the perfect mascara that doesn't flake or run. But in matters of the heart . . ."

"I wasn't talking about marrying him, Mother. Only that I like being with him. There's a big difference."

"Just make sure he knows that, dear."

I thought about how he hadn't kissed me yet, although I'd been pretty sure on several occasions that he wanted to. "He does," I said.

The front door opened and we turned to see General Lee loping into the room with his tongue dangling, my father panting behind him.

"How old is that dog? He acts like a puppy. Just about wore me out going around the block. It was like he was chasing something."

I exchanged a glance with my mother, both of us recalling Julia Manigault's childhood pet dog, whose lingering spirit still sometimes came out to play.

"I inherited him, remember? I have no idea how old he is, but Mrs Houlihan said he'd been with Mr. Vanderhorst since before she came to work for him ten years ago."

We watched as the little dog put his front paws on the coffee table so he could sniff the cookies and tea sandwiches before giving what could only be called a disdainful sigh as he got back down on the floor without taking any food, and curled up under my chair.

"Smart dog," I said, grinning with self-satisfaction. "So, what is it that you wanted to tell me?"

My mother moved to sit next to my father opposite me. He took her hand in both of his, and that was when the alarm bells started sounding in my head.

My father spoke first. "Your mother has done me the great honor of agreeing to be my wife. Again. I suppose you can say that we both believe in second chances."

"But . . ." I stopped, my gaze going from one familiar face to the other, wondering why they suddenly looked like strangers. "But you're divorced. Because Dad couldn't come to terms with who you are."

"And because of my drinking, don't forget," my father added. "But that was nearly thirty-five years ago. We're different people now."

I stood, not really sure why I was so agitated. "True, but you still call what Mother and I do 'mumbo jumbo.' You just had to leave the room so she and I could discuss my ability to see dead people and how it might affect my career if the fact was publicized." I hit the heel of my hand against my forehead. "For crying out loud, Dad. I've been in denial about my abilities almost my whole life because of that. I don't know how you can just say, 'Never mind,' and get married as if it didn't matter."

My mother dropped his hand to come stand by my side. "Mellie, I know what you're saying. And so does your father. We both know there are things we need to work on, and we both believe strongly that our relationship is worth fighting for."

I stared into her eyes, trying very hard to understand her logic, but failing miserably. "But you couldn't before, and look what happened. Now you know better—why wouldn't you wait until you solved all of your differences before you make such a giant leap?"

She smiled patiently at me, the same smile she'd used when she taught me how to tie my shoes. "Because we've realized that if you wait until everything's perfect, until all your differences have been settled and all the stars have aligned just right, then you miss your chance at happiness. That's what real and enduring love is. It's being able to see past the disagreements so what's left is the knowledge that you'll never be complete without the other person."

I blinked back tears that I had no idea why I was shedding. Her words were like flung arrows that seemed to bounce off of me as if I were wearing armor. I suppose forty years of believing that love was fickle and fleeting could become a mind-set that was as impenetrable as a coat of armor.

I pushed back my doubts and took a step toward them. "Congratulations," I said, kissing them both. "At least you won't have to pick out wedding china or find a place to live!" My voice had a forced cheerfulness.

"Thank you, darling," my mother said, looking relieved. "We were thinking of just a small ceremony around the first of the year. You'll still be three months away from your due date, and it's past all the excitement and busyness of Christmas. Did I mention I'm on the tour of homes again?"

"No, you didn't—but if you need me to wear green boughs to look like a Christmas tree, since I'll be about the same size by then, I'm going to decline." I smiled. "But instead of January, could you please make it on the same day as Rebecca's wedding? Then I'll have an excuse not to go."

My mother put her arm around me. "Come, dear, she *is* family. Besides, isn't her wedding set for the twenty-second of March? Chances are you'll have two of the cutest excuses not to go."

"We can only hope." I let out a heavy sigh. "I need to get back to the house. The furniture Amelia ordered for the nursery is arriving today, and I have to corral all of the packages and gifts so that there's room."

"Which reminds me," my mother said. "Nancy Flaherty called. She wants to give you a baby shower. She wasn't sure how you'd feel about it, so she wanted to ask me first. I think it's a lovely idea, but it's up to you."

"Well, considering we need two of everything, it would certainly help. All of these recent home repairs have pretty much depleted my bank account. Thank goodness for the trust."

My father coughed, then took a large gulp of water. "That's right. Thank goodness for that." He leaned down to pet General Lee, so I couldn't read his expression.

I turned back to my mother. "So, January?"

"Yes, if that's okay with you."

"What else am I going to be doing, Mother, besides working and getting bigger?"

She kissed my cheek, then gave me a tight hug, startling me. "But you also just keep getting prettier and prettier."

"Really? I swear only you and Thomas don't see the real me that I see in the mirror."

"And Jack," my mother added.

"And Jack," I reluctantly agreed. "At least that's three people."

"Don't be silly. You've always been your own worst enemy and fiercest critic. It's time to give yourself a break. You're growing two healthy children, Mellie. And that's the most important thing right now."

I reached my arm around her shoulders and squeezed. "Thanks, Mother. I really needed to hear that."

I picked up my purse and General Lee's leash, then walked to the door, my parents following with linked arms. "Hopefully we'll get the DNA results soon so I can get all of this behind me before the babies arrive."

We said our good-byes and I left, hesitating on the bottom step as I considered going back to ask my dad for a ride. Before I could, General Lee took off, leaving me with no choice but to follow, barely hanging onto the leash. Instead of heading down the sidewalk, he ran to the side garden and to the wrought-iron table where I'd once had doll tea parties with my beloved grandmother.

He stopped in front of the chair where she'd once sat, and bowed his head. I watched as the fur was ruffled as if by an unseen hand.

"Grandmother?" I whispered to the winter garden. I wanted so badly to see her again, to be the little girl still small enough to crawl into her lap and know that I was safe.

Be ready. The words were almost too quiet to hear, the sound broken, as if my connection to her world were already lost.

"Be ready for what?" I asked the scattered leaves that blew at my feet and twisted around the table legs like a snake.

I strained to hear over the rustle of the leaves and the wind, but the words were too faint. I waited for a long moment for her to come back, but I knew that I was alone. Tugging on General Lee's leash, I walked slowly from the garden to the sidewalk, wondering whether my grandmother had answered my question at all, or if she'd remained silent with the certainty that I already knew the answer.

CHAPTER 22

On Sunday morning, I parked my car on South Battery near White Point Gardens and walked to the pavilion. The temperature hovered in the fifties, but the sky was sunny and clear enough that one could see Fort Sumter and a spectacular view of Charleston Harbor.

It would have been a lovely day for a stroll along the Battery except that I was dressed in maternity-size Lycra and was meeting Sophie, who had come up with the brilliant idea that we should start exercising together. I told her I would if it would mean she'd stop mentioning the words "water" and "birth" together in the same sentence as "your" and "labor." Besides, she'd promised me some new information regarding the Vanderhorsts that she assured me would be worth the exertion of a power walk with her along the water.

I spotted her with her leg up on one of the benches, stretching her calves. She wore a pretty blue Windbreaker that covered her cute baby bump, along with lime green leggings that showed off her petite legs and ankles. She actually wore sneakers, and I wondered whether they were made by Birkenstock, since I didn't think she knew of any other shoe brand. Her rainbow-hued gloves matched the thick headband that covered her ears and tamed most of her dark curls.

I wore the same thing I usually did when I walked with my mother and Amelia—mostly a pulled-together ensemble in which my father's castoffs were prominently featured. At least I had new sneakers, courtesy of my mother. She had told me that wearing my old ones with all the laces pulled out to accommodate my larger feet and ankles was not a good idea, and she was not going to wait until Louboutin or Manolo Blahnik started making athletic shoes.

I slowed my steps as I approached, the alarming reality dawning on me that for the first time in the years we'd been friends, Sophie was actually better dressed than I was.

She spotted me and waved, and I waved back, quickly yanking my hand down as my father's oversize ski gloves flopped back and forth.

She looked at me suspiciously. "You don't look like you've been walking for several blocks already."

"That's because I haven't. I drove. I figured that in your condition you couldn't carry me back if I collapsed from exhaustion."

"Right." She shook her head, then picked up a small backpack from the bench and handed me a water bottle. "I figured you'd forget one, so here you go. Drink some before we get started."

Handing it back to her, I said, "I promise to drink all of it when we're finished. But if I take a sip now, we'll be stopping for me to go to the bathroom every five minutes." I patted my belly. "These two have successfully squished my bladder into a space that's only big enough for a pea. I'm thinking of setting up a cot in the bathroom to save myself the trips back and forth every night."

"Is Jack still staying with you?" She took a swig of water from her own bottle.

I looked at my watch. "Gee, it's getting late. We should start."

"Nice try, Melanie. I'm taking that as a yes."

I sighed. "It's just that Nola and Jack are still working on some issues, and they apparently need me as a referee and someone to listen to them vent. I'm like a cheap psychiatrist."

She raised one eyebrow. "And that's why Jack is still sleeping two doors down from you?"

Thank goodness I hadn't mentioned that he'd slept an entire night in my bed. I almost sighed out loud, remembering how nice it had felt to have him there. "Mostly. But I'm still pretty disturbed about the whole window incident. He says he's happy to stay until they're replaced."

"Do you want me to delay them for another month?"

I shook my head more vehemently than I felt. "No. Really. I think I'm close to finding Jack the perfect home, so it's just a matter of time before they're in their own place with plenty of space for both of them—and the babies."

"Uh-huh."

I narrowed my eyes. "What's that supposed to mean?"

A small group of elderly tourists congregated at an adjoining bench, clustering around their leader like Martians around a mother ship. Most wore caps over their white hair, with mitten-covered hands resting on more fanny packs than I'd seen in one place.

The tour guide's voice wafted over to me. Indicating one of the many cannons facing the harbor, he said, "These cannons were not used on the attack on Fort Sumter that started the War of Northern Aggression. They would have been out of range. But you can imagine, if you will"—he swept his arm in the direction of the old mansions across the street from the park—"the sheer spectacle afforded those people who stood on their piazzas to enjoy the show."

I turned to look, along with the tourists, at the lovely homes that had welcomed visitors and marauders alike to the Holy City for nearly two hundred years, expecting to see the specters of the old residents. But the piazzas and windows were empty and still, like an unfinished painting.

The tour guide continued. "In addition to the wartime history of the Battery, there's a seedy history, too. Dozens of pirates were hanged from oak trees and gallows in the early seventeen hundreds and left dangling for days. This was to deter other pirates from entering Charleston Harbor. Many people still believe that there is sunken treasure just waiting to be discovered in the waters."

My gaze strayed toward the spot where the gallows had stood, and where I'd once been able to see the twitching bodies of doomed pirates swinging for eternity.

"Still nothing?" Sophie asked quietly.

I shook my head, my frustration sprouting wings of apprehension.

She was silent for a moment. "Have you had a chance to figure out if your ghost is Charlotte or Camille?"

I met her eyes. "Not yet. Whoever it is doesn't like my saying their names." I shrugged. "It's a little scary when I can't see them coming."

"But you're probably more scared of what they might tell you."

I began stretching my own quads, suddenly eager to begin. "Do you want to walk the boardwalk on the waterfront and then head down East Bay Street?"

"Come on, Melanie. It's me you're talking to. What is it that you're so afraid of?"

"You're almost worse than my mother, you know?" I tried to laugh, but couldn't. "It's just the feeling I get that they're . . . waiting."

"Who?"

"All the ghosts in the house. Camille/Charlotte—or whoever she is. And Louisa, and my grandmother. And I think Nevin might be hanging around now, too."

She was silent for a moment. "What do you think they're waiting for?"

I blurted out the words that I hadn't realized I was thinking before I'd said them. "For me to *see*. It's like they're as frustrated as I am. I get the feeling that they're waiting for me to see more than just ghosts."

Sophie's eyes widened. "Well, this pregnancy is good for you in more ways than one." She began walking across the park toward the walkway that edged the harbor along East and South Battery.

I rushed to follow her. "What's that supposed to mean?"

"That you're a lot more insightful than you were before. It's sort of poetic, don't you think? How you can see things better in your head now that you *can't* see ghosts."

I hated that she was always right, but I was already too winded to argue. We walked almost the entire length of the park before I'd managed to regulate my breathing enough to ask a question.

"You can tell me what you found out about the Vanderhorsts now. I'm walking."

She glanced over at me and something she saw made her slow her pace. "I went back to the college's archives on the Vanderhorst house, where I'd found that postcard from Camille to her mother about the dining room table, and I was right. The friend she mentioned is Charlotte Pringle. It might not be the same Charlotte, but that's the same name as John's second wife."

"Charlotte and Camille." I gasped from exertion. "It certainly gets a little more interesting if both wives knew each other."

Sophie's voice was steady, as if she were sitting in a rocking chair instead of pounding the pavement. "You could ask them. That's worked before."

"I'm just not sure I can afford more replacement windows or chandeliers. Not to mention that I can barely hear the spirits anymore. The voices I've been hearing since our trip to the museum have begun to sound like an AM radio—lots of fading in and out, and filled with static. Besides, I need to get my mother to be with me, and she's a little preoccupied." I took a few deep breaths. "What was the context of the mention of Charlotte's name?"

When she looked at me she was grinning, as if she'd been waiting for me to ask. "Charlotte was traveling with them, apparently. Yvonne might be able to dig up more information, but Charlotte was Camille's childhood friend. It wasn't that unusual for friends and family to accompany a newlywed couple on their extended honeymoon."

"Awkward," I said, borrowing one of Nola's favorite words. We descended the steps that led from the boardwalk, then walked across the street to the sidewalk in front of the stately houses facing the harbor that I'd once called money-sucking pits. It wasn't that I no longer considered old houses to be like holes in the ground into which their owners shoveled their hard-earned money, because no matter how much one loved antique architecture and creaking floors and warped doors, there was no denying that they were like a downtown parking meter, always requiring an influx of money.

But now when I looked up at their elegant facades, their painted blue porch ceilings and overflowing window boxes, their tall windows with wavy glass and hand-hewn pediments, I could sense the passage of time and the weight of years these houses and their inhabitants had witnessed. In my own house I'd begun to awaken to the pitter-patter of little feet running down the halls, and I could imagine the house smiling. *It's like a piece of history you can hold in your hand.* Maybe I was

finally beginning to understand what Mr. Vanderhorst had been trying
to tell me.

Just as we reached the line of houses in pastel hues known as Rain-
bow Row, we turned around and began walking back the way we'd
come. We were silent for a long time, our thoughts churning in rhythm
to our steps. The sidewalk was uneven and I had to focus more on my
feet than the houses, which didn't stop me from attempting peeks at
the windows to see whether I could catch a brief glimpse of a ghost.
Finally I faced Sophie, my thoughts focusing on something she'd said.
"What did you say Charlotte's last name was?"

"Pringle. Charlotte Pringle. Why? Have you heard it before?"

I thought for a moment. "Yes, I'm pretty sure I have. I don't remember where, but it'll come to me."

We'd reached the pavilion where we'd started, and I was surprised
that I wasn't as out of breath as I had thought I'd be. I sat down while
Sophie dug the water bottles from her backpack. She handed one to
me, then pulled out something else. "Wasn't sure if you'd gotten
around to reading your own copy yet, but thought I'd show you mine
just in case."

I peered over the bottom of my bottle to see the Sunday edition of
the *Post and Courier*. I almost spit out my water. "I can't believe I forgot
that came out today. This pregnancy has turned my brain to mush." I
reached for the paper. "How bad is it?"

"As an impartial observer, I don't think it's bad at all, but you might
freak out a bit. It's only a single column, since they're apparently running three serial stories simultaneously. But there's a nice picture of
you at the cemetery."

I slapped the paper across my legs and began thumbing through it
until I found the right page. The picture under the headline showed
me in all of my pregnant glory, my hair looking like somebody had
rubbed a balloon on it to give it static, and my expression was a definite
scowl. They'd cut Thomas out of the picture completely, not realizing
that leaving him in it would have been the only thing saving the photo
from being classified as wretched. "Why did they even bother to put

this in there? To make people hate me?" I read the headline and groaned. "Nevin Vanderhorst Speaks from Beyond the Grave."

For a moment, I thought that Suzy Dorf had managed to overhear the voice that had spoken to me at Magnolia Cemetery. Flattening the page on my lap, I began to read:

On a rainy and cold Tuesday morning, the Charleston County coroner's office exhumed the remains of Nevin Vanderhorst at the request of New York residents Irene and George Gilbert. After months of legal delays, their claim to be Vanderhorst heirs is about to be put to the litmus test.

Present at the exhumation was the current heir apparent, Melanie Middleton. In *Lust, Greed and Murder in the Holy City*, an upcoming book by Charleston resident and debut author Marc Longo, Mr. Longo hints at the possibility of help from the "other side" that may have assisted Ms. Middleton in attaining her current status as heir.

Although reluctant to be interviewed, Ms. Middleton did speak a few words at the exhumation, defending her position by saying that Mr. Vanderhorst was a kind old man and she allowed him to believe what he wanted to believe to make him happy. Whether or not that included telling him that she saw his late mother in the garden will never be known, as one of the witnesses won't say and the other one can't.

When asked about Ms. Middleton and her affinity for old houses (she lived for several years as a child at the Prioleau house on Legare Street), Middleton family friend and author Jack Trenholm would comment only that Ms. Middleton's "thoughts and feelings are rarely shared with even those closest to her, including herself."

The results of the DNA tests on Mr. Vanderhorst and the remains found in the foundation of his house are expected to take a few months, and will not be announced until after the first of the year.

As for Ms. Middleton, all she would say when asked whether she would fight the Gilberts if their claims turned out to be legitimate was, "The Gilberts and I both want the truth."

But what the truth might be remains to be seen.

I looked up at Sophie, resisting the impulse to shred the entire newspaper. "I'm not sure who I should kill first—the journalist or Jack."

Sophie steadied me with her professor look. "Did she write anything in the article that wasn't true?"

"No, but . . ."

"And did Jack say anything that wasn't true?"

"Of course not. I mean . . ." My mouth worked as if I were speaking, but nothing was coming out. "Well, it was his opinion, I suppose, however misguided it is. People are going to think I'm some sort of adolescent who is afraid of her feelings."

I glanced up at Sophie, hoping to see a look of compassion and understanding. Instead, she continued to regard me with her professor look, the one that prodded a student who had given a partially correct answer and was still working on figuring out the rest.

I folded up the newspaper as best I could, then handed it back to Sophie. "I've got to go. Jack and Nola went out to brunch, so I've got the house to myself. I'd like to start organizing all of the gifts in the nursery, and sorting the children's books alphabetically by author on the little bookcase my dad made."

After taking a final swig of my water, I stood up. Sophie hadn't moved, her expression unchanged, her arms crossed over her still-small chest. "You know, Melanie, one day you'll realize that all of life's problems can't be solved by immersing yourself in spreadsheets and perfectly organized drawers."

I forced a smile. "Yes, well, it's all I know how to do." I swallowed, my throat thick. "Do you want a lift?"

She shook her head. "No, thanks. I think I'll call Chad and see if he wants to meet me at goat. sheep. cow. I'm craving cheese in the worst way."

I gave her a quick hug to hide my teary eyes. "Okay. Say hi to Chad for me."

"Will do. Have fun with your organizing."

I'd already started walking away and gave a quick wave to show that I'd heard her. I walked briskly to my car, trying to fake pep in my step, because I knew she was watching me. I made it all the way to my driveway before I realized I was crying and had no idea why.

CHAPTER 23

I smoothed down the red maternity dress, noticing how it fit much more snugly than when my mother had purchased it for me only a few months before. I'd resisted wearing it, but it was Nola's Christmas play and I wanted to look festive. I wore my mother's diamond pendant earrings that, according to her, would draw the eye upward, away from my expanding girth. As I stared at myself in the vestibule mirror, I knew it was like planting flowers in the window boxes of a burned-out house so nobody would notice it needed painting.

"I do like you in red."

I turned toward Jack's voice, ready with a retort, but the words stuck to the inside of my mouth. He was walking down the stairs wearing a dark suit and red tie, his face freshly shaven, his hair combed and tamed. Even his shoes gleamed like the star on top of a Christmas tree. I could only hope that standing next to him, I wouldn't be noticed.

He stopped in front of me, smelling nicely of soap with a hint of cologne, and I resisted the impulse to lean toward him like a thirsty giraffe spotting an engorged creek. "It's been so long since I wore a tie that I can't seem to get the knot right. Can you help?"

I took a step forward, glad that my belly created just enough of a barrier so I couldn't melt into him. "I used to do this for my dad every morning, so I'm a bit of an expert." I didn't tell him that I'd had to learn to knot a tie because my dad's hands were never steady following his nightly benders. Jack already knew this about me, and there was something comforting about that, knowing he would never judge me, or my dad, because we shared the same demons.

Ever since the column in the *Post and Courier* had come out, I'd been avoiding him, leaving for work early, and returning only after I knew he was at his condo writing, or out with Nola or friends. If Nola was home alone in the evenings, I made it a point to sit down and have dinner with her—even if it meant I was forced to share a vegan meal—but most of the time I found myself a shadow in my own house. My anger at him for telling the reporter that my "thoughts and feelings are rarely shared with even those closest to her, including herself" had faded to a slow burn, then disappeared completely when I'd finally accepted that there may have been some truth to his words. But I continued to avoid him so I wouldn't have to actually acknowledge it.

I also didn't want to give him an excuse to move back to his condo. The windows had been replaced at a cost that still made my eyes sting when I thought about it, but I felt safer having him so near. There had been no more big incidents like shattering windows, but I couldn't help but feel as if I were sitting on a fault line, knowing that it was a matter of when and not if the angry spirit would make her presence known again.

I felt his eyes on me as I undid his tie and reknotted it, moving slower than necessary as I kept brushing his neck with my fingers, pretending I wasn't doing it on purpose. When I was finished, I stepped back to admire my handiwork, eventually lifting my gaze to meet his.

"Like what you see?" he asked evenly, without even a hint of a smirk.

"It'll do." I stepped back, then slid my purse over my shoulder. "Let's hurry—I don't want to be late. It's open seating, and I hate to think of our parents lying across the front pews to block other people from getting our seats."

He chuckled at the mental image. "Personally, I think a well-placed look from either of our mothers would suffice. Not to mention being intimidated by Cooper in dress uniform."

I walked toward the door, waiting for him to open it for me.

"Don't you need a coat?"

"It's pretty mild outside. Besides, these babies have made me into a little furnace. I swear they're burning logs in there, because I can't seem to cool off. I actually had to take off my nightgown to sleep last night."

He pulled open the door, and I welcomed the cool air on my face. "Be still, my beating heart. The mental image is doing all sorts of wonderful things for me."

I turned to face him, our noses almost touching as we stood in the doorway. "Really, Jack? I'm as big as a house."

"Really," he said, his tone so suggestive that I felt as if two more logs had been thrown onto my internal stove.

I pressed my fingers against my temples while I waited on the piazza as he set the alarm and locked the door.

"Mellie?" His voice was full of concern.

"I have a headache, that's all. I haven't been sleeping well."

Jack's eyebrow lifted, and I fleetingly thought to ask whether he'd considered patenting the look. "I have a remedy for sleeplessness, and it works quite well if you'll recall."

"So does General Lee, and his snores are softer."

"I don't snore," he said, his voice low. More seriously, he asked, "So, what's wrong?"

I looked at him, surprised for a moment that he hadn't heard the noises, too, until I remembered that much of what happened in my house was for my benefit only. "I hear footsteps all night long. From little feet, as if small children are racing up and down the hallways and stairs. It's not scary—at least, not until I remember the baby being bricked up in the foundation. Then it just makes me sad. When I get to that point, I hear the baby crying again. Even with earplugs, I can still hear it."

"You have earplugs?"

I knew he was trying to distract my thoughts, and I eagerly allowed him. "So that if you fall asleep in my room again I can block out your snores."

He leaned in close to me. "I told you, I don't snore. And if you spent more time with me in bed, you'd know that."

A cool breeze swept dead leaves across the marble floor of the piazza, making me shiver despite my overheated internal temperature. My temples throbbed and I pressed my fingers against my skull in an attempt to make it stop. "Dr. Wise said I could take a Tylenol, but I really hate taking any medication. I was just wondering if I should anyway."

"If Dr. Wise says it's okay, then maybe you should."

I shook my head. "No, it's all right. I'll be fine. It's only a couple of hours, right?"

He sent me a dubious look, but held out his arm for me. "My mother carries an entire drugstore in her purse, so she's bound to have something if you change your mind."

As he helped me into the van, he paused. "Mellie, if I say something to you, will you promise not to be mad?"

I frowned at him. "What are we—still in high school?"

His eyes widened like those of a judge in a spelling bee, waiting for the correct answer.

"Never mind," I said. "Just tell me. I promise not to get mad."

He put a hand on my ankle, but I barely felt it through all the padding. "You seem a little . . . puffier than usual. Are you sure everything's okay?"

I jerked my leg away. "I just saw Dr. Wise last week. She told me to drink more water and I have been—even though it makes me go to the bathroom every five minutes. I haven't had much to drink today, because I didn't want to have to get up in the middle of the play. She also told me to get a blood pressure monitor so I can keep track at home, and two days ago it was fine. I kind of forgot the last two days, but I'm sure everything's still fine." I sighed. "Jack, I'm over forty and I'm having twins. My body is just freaking out a bit. Kind of like my brain did at the beginning."

He hesitated, as if not completely convinced, before shutting the door of the van and moving over to the driver's side. He was already driving down Tradd Street before he spoke again. "I still find you incredibly sexy, by the way."

I rolled my eyes and sighed, even though my heart was doing somersaults as more logs were thrown onto the stove.

As usual, Jack found a parking spot at the curb barely a block from

St. Matthew's Lutheran Church, where the eighty-ninth annual Ashley Hall Christmas play was being held. Two stragglers, small angels in white robes, ran past us, a frazzled mother clutching a toddler with a missing shoe walking quickly behind them. "Speak clearly, and don't forget to smile!" she called after them.

It was twenty minutes before showtime, so clusters of parents and attendees stood outside chatting in front of the tall red Gothic doors of the imposing brick church with the tall steeple that towered over this portion of King Street.

I spotted Cooper and Alston Ravenel as soon as they saw us. Alston came rushing toward us, while Cooper walked more sedately, as befitted his status as a Citadel cadet. Alston hugged me and kissed my cheek, then surprised Jack by doing the same to him.

"I'm surprised you're not in the play," I told her.

"I get stage fright. I'm helping with the lighting, though, so I've got to run. I just wanted to say hi and let Nola know you're here. I think she's nervous, but don't tell her I said that." She gave us a quick wave, then walked away quickly, her posture still perfect and straight enough to carry a stack of books despite her rapid pace.

Cooper extended his hand to me and I shook it, and then he did the same to Jack. Jack hesitated for just a second longer than necessary before accepting it. "Cooper," he said curtly.

"Sir," Cooper said.

I looked down at their clasped hands, wondering whether they were perhaps clasped more tightly than the situation warranted.

"Are you sitting with your parents?" Jack asked.

"No, sir. Nola's grandparents were kind enough to save a seat for me in the front row."

"Terrific," Jack said, unsmiling.

"Yes, sir, it is," Cooper said, his smile showing that he was unfazed by Jack's chilly reception.

Cooper excused himself to go talk with friends, Jack glaring after him.

"Jack, he's a nice kid. Would you prefer some tattooed convict on a motorcycle with a cigarette pack rolled up in his sleeve?"

"I'd prefer Nola to be in a convent in Ireland for the next ten years." He snorted, making me want to laugh. "I know what he's after—all guys are the same. Her money's just a bonus."

"What are you talking about? They're not even dating. And even if they were, I doubt money would be an issue."

"Yeah, well, she just got her first royalty check for 'My Daughter's Eyes.' It's enough to pay for her college, with a bit left over to invest. And that's just the first one. They're still playing it heavily on the radio, and Apple might be interested in using it in one of their iPod commercials."

"That's fabulous! I'm just surprised she hasn't told me."

"She just found out yesterday. She was planning on telling everybody tonight at dinner, after the play."

I felt an absurd relief, as if I'd believed that her omission meant that I didn't rate as high in Nola's affections as she rated in mine. "Don't worry—I'll pretend to be surprised."

We stepped through the black iron gates and onto the black-and-white-tiled flooring that led up to steps and the main door. I stared down at the squares, laid down to look like diamonds, and they seemed to float up to me, then swim back and forth as if they were liquid. I stopped, clutching at Jack's arm.

"Mellie? Are you all right?"

"Yes. I think so. I just think my headache is becoming some sort of migraine. It's messing with my vision."

He took hold of both of my elbows and led me to the church steps and made me sit down. Taking his phone from his jacket pocket, he said, "I'm calling Dr. Wise."

I wanted to argue, but my head was throbbing and the black and white tiles continued to move around my feet. Without thinking too much about it, I tilted to the side until my cheek was resting against the top step.

"Mellie!" Jack's voice sounded as if it were coming from very far away.

"Thanks for letting me rest my head on your lap," I mumbled.

"I'm not."

"Hmm?" His words made no sense. I definitely felt a soft lap underneath my head and a hand brushing my hair from my face.

Jack began speaking into the phone, but his words were no longer registering with me. I saw Cooper within my fading field of vision, and then Jack was saying something to him before Cooper disappeared into the building. A group of people had congregated in front of me, but I ignored them, focusing instead on the gentle hand on my forehead that was easing my headache.

A siren broke through the fog, and I heard Jack's voice very close to my ear. "Hang on, Mellie. Hang on, all right? The ambulance is almost here. You're going to be fine. Just hang on."

I heard my mother, and then Amelia, their voices low and soothing, but they were talking to Jack and not me. But I felt Jack's hands on mine, and then he was cradling my head and I wanted to protest, to ask what had happened to the other gentle hands, but once he touched me nothing else mattered.

The siren grew louder, but it seemed the shrillness was muted, like somebody had placed their hands over my ears so I wouldn't be disturbed. I sensed the movement of people as a new person wearing some sort of uniform shirt appeared in front of me. I was suddenly being lifted in the air, then set on something firm. Jack's hands slid from mine, and I tried to call his name, but my words disintegrated before they'd left my mouth.

And then I felt Jack's lips on my forehead. Then, very softly, as if it came from a great distance, I heard, "I love you, Mellie." The gentle hand returned to my face, stroking softly, and I realized that Jack was gone.

A needle prick stung my arm, followed by the sound of slamming doors. I opened my mouth to shout Jack's name, to ask him to repeat what he'd just said, because I wasn't sure whether I'd imagined it or not. "I love you, too," I said, but the words dissolved on my tongue like a bitter pill, leaving me hollow and empty as I finally closed my eyes and allowed myself to slip into oblivion.

CHAPTER 24

"It's not fair," I said, my voice sounding small and scared, just like I felt. "I've always been so healthy. Maybe it's a mistake."

My mother sat on the edge of my bed, stroking my hair, the action enveloping me in strong sense of déjà vu. "Nobody ever said life was supposed to be fair, Mellie. You need to look at the bright side: You're healthy, the babies are healthy, and your doctor isn't making you stay in the hospital."

I sighed. "On one level, I do realize you're right. But Dr. Wise is making me lie on my left side in my bed for three months. I think she just looked that up in the *Journal of Medieval Torture*. She probably has a subscription."

"Sweetheart, preeclampsia is serious. You're lucky Jack was there and knew to call an ambulance. And you've got me. Between the two of us and Mrs. Houlihan, we'll be able to constantly monitor you and the babies until they're strong enough to be born. We're in this together, okay?"

"I know—and I'm so grateful that the babies are okay. But that doesn't make being a prisoner in my own room any easier to take."

She leaned down to kiss my cheek. "Sometimes I am very glad that we didn't spend your teenage years together. We might not have survived." Straightening, she said, "Mrs. Houlihan will bring your dinner up in a few moments, and I'll be back when you're finished to give you your prenatal vitamins."

"What's for dinner?" I asked, imagining all the comfort foods Mrs. Houlihan usually made for me when I was feeling low.

"Steamed vegetables, grilled chicken, potatoes with no butter or gravy, and an apple for dessert."

I stared at her. "Do you want me to cry now or wait until you leave?"

"Mellie, please try. Mrs. Houlihan is an excellent cook and I know she'll make it all very tasty."

"Without salt. Or a real dessert."

"Think of the babies." She sent me a pointed look.

I closed my eyes, feeling the self-pity quickly replaced with shame. "I will—promise. It's just . . . a lot to take in." My gaze strayed behind her to the wall by the bathroom door, where somebody had set up a cot and bedding while I'd been in the hospital. "Is that yours?"

"No. It's Jack's. He insisted on sleeping in here. I'm taking over the guest room."

A warm flush threaded through my veins as I tried to remember something Jack had said while I'd been floating in and out of consciousness. But all I could recall was the sound of doors slamming and the compulsion to ask him something.

She opened the bedroom door and a black-and-white ball of fur raced inside before jumping up on the bed and settling himself in his usual spot of honor on top of my pillow.

"I'm assuming General Lee is allowed?" I asked.

"Of course. I asked Dr. Wise, and she said that he might actually help to keep your blood pressure down. You should pet him as much as possible."

I reached up to stroke his silky fur, but paused as I realized that his ears were at attention, along with his tail, and his eyes were following movement where no movement should have been. It was unnerving because I couldn't see what it was, but even more unnerving because the little dog wasn't barking.

"Mother?" I whispered.

"I know," she whispered back.

"Why isn't he barking?"

"Because he doesn't feel threatened, and he doesn't feel as if you should be either."

General Lee's head went back as if the unseen visitor were now standing at the bed, looking down at us. And then he tilted his head back and forth as something or someone scratched behind his ears.

"I smell roses," my mother said quietly.

As soon as she'd said the words, General Lee stopped moving his head and whimpered, as if the scratching had suddenly ceased. But not before I'd felt the press of cold fingers being laid gently on my cheek.

"It was Louisa," I said with certainty, remembering again a soft lap and gentle hands on my face as sirens screamed in the distance.

"She's here to protect you," my mother said, her tone anything but comforting.

My eyes met hers. "But from what?"

Our gazes held for a long moment before she turned away. "I'll be back in a little bit."

"Mother?"

She faced me again.

"Would you mind getting me a few fresh thin-tipped Sharpies and a blank pad to put on my easel? I want to make a flowchart of all the information we've gathered so far about the Vanderhorsts."

"Sure. Anything else?"

I nodded. "And if you wouldn't mind, could you move my easel closer? You can put the new pad and pens at the foot of the bed so I can reach them."

My mother lifted the easel and brought it nearer the bed, scrutinizing the chart as if for the first time. "You're still planning on giving birth on March twenty-third, I see."

I nodded. "I'll ask Dr. Wise if my condition might mean an earlier delivery, but unless I hear otherwise, that's still what I'm aiming for."

She gave me an odd smile before heading out the door, muttering something under her breath, the only two words I could understand being "reality" and "check." I lay back on my pillow and closed my eyes, imagining for a moment that I could smell the sweet scent of roses.

I'd just finished losing my fourth game of tic-tac-toe on Nola's iPad when I looked up at a gentle tapping on the doorframe. Jack stood there in a white T-shirt that outlined his abs, barefoot and wearing plaid pajama bottoms, looking as devastating as he had the first time I'd seen him. In the week I'd been on bed rest, he'd moved his writing desk into the music room, where both he and Nola had found some sort of positive vibe in working together. Nola had explained it as an exchange of creative juices. I considered it a neutral way for them to be in the same room without a reason to shout at each other.

Since my return from the hospital, I'd hardly seen him alone at all. It was as if he were avoiding any chance to be alone with me. He helped with my blood pressure monitoring and clearing my food trays, and slept on the cot—only after I'd fallen asleep—so that if I needed help at night he was there. I felt his presence in the house like a person in daylight knows there's a sun shining somewhere in the sky without actually looking up.

"I thought you'd already be asleep," he said, sounding almost apologetic.

I shook my head, then tossed the iPad on my nightstand with disgust. "I was hoping the stupid thing would take pity on me and let me win just once."

"I'd be happy to show you some pointers on how to win. Every writer I know is great at online games, because we're pros at procrastination. I could teach you a thing or two about solitaire and sudoku, too."

"Well, there's something to look forward to, I guess. Maybe I can find other bedridden pregnant women out there in some online-gaming chat room."

"It's probably right next to the one for writers," he said with a smile. He stepped toward me but didn't sit on the bed. "You know, if you really don't want to take those Lamaze classes, there are easier ways to get out of it than preeclampsia. That's a little extreme, even for you."

I pursed my lips. "I wish I'd known there was a choice. Panting in a room with a lot of pregnant women almost sounds fun to me now."

He lifted his hand as if to touch me, then let it drop. "I'm sorry you're stuck in bed for the duration. You know we're all here to help."

I nodded. "I know. It's just that, well, there's stuff I need to be doing. Like selling houses. And walking General Lee. And it's Christmas. Fortunately, I'd finished with my shopping and cataloging everything in my gift closet by November first, but I haven't wrapped anything yet. I probably won't even be allowed to go downstairs to decorate the tree, and I know I won't be allowed near the turkey or ham. Or pecan pie." I'd started to salivate and stopped.

Very slowly, he said, "You finished with all of your shopping by November first?"

I nodded. "That's my deadline every year, and I've never missed it. I usually have it all wrapped by December tenth, but it looks like that's not going to happen."

"You know that's not normal, right?"

"It is for me."

He just looked at me for a long moment. "I can wrap for you. I used to help out at Trenholm's Antiques when I was in high school, and I can tie a mean bow, if I do say so myself. Where are the presents?"

I pointed to the old mahogany armoire that had once been the room's only clothes storage until I'd knocked down a wall to add the master bath and walk-in closet. "In there."

He opened the doors and stood there not saying anything for a full minute. "All of the shelves are labeled. With one of those labeling-gun things."

"Actually, I used five different labeling guns so that I could color-code for specific people without having to reload the tape. My mother is gold, my father silver, Sophie is green, Nola purple, and you're black."

He turned to regard me with one raised eyebrow, then turned back to view my masterpiece again. "This is pretty amazing."

"Thank you," I said, feeling better than I had in more than a week. "The miscellaneous shelf at the bottom is for people at work and Ruth at the bakery. I just used different-colored Sharpies on masking tape for those."

"You should be on one of those TV reality shows."

"Like one of the HGTV programs about home improvement?"

He shook his head. "No, I was thinking about one of the shows about people with weird obsessions." He leaned down and lifted something from one of the shelves. "What's this?"

I struggled to sit upright and then gave up, flopping back on my pillows and General Lee. "That's one of your presents. You weren't supposed to look."

"What is it?" He held it flat in his hands.

"It's a leather expanding file. It has your initials on the other side," I said shyly.

He flipped it over and examined the three letters. "It's very nice."

"Your workspace is such a mess that I thought this would help organize all your notes when you're writing. That way you won't have paper strewn over every flat surface."

His eyes sparkled as he regarded me. "Some people actually work better that way, you know."

"I don't see how. It would drive me nuts."

He leaned down again and picked up the small leather box with the words "Croghan's Jewel Box" embossed on top. "What's this?"

I sighed with exasperation. "I bet you were one of those kids who crept downstairs when your parents weren't looking and opened all the presents before taping them shut again."

"And you weren't?"

"I wasn't really given the chance. Christmas was some sort of haphazard thing. My dad and I usually didn't even have a tree. I think that's why I go a little crazy with all the decorations and preparations. I don't mean this to sound shallow, but one of the things I'm most looking forward to as a parent is Christmas mornings. Especially when they're small." I paused. "Hopefully we can work it out so that we don't have to take turns with them on holidays. I figure since Nola is practically mine already, and your parents and my parents are good friends, we could just all be together for holidays and birthdays."

He looked down at the box in his hands, but not before I'd seen the look in his eyes. I figured it was a trick of the light that made them seem angry.

"You've already worked it all out, I see. You and your planning. You should have been a five-star general."

There was a hard edge to his voice, but before I could ask him about it, he said, "Can I go ahead and open this one? That way I won't have to wrap it."

"Go ahead. But I'm still going to make you wrap it so you can open it again on Christmas morning."

He moved toward the bed and this time he did sit down, but was very careful not to touch me. He took the lid off the box and placed it on the folded-down bedspread, then parted the tissue so he could see the sterling-silver three-part frame. I'd already put Nola's freshman-year photo in the center, and the sonogram pictures of the twins on either side. He regarded them intently, not saying a single word.

"I figure after the twins are born you can replace those with real photos. I'm assuming it will be hard to narrow it down to two good ones, because it seems the Trenholm family trait is to be highly pho-togenic. I mean, even the sonogram photos are cute—in one of them I swear the baby is smiling for the camera. And Nola's photo looks like it belongs on the cover of *Vogue*. I'm not even going to mention your author photo on the backs of your books, or your driver's license photo. I mean, who takes good pictures at the DMV?"

He was staring hard at the frames without saying anything, so I'd started to babble to fill the silence and maybe to block out whatever it was he would say.

Jack's lips lifted, but his smile was sad. "Just when I'm beginning to think that you have no heart at all, you do something like this."

I didn't know how to respond. I was hurt and touched at the same time, and anything I wanted to say would have just come out wrong, so I remained silent.

Jack stood and replaced the box with the frame back in the armoire and closed the doors.

"I'm assuming you have another closet somewhere in the house for just wrapping paper and supplies?" He held his finger to his lips, silencing me. "Don't tell me now—wait until tomorrow. I don't think I could handle two Mellie-isms in one night. It might overwhelm me."

I narrowed my eyes at him, but he'd already walked to the cot and lain down.

"Jack?"

"Um?"

"Can you turn out the light? It's hard for me to get out of bed."

He stood and walked across the room to flip the switch, giving me a nice view of his T-shirt-clad torso. Maybe I'd get lucky and dream about it.

He crawled back onto the cot and I lay very still, listening to him breathe.

"Jack?"

"Yes, Mellie?"

"Remember before, how you slept with me in my bed so we could both be more comfortable?"

"Yes."

"You could do that again. If you like. I don't think that cot's easy on your back. And you'll need your back for all the baby lifting."

He didn't say anything, but I heard him leave the cot, and then felt movement from the other side of the mattress.

I barely breathed while I waited for him to get closer.

"Are you comfortable?" he asked.

"No," I said, finding it easier to be honest with him in the dark.

Without a word he moved closer until he was curled up behind me like a spoon. He snagged one of the small pillows that were now a permanent fixture on my bed and began to arrange them right where I needed them without my having to tell him.

"How about now?"

"That'll do," I said, relaxing into him.

"Jack?"

"Hmm?"

Did you really say that you loved me or was I just dreaming? But all the darkness in the world could not force that question past my lips. "Can we do this again tomorrow night?"

"Um-hmm."

"And the next?"

"Um-hmm."

"But don't tell Nola or my mother, okay? We'll mess up the sheets on the cot every morning so no one will know."

His chest rumbled against my back. "Mellie?"

"Yes?"

"Go to sleep. I can't take any more."

I stayed awake long after Jack's breathing slowed into a heavy sleep rhythm, wondering what he'd meant. Then I closed my eyes, pressing myself against him, and fell asleep to the sound of little feet running up and down the halls of the old house.

CHAPTER 25

I picked at my plate of black-eyed peas and collard greens, unable to find the enthusiasm needed to place a bite on my fork and lift it to my mouth. "It tastes a lot better with lots of salt and fatback."

Nola sat on a chair beside my bed, her own plate perched on her lap. "I don't think I want to know exactly what 'fatback' is." She put a bite of the peas into her mouth and chewed. "It's not bad at all—you should try it." She smiled encouragingly.

"I figured you'd like it, because you've never eaten it the way it should be. It's kind of like eating chocolate that doesn't have any sugar in it."

She looked up with wide eyes. "I've had that—and it's pretty good."

"Never mind," I muttered, putting a small bite of unseasoned black-eyed peas into my mouth. I hadn't minded the bland diet I'd been on for almost a month because I knew it was best for my babies. But this was New Year's Day, and the plate in front of me was just a glaring reminder of everything I'd willingly given up and forgotten to miss. Until now.

Nola put a mouthful of collard greens into her mouth and almost choked. She quickly took a drink of water and shook her head, as if trying to negate the taste that was probably still lingering. "Ugh. How can people eat that?"

"Like I said, it's a lot better cooked in fatback. You have to finish it, though, to bring you good luck throughout the year. It's a Southern tradition."

She eyed the collard greens with suspicion. "Tradition or punishment?"

"If you're going to grow up in South Carolina, you really need to know these things." I took a deep breath, remembering what my grandmother had taught me at about the same time I was learning to walk. "Back during the Civil War, when the Yankees traipsed through the South burning everything in sight, they left behind the black-eyed peas and greens to feed their animals, not destroying what was left because they didn't think it edible for humans."

"They got that right," Nola said under her breath before taking another long drink of water.

I continued. "The Southerners were grateful for the leftovers, because it was the only thing that saved them from dying of starvation. So each January first, we eat our collard greens and black-eyed peas with grateful hearts and a renewed sense of hope for the coming year."

"Do you really believe that?" Nola asked dubiously.

I rubbed my belly. "I will admit that every New Year does give me a little spark of excitement and enthusiasm, and even a renewed sense of purpose. Especially this year, since I'm expecting the twins."

My eyes met her skeptical ones.

I pushed away my plate. "Oh, all right. I confess that starving might be a viable alternative to eating these plain. I might even feel a little more hopeful and enthused if I could just have a tiny bit of fat and salt to go with my greens and peas."

General Lee sat up, his face turned toward the open bedroom door as Nola and I both became aware of the sound of somebody walking up the stairs. The dog gave a high-pitched whine—something he usually reserved for those he loved best, or whoever was holding the dog food—while we waited for the visitor to appear in the doorway.

Both Nola and I slumped when we spotted Rebecca, a vision in pink cashmere and wool tweed, holding Pucci, who was wearing a matching tweed sweater.

"I think I'm going to puke," Nola said quietly through clenched teeth and what might pass as a smile.

"Melanie! Nola! It's been for*ever*!" Rebecca burst into the room in a cloud of perfume and hair spray, but before I had a chance to cough, she was kissing me on both cheeks and then Nola. "Your mother let me in, saying a visitor was just what you needed to perk you up."

Nola and I made a big show of gathering and stacking plates so we wouldn't have to respond, while Pucci and General Lee became reacquainted by sniffing each other's posterior. Without being asked, Rebecca dragged over the low upholstered slipper chair by the window and parked it next to Nola's.

"I can't tell you how disappointed I am that you can't be in my wedding now, Mellie. It's important to both Marc and me that our families play a big part in our wedding. Maybe you can be godmother to one of our children instead." She looked pointedly at my belly, which I inadequately tried to cover with my hands. I hadn't thought about godmothers yet, but I was pretty certain that Rebecca wouldn't be one of them.

"How nice," I said.

She didn't seem to have heard, as she was staring intently at Nola. "What size are you? A two? Or maybe a four? I think you might fit into Melanie's—"

Nola stood suddenly, her chair wobbling in her wake. "I need to get these dishes down to the kitchen. And I've got tons of homework. . . ."

"I thought you'd have at least another week for your Christmas break," Rebecca said.

"Yes, well, I do, but Ashley Hall is pretty tough. You have no idea how much homework they give even over breaks." She gathered up the tray and smiled at us before backing out the door. As she descended the stairs, I thought I heard her fading litany, "And then I have to milk the cows, plow a field, scrub the floors. . . ."

"Sweet girl," Rebecca said, diverting my attention. "A little excitable, perhaps, but sweet. I guess that comes from growing up in California."

I yawned, not bothering to hide it. "Sorry," I said. "I guess it's my nap time."

She laughed. "My mother and grandmother have to take naps, too. I guess I'm not old enough for that yet."

I was grateful that my bulkiness precluded me from leaping on her and squashing her like a bug. Instead, I said, "I am sorry about not being able to be in your wedding. Even my parents have postponed their wedding until after the babies are born so that I can participate. I don't expect you to do that, of course," I added quickly, hoping I wasn't giving her any ideas, "but I will pay for my dress, since we already ordered it."

She smiled, and I began to have a very bad feeling about the purpose of her visit. "Actually," she said slowly, "all might not be lost, and you might have a reason to wear it after all. It *is* in the most beautiful shade of pink, and if we get it altered just a bit to show that it's different from the bridesmaids' dresses, I think we could make it work."

"Make it work?"

She beamed. "Well, since we're practically sisters, I thought I could ask you this favor. Actually, it was Marc's idea, but since you and he have a . . . history, we thought it best that I ask."

My phone buzzed and I looked down at the screen to see it was Detective Riley. We spoke almost daily, but not in person. The two times he'd come to the house, Jack had hovered like a chaperone, and the second time he'd actually lain down on the cot and pretended to nap while Thomas and I talked. It was awkward and unnerving, and we'd decided to chat by phone for the duration of my pregnancy unless I knew that Jack was out of the house for at least an hour.

After making a mental note to call him back later, I hit mute and looked back at Rebecca. "I'm sorry. You were saying you wanted to ask a favor? Look, if you want to borrow any of the family jewelry for your wedding day, you're welcome to it."

"Actually, we want to borrow your house."

I was silent for a moment, trying to unscramble her words into an order that made sense. "Excuse me?" There was a scuffling sound from the other side of the bed, out of our line of sight, but I was too focused on what Rebecca was saying to give it my full attention.

"It's such a perfect idea, I'm just ashamed that I didn't think about it first!" She practically bounced up and down in her chair. "Since it's technically because of this house and your connection to it and to

Marc that he and I met, we thought it would be the *perfect* location for the rehearsal dinner."

"The rehearsal dinner," I repeated, just to make sure I'd heard her correctly.

She nodded multiple times, reminding me of a bobblehead on a dashboard. "Yes! Isn't that the most amazing idea? We've already paid our deposit at the yacht club, but we would happily forfeit it, because having the rehearsal dinner at your house would just be the icing on the cake of our wedding plans. And you won't even have to lift a finger. We'll have our wedding planner take care of everything—hire the caterers, do the decorations, the cleaning, and all the prep work. All you have to do is smile."

Her gaze slid down to my abdomen. "Maybe I can get the alterations lady at the bridal shop to make a sash or something to cinch you in. You know, give you a waist."

The sounds on the other side of the bed were becoming more frantic now, but I was too busy wondering how I could grab a pillow and toss it at her while making it look like an accident.

"Actually, Rebecca, I'm not supposed to leave my bed. Except to go to the bathroom or sit up and eat, I'm supposed to be lying on my side."

She stood and walked toward the cot, her thoughts so focused that she didn't even think to ask why it was there. "This would be perfect! You could be carried down the stairs on this—sort of like Cleopatra!—and moved from room to room with the guests."

I needed her to leave before I'd be forced into an act of violence that I couldn't even pretend later that I regretted. "I need to think about it. Can we talk about this later?"

She returned to her chair, her expression solemn. "It might be the very last function you will ever have in this house, you know. It would be like a huge farewell celebration—everything shimmering and gleaming just like when it was new. It would be something you'd remember for the rest of your life."

I narrowed my eyes. "Do you know something you're not telling me?"

Her own eyes were round and innocent. "It's nothing I've read or been told. I'm waiting with bated breath along with everyone else to find out what the DNA results will be. But I did have a peculiar dream. That's the other thing I wanted to tell you. But only after you agreed to do the rehearsal dinner."

"You're bribing me? What's this 'we're all family' stuff?"

"I'm not the one who has trouble recognizing that we're related, Melanie. I'm always having to remind you. I know our connection is a distant one, but we *are* blood relations. Marc and I both think it makes perfect sense for our rehearsal dinner to be here. I just figured you might need a little . . . incentive."

I leaned back against my pillows, wishing for a giant flyswatter so I could just shoo her away. But somewhere inside of me, buried in all of my annoyance, I knew she might be right—that it could be the last party and gathering of family and friends in this house that I'd called home for such a short time, but that seemed like a lifetime.

With a sigh, I said, "Do you promise I won't have to do a thing? Because I really can't. And there's no guarantee that the ghosts will behave, either."

She was bouncing up and down in her chair again. "Oh, I can manage them." She reached over and hugged me, then sat back. "So, do we have a deal?"

I sighed, seeing no alternative and lacking the will or energy to argue. "Whatevs," I said, feeling a small sense of satisfaction as I watched her mentally translate. "So what was your dream?"

She moved her chair up a little closer next to the bed, as if the ghosts couldn't hear her if she whispered. "I dreamed of that woman again. The woman I saw before with the cradles."

I felt a stab of disappointment. "And that was all? You just saw the woman with two cradles again?"

She shook her head. "Sort of. Except that there were three cradles this time. And one of them had a baby in it."

"Were the cradles all the same?"

She nodded slowly. "They were black with twisted spindles, and rockers carved to look like egrets." Her eyes opened wide. "And there was one more thing that was different this time."

Her face was so close to mine that I could feel her breath as she spoke. "What?" I whispered.

"She was holding something in her hand, a piece of paper. There were lots of lines on it, like some type of official form, like a birth certificate or something, but I couldn't read any of the writing. She kept holding it up to my face and pointing at a signature at the bottom. I couldn't read it, so I was hoping you might know what it's all about so that she won't come back and disturb my sleep. Wouldn't do for me to have dark circles under my eyes in my engagement photos."

"Thank goodness for Photoshop," I said, my attention distracted by what she'd just told me.

"Excuse me?"

I refocused on Rebecca. "I said that I doubted you could take a bad picture."

The table on the other side of the bed began wobbling back and forth, accompanied by a grunt and a whine, the crystal lamp on top of the table beginning to shimmy.

Rebecca jerked to her feet. "What on earth . . . ?" When she reached the foot of the bed, she shrieked. "Pucci!"

In the same moment that I realized I couldn't get out of bed fast enough to help, I noticed that General Lee was MIA. I turned to Rebecca with horror. "Is my dog . . . ?"

"General Lee!" she shrieked again before leaning down.

It was like watching a movie where the bottom half of the screen was blocked, meaning all I could do was hear the sounds of a little dog squealing, another dog growling, and Rebecca screaming while I watched her bob up and down as if looking for a suitable stance from which to rescue her dog.

A fierce growl sounded from beyond my vision, making Rebecca jump back. The image of my marshmallow-like dog getting territorial almost made me laugh.

"Maybe you should just let them finish . . ." I began, but quickly stopped at the venomous look Rebecca gave me.

Without a word, she grabbed one of the pillows and began advancing on the unseen amorous pair before stopping abruptly. "I think they're through," she said. Dropping the pillow, she leaned down and picked up Pucci, who, I thought, looked quite happy and not despoiled at all.

"Do I need to find a couple of cigarettes?"

She glared at me. "I thought you said your dog was old!"

"He is. But old doesn't mean dead, Rebecca. Just look at my parents!"

With a disgusted look at my dog, Rebecca stormed to the door. "I can only hope there aren't any . . . repercussions." She stared pointedly at my swollen girth. After a deep breath and a moment apparently needed to compose herself, she said, "My wedding planner will be calling you. His name is Daniel—just the first name. Like Madonna."

"I thought you said I wouldn't have to do anything . . ." I began, but she'd already slipped through the door and was headed for the stairs.

With a sigh, I leaned back against my pillows, then immediately jerked myself upright again, remembering my conversation with Sophie during our walk on the Battery. She'd mentioned the last name of Camille's friend Charlotte, and the name had rung a bell with me. At the time I couldn't place it. But now, after what Rebecca had just told me, I thought I knew.

Gently rolling myself into a sitting position, I reached for the folder Yvonne had given me that I'd set on the easel. I'd already started making a time line of all the information we'd discovered so far, but what I was looking for wouldn't be there.

I began flipping through the papers until I'd reached the copy of Camille's death certificate. Running my fingers down the page, I stopped at the bottom, right where in bold black ink was the signature of the attending physician who verified the death. Robert Pringle.

Icy crystals seemed to form down the line of my spine as I flipped through more pages until I'd found the second piece of paper, a later addition that Sophie had asked Yvonne to include in the folder. It was a copy of the postcard that Camille Vanderhorst had sent to her mother while on her honeymoon in Italy, the postcard where she'd mentioned the name of her friend who'd accompanied Camille and her husband.

There, in Camille's own elegant cursive writing, was the name I'd been looking for: Charlotte Pringle.

I turned back to the front of the folder, where Yvonne had stapled the Vanderhorst family tree. I found John and his lone descendant, William. And there, on the same branch with John were the names of his two wives, Camille and Charlotte.

It could be a different Charlotte; Pringle was a common Charleston family name, and it could just be a coincidence. But, as Jack was so fond of reminding me, there was no such thing as coincidences.

I hadn't realized that I'd said the two names out loud until the lamp on the bedside table began to wobble. I was about to call out General Lee's name to get him to stop until I realized that he was curled into a ball on the floor by my dressing table.

With alarm, I turned back to the lamp as it continued to move from side to side, gaining momentum until it seemed to perch itself on the edge of its brass base for a moment before swinging back in the other direction with such force that it toppled over, hitting the table with a loud cracking sound before smashing to the wood floor.

Jack, my mother, and Nola were at the doorway within minutes, Mrs. Houlihan panting behind them a few moments later. Jack came right to the bed and began touching me, as if to reassure himself that I was still in one piece, while my mother and Nola moved around the bed and spotted the lamp.

"Are you all right?" Jack asked.

I nodded. "I'm fine—really."

Mrs. Houlihan moved to the windows, rubbing her arms. "It's freezing in here."

My mother lifted the top half of the lamp from the floor and we all stared at the shade that seemed to have been shredded by what looked like claws. Or the fingers of a very angry woman. "What happened?" she asked, although it was clear from her expression that she'd already guessed.

I felt three pairs of eyes on me while Mrs. Houlihan tested the window locks and moved aside curtains to check for cracks. Looking at Jack, I said, "I think things just got a little more complicated."

CHAPTER 26

The last week of February, Detective Riley had let me know that the forensics lab had finally begun to work on the DNA procured during Nevin Vanderhorst's exhumation and that the results were imminent. I wouldn't risk the health of the babies by asking questions and antagonizing the ghost I couldn't yet see, and whose restlessness I sensed near me almost daily, but my pregnancy was a temporary thing. As I lay in my bed each day, waiting for the babies to be born, I felt as if the house and its spirits were waiting, too.

I was still on bed rest as the babies thrived and I grew even larger, something I hadn't thought possible the previous month. My mother and Amelia had taken over setting up the nursery, including the addition of a new closet to hold all of the accumulated baby gifts from extended family and friends, as well as from the baby shower Nancy Flaherty and Joyce Challis had thrown for me. I thought I'd be upset relinquishing control over the babies' room, but I'd secretly found it a little liberating knowing that something was being done without my having to manage it. Perhaps my impending motherhood was changing me in spite of myself.

To keep my sanity, I tried to keep to a schedule, eating and sleeping at the same times every day, making business calls and checking in with my coworkers who were handling my clients, and updating my essential charts. I meticulously noted my weight and the baby's statistics after every checkup with Dr. Wise, along with my blood pressure and urine test results. I made lists of baby clothes we'd received, the number of diapers we had on hand, the safety ratings of every piece of baby equipment we did or would own during the first five years of life. I'd even already addressed all of the birth announcement envelopes and stamped them. All we needed to do was call the printer with the baby's names and weights after they were born. I tried to get the company to go ahead and print the birth date, but they had declined.

I had filled three large sheets of easel paper with everything I'd discovered about the Vanderhorsts and the house since the baby's remains had been found—the three christening gowns and bonnets, the package that had been mailed one hundred years before and had just been delivered to my front porch. In a corner I listed baby William and his physically deformed brother, Cornelius, a line drawn from their names to Camille's name and a note of her death in 1861 in an insane asylum. Underneath Camille's name I had printed John's name and Charlotte's name on the same line, a question mark connecting Charlotte with Dr. Robert Pringle. Their connection—if there was one—had remained elusive, although neither Sophie nor Yvonne had yet to accept defeat.

All of the bits and pieces reminded me of a game I'd once played with my grandmother where long, skinny sticks were poked into a clear canister and marbles placed on top. One by one we'd pull a stick, trying not to let any marbles fall. In this game, however, all of the sticks were questions, the marbles answers. Yet no matter how many sticks I tugged on, the marbles stubbornly remained where they were.

I looked up at the ceiling as I heard another bump and scrape in the attic, followed by my mother's voice as she instructed Jack and my father where to put something. She'd decided it was time the attic was scoured in the hopes of finding some last-minute additions to the nursery—as long as anything she brought down didn't have any hangers-on.

Her heels tapped on the attic stairs and then down the hallway into my room. She carried what looked like a polished wooden box the size of a pillow, and which could have once been a cigar humidor. She wore her gloves and used them to wipe off the bottom of the box before setting it down on the foot of my bed.

Using the back of her arm, she swept a lock of dark hair from her forehead. "As OCD as you are, I can't believe you've left the attic in such a state."

"I'm not obsessive-compulsive. That's just what Jack says to annoy me. But to answer your question, I have done some cleanup. Before I had the roof repaired, I had Amelia and John come to take away anything valuable and give me an appraisal. A lot of it is still in their shop waiting for me to decide what I want to do with it. I also got rid of the large buffalo head, because it was beginning to smell with all of the pigeon poop on it. But the rest of it I just left where it was, because I haven't had time with all the house repairs, my job, and the pregnancy."

She raised her eyebrows, as if she knew I was telling her only part of the truth.

I sighed. "And because it's a little scary up there. The Vanderhorsts never threw anything away, and I think a lot of them have chosen to remain in the attic with their favorite possessions. Like that cradle. Which, for the record, I don't want anywhere near the babies."

"You're not going to hear me arguing about that. Besides, your father is almost finished with the cradles he's making. Don't worry—they're being made with current safety specifications, and Amelia is going to a lot of trouble getting custom-made bedding that is also current with today's standards. I'll make a chart if you want me to."

"Very funny. By the way, has anybody called or brought over the Manigault cradle that Julia left for me in her will? I've got so many cradles to choose from, I guess I let that one slip from my mind."

She shook her head. "No, but I'll find out." She was thoughtful for a moment. "I am curious, though, why Julia Manigault left it to you. I'm not even going to try to guess how she knew you were pregnant, but I suppose she knew in the same way that you'd need another cradle."

"Technically, I didn't need another cradle—the second one is in the museum. Knowing Julia, she would have assumed that I would demand that the museum return it to its rightful owner until it was no longer needed." I thought for a moment. "Which makes me think she was giving me a third cradle on purpose." Shrugging, I said, "Who knows? Nothing's making sense anymore, and the more I speculate, the more confusing it gets."

My mother sat down on the edge of the bed, a soft smile on her face. "I think it's conversations like this that drive your father crazy. If it doesn't make sense to us, it will make even less sense to him, so let's keep that little tidbit of information to ourselves for the time being, all right?"

Another screech and bump sounded from above. Looking up at the ceiling, my mother said, "Your father found a few crated paintings under a tarp that must have been left over from the roof repair. He's going to bring them to Trenholm's Antiques to see if they're worth anything. You can look at them first to see if there're any you want to keep, but he's hoping he might be able to sell most of them."

"Why does he want to sell them? Surely in today's market it would make more sense to hold on to them until the economy improves."

She was silent for a moment, allowing doubt to tiptoe across my scalp.

"He's eager to repay your generous loans to the trust, because we're aware how deep you had to dig into your own personal accounts to pay for a few recent repairs. He's liquidated some of the trust's assets, but unfortunately the market value today isn't all he had hoped. He's waiting for a better opportunity to liquidate more, but in the meantime was hoping the paintings could be a welcome windfall that would enable him to pay you back and also give us a little more time."

I kept my expression neutral as I tried to tamp down my own worries. Without a steady income due to my leave of absence from my job, my own accounts were getting low enough that I'd started to worry about how I was going to make ends meet if I didn't sell another house within the next six months. "I have enough art on the walls. Just tell Dad to do what he needs to do. If it gets serious enough, then we can have the Trenholms appraise some of the stuff hanging on the walls, too."

My mother's eyes met mine as if she'd also felt the chilling breeze that had rushed through the room.

She lifted the wooden box and placed it on her lap. "We found Louisa's trunk—where you and Jack discovered her camera and albums. It's also where I saw this—under an old gramophone." She lifted the lid of the box and placed it on the bed beside her.

Reaching inside, she pulled out a silver frame, tarnished to a deep smudge of black. "I'm thinking these belonged to her, but they didn't make it into her scrapbooks because they were in frames. Maybe her husband boxed these up after she disappeared, in an attempt to forget her."

I sat up, remembering my conversation with Yvonne about nesting before a baby is born. "Louisa donated one of the cradles and a bunch of useless papers around the time Nevin was born in 1922. I'm surprised she didn't clean up the rest of the attic. Like that buffalo. Yvonne found references to a hunting trip to Montana in the eighteen eighties, which is where we assumed it came from, so it would definitely have been here when Louisa was doing her cleanup."

"Her baby might have arrived before she finished," my mother suggested.

I barely heard her, I was so preoccupied with my own thoughts. "But why would she just donate the one cradle? She was a Charlestonian and had probably seen the Vanderhorst family tree with all the twins hanging from it. Well, at least until William. According to the family tree, at least, he was an only child, as was his son. But I wouldn't think that would be enough to convince her that she wouldn't have twins in her first pregnancy or any other pregnancies."

My mother was thoughtful for a moment. "Louisa was a Gibbes. Maybe she figured that since her husband hadn't married a cousin they probably wouldn't have twins."

"Or maybe she knew something that we don't. Maybe she found something in the attic while she was cleaning it up. That would explain why she stopped before she'd finished."

Mother began pressing her thumbs into the tarnish on the frame, revealing the silver underneath. If only uncovering the truths hidden in this house could be so easy. With her voice barely louder than a whisper, she said, "The roses are back."

"Louisa?"

She nodded.

The stab of disappointment I'd begun to feel each time I was reminded of my extrasensory loss hurt a little more this time. As I neared my due date, I wanted to know that Louisa was close by. She was the only spirit in the house who seemed to do more than just watch and wait. And I couldn't help but wonder whether it was the sound of Nevin's baby feet I heard racing down the halls each night as I drifted off to sleep.

Eager to shake my sadness, I indicated the frame and said, "What did you find?"

She turned the frame so that I could see the old black-and-white photo inside it. "I think it's an early print made from taking a photograph of a painting of two babies. If you look closely enough, you can see the canvas markings."

I plucked my reading glasses off of my night table—my increasing girth and a wardrobe consisting mostly of nightgowns had made me decidedly less vain in the past months—and stuck them on my nose.

Her gloved finger tapped on the glass. "Whoever took the photograph and put it in the frame wrote on the back—John and Henry. And they're wearing matching christening gowns."

I nodded. "The gowns are identical—and just like the one I found in the package that showed up on my doorstep. The bonnets are the same as well." I studied the round babies' faces, my finger slowly moving across the glass as if something in the shape of the eyes or curve of a chin could tell me what I needed to know.

My mother reached back into the box and pulled out another tarnished frame. "I think this must be baby Nevin. He looks so much like the little boy at the piano you have in the photograph downstairs. It appears to be the right time period, too."

"Yes," I said, nodding vaguely, my attention focused on the christening gown the baby wore. "Can you take it out of the frame?"

She shook her head. "I tried. It's stuck to the glass and I don't want to damage the photograph. But I did look on the back, and there's nothing written on it." She handed the frame to me and I took it.

After examining it closely, I lifted my gaze. "This gown and bonnet definitely match those worn by John and Henry. I could pull the one from the package to compare, but I'm positive it's identical."

"But if one of the gowns was in the foundation, and the other was sent up north with Cornelius in 1860, why is Nevin wearing one, too?"

"Because," I said slowly, remembering standing next to Yvonne while she pulled out an old sales slip from the archives, "a third gown and bonnet set was made by the Susan Bivens shop—the same store that had made the original two—in 1860. I saw the invoice. It was commissioned by a C. Vanderhorst."

I slid the glasses from my nose and began cleaning them with the edge of my sheet as I considered the box. "Is there anything else in there?"

My mother shook her head. "Just those two photographs in frames."

"Which makes me believe they were selected on purpose instead of randomly gathered by Louisa's husband and tucked away. It almost seems like they were hidden."

"But why?" she asked, her eyes wide. "And by whom?"

Our heads swiveled toward the bathroom door and the sound of the water being pumped through the fixtures at full force.

"What . . . ?" My mother stood and began walking toward the bathroom door just as it slammed shut, shaking the frame.

She stared at the closed door while the water continued to run, both of us unsure what to do. My first thought was that I hoped the tub and sink weren't stoppered, because that would mean an overflow of water and a leaky ceiling below that I couldn't afford to fix. I shook myself, wondering when I'd become Sophie.

My mother's head was bent, her eyes closed, as if she were listening closely.

"What is it?" I asked.

She raised her finger to her lips. "I smell roses," she said quietly. "But she's not alone."

We faced the door again as it unlatched and then slowly opened, a billow of steam escaping through the doorway like an expelled breath.

"Wait," I said, rolling carefully out of bed.

She held up her hand. "Don't come yet. I think they're gone, but I want to make sure."

I nodded, my hands resting on my belly, watching as my mother entered the bathroom. I felt a small twinge in my abdomen, stronger than one of the kicks I'd grown used to. I waited for a moment to catch my breath, listening as my mother moved around the bathroom.

"Louisa was here," she said from inside the bathroom. "But the other one was, too. I got the impression that they were arguing. I don't know about what." She paused, and when she spoke again, the tone of her voice had risen. "Mellie? I think you need to come in here."

Walking as quickly as I could, I stepped into the steamy bathroom, finding it hard for a moment to catch my breath as another twinge squeezed me from the inside. My mother took my arm and led me to the long marble vanity, then pointed at the mirror above it.

There, written by what appeared to be a narrow finger, somebody had rubbed out the steam on the mirror to write a single word: *Mine.*

I opened my mouth to say something, but was distracted by the feel of water beneath my bare feet. "Oh, no. They flooded the bathroom."

Instead of rushing to the tub or sink to pull out the stops, my mother stepped forward and lifted my nightgown. "I don't think so, Mellie." She dropped the hem and gave me a wobbly smile. "But I do think you're about to have your babies."

CHAPTER 27

I sat in the back of the van with my mother while Jack drove very, very slowly through the streets of Charleston, although he claimed he was speeding. My father and Nola were in his car behind us as my dad flashed his lights and honked his horn like an emergency vehicle. I could only hope that he wouldn't be stopped by the actual police for reckless driving.

Despite the constant pains that were now about five minutes apart, I was still in denial that I was in labor. "It's not March twenty-third," I continued to insist to both my mother and Jack, until they both pretended to be hard of hearing.

"It's too early," I insisted, trying a new tack. "The babies are too small."

My mother sent me a dubious look. "At your last visit with Dr. Wise, she said she thought the babies were well over six pounds. You were six pounds, four ounces when you were born, and you turned out just fine."

She and Jack exchanged a glance in the rearview mirror that I had to ignore because another pain gripped me. When it was finished, I gasped out, "Where's my phone? I need to change my nail appointments, and . . ." I stopped as another thought occurred to me. "Did you call Dr. Wise to tell her to have the epidural ready as soon as we hit the parking lot?"

My mother clasped my hands in hers. "She'll have to examine you first. You might be completely dilated when we get there, which means there won't be time for an epidural. These babies are calling the shots right now and we just have to go with it."

I shot a malevolent look toward Jack. "They got their bossiness from their father. He's always wanting to call the shots."

"What? *I'm* the one calling the shots? What planet have you been living on for the last two years, Mellie?"

I was prevented from answering by another stabbing pain. My mother glanced at her watch. "They're coming a little closer together now," she said calmly. "Don't worry; we're almost there."

I pressed my head against the back of my seat. "I'm not ready! My calendar is full of things I need to take care of before the babies get here. I still need to organize their little sock drawer—have you seen how many they have, and how tiny? And I hadn't decided which toy organizing system to order—the catalogs are still in the basket by my bed." I closed my eyes. "And preschools! I'm still collecting all the brochures. How will I ever get it all done?"

My mother squeezed my hands. "Mellie, you are not alone, all right? You have lots of family here to help. And what doesn't get done? Well, I think you're about to find out the hard way that some-times you just have to let it go. You might even find that you'll enjoy the ride."

I stared at her in panic as another pain gripped me, worse than any of the ones before. I looked at the back of Jack's head. "Hurry," I said in a gasp. "I don't want to give birth in a minivan!"

I wasn't sure whether it was my imagination, but I thought I heard the engine race as the van jumped forward. I sat up, another thought sending me into a near panic. "We haven't even settled on names!"

"We have," Jack corrected me. "Two girl names and two boy names. You wrote them down on a notepad and stuck it in my glove box just in case."

I shook my head. "No—their last name. We haven't even talked about it."

"Yes, we did," he said steadily. "Right after you told me you were pregnant."

My hands tightened over my belly at the approach of another contraction. "We weren't talking about names then. . . ." I forgot what I'd been about to say as I felt my muscles tighten again.

The contraction hit like a fist from the inside, taking all of my breath.

My mother kept her voice soft as she patted my hand. "Keep breathing, Mellie. That will help. Like this." She began panting like General Lee after a long walk on a hot summer afternoon, but without the lolling tongue.

The contraction subsided and I stared at her. "What are you doing?"

"It's Lamaze breathing. I've seen it enough on televisions that I thought—"

"Please stop. I appreciate it; I do—but you look ridiculous and it's not helping."

I shifted in my seat, trying to get more comfortable, before I realized that there really weren't any options at this point. I held the seat belt strap away from my neck—that was the only place it would fit, since it wouldn't stretch over my belly—then glared at the back of Jack's head.

"What did you mean that we talked about the babies' last names? I don't rememb—" I stopped, remembering.

He completed my thought out loud. "When I asked you to marry me and you said no. That would have settled it."

My eyes stung, and I told myself it was from the labor pains. "But that's why I said no. I didn't want you to marry me only because you felt obligated to do the right thing."

"That's what you thought? Do you actually believe—" he began, but was cut off by a bloodcurdling scream that seemed to be coming out of my mouth.

The contraction this time was longer, the pain sharper, my scream higher-pitched. As I came through the other side of it, my mother gave me a reassuring pat. "At least that means you're breathing."

"What else was I supposed to think?" I screamed at Jack, my voice raw. "I'd already told you how I felt, and all you could say was, 'I'm sorry.' So what was I supposed to think when all of a sudden you ask me to marry you right after you found out that I was pregnant?"

I heard a screech of tires as Jack made a sharp turn into the hospital parking lot before the van came to an abrupt stop at the emergency entrance. My dad's car drove past, still honking and blinking the lights, toward the visitor parking lot. Jack hopped out, then slid open the back panel where I was sitting. He leaned in and unbuckled my seat belt, but didn't step back.

"Do you still love me?" he asked.

The skin over my belly tightened while both sets of little arms and legs seemed to start pummeling me from the inside, demanding an answer.

"Yes," I gasped out as another contraction hit, taking with it my powers of dissembling along with my ability to evade difficult questions.

He rubbed my arm as I began to scream, waiting patiently until I'd stopped. "Good," he said, stroking my cheek. "That will make this a whole lot easier. I'm going to ask you again, but I promise it will be the last time. I'm not good with rejection. As a matter of fact, until I'd met you I hadn't had that much experience with it."

I felt the perspiration dotting my skin, making my hair cling to my face, a pair of maternity sweatpants and a trapeze top in tie-dye—a gift from Sophie that I'd hidden until my mother discovered it when trying to dress me for the trip to the hospital—draped over my voluminous body. I felt like a character from the bar scene in the original *Star Wars* movie, without benefit of cool weaponry. In none of my schoolgirl fantasies had I ever imagined this scenario when daydreaming about a marriage proposal.

His face was very close to mine, his eyes bluer than I remembered. "Mellie—will you marry me?"

My mother appeared behind him on the sidewalk. "Jack, shouldn't you wait until she has regained all of her mental faculties?"

"Absolutely not," he said, his eyes not leaving mine. "I want her to make a decision using her heart for once instead of her head."

I listened to my grandmother's voice, very distant and very small, but crystal clear. *You need to decide sooner rather than later what you want.*

And then be ready to fight for it. Despite months of denial, it suddenly become very clear what it was that I wanted, and what I needed to do.

The next contraction began creeping closer, starting in my back this time before sweeping forward. "Yes," I whispered, and then, "Yes," I screamed as the contraction hit, just in case he hadn't heard me the first time.

"Good," he said after it had passed, kissing me gently on the lips and wiping away the hair that was clinging to my forehead. "I know a probate court judge who can be at the hospital within the hour so we can get our license, and I'll put in a call to the minister at my parents' church. He's a big fan of mine, and I'll promise to put him in a book. We'll have a real wedding later—if that's what you want."

He slid his arms underneath me and lifted me out of the van before carrying me into the reception area of the hospital.

"Jack?"

He stopped walking, his expression worried. "Yes?"

"I'm going to need your help to keep my house. I can't let it go without a fight."

"I can't wait," he said, placing me in a wheelchair that had been brought by a nurse. "We make a good team, Mellie. We always have."

The nurse began to wheel me toward labor and delivery while Jack jogged along beside me. I turned toward him, wanting to ask one last question about half-remembered words spoken before I'd been taken away in the ambulance from Maddie's Christmas play. But another contraction gripped me, the worst one yet, making me feel as if I'd just been knocked into next week by a three-hundred-pound linebacker.

The pain consumed me, altering my reality, and any claim I might have once possessed to sobriety and gentility disintegrated completely. I tilted my head back like a shrieking hyena and screamed out what every laboring woman since Eve has at least thought about the man who'd put her in that predicament: "This is all your fault, Jack Trenholm! I hate you!"

Both Jack and the nurse looked nonplussed. She turned to Jack as she backed us into an elevator. "Don't pay any attention. They all say that."

"Good to know," he said, taking my hand and squeezing as the elevator doors closed.

Just slightly more than twenty-four hours later, I was sitting up in my hospital bed with two bassinets beside me, one with a pink blanket and the other with a blue one. The boy, JJ—for Jack Junior—had already outdone his sister in size, weight, enthusiasm for breast-feeding, and ability to perform amazing sleep marathons. The only time he wasn't sleeping was when he was eating. I had been more than a little alarmed when Amelia told me that Jack had been the same way.

Sarah Ginnette—named after my grandmother and mother—was smaller by eight ounces and one and a half inches, with a strong chin and a delicate nose. The only thing the twins seemed to share besides their last name and birthday was their identical heads of thick, black hair and deep blue eyes. Although the nurses kept reminding us that all babies had blue eyes, I was confident that they would look just like their father's and half sister's. Jack's DNA was most likely as persistent as he was.

Despite feeling like I'd been run over by a tractor-trailer twice, I felt startlingly content every time I looked at their tiny precious faces, or counted their adorable fingers and toes, and I was already looking back at my labor and delivery through a hazy fuzz. Jack had been with me the whole time, coaching me as if he knew what he was doing. I had a slight memory of shouting things at him that made one of the nurses blush, but I was happy not to remember it too clearly.

He had turned green around the mouth at one point and had to briefly sit down, but he'd never once let go of my hand, even when the judge and minister came into the room to ensure that our children weren't born out of wedlock. I considered the possibility that Jack couldn't let go of my hand because I'd squeezed too tightly and broken all of his fingers when I learned that it was too late for an epidural, but I quickly dismissed the thought.

Still, even though we had the papers to prove it, I didn't feel married. He'd promised me a church wedding later, the kind I'd once dreamed about as a little girl walking around in my mother's shoes and grandmother's jewelry, but I was unsure whether even that would solidify our relationship as husband and wife. I'd told him that I loved him, and then he'd asked me to marry him—again—and I'd said yes. But there was one important element missing from that scenario, yet I hesitated to bring it up for fear that I might not like the answer. If I was to walk down a long center aisle toward a minister while wearing white and my grandmother's pearls, I needed to hear those three little words. So far we'd done everything in our relationship backward, and I allowed myself to hope that there was still more to come.

I looked up at the sound of gentle tapping on my door and smiled when I saw Detective Riley hanging back in the doorway with a huge bouquet of yellow roses.

"It is visiting hours, right? I thought you'd have a crowd."

"Jack's parents just left, and my parents, Jack, and Nola went home to shower and change and put the car seats in the van before coming back for us."

"They don't keep you very long at the hospital, do they?"

I shook my head. "I'm lucky to be here this long. Dr. Wise wanted to make sure that all of my preeclampsia symptoms were gone before she'd release me."

He walked across the room to place the roses on the table by the window that was already crowded with bouquets of balloons and flowers from family and friends. "News travels fast," he said, indicating my collection.

"Charleston might be a city, but it's a small town, too."

"That's for sure," he said, stopping by the bassinets. He was silent for a moment as he studied the babies. "Not that I'm surprised, but those are probably two of the prettiest babies I've ever seen. And with my family, I've seen a bunch."

I grinned. "Thank you, but I can't take any credit. I seem to have been an incubator for their father's clones."

He chuckled as he pulled up a bright yellow metal-and-plastic chair and sat down next to my bed. "Don't sell yourself short, Melanie. You're not hurting in the looks department, either."

Blushing, I swatted a hand at him. "Detective Riley, you have inherited the Irish gift of blarney. But thank you. I haven't seen a mirror yet, but knowing what I've gone through in the last twenty-four hours, I can only imagine what I look like."

The expression on his face told me that he didn't see anything lacking, and I blushed again.

He cleared his throat. "So, I hear you're married."

"Wow, I knew news traveled fast here, but I didn't know it was supersonic. How did you find out?"

"I'm a detective, remember?" He gave me a self-deprecating smile. "I also have a cousin who works downstairs in reception. She owed me a favor."

"Yes, Jack and I are legally married. We both decided last-minute that it was the right thing to do—for the children. It was all sort of . . . sudden."

He leaned back in his chair, stretching out his long legs. "Oh, I wouldn't say that. I'd even say that it's been a long time coming."

I opened my mouth to argue, but he cut me off. "Even a blind man could see that you two were meant to be together. I tried to fool myself that maybe I was wrong, but I knew. Can't blame a man for trying, though."

"Oh, Thomas. You've been such a great friend to me—and a wonderful companion during my whole pregnancy, not to mention the fact that I now know how to make the best omelet on the planet because of you. You made me feel pretty and desirable when I felt anything but, and you didn't point and laugh when I told you I could see dead people."

"Point and laugh?"

"You know—what the mean kids at school do to kids who are a little different."

He grinned. "I already told you—you're quirky. And I happen to like quirky."

"Well," I said, clasping my hands on top of the blanket, "I guess what I'm trying to say is that I treasure your friendship, and I don't want it to end."

"Thank you, Melanie. That means a lot to me." He leaned forward, his elbows on his knees. "Is it back yet—your sixth sense? Because if you're still interested, I'd love your help with some of my cold cases."

I shook my head. "Not yet. My mother's came back right away, but mine seems to be taking its time. I guess it's a good thing, since I'm in the hospital. They're like cemeteries—somebody's always wanting something."

"Sounds like fun."

"I used to not think so, but I miss it now. It's funny, isn't it, how we don't always know what we want until we think we've lost it?"

His smile was sad. "Yep. I know exactly what you mean." His face became serious. "I actually had a piece of business to share with you, but it can wait if you'd prefer."

I sat up. "If it's about the DNA tests, I'd like to know now."

He nodded. "I heard from the coroner's office that the final reports should be ready in the next couple of weeks. I wanted to give you the heads-up so you can make sure your lawyer is available, just in case."

Our eyes met. He didn't need to elaborate.

He stood, then leaned over to kiss me on the cheek. "Congratulations, Melanie. I'm happy for you. For both of you."

"Thank you, Thomas. You'll make a great husband and father one day."

"I hope so. But what are my chances of finding another beautiful woman with a quirky talent? Hey—what about your cousin Rebecca? Is she single?"

I almost choked. "Thomas—I said I liked you. I couldn't do that to you. Besides, she's engaged."

He grinned. "It was worth a try. I'll keep looking. And let me know if your sixth sense comes back. Not just because I need your help, but because I know how important it is to you."

"I will—promise."

We said good-bye and he left. I lay back against my pillows, listening to the soft breathing of my babies and thinking about Thomas's words, wondering why it had taken me an entire lifetime to know that he was right.

CHAPTER 28

I awoke to the sound of a crying baby, jerking me out of a dream where I was on the swing in the garden and there were three empty cradles in front of me with the Louisa roses blooming from one of them.

I sat up, my left hand moving instinctively toward my abdomen. As usual, I was surprised to find it smaller—although not down to its prepregnancy size—as well as to feel the weight of Jack's grandmother's platinum wedding ring on my third finger. The twins had been home for more than two weeks, yet I still awoke each time with utter surprise and astonishment that this was my life.

Despite our new status as man and wife and parents, my relationship with Jack remained difficult to qualify, our emotions like a riptide under soft waves. But there was something about sleeping in the same bed with him, with our children nearby, that anchored whatever had been loose inside of me since I was a little girl. For now, as I was still recovering from my pregnancy and childbirth, it was enough.

"Mellie? What is it?" Jack's voice wasn't heavy with sleep, as if he'd been lying awake with his own thoughts.

"I heard a baby crying."

He looked over the side of the bed where the two cradles my father had made rested next to each other. In the glow of the night-light, which was shaped like a crescent moon with a cow perpetually leaping over it, we could see the outlines of the babies sleeping on their backs, as we'd been instructed by our new pediatrician.

"It's not one of ours," I whispered.

General Lee, in his new sleeping spot between the cradles, lifted his head as if to tell me that all was well before resting it again on his outstretched paws. With a sigh, I settled back against Jack, resigned to yet another sleepless night.

Jack stroked my hair. "Go to sleep, Mellie. I'll get up with the babies when they awaken and do diaper duty."

"Are you going to breast-feed them, too?" I squinted at my new digital clock with bigger, glowing numbers I could read at all hours of the night. A necessity for breast-feeding mothers. "They'll need to eat soon, so I'm just going to stay awake. It's easier than being jerked out of a sound sleep again."

He yawned. "I never thought it was possible to be this bushed. Babies should come with a warning label. Not that I would have been deterred, of course."

Despite myself, I felt my eyelids beginning to droop. "It would have been helpful if they at least came with some kind of regular internal clock. JJ's a champion eater and wants to eat all the time, but Sarah chooses her eating times at random. It's exhausting."

A soft cooing came from one of the cradles, and I smiled through my sleepiness at the sweet sound. "That's Sarah. She's always singing to herself. Maybe she'll be a famous opera singer like her grandmother."

"Umm," Jack mumbled, already almost asleep.

I began to drift off myself, only to have my eyes shoot open again. I grabbed his arm. "Jack? Do you smell that?"

Half-asleep, he was already taking the covers off. "I'll change them."

I held him back. "No. Roses. I smell roses."

He turned back to me, and I could hear his smile in his voice. "It's come back. Your gift is back."

"At least part of it. I still don't know if I can see them yet."

We both sat up against the headboard, our gazes focused on the cradle where Sarah lay kicking her tiny hands and feet beneath her pink blanket, her newborn gaze riveted on movement above her. The night-light dimmed, as if something translucent had passed between me and her cradle. I focused harder, my gaze traveling to the spot where Sarah was looking, sucking in my breath when I realized I was staring at the shadowed outline of a woman wearing a rose in her blunt-cut hair.

"Louisa?" I whispered.

As soon as the word was out of my mouth, she vanished, making me wonder whether she'd even been there at all.

"Why is she here?" Jack asked, both of us on alert as Sarah began to quiet now that her entertainment had been taken away.

"Because she thinks we still need her." I slid from the bed and reswaddled Sarah in her pink blanket, wondering how it had all become untucked.

I felt Jack's eyes on me in the darkness. "Because of everything still being so unsettled?"

Because I'm still not sure how you really feel about me. "Yes. Because of the house. We're all in limbo right now, and the other ghost is still trying to stake her claim." I waved my hand in the direction of the bathroom, where, despite my scrubbing with various cleaning products, the word "Mine" still showed up every time hot water was used.

"Do you think Sarah might have inherited more than her singing voice from your mother?"

My eyes widened in alarm. "It does run in our family through the females, so it's a possibility, I guess." I continued to stare into the darkness, not sure how I felt about it. "But JJ's such a sound sleeper; he could be seeing them, too, if he were ever awake longer than it takes to fill his tank with milk."

My phone alarm buzzed on my nightstand and I picked it up to silence it. "It's time to feed them."

Jack leaned over the side of the bed to get a better view of the babies. "But they're both sound asleep."

"I know. But I'm trying to get them on a feeding schedule, and in the first few weeks it should be every four hours. I read that in one of the parenting books you bought for me."

"But they're sleeping," he repeated, emphasizing the last word in case I hadn't understood it the first time. "Besides, I think the every-four-hours schedule is for bottle-fed babies. Breast-fed babies are supposed to eat on demand."

"How am I supposed to get them on any kind of schedule if I feed them whenever they want—which is never at the same time for both of them?"

He massaged the back of my neck with strong fingers, making me almost forget what we were discussing. I leaned toward him, waiting for him to speak, waiting for him to tell me what I was so desperate to hear. But when he finally said something, my shoulders slumped. "They're only two weeks old, Mellie. I don't think the fact that they're not on a schedule yet will mean they won't get into college. Besides, there's just something inherently wrong about waking a sleeping baby."

Still weighing my options, I looked down at my phone and saw that I had two text messages that had arrived the previous evening and gone unnoticed. Nobody called me anymore, as if they were afraid they'd wake me up, or the babies—which was a near impossibility, seeing as it was next to hopeless to awaken JJ, Sarah was too content to be disturbed by the sound of a ringing phone, and I was never asleep anyway.

"I have texts from both Yvonne and Detective Riley."

Jack moved up behind me to see. "What does Yvonne say?"

I handed the phone to him. "I can't read those tiny letters."

"I told you to go into settings and change the font size. Do you want me to do it for you?"

I set my chin, making me think of my little Sarah when she didn't feel like eating. "I'm perfectly capable of changing my settings. I just prefer not to."

He pressed his lips against the back of my neck, reminding every single nerve ending in my body that I was still a woman and that his effect on me had not changed, despite the fact that I was only two weeks postpartum. "You're so cute when you're being vain, Mellie. But you look adorable in your glasses, too."

"Just read the text, please."

He took the phone from me. "You know, they say that your eyesight goes downhill once you hit forty. I'm glad I've still got a couple years to go."

I elbowed him, but his quick reflexes saved his abdomen from a bruising. "Read," I repeated.

He was silent for a moment as he read the screen. "This is amazing."

"What is?"

"That Yvonne can text so well. There's not a single mistake."

"Jack, please! What did she say?"

"That she's found information on Charlotte Pringle and to call her when you get her message. I'm assuming she thought you'd get the message before three o'clock in the morning."

"Great—now I definitely won't be able to sleep, because I'm too excited to hear what she found. What about Thomas—what does he say?"

He read the screen in silence, then slowly lowered the phone. I felt his eyes on me, but he didn't say anything.

"Jack, what is it?"

"He has the DNA report, and he can bring it by tomorrow. Give him a call first thing to let him know what time." He paused. "He said you'll want your lawyer here, too."

"No," I said, unaware that I'd spoken out loud until Jack's arms came around me, taking away some of my anxiety.

He spoke softly into my ear. "We're a team, remember? And whatever happens, we'll face it together."

My heart contracted and then expanded, as if absorbing grief and happiness simultaneously had left it confused.

I nodded against his chest, where I stayed until we both became aware of Sarah cooing again as the scent of roses drifted from the floor to the tall ceilings, reminding us that there were more than just two players on our team.

CHAPTER 29

Thomas rang the doorbell promptly at nine o'clock the following morning, my lawyer arriving behind him as I opened the door.

Thomas greeted me with a kiss on the cheek. "Melanie—you look wonderful!"

"You're only saying that because you've never seen me with a waist before. And I'm wearing under-eye concealer. Otherwise you might be leaping off the piazza into traffic, screaming that you've seen a ghost."

He winked at my reference to spirits, then walked into the house as I greeted my lawyer. Sterling Zerbe was a tall man in his mid to late forties, with prematurely white hair and the build of a former football player—which my dad said he was. Despite their age difference, he and my father had bonded over their love of their home city of Charleston while stationed with the army in Germany.

He kissed me on the cheek. "When do I get to meet the babies?" he asked.

"They're sleeping right now, but I can pretty much guarantee that one of them will awaken within the hour, if only because on the schedule I've made for them they're not supposed to want to eat for another three."

He gave me a confused smile and a nod before walking into the foyer.

Jack shook hands with both men, then led them into the parlor, where Mrs. Houlihan had set out coffee and doughnuts. I noticed a separate tray set next to the baby monitor and apparently meant for the breast-feeding mother among us. It contained a tall crystal glass of water with fresh lemon and an unappetizing bran muffin. Next to the doughnuts, it stood out like Cinderella with her ugly stepsisters. Thanks to Jack Junior and his voracious eating habits, I could eat as many calories as I liked. Unfortunately, those calories had to come from sources that were scrutinized and approved by my personal food-police squad.

As soon as Thomas sat down, he reached for one of the doughnuts and took a bite. He chewed slowly, his eyes closed. "These have to be from Glazed Gourmet on King Street. Best doughnuts on the planet. And believe me—I'm a policeman, so I know doughnuts."

"Naturally," said Jack, ignoring the sweet pastries and going right for the coffee.

I closed my eyes and sniffed the coffee, remembering what it had once been like to drink large quantities of caffeine without anybody complaining. I picked up my muffin and bit into it, staring at the doughnuts while I chewed, and trying to pretend I was eating something other than sand. It didn't work.

"So," Thomas said, wiping crumbs from his mouth with a napkin. "Let's get down to business, shall we?"

Sterling and I each pulled out notebooks and pens, while Thomas reached into the briefcase he'd brought with him. Jack sat back with a fresh cup of coffee and crossed an ankle over the opposite knee.

Thomas moved aside plates and cups and spread a few papers on the coffee table in front of him. "I spent a lot of time talking with a DNA expert to make sure I understood it all enough to be able to explain it without a lot of scientific mumbo jumbo."

He looked up and smiled at me, but it did nothing to reassure me. I sat on the edge of my seat, my pen in hand, fighting the urge to start making a plan-of-action spreadsheet. It was hard not being in control of this situation, the feeling bringing me back to that place I'd been as a young girl, when I'd awakened to find my mother gone.

Thomas continued. "I'm just going to lay it all out and explain what is in the report, and then open it up for questions. Anything I can't answer, I promise to find the answer for you. So," he said, clamping his hands down on his knees as if he were a teacher getting ready for story time. "They were able to confirm their original finding that the skeletal remains were those of a male. This meant that they were able to compare the Y chromosome in the DNA of the remains to those of Mr. Vanderhorst and Mr. Gilbert." He paused, his gaze sliding to me. "There was a match." He cleared his throat. "That means that all three males were related on their paternal side."

My eyes met Jack's briefly before I turned back to Thomas. "So Nevin Vanderhorst and George Gilbert are related. And so is the baby found in the foundation."

"Yes, it would appear so. An analysis of the christening gown and bonnet found with the remains estimates that they were made near the beginning of the eighteenth century, while the actual remains are approximately fifty years younger, sometime in the mid-to-late– eighteen hundreds range. In addition, an examination of the skull revealed that the anterior fontanel had not been closed, indicating that the baby was less than two years old at the time of death, with further skeletal examination showing that it was most likely a newborn."

A heavy stone seemed to lodge itself in the middle of my chest. "So it's probable that what Bridget Monahan Gilbert said is true." I hesitated, wanting to make sure that my voice was strong when I spoke again. "That William had a twin brother, Cornelius, who was taken up north and raised by another family. And that George Gilbert is one of his descendants. A Vanderhorst heir." I looked at Sterling Zerbe, who was busily scratching notes on his notepad.

He stopped writing and looked at me, his expression grave. "That's certainly the most plausible explanation one can conclude from the scientific evidence, and most likely the angle the Gilberts will be taking if they take their case to court. I have to admit, the evidence is pretty compelling, but that doesn't mean you don't have an argument. The house belonged to Mr. Vanderhorst and he left it to you in his will. There is no clear-cut winner or loser here." Turning back to Thomas, he asked, "Is there anything else?"

"Oh, yes. And here's where it gets interesting. They were also able to extract mitochondrial DNA from the skeletal remains as well as from Mr. Vanderhorst—that's the DNA that's passed down on the maternal side. There was no mitochondrial match between Mr. Vanderhorst and the remains—meaning their relationship is only on the paternal side. We also compared it to Mr. Gilbert's."

"And?" I asked, my voice sounding much stronger than I felt.

"His mitochondrial DNA matched that found in the remains, but not Mr. Vanderhorst's."

I put my pen down and rubbed my hands over my tired eyes, wondering whether it was the lack of sleep that was making all of this so hard to comprehend. "So what does all of this *mean?*"

Thomas slid a piece of paper in my direction, then turned it around so it was facing me. It was a chart with three boxes at the top. The first was labeled with the single word *remains*, the second one *Nevin Vanderhorst*, and the third *George/Cornelius*, with arrows connecting the boxes drawn in two different colors. The color scheme was explained at the bottom, with little colored squares indicating that red was mitochondrial DNA and yellow the Y chromosome. It was like something I might have drawn if I'd understood half of what Thomas had just told us.

Despite the churning in my stomach, I couldn't help but smile at him and wonder whether maybe we should have our DNA tested to see whether we might have somehow been separated at birth.

I placed my index finger on the chart—the nail unvarnished and clipped short so that I wouldn't scratch delicate skin when changing diapers—and followed the red and yellow lines that led from the *remains*-labeled box to the one labeled *Cornelius*. "So these two are connected on both their mother's and father's side. We also know that Cornelius was born in 1860, and the remains are approximately from that time period, too. Meaning they could be full brothers."

Jack moved to sit beside me, placing one hand on my back while the other traced the yellow line that connected all three of the boxes. "And all three of these are related on their father's side."

Thomas nodded. "That's correct."

My brain felt as if it had been tied in a knot, but I could feel the strings suddenly loosening. "So they couldn't have been triplets," I said.

Sterling continued to write in his pad as Thomas leaned over to study the chart again. "No—because only two of them are related on the mother's side. One scenario that I came up with that might explain this would be that perhaps there was a pair of twins born at about the same time as a single birth—from the same father, but with two separate mothers."

I thought for a moment. "But wouldn't the DNA be able to tell us there were twins?"

"Not if they were fraternal. Fraternal twins have their own DNA, just as if they were regular full siblings."

The soft sound of a baby's cries undulated in the air around me like ripples on a still lake, but it wasn't coming from the baby monitor. "Do you hear that?" I asked softly, turning toward Jack. "It's a baby crying."

"No," he answered. "One of ours?"

I shook my head, belatedly realizing that both Thomas and Sterling had been listening to our exchange. For Sterling's benefit, I said, "I think we might have a stray kitten that comes to our garden and cries. Sounds just like a baby."

He nodded, then went back to his note making, but Thomas sat back in his chair, understanding dawning on his face.

My phone that I'd placed on the coffee table rang and I looked down at the screen. "It's Yvonne. I haven't had a chance to call her. Hang on a second and I'll tell her I'll call her back when we're through here."

Jack put his hand on my arm. "No. I think you should take it. It's about the Vanderhorsts and might further explain what's going on."

I nodded, then quickly excused myself and walked into the foyer.

"Hi, Yvonne. I got your text too early this morning to call you, and I haven't had a chance yet."

"And I know how busy you are with those little ones, but I'm too excited to keep this information all to myself. I think I just might explode if I can't tell someone right now. I promise it will only take a minute."

I pictured her pearls, reading glasses, and sensible pumps being flung against the walls and ceiling of the Fireproof Building and stifled a grin. "I wouldn't want that to happen. And this is actually perfect timing. We were just talking about various members of the Vanderhorst family tree, so I hope you might have information to add to the discussion."

Something like fear and adrenaline braided together before racing through my veins, filling me with an odd mixture of dread and hope. "Go ahead, Yvonne. I'm listening."

I could almost imagine her clapping her hands together. "It's been driving me crazy that I couldn't find the maiden name of John Vanderhorst's second wife, Charlotte, to verify that she was Charlotte Pringle, Camille's friend and honeymoon companion. It occurred to me two days ago that I was looking at the question in the wrong way. As Jack once told me, sometimes you have to turn the question upside down and attack it that way. So that's what I did."

I stole a glance into the parlor, where the men had refilled their coffees. "I have no idea what that means, Yvonne. So what did you find?"

She continued as if I hadn't said anything. "When I couldn't find anything as far as a wedding announcement or invitation anywhere in the archives, I thought I'd have to disappoint you and tell you I came up empty-handed. Of course, with John marrying so soon after his first wife's death, it could have been a very private affair and therefore not broadcast in the papers. It was also the beginning of the Civil War, and most of the news was, of course, about that. I'd like to take credit for this next tidbit, but I actually came across it by accident when looking for a wedding announcement. It was an invitation to a meeting of the Ladies' Auxiliary Club to discuss their making bandages for the 'glorious cause.'" She paused for effect. "At the home of Charlotte Pringle Vanderhorst at fifty-five Tradd Street."

My mouth went dry. "So it is the same Charlotte. Which means she married her best friend's husband a year after the friend died."

"Yes. But as I mentioned before, that wasn't so unusual back then. But there's more unusual information about Charlotte Pringle Vanderhorst that you will understand after I tell you why I just had to call you."

I could almost see her bouncing with delight. "I then needed to find out if there was a connection between Charlotte and Dr. Pringle. It was too much of a coincidence that Camille's best friend would have the same last name as her doctor. So I turned the question upside down and it became clear to me where I had to look. I realized that if Charlotte and Camille were good enough friends to share a honeymoon, surely Charlotte would have been in Camille's wedding. I felt silly for not thinking of it before! John was a Vanderhorst, so of course it would have been a huge society wedding, with some sort of announcement in the paper. And there it was! A wedding announcement in the newspaper for Camille and John. They listed the maid of honor as Miss Charlotte Pringle, daughter of a Dr. and Mrs. Robert M. Pringle."

I felt somebody watching me, and I turned around to face the parlor again, but the three men were still drinking coffee and talking, paying no attention to me. "And then what?" I said, watching my breath float up toward the ceiling.

"Well, I knew you'd be asking me if it was the same Dr. Pringle who'd signed Camille's death certificate. So I dived back into the archives, this time searching for anything I could find regarding the South Carolina State Hospital in the eighteen fifties and sixties."

She fell silent again, so I immediately asked, "And what did you find?" I closed my eyes, hoping she'd speak quickly as pinpricks of fear tiptoed across my scalp.

"A book. Written by one of the asylum's doctors, in which there is a brief passage regarding Dr. Pringle and his assistant." I heard the smile of triumph in her voice. "His daughter, Charlotte."

"She worked with him?" I shivered in my thin long-sleeved blouse, watching out of the corner of my eye as a small cloudlike vapor began to form at the top of the stairs.

"Yes. The author praised her intelligence and abilities, despite the fact that she was a woman. He said she was well trained by her father and allowed to administer medications without supervision, and that she had a calming impact on the patients."

It was so cold now that I felt my lungs tighten, making it hard to breathe. I watched the vapor cloud begin to take the shape of a woman as I recalled a part of Bridget Gilbert's letter. *After some discussion, which I did not hear, the doctor's daughter, acting as his nurse, wrapped the child in a blanket before handing him to me. She said it was a blessing that his mother had fainted from the pain and was not awake to see the horror.*

I whispered into the phone, "Thank you, Yvonne. I have to go now. One of the children . . ." I ended the call, my attention focused on what was happening in front of me.

The woman at the top of the stairs wore a long dress with a tightly fitted bodice and a large bell-shaped long skirt, an oval cameo pinned to the high neck of her gown. Her dark brown hair was swept off of her face, with a curl dangling on each cheek. She was solid, and so real that for a brief moment I thought that an intruder might be in the house. Until I noticed that instead of eyes, there were only empty sockets.

I didn't move. I couldn't. It was as if her empty gaze held me to the floor. And then the most terrifying thought of all: *She's between me and my children.* I began to tremble, more afraid than I'd ever been. I thought of what Yvonne had just told me, about one friend's betrayal, and I forced myself to speak. "Camille?"

The air sizzled and popped around me as the apparition wavered and weakened, allowing me to take a step toward the stairs. She turned and began moving down the hallway, toward the open bedroom door where my babies were sleeping.

"Jack," I shouted, half sobbing, as I began to run up the stairs, hearing him running up behind me.

I watched as the specter moved to my doorway, floating about a foot off the ground, a storm cloud about to make rain. I was running up the stairs as hard as I could, but it was like a dream run where my legs were stuck in molasses, making it impossible to lift them with any speed. Jack came up behind me in time to watch the door slam in front of the now cloudy apparition, blocking her from entering the room.

I ran toward her, moving fast now, then feeling only bone-shattering cold as I ran through her. When I turned around to look, she had completely vanished, only a lingering chill on my skin remaining. Jack was already turning the door handle. It didn't move at first, but on the second try it turned easily, and the door swung open into the room.

We moved quickly toward the two cradles, where General Lee lay between the sleeping children, the overwhelming scent of roses saturating the air. I dropped to my knees, an arm stretched over the top of each cradle, as drained as if I'd just given birth again.

"Thank you, Louisa," I said to the room, my thoughts jumbled. Louisa was protecting something precious, something Camille thought was hers. And somehow Jack, I, and the children were caught in the middle of a struggle I neither understood nor knew how to end.

CHAPTER 30

Jack and I sat outside in the garden, listening to the fall and splash of the fountain as the children slept like tiny flower buds in their double pram. It was a warm day for early March, the wisteria and gardenias pregnant with upcoming blooms, the Louisa roses hibernating in their waxy green bushes. It was comforting, somehow, to find the world waiting alongside us as we prepared for what would happen next.

Jack's arm was around me, his hand resting on my shoulder as we contemplated the perfection of the two sleeping babies. "Have you spoken to Sophie?"

"Yes. She's as confused as I am, because there are too many pieces in this puzzle that don't seem to fit. She even admitted that she might appreciate one of my charts to illustrate what Yvonne told us yesterday, the DNA results and what we already knew. She thinks it's her pregnancy brain, but I think that's just her excuse not to tell me that my chart making might actually be a useful tool."

"With figuring out an old murder, sure. For tracking the color and consistency of an infant's diaper contents, not so much."

I scowled at him. "You never know if that sort of information could be handy. And maybe one day they'll want that kind of stuff in their scrapbooks."

His eyes narrowed. "You're kidding, right?"

I paused, trying to think of the right answer. "Sure," I said slowly. "But I still think it's a good idea."

After studying me for a moment, he said, "We need to figure this out. JJ and Sarah aren't sleeping another night in this house until I know they're safe. And I don't want all five of us to move into my condo. Last night was enough to convince me that it's way too small."

"I know. I feel the same. But even after what I saw, I'm not convinced that Camille—and I'm almost positive it was her—meant to harm the babies."

Jack jerked back, dropping his arm. "She was trying to get into the room."

I held up my hand. "Yes, but there was such a feeling of . . . sadness I absorbed when I ran through her. It was the same feeling I got every time I saw Nola's mother." I was silent for a moment, thinking. "Even my mother believes that the ghost is the wronged party, that whatever she's claiming is hers is a legitimate claim. And yesterday . . ." I shrugged, not even sure I could voice my confused feelings. "Yesterday I got the feeling that she was using the children to show me the intensity of what she'd lost. As a mother to another mother."

"And Louisa?"

"She's definitely here as a sort of guardian angel for the children, returning the favor, I think, for my granting her only child his dying wish. But again, I have a feeling where she's concerned, too."

"A feeling?"

I nodded. "You know how you're always saying there's no such thing as a coincidence? I also believe that there's no such thing as a stray feeling. I think more people are psychic than we think. It's just that too many of us brush aside these feelings, or gut reactions, or intuition—whatever you want to call it. I've learned not to. And the feeling I get about Louisa is that she's here because she shares a connection with our ghost. That whatever it is the ghost thinks is hers, Louisa disagrees."

Jack was silent, his thumb rubbing the top of my hand. "When is your mother getting here?"

"I told her not before nine o'clock—Nola and the babies will be out of the house, and it should be full dark by then. That's one thing about ghosts that Hollywood usually gets right. Although I've had my fair share of experiences during broad daylight, there's always more activity at night."

He put his arm around me again, his finger absently tracing a pattern on my shoulder, making me shiver. "It feeds on the elemental fear in all of us. It's usually what we can't see that scares us the most."

I faced him, wanting him to tell me what it was that scared him, but he was studying the side of the house with such focus that my words stumbled.

His gaze moved from the slate roof down the clapboard sides and tall, mullioned windows, then swept across the Loutrel Briggs garden with the Louisa roses that had once been the pride of the Vanderhorsts— the same roses that my father had brought back to their original glory with love and care. "It really is like a piece of history you can touch, isn't it?"

"Yes," I said, remembering Nevin Vanderhorst's letter telling me about the strength of the Vanderhorst women, and how I reminded him of them. It was his way of explaining why he'd left me his house. *They sent men off to war and kept food on the table long after money ran out. They camped out on the front porch during hurricanes and after the earthquake of 1886, armed with whatever they could find to protect what was theirs for their family. They were like the foundations of this house—too strong to be swayed by little matters such as war, pestilence, and ruin.*

"He'd want me to fight for it," I said.

"I know," Jack replied. Our thoughts had always seemed to run on a parallel course, whether or not we wanted to admit it. "And we will. I'm hoping the intervention you and your mother are staging tonight will give us a little more ammunition."

"Me, too."

Jack continued to stare at the house, at its beautiful lines and elegant proportions, as if he were seeing it for the first time. "You know . . ." he said, his voice trailing away.

"What?" I asked, hoping and praying he hadn't spotted another hairline crack somewhere.

"Do you remember what I told you about the perfect family home I wanted you to find for me? I said I wanted something large so I could throw huge parties for Nola and the babies. And a big enough yard so there's room for a swing set and maybe a little lap pool, something with architectural charm and character. Even a ghost or two."

I turned to him with surprise. "You just described my house—right down to the 'ghost or two.' Was that on purpose?"

He shook his head, amusement making his eyes sparkle. "Believe it or not, no. Maybe subconsciously, but I promise it wasn't intentional." He laughed. "It's funny how it all worked out, though, isn't it?"

I looked down at my hands, not wanting him to read the uncertainty in my eyes. I twisted the platinum band on my left hand, still amazed at the perfect fit, as if it had been made for me. The metal seemed to warm beneath my touch as I remembered Jack putting it on my finger in the hospital, telling me the story of how his grandparents had been married for more than seventy years. The memory gave me the courage to meet his gaze again. "Did you marry me for my house, Jack?" I said it with a smile, but the rest of me tensed, waiting for the answer I so desperately needed to hear.

"Alston, they're over here!"

We turned to see Nola and Alston, wearing matching Ashley Hall uniforms, come through the garden gate. They rushed over to us and plopped their backpacks on the ground. General Lee sat up from his now permanent perch near the babies, letting out a low growl before he realized the two girls weren't intruders. What his plans were for an actual intruder remained to be seen, and would probably conclude with the criminal being easily apprehended because he was laughing too hard to move.

"I can't believe it's already so late in the day," I said, amazing myself again how an entire day could go by without my actually doing anything, yet I could look up and see it was late afternoon and I was bone tired.

"Hello, Mr. and Mrs. Trenholm," Alston said with a shy smile. "Nola told my mom it was okay to drop me off here for a little bit so I could see the babies. Mom had some errands to run, but she said she'd be back in an hour to pick us up."

"We really appreciate you taking Nola in tonight. But we all have to leave the house while it's being fumigated."

"Nola told me about all the palmetto bugs." She gave a delicate shudder. "I can't imagine what it must have been like to wake up with two of them in your hair."

I eyed Nola, wondering what kinds of embellishments she'd given to our fumigation story. I'd been trying to keep everything as close to the truth as possible, which was why I'd chosen fumigation in the first place. Except the bugs we were going to try to eradicate were bigger and just as hard to get rid of.

"I'm glad you came by. I'm afraid the babies won't be much entertainment for you, but if they wake up while you're here, you can hold them if you like."

"But you'll have to wash your hands first," Nola said.

She said it without any angst or drama, but as the responsible older sister of two small babies. During the pregnancy she hadn't shown any jealousy toward the two new interlopers, but all of the parenting books Jack and I had read said it would be the natural course of things, and to be prepared to deal with it. We should have known that Nola Trenholm was no ordinary teenager.

Both girls moved to stand in front of the pram to see the babies.

"They're so *cute*," Alston whispered.

"Like fun-size people," Nola said. "If you make faces at JJ, he'll smile at you. But if you do it to Sarah, she just stares at you like you're an idiot." She grinned. "I can't wait until they get a little older and we can do stuff together. I'm going to teach them each to play an instrument so we can have our own band. Sarah already sings, so we can harmonize together. We don't know if JJ sings. He spends most of his time eating or sleeping."

Alston leaned into the pram, gently tweaking one of JJ's small feet clad in socks made to look like blue Birkenstocks. "These are adorable. Where did they come from?"

I moved aside the blanket so she could see Sarah's pink ones. "My friend Dr. Wallen-Arasi. She's a big fan of the real things. She's expecting a baby girl in May, and I already bought her a pair of socks made to look like black patent-leather Mary Janes with lace around the ankles."

Smiling, I stood. "I'll let the three of you babysit while I go inside and pump some milk for tonight."

Alston looked confused but Nola said, "Ew."

"Unless you want your grandparents having to deal with two very cranky babies who like only breast milk and who won't be very happy when they're fed formula in a bottle instead."

With a small shudder, she said, "I've learned more about the human reproductive system and childbirth than I think is healthy for a young girl. It's enough to make me want to become a nun."

"That's a plan," Jack chimed in.

"Well, I don't think Cooper would be too happy to hear that," Alston said matter of factly, until she caught Jack's expression and began to blush profusely.

I said good-bye, then left them in the garden under the watchful eyes of the old oak tree, its swing swaying gently.

I walked through the house to the kitchen and stopped, surprised to see a cup of coffee on the kitchen table. Mrs. Houlihan always left at noon on Wednesdays, and she didn't drink coffee. Neither thought occurred to me until I was already halfway into the room and felt a presence by the pantry. It was definitely the living, breathing type of presence, because to my knowledge, the dead didn't drink coffee.

As I spun to face whoever it was, I fleetingly wished for General Lee's protection. He could have at least latched onto an ankle long enough to give me ample time to make my escape.

"Sorry to startle you, Melanie. I was just hoping to find a doughnut to go with my coffee. All I can find is this organic and whole-grain stuff."

"Dad," I said, pressing my hand against my heart. "I wasn't expecting you, was I?"

"No, sorry. I dropped in unannounced. I used my key—hope you don't mind."

"Of course not. You don't need an excuse to come visit. If you want to see the babies, Jack's with them in the—"

"I know. But I wanted to get you alone first, if that's all right. I figured if I waited in the kitchen, you'd show up eventually. Growing up, it was always your favorite spot."

I walked past him with a grimace. "That's because I knew I'd always find something in there I liked. Now I have to be a little more creative."

I reached behind the plastic containers of flaxseed and granola and grabbed an old familiar paper sack with the beloved grease stains on the sides. "I picked these up at Ruth's Bakery yesterday, so they should still be fresh." I put them on a plate, then placed them on the kitchen table.

"I'm surprised there're any left," he said.

"Actually, I haven't had any yet. Nola spotted them yesterday after I'd brought them home, and made a point of telling me how many calories were in each one and how much harder it is for women to lose weight after they're forty. Pretty much killed it for me."

He stood and retrieved a knife from a drawer, then cut a doughnut in half before placing one half on a napkin and sliding it over to me; then he took the other half for himself. "You know you'll always look beautiful to me, and you've inherited your knockout figure from your mother. But if you want to lose weight, depriving yourself isn't the answer. Portion control is."

Smiling, I picked up my half and took a bite, chewing slowly and savoring it. It was the first sweet thing I'd had in months, and I wanted to make it last as long as possible. I was enjoying it immensely until I opened my eyes and caught my dad's expression.

"What's wrong?" I asked, forcing myself to swallow.

He looked down at his untouched doughnut half. "I'm afraid I have some bad news."

"Is it Mother? Is she okay?"

He reached across the table and patted my hand. "She's fine. We're fine. Still healthy—nothing to worry about there." He gave me a weak smile, then withdrew his hand.

"So what's wrong?"

He picked up the mug of coffee, then set it down. "There's really no easy way to say this, so I'm just going to give it to you straight. The trust is out of money. There's nothing left."

I blinked, trying to get the words to register. "But what about the Confederate diamonds that Jack and I found? There were three of them and all very valuable. Surely . . . ?"

He slowly shook his head. "I sold them. I consulted with a financial adviser—at your suggestion—and he advised that I sell the diamonds and invest in what we both agreed at the time were good solid stocks that were expected to triple in value."

"No." I was shaking my head, trying to make all of this go away. "No," I said again, as if repeating the word might make it true.

"That was about the time that the market crashed. I was able to salvage some of it, but with all the repairs, it just completely wiped out the rest." My father seemed diminished all of a sudden, his military bearing completely deserting him. "I don't know what to say," he said. "Sorry is so completely inadequate. I thought I was being so careful, seeking professional advice. And then . . ."

"It's not your fault, Dad. And I was the one who told you to consult with the adviser, and I agreed with everything he said. It was just bad timing." I stood and got a drink of water from the tap, but I still couldn't wash away the horrible taste in my mouth.

"Your mother and I talked about selling her house, but she bought it at the top of the market and nobody's willing to pay what it's worth right now. And she can't get a second mortgage because it's worth less now than what she paid for it, so she hasn't built any equity."

"Dad, stop. I would never ask Mother to sell her house. This is separate—something I need to deal with. Somehow. We just put Jack's condo on the market, and although it's not the right time to be selling a condo in the French Quarter, we can take a loss on a sale if we really find ourselves cash-strapped. But I'm going back to work next week, and Jack's book just sold at auction for a really nice advance. We finally have an income again. We'll be fine. And hopefully all the major repairs are behind us."

My words seemed to have no effect on him. "That's all well and good, Melanie. But there's something else to consider."

I sat back in my chair, mentally bracing myself. "What?"

"The Gilberts. The DNA evidence doesn't look good for you, sweetheart. If they want this house, and the legal system says it's theirs, then you lose. But I met them. They're a great couple, really nice, but I didn't get the impression that they really wanted to uproot their family and move to Charleston. But what's theirs is theirs. Unless . . ."

"Unless what?"

"Unless you wanted to buy them out."

I was silent for a moment, understanding finally dawning on me. "But now I don't have the money to do that."

"No," he said, choking on the word, and for a horrible moment I thought my father would start crying.

The grandfather clock chimed in the front of the house, the sound somehow unbearably sad. "Daddy?" I said. I suppose in moments of crisis, we all revert to our childhoods, when questions usually had answers. "What am I supposed to do?"

He stared into his coffee mug for a long moment before looking at me. "The DNA evidence tells only part of the story. Maybe the rest of it will back you up. You just need to find out what it is." He shook his head as if he were arguing with himself. "I know your mother is coming here tonight, and I can guess why. Just do whatever it takes to get the whole story."

My eyes widened in surprise. "Are you saying that you believe us now?"

"I believe," he said, stabbing his index finger into the top of the table, "in anything that will fix this and make it right for you. Just do what you need to do."

A mewling cry of a newborn came from the monitor sitting on the kitchen counter. He looked at it as if seeing it for the first time. "I thought the babies were outside."

"They are." I watched as his gaze followed the cord to where the plug had been pulled out of the outlet.

"Is there a battery in there?"

I shook my head. "It died and I haven't had a chance to replace it."

He turned back to me, and our gazes locked. Finally he stood, then leaned over and kissed my cheek. "Just do what needs to be done."

I watched him let himself out the back door while the crying of the baby suddenly stopped, replaced by a heavy silence. And then in a deep, hollow voice that had no heartbeat behind it, a single word: *Mine*.

CHAPTER 31

After Amelia and James had left with the babies, and Alston's mother left with the girls, I collapsed on one of the white wicker rockers on the front porch, barely able to breathe.

Jack climbed the steps to the piazza and stopped in front of me. "The babies will be fine with my parents, Mellie. They already have one great success story behind them."

I couldn't even smile. "My dad was here earlier. He was waiting for me when I came inside." I swallowed, promising myself that I was going to keep it all together. "He came to tell me that we're broke. If it comes down to us having to buy out the Gilberts, we can't."

He sat down in the rocker next to me. "I know."

I met his gaze, happy to let anger sweep over my feelings of helplessness. "You know? But how? And how could you not tell me?"

He expelled a deep breath, making me wonder exactly how long he'd been holding it in, waiting for me to find out. "Right before the babies were born, Rich Kobylt came to see me. He said your father's check to him had bounced, and he was wondering if maybe I could help with getting him his money. I went ahead and paid him, then went to see your dad. He told me the whole story."

I stood up quickly, too angry and restless to sit down and rock. "But you didn't tell me! It's *my* house, Jack. Didn't you think I should know?"

"You were on bed rest, Mellie. I told your dad to wait until after the twins were born before he told you. He's waited this long because he's been talking to people to see what can be done. He'd hoped to bring you good news."

I slapped my palm against the porch railings, making the skin sting. "Great. Is there anything else you've been holding back from me?"

"Sit down, Mellie. Sit down so we can talk."

Slowly I turned, my stomach suddenly queasy. "Why? There's more?"

He reached out his leg to hook onto my rocker and pull it closer. "Sit down, and we'll talk."

Instead I leaned back against the piazza railing and crossed my arms over my chest, trying to make myself look as if I were in control, even if I didn't feel it. Especially with him looking at me that way, the fading light making his eyes seem darker. "Just tell me."

"Fine," he said, leaning back in his chair. "I'm going to tell you what I think is the real story of this house and how it came to be yours. I think you need to hear this first before you decide what you're going to do next, all right?"

I gave him a reluctant nod.

He continued. "Anytime you think what I'm saying contradicts the facts, let me know. But I don't think that you will."

"Go on," I said.

"So much of what I'm about to say seems circumstantial, but when you put it all together, it starts to make sense," Jack said softly, as if he could imagine my mind working to see past the obvious to only what I wanted to see. "I think that Camille Vanderhorst gave birth to twin boys in March 1860. One died, either as a stillborn or shortly afterward, and was buried in the foundation, since, as we know, work was being done to the house at the same time."

"But why would they hide the body? Why not just have a funeral and bury it in the family mausoleum in Magnolia Cemetery?"

"Because there was a third baby." He paused, letting me absorb what he'd just said. "Not a triplet, because even though all three babies shared the same father, this third baby had a different mother than the twins."

"But who . . . ?" I stopped, beginning to understand where his story was heading.

"Charlotte was Camille's best friend, and joined the newlyweds on their honeymoon. When they returned, Camille was pregnant with twins, although it's likely she didn't know there was more than one baby. What if John strayed while on his honeymoon and Charlotte was pregnant, too? Charlotte—as an unmarried pregnant woman—could have gone into seclusion—maybe even at the mental hospital where her father saw patients—to hide the pregnancy. It's been known to happen."

I was shaking my head. "But Bridget Gilbert said she heard the healthy cry of Cornelius's brother, William. She *saw* the baby." My fingernails bit into my palms, helping me to focus. I needed to prove that he was wrong. I *had* to.

"Bridget saw only what they allowed her to see, Mellie. Charlotte's baby might have been close by. She might have been living in a nearby house, set up as John's mistress, right under Camille's nose. Charlotte was in the room, assisting with the birth. When the first baby was born, and it wasn't breathing, she must have seen her chance. Somebody—it could have been John, or Charlotte, or even her father—made the decision to switch babies, and hide the body of the dead child so nobody would know."

"Wouldn't Camille have known it wasn't her baby?" I protested. "I look at Sarah and JJ and I know in my heart that they're mine. I could have picked them out in a nursery with hundreds of babies—by their smell, their expressions. What they look like. A mother knows these things, Jack. You can't just plop any baby in a mother's arms and tell her it's her baby."

He watched me in the soft light of late afternoon, his eyes sympathetic. I wished I'd sat down, as he'd asked me to, but I wouldn't give him the satisfaction of sitting down now. Gently, he said, "Camille died in a mental institution. Maybe that's why people thought she was crazy—because she didn't believe the baby everybody said she'd given birth to was hers.

"Think, Mellie. Think how simple it would have been back then.

Dr. Pringle, perhaps a family friend or at least a well-compensated one, has Camille committed to an asylum for psychosis. It would have been easy to call a mother crazy who denies her own child."

I shook my head. "That doesn't make any sense. How would that kill her at only twenty-one?"

Our eyes met with mutual understanding. *Oh.* My mouth formed the word, but nothing came out.

Jack continued, his voice soft. "Camille was young, and a year before her death she was writing to her mother about a dining room table and what a lovely time she was having on her honeymoon. It's hard to imagine a young woman with so much to live for dying so soon from psychosis." He paused. "Unless it wasn't from that. Charlotte's father signed the death certificate. He was a well-respected physician, so no one would have questioned him."

"No, Jack. No. That's murder. They were best friends."

"It wouldn't be the first time, unfortunately. Think how much Charlotte stood to gain. She would be the wife, a mother to a son being raised as the legitimate heir, the mistress of this beautiful house. In 1861, that was a lot better than being her friend's husband's mistress."

When I didn't say anything, he continued, his voice still soft and cajoling, as if he needed me to understand what he was saying as much as I didn't want to. "I believe that's why Camille didn't start haunting until her baby's remains were found. She'd finally found out what had happened to her babies. To both of them."

I couldn't stand any more, so I sat back down in my rocking chair. Jack tried to take my hand, but I brushed him away.

"Mellie, it all makes sense. Nevin Vanderhorst is the direct descendant of Charlotte's illegitimate son, whom they named William after passing him off as John and Camille's baby. George Gilbert is descended from Cornelius, one of two legitimate sons born to John and Camille, but given away because of his physical deformity. If he had not been given to Bridget Gilbert, and was brought up here with his biological parents instead, this house would rightfully belong to his heirs."

"But inheritance laws don't work that way anymore," I protested, seeing a glimmer of hope. "How can they claim something that I inherited in good faith?"

"Because if they contest Nevin Vanderhorst's will in a court of law, the court could decide in their favor because they *are* the legitimate heirs. They have Vanderhorst blood. You don't, and you inherited it from somebody whose bloodline was illegitimate. And whose very existence on the family tree might be due to murder."

"This is the twenty-first century. What jury wouldn't understand that things are done differently now?"

"It's a matter of a jury's sympathy for the victims—in this case poor Cornelius and his heirs. Seemingly unwinnable cases have been won in the past for just that reason."

I closed my eyes to block my sight of the porch with its tower-of-the-winds columns and the front door with its Tiffany glass, and the way the light slanted across the garden, bathing everything in the same golden light as it had for over a century. *It's a piece of history you can hold in your hands.* "I thought you were on my side, Jack."

"I am, Mellie. I always have been. But I thought you wanted the truth."

I jerked out of my chair again, wincing as it hit the side of the house. "It's only your version of the truth. I'm sure if I thought long and hard, I could figure a way to make all the pieces fit to show a completely different picture."

He looked at me, waiting, his eyes not unkind. "Even your mother believed that the ghost was the wronged party, and you just told me that you thought that she wasn't trying to harm the babies, that she was using your own love for your children to show her own grief. It all fits—don't you see? Even Louisa's presence makes sense. Nevin was her son, and he gave the house to you. As his mother, she's here to protect his interests."

Leaning closer to me, he said, "Why do you think Louisa donated the cradle to the museum? She must have discovered the package from Bridget Gilbert containing Cornelius's christening gown, and to assert her own position as mother of the only known Vanderhorst heir, she gave away the cradle. It was her way of protecting her son, of telling Bridget Gilbert and everybody else that there was only one heir, and his name was Nevin."

I massaged my temples, trying to sort everything into a manageable list, trying to resurrect one lost piece of information. "But how did she know about the package? It was mailed in 1898. Where had it been between 1898 and 1922?"

He was silent for a moment, organizing his thoughts in his head the way I liked to do it on paper. "I don't know," he said. "But you know how to find out."

A tremble rippled through me as I remembered the eyeless woman staring at me from the top of the stairs, and the violence of the exploding windows and the falling light fixture. But I thought of Louisa, too, and the mailed package, and I grabbed onto both of them as proof that Jack didn't know all the answers. That there was still a chance that he was wrong.

I turned my back on him and headed toward the piazza steps. "I'm going for a walk. I've got to clear my head so I'm ready for tonight. I'll be back before my mother gets here."

"We're on the same side, Mellie. Don't treat me like I'm the enemy."

My answer was the slamming of the piazza door behind me. The shock of the sound shamed me into the realization that it was easier to be angry with Jack than to admit to myself that I'd been so wrong about so many things for far too long.

*

By the time I returned to the house, it was near full dark and my mother was waiting on the piazza with Jack. An open sack from Sticky Fingers sat on the floor between them, the aroma of barbecue having no effect on my twisted stomach.

"I called Jack, and he said you hadn't eaten. I thought I'd bring you dinner. You'll need your strength."

I shook my head, avoiding both of their gazes. "Thanks, but I can't eat right now. I'll be fine."

Jack handed me a bottle of water. "Drink this."

I took it with mumbled thanks and drank it, realizing how thirsty I was. When I was finished, I screwed the top back on and placed the bottle next to the paper sack. "Are you ready?"

My mother nodded, then turned to Jack. "I think it's best if you stay here for now. I'll call you if we need you."

"I really don't think—" he began.

"They might be more talkative if it's just us women. We're all mothers, so we can relate to that." She frowned. "Besides, you can be too much of a distraction to most females."

She extended her hand to me, and I took it before we entered the darkened foyer. I reached to turn on the table lamp in the vestibule, but my mother held me back. "Spirits are usually more active without electric lights." She set her purse on the small table and pulled out a flashlight before handing it to me. "We'll use this instead."

I spotted her gloves tucked neatly inside her purse, and another tremor swept through me. Looking behind us, I found Jack standing on the threshold. "I'm keeping this door open, and I'm waiting right here."

I felt a warm flush of gratitude and other feelings—some I could and others I couldn't identify—all rolled up in one. "Thank you," I managed before I turned around and followed my mother into the house.

The house breathed silently around us, the sensation of unseen eyes watching us in the darkened spaces more than a little unnerving. "Louisa?" I called out, my quiet voice amplified by the tall ceilings. "Are you here? We need your help."

We waited a moment, then moved forward into the foyer. She was waiting for us at the bottom of the stairs. I couldn't see her, but I felt her, sensed her maternal presence even before I smelled the roses. A tingling in the fingertips of the hand that held my mother's zipped up my arm, as if a supernatural switch had suddenly been flicked on.

My mother gripped my hand tighter. "Don't let go," she whispered.

"Try to make me," I whispered back, leading her to the steps. I could suddenly hear a babble of voices, men and women and children;

could hear the slash of sabers from Yankee soldiers as they hacked at the banister, leaving scars that could still be seen today. A pattering of feet ran past us up the steps, and I felt the brush of a small hand against my arm. It was as if all the house's residents of the past had come to witness whatever was going to happen next.

I began to tremble, my fingers threatening to slip from my mother's grasp.

"We are stronger than them," she said softly, reminding me of all the times she'd said those words to me, and how they'd never failed us. I clung to the thought as much as I clung to her hand, knowing that with all of my uncertainties, it was the one thing I could believe.

I aimed the flashlight toward the top of the stairs, spotting disappearing feet wearing twenties-era shoes and pale stockings. "She's taking us to the attic."

My mother looked at me, and for a moment I thought she was going to tell me that we should rethink our plan. Instead she said, "Then let's follow. She wants to show us something."

We walked slowly up the stairs, sensing the presence of all the spirits on either side of us, making me feel as if we were running the gauntlet through a potentially hostile crowd. I quickened our pace and made it to the top step just as the door that led to the attic stairs flew open.

"Great," I muttered, working hard to control my trembling as we slowly walked down the hallway to the attic, pausing only briefly before climbing the narrow steps one in front of the other, our hands awkwardly clasped together.

The full moon outside bled a milky light through the two short windows, illuminating most of the room and throwing the rest in shadow, creating a cityscape of dark shapes along the perimeter. I flicked off my flashlight, allowing us to see a blue glow that was not coming from the windows.

The odd light pulsed and moved, mimicking breathing, its darker center expanding as it moved across the ceiling, then settled in the back corner of the attic. It was the same corner where I'd found Louisa's trunk containing her scrapbooks, and my mother had found the framed photographs of the babies in christening gowns. "Louisa? Are you showing us this part of the attic to acknowledge this is you?"

We waited for a long moment, listening as the grandfather clocked chimed nine times, the last chime echoing throughout the empty house like a child calling for his mother. There was no response from the spirit, but the light shrank suddenly into a small, glowing ball, centered on the corner floorboard.

I tried again. "Why did you donate one of the cradles? Was it because you knew you weren't going to have any more children, or is there another reason?"

I was answered again with silence, the ball of light growing small as its intensity increased to the point where it was hard to look at it directly. I swallowed, then forced myself to ask the next question. "Did your reasons have anything to do with Charlotte Vanderhorst and her son William?"

A sound like taffeta rustled behind us near the steps. I flicked on the flashlight and aimed it in that direction, but we saw nothing. The air seemed to thicken, making it harder to breathe. My mother clenched my hand even harder, letting me know she'd sensed the change in the atmosphere, too.

I tried again. "Why did you donate the cradle?" I needed her to tell me that it was because she had only the one child and didn't need two cradles. Anything that would prove to me how all of Jack's conclusions were wrong.

The light began moving in a small circle, still centered over the floorboard, pulsing like a heartbeat. My mother gasped, and we turned toward each other as the same thought hit us simultaneously.

"There's something under the floorboard," I whispered, mesmerized by the blue dancing dot of light that seemed to be nodding in assent.

I closed my eyes, trying to remember where I'd seen my father's toolbox, jerking them open as soon as I remembered. "Daddy's toolbox is over by the steps. He brought it up yesterday to shave the bottom of the door because it kept sticking."

We retraced our steps as I tried not to recall the rustling sound we'd heard earlier, stopping when my foot kicked the black metal box. "I've got to let go of your hand just for a few moments. Stay close."

My mother hesitated before nodding. I trained the beam of my flashlight inside the toolbox as we picked up whatever tools we thought might work to pry up an old floorboard.

Sliding back a box of shoes so both of us could fit in the corner, we knelt to examine the spot where the blue light had been reduced to a single pinpoint. In the small circle of light from my flashlight, we examined the floorboard, relieved that instead of being nailed down with four nails like the rest of the boards, this one had been nailed using only two, one of which had been placed at a forty-five-degree angle, making it easy for me to wedge it out using the claw of my father's hammer.

"I think someone has done this before," I whispered as I discarded the bent nail on the ground.

For the second nail, I handed the flashlight to my mother. "Shine this here."

Using both hands, I worked the old timber up and down, prying the nail loose enough so that I could pull the rest of it out with my hammer. When I heard the board crack after only a few tugs, I cringed as if I'd hurt the house, feeling bad enough about it myself without wondering what Sophie would say.

When it gave way in my hands, I fell backward, then scrambled back to the small hole. The beam from the flashlight threw a triangle of light into the blackness, illuminating a length of what seemed like twine. Reaching inside, I grabbed it between my thumb and forefinger, and slowly pulled it up.

It was frayed and brittle, not completely immune to humidity and age despite the protection of its hiding place. A hiding place, I thought, that was never meant to be permanent.

"It's twine," I said, rolling it between my fingers. "Just like the twine used to wrap the old package I found on the porch."

Our eyes met for a moment before we looked back at the hole beneath the floorboard. "Could the package have been hidden here?" she asked. "It must be bigger than we think."

Getting down on my stomach, I said, "Shine the light back in the hole."

I peered inside, realizing that the hole was much deeper and wider than it had originally appeared, reminding me of stories I'd heard of Charlestonians hiding their silver from the Yankees who'd besieged the city in 1864. I imagined Louisa up here in the attic, cleaning up this corner as part of her nesting before giving birth to her first child, and finding the hiding place.

"To the right," I said, following the light as my mother slowly aimed the beam into the deep recess until it found something to reflect against. With a deep breath and a prayer that there weren't any lurking spiders, I reached inside and grabbed what felt like a handful of tissue, knowing what it was before I'd even lifted it out.

"What is it?" my mother asked as I carefully pulled away the paper.

I inhaled deeply as we both recognized the christening gown and bonnet. Already knowing what I'd find, I pulled back the neck of the gown to see what had been embroidered there. *Susan Bivens.*

"It's the missing third set," my mother said unnecessarily.

Ignoring the squeezing feeling in my chest, I focused instead on making a mental list of everything I knew, and how what we'd just discovered fit in. Or didn't. "The invoice Yvonne showed us said it had been ordered in March 1860 by C. Vanderhorst. I'm guessing it would have been Charlotte, since she's the only one who'd have had a reason. She probably pretended to be Camille when she ordered it."

"But why would she have another set made?" my mother asked.

I thought hard for a moment, wishing that all the pieces weren't falling so easily into the spots where Jack wanted them to be. "When she realized that she needed to have a Vanderhorst christening gown and bonnet to baptize her son in. Because one had been buried in the foundation and the other was taken by Bridget. This would have been the set that Nevin wore in his christening photograph, because it had the bonnet. The original bonnet would have been with Cornelius's family."

My mother touched my arm, and I stiffened, focusing very hard on just the facts and not what they might mean. "Charlotte hid this here, and Louisa must have found it, along with Bridget's package." I swallowed. "Charlotte didn't die until 1902, which means she most likely received the package when Bridget mailed it in 1898, but for whatever reason decided to hide it instead of destroying it. Allowing Louisa to find it nearly twenty years later. I'm not sure why she would have put the new gown and bonnet in here. I can only hope it was shame."

I stood, hardly feeling my aching knees from squatting in front of the ruined floorboard. I spun around, looking for Louisa, still hoping she'd tell me I was wrong. "Is this where you found the package from Bridget Gilbert? Is that how you found out that your son wasn't the legitimate heir?" The pain in my chest was nearly choking me now. "There must have been a letter in the package from Bridget that Charlotte saved with the package, but you destroyed it, didn't you? You were scared, but not so scared that you felt you should destroy the rest of the package's contents."

I wiped at my face, surprised to find tears, and angrily brushed them away. "So why, Louisa? Why did you send me the package? What did you hope to accomplish?"

The air suddenly became charged, like the sky before a tornado hits, the smell of roses now mixing with the dank smell of damp earth. Then softly, I heard her voice, recognizing it from the time when I'd first begun living in this house and Louisa had been protecting me from Joseph Longo. *We both want the truth, Melanie. It is time that old wrongs are put right.*

"But what *is* the truth?"

You know the truth. You can see it. But it is not the end of your story. Listen to your heart and remember that sometimes when you think you have lost everything, you have won your heart's desire.

"No!" I shouted, the word drowned by the sound of the Vanderhorst cradle dragging itself against the wooden floorboards, blocking the exit down the attic steps.

As if propelled by instinct, my mother rushed forward, reaching out to grab the cradle as if to shove it out of the way so we could escape.

"Mother!" I screamed, but I was too late. Her body went rigid as her hands made contact with the wood, like a bird trapped on a live wire. *We are stronger than you,* I whispered inside my head, and then, as loudly as I could, "We are stronger than you." I pried one of my mother's hands from the side of the cradle and clasped it in mine, and then watched as the world disintegrated around me, a tidal wave of sights and sounds that weren't my own obliterating the attic, the light from the moon, and the gentle presence of Louisa Vanderhorst.

CHAPTER 32

Mine. The word came from inside my head, but also seemed to echo off the high rafters of the ceiling, shaking the fragile glass in the attic windows. My mother's hand was still clenched in my own, her eyes struggling to stay open. A pounding on the door and Jack's voice shouting my name and my mother's name seemed to be coming from very far away.

I wasn't sure whether I'd passed out, or if time had somehow shot forward. I was lying on my back looking up at the rafters, where the moonlight had been replaced by an eerie fog of ambient light. The pungent scents of rotting wood and damp earth permeated the space, the staccato sound of wood scraping wood echoing throughout the attic, shaking my bones.

"Mother," I shouted, tugging on her hand. "Let go! Let go of the cradle! We have to get out of here."

She shook her head slowly, as if she weren't sure what I'd just said. I tried to stand and pull her with me, but a heavy weight across my calves pinned them to the floor. My toes had already started to tingle from the loss of circulation. Twisting my body, I saw Louisa's trunk had come to rest on top of my legs. And that was when I realized what the scraping noise was. All around us the furniture was moving, closing in on us like hounds at a hunt—like bricks around a small coffin.

I tried to straighten my body, to find leverage to sit up, but my head hit something hard and unforgiving. Tilting my head back, I saw what it was, and a deep hole of fear burned itself into the pit of my stomach. The tall armoire towered above me, wobbling slightly each time something else bumped into it.

"Mellie! Ginnette! Are you in there? Can you open the door?" Jack's frantic voice called from the other side of the attic door.

I felt momentary relief until I realized that if Camille didn't want him to come inside, then he couldn't. I had to figure this one out on my own.

Slide, scrape, slide. I tried to shimmy my way out from under the trunk, but I couldn't move at all, making me wonder whether it was only the trunk pinning me down. Something struck the armoire from behind, making it tip forward, balancing precariously for a moment before settling back down.

I closed my eyes, allowing my despair to consume me, to convince me that everything was hopeless. My mother's hand was still held tightly inside my own, but it had gone slack. I had never felt so utterly and completely alone.

Pounding began on the door again, something heavier than fists this time, and then Jack's voice. "I'm coming, Mellie. Keep fighting; I'm coming."

His voice forced me to open my eyes. As I lay there trying to find a focus, to find a place to start, I heard the high-pitched cry of a newborn winding its way around the furniture and the rafters of the old attic like a ribbon. *JJ. Sarah.* My brain shouted their names over and over like a mantra as I began to struggle with renewed vigor. I *had* to get free. Not for me, or for my mother, or even for Jack. I had to do it for the two children who'd just begun this life and would need their mother to help navigate it.

Keep fighting, Mellie. "Mother! Open your eyes. I need you to open your eyes."

They opened to slits, her eyeballs moving beneath the lids.

"Mother, please. I need you to open your eyes and give me your other hand. Please." I sucked in my breath, my mind searching for a way to convince her. "If there was ever a time when you felt you needed to make up for thirty-three years of abandonment, this is it."

Her eyes fluttered open in understanding as her hand pulsed to life inside of mine.

"Let go of the cradle, and then grab my other hand. We are stronger than she is. But we have to do this together."

She nodded, and I watched her forehead crease in concentration. I tightened my hand on hers and then shouted, "Now!" With a loud gasp she wrenched her hand off the cradle, then rolled closer to me, slipping her other hand into mine. I held on tightly, afraid to let her go.

Scrape, slide, scrape. My mother glanced around her, her eyes widening as she watched a rustic oak bookcase edge its way toward her. When she looked at me, her eyes held only questions instead of answers, and desperation quickly overtook my fear.

"Camille? It's you, isn't it? Please don't do this. I have two babies, and they need their mother."

My words did nothing to slow down the approach of furniture and boxes toward the tiny space where my mother and I lay.

"Let us send you into the light. Let us give you peace."

A loud crash sounded from somewhere out of my line of vision, and I remembered the pine curio cabinet with its dusty collection of Depression glass that had been tucked beneath the window, now imagining the floor studded with bright shards of glass.

My mother tugged on my hand. "Tell her what she needs to hear, Mellie. Tell her what you both need to hear."

I blinked my eyes in confusion for a moment, trying to understand what she was telling me, wondering why her lips were moving but it wasn't her voice emerging from her mouth. *You know the truth. You can see it. But it is not the end of your story. Listen to your heart and remember that sometimes when you think you have lost everything, you have won your heart's desire.*

I blinked my eyes again, but this time it was to clear the tears that had begun to well up inside them. I now understood what Louisa had been telling me, understood why she'd sent me the package containing the christening gown. Because Camille Vanderhorst had been grievously wronged, and after more than one hundred and fifty years, it was time to make restitution.

"Camille," I shouted again. "I know what happened, and I will see to it that the world knows, too. You didn't deserve what happened to you. You were robbed of the most precious thing—your children. I understand that now. This is your house, and your children's house. It belongs to their descendants. I will do the right thing for them; I promise."

The sound of moving furniture ceased as a crushing silence descended, the air seeming to wait with held breath. My mother squeezed both of my hands, a silent *we are stronger than you* between us. When she spoke, her voice was firm, the love between mothers and their children a bond that reached across time.

"It's time for you to join them," my mother said. "It's time for you to all be together again. They are waiting for you inside the light."

The electric buzzing sound that had been zipping around the corners of the room suddenly stopped, replaced by the cries of the baby I'd been hearing since the day the remains of a newborn had been discovered in the foundation.

"Go to them," my mother said. "Go to them and rest now. We will take care of things here."

The weight of the trunk lessened, and I was able to push it off my legs and slide out from under it. I quickly stood, pulling my mother up with me. I listened as sirens wailed in the distance, the sound growing louder, the pounding on the door and Jack's voice resuming.

We turned at the rustling of taffeta and watched as the figure of a woman knelt by the cradle, now tucked against the armoire, and lifted a baby into her arms. The beautiful folds of a linen-and-lace christening gown flowed softly against the satin of her voluminous skirts. She glanced at me, and her eyes were no longer empty, but ovals of shining light as she held the child she'd been denied all those years ago. She nodded in our direction and, with one last glance, slowly began to walk toward the window, disappearing through it with a shimmer of blue light before the attic fell dark again, lit only by the light of the moon.

The attic door opened as easily as if it had taken only a turn of the doorknob, and Jack stumbled in, outlined by the hallway light and holding the saber-scared pineapple finial from the top of the main staircase. He ran up the attic steps and pulled the chain switch that flipped on the overhead single bulb. Pausing at the top step, he stared at my mother and me huddled together in the middle of the attic, furniture crowded around us like spectators at a boxing match.

He was breathing heavily, sweat dripping down his forehead, his hair porcupine-like. There was worry and concern in his expression, as well as confusion. "Are you all right?" he asked with hesitation. Then, with more emphasis: "Why didn't you open the door? It wouldn't open and I was panicking. I called the fire department. . . ."

He stopped when he saw my gaze settle on the finial, and I knew what that extra pounding on the door had been. "Sorry," he said. "I hope Sophie can forgive me."

I looked at the scarred wood of the door and winced before I realized that I didn't need to worry about the house anymore. My term as caretaker of the house on Tradd Street was over.

I made my way amid the furniture to Jack, throwing my arms around him as if I hadn't seen him for a very long time. I pressed my face into his chest, finding comfort in the smell of him even as my enormous loss threatened to drag me under.

"Tell me I'm doing the right thing, Jack. Please tell me that everything's going to be all right."

With lips close to my ear, he whispered, "We're together, Mellie. It's all going to be fine."

I nodded into his chest, afraid to meet his eyes and allow him to see my doubt. Pulling away, I turned to my mother. "Are you okay?"

She nodded. To Jack, she said, "Mellie will tell you everything later. But first, we need to get out of this attic. And I think the fire department is here."

On not-so-steady legs, she began to thread her way toward the stairs. Jack took her arm to assist her, sending a questioning look in my direction. *Later,* I mouthed, not quite ready to relate what had just transpired in the confines of the attic.

I pulled on the chain, turning out the light and throwing the attic back into darkness, the moonlight casting fingerlike shadows through the spindles of the old cradle.

I followed Jack and my mother out of the attic and closed the battered door, leaving the cradle and all of its ghosts behind me.

CHAPTER 33

I bent down to untangle a strand of fig vine that wound its way through the small topiary in one of the new planters my father had just delivered to grace either side of the front door.

Daniel—"Just Daniel, please"—Rebecca's wedding planner, stood behind me with his wrist on his hip, tut-tutting his displeasure. "Melanie," he said, his rich Charleston accent heavy on the vowels. "These planters don't go with the theme of tonight's party. They look like baby cradles, which, I'm afraid, will give the wrong impression to the guests about the wedding couple."

"They look like cradles because they *are* cradles. And there are two of them because the family that built this house has a history of twins. I thought it appropriate."

I studied the two planters—one from the attic and the other a replica my father had made—marveling at what a beautiful job my father had done with the conversion from open-sided cradles to planters with an assortment of blooms and greenery that could only be described as eye candy. The Manigault family cradle had finally arrived, too, and it now held a place of honor outside near the kitchen door as a container garden for Nola's herbs. At least, they would be her herbs until Irene Gilbert decided what to do with the planter.

Daniel looked heavenward, his pencil-thin eyebrows and mustache making him look like a silent-film star. "Could I at least put a pink bow on them?"

"Absolutely not. And I must insist that the large bow on the Baccarat chandelier be removed. It's almost sacrilege."

"But Ms. Edgerton—" he started to protest.

"Yes, as you've said dozens of times, it's her party. But it's my house. At least for now. So I get the final word. I agreed to allow my dog to wear a pink bow tie, but that's my last concession."

With compressed lips, he turned and left, his cell phone already pressed to his ear, undoubtedly to call Rebecca and let her know about another one of my ill-designed changes to his plans.

"I love you in red, but I must admit that you look quite delicious in pink, too."

I turned around to see Jack in the doorway, the look on his face close to a lascivious leer without actually being one. He was dressed in a dark suit with a cobalt blue tie that brought out the color of his eyes. I might have swooned if I didn't have the porch railing to hold on to.

"Thanks, but I feel like a cupcake. What's with this bell-shaped skirt? I haven't worn a dress like this since I was six."

"I'm not sure what a bell-shaped skirt is, but I like the way it shows off your legs."

I wanted to roll my eyes, but I didn't want to look anything like Daniel. Instead, I walked toward Jack. "Need me to fix your tie?"

"Sure." He grinned, straightening as I reached him.

He placed his hands on my hips as I played with his tie, making it impossible to suck enough breath into my lungs. "Six weeks is like an eternity," he said softly, and I blushed. That was the time Dr. Wise said I needed after the birth of the twins until we could "resume marital relations." I'd been too embarrassed to tell her that there'd been no relations to resume. At least not marital ones. And definitely not plural.

I focused on his already perfect tie instead of meeting his eyes. "She said it could be longer depending on how I feel."

He smoothed down my dress with the palms of his hands, skimming my waist and hips. "I think you feel pretty good."

My hormones, most recently consumed with growing babies inside of me and producing milk, began to awaken and stretch like bears after a long winter. But I held myself back, resisting the urge to press him against the door. I had reconciled myself to the fact that I loved him, and had admitted it when I'd been about to give birth and he'd asked. I'd even reconciled myself to the fact that I was not the rightful owner of the house I'd only begun to call my home. But I couldn't yet reconcile myself to the fact that I was married to a man who had never said he loved me.

"Is everything all right?" he asked.

I patted his tie and stepped back, a prim smile on my face. "As well as it can be. Mr. Drayton called earlier. The Gilberts flew in yesterday. He's setting up a meeting for tomorrow afternoon—he'll let us know what time once he speaks with my lawyer. When I spoke with Sterling yesterday, we talked about what I might expect. He thinks we should be able to get some reimbursement for my out-of-pocket costs associated with the house's restoration."

The familiar sting behind my eyes began again, so I focused on picking imaginary lint from his suit. "Hopefully we'll have enough time to find a new house before we have to move. With no offers on your condo yet, and your insistence that we find another historic home South of Broad, I'm afraid even your advance would barely cover a down payment. I'm a little short on cash right now, too, so we'll probably have to rent for a while until I sell a few more houses and you start making royalties again."

I tried to smile, but my lips wobbled too much to be convincing. "The house I showed you in Ansonborough is still available, by the way. I thought maybe we could bring Nola to look at it with us, see what she thinks. I put a call in to the listing agent to see how desperate the owners are to sell and whether or not they'd consider long-term renters with the possibility of buying in the next couple of years."

"Mellie . . ." he began.

I shook my head. "Don't. Please. I'm sorry I brought it up, but I really can't talk about this right now. I went to a lot of trouble with my makeup and I don't want to mess it up."

He kissed the top of my nose. "All right. But we'll figure this all out. Together, remember?"

I nodded, staring at the crease between his eyebrows. "What is it?"

"I was just wondering about something. It's been bothering me ever since you told me about what happened in the attic. It's about Charlotte. Why isn't she haunting the house?"

I shrugged. "I can only guess, but I'm thinking it's because she got what she wanted in life. I hope she's now facing due penance in the next one."

"And Louisa and Camille—do you think they've moved on and are at peace now?"

"I'd like to think so—I mean, it's not like I get postcards or anything to let me know. But I still feel a presence, a maternal one. It might be Louisa, or it could be Camille, making sure I keep my end of the bargain. But it's a gentle presence, whoever it is, and I don't mind it. I'm almost thinking we should make sure our next house has ghosts, just to keep it interesting."

Jack chuckled. "At least it would give me an unending source of plots for future books. That and anything you pick up from cold cases, if you decide to work with Detective Riley." He raised an eyebrow. I'd mentioned the offer from Thomas, and Jack had actually said he thought it was a good idea if I found a positive way to use my gift, whether or not it gave him book ideas. And even if it meant my working with Detective Riley.

"If somebody doesn't beat me to it, I'm thinking about making Camille's story my next book after the Manigault book."

"Don't worry about Marc scooping you again, because I'm not saying a word to anybody—especially not Rebecca. As for telling Camille's story, she'd like that," I said with confidence. "She'd want the world to know the truth."

A car door slammed and we looked over at the street to see a new navy blue Jaguar pulled up to the curb. It was too early for either guests or the valet parkers Daniel had hired, so I assumed it had to be the guests of honor. "Great. They're here," I said through gritted teeth.

I couldn't believe that I'd agreed to host Marc and Rebecca's rehearsal dinner. My only excuse was that the pregnancy hormones had made me temporarily insane. Still, I was grateful that I had a reason to dress up the house one last time and open the doors to guests. It was bittersweet, but still a better way to say good-bye than just locking the door behind us and loading up the van.

"Have you fed the babies yet?" Jack asked.

"No, I was just about to, so their tanks will be full before Nola takes over. She's not too crazy about feeding the babies breast milk, even if it is in a bottle. She's afraid some might touch her."

"I think you're going to need to go change, too."

"I thought you said you liked this dress," I said, my gaze following his to my chest. "Oh." I looked down at the two wet spots staining my bodice. The garden gate clanged shut, and I turned to Jack in panic. "Please make my excuses—and don't you dare tell them the real reason I had to change my dress. Tell them one of the babies puked on it or something."

"That's better than breast milk?" he asked.

Instead of answering, I turned and ran inside the house, listening as Jack greeted Marc and Rebecca. "Hello, Matt. It's good to see you again."

I snorted with laughter as I ran upstairs to feed the twins.

The scent of flowers saturated the house from the elaborate bouquets Daniel had set up and from the open doors and windows that brought in the sweet scents of tea olives and Confederate jasmine from the garden. The Baccarat chandelier, which Sophie had helped repair and restore after it had smashed onto the floor the first year I'd owned the house, sparkled as prisms of light shot through its crystal pendants. The wood floors had been polished with old-fashioned beeswax per Sophie's instructions—but without her help, since her own due date was quickly approaching—and the Tiffany glass on the front door had been cleaned by hand using Q-tips to get into all of the crevices. I had actually volunteered for that project, wanting it to be my good-bye gift to the house.

There were forty guests for dinner, twenty-four of them to be seated at Camille Vanderhorst's dining room table, the other sixteen at smaller tables set up in the large dining room. Daniel had been delighted to use the Vanderhorst china, mixing and matching the set with the roses dancing delicately along the edges of the plates with the gold Haviland Limoges china with the large "V" emblazoned in the middle.

Silver candelabras blazed from the table and every surface, festooned by pink roses, pink toile, and pink satin. Even I had to admit that everything looked beautiful against the pink lace tablecloths—custom-made to fit the tables—the candlelight reflecting off the antique mirrors and hand-painted wallpaper. All the possessions I had once looked at as just one more thing that would eventually need repairing or replacing.

I tried not to think where all the money had come from to pay for the party, despite Jack's label of "blood money"—referring to Marc's well-publicized high-six-figure advance for his book. It was all too beautiful, and too poignant, for me to want any negative emotions to cloud this sweet good-bye.

I had changed into my red maternity dress, belting it in the middle so that it would fit better. Everything else in my closet was still a little tight, and Jack seemed to appreciate the neckline of this dress and the way my new lactating bustline filled out the bodice.

Jack and I moved among the guests, brushing up against each other often yet seemingly accidentally, our eyes finding each other across the room with an odd regularity. We both knew enough of the guests to feel included, and if it hadn't been for the constant reminders that this was as much a going-away party as a rehearsal dinner, I might have actually enjoyed myself.

We had just been seated for dinner—Jack and I at each head of the main table—when Nola appeared at the dining room door, beckoning to me. Jack saw her, and we both excused ourselves with the insistence that the meal continue as planned, then moved to join her in the foyer.

"Are JJ and Sarah all right?" I asked, already taking a step toward the stairway. It was then that I noticed the couple hanging back in the vestibule, looking very self-conscious and uncomfortable.

"Irene? George?"

The Gilberts stepped out into the foyer, holding hands and looking pretty much the same as when I'd last seen them, with jeans and matching T-shirts. "We're so sorry to bother you—we didn't know you were having company." Irene looked behind me toward the dining room, where the babble of voices and the smell of food wafted out to us. She returned her gaze to me. "But it was important we speak with you today—without lawyers."

Jack and I exchanged a glance before I said, "Why don't we go into the parlor and sit down . . . ?"

Irene shook her head. "No. We just want to say what we need to say."

"Which is . . . ?" Jack prompted.

George put his hand around his wife's shoulders and she sent him a look of gratitude. Turning back to us, she said, "George and I have been doing a lot of talking between each other, our extended families, and our kids. But it comes down to this—New York is our home. As beautiful as this house is, and how great Charleston is, it doesn't matter. It's not our home. And I can't see us ever really feeling at home here."

My heart began to sink as I guessed where this conversation was heading. I wanted to stop them before they dangled that unreachable fruit in front of me, but I stood there and listened anyway as my last chance to hold on to the house was lost.

Irene continued. "We were hoping that we could come to an agreement, an offer of fair market value for the house, minus all of your own money you've put into it. We're assuming, of course, that you want to stay here."

A large knot seemed to be blocking my throat, prohibiting me from speaking, so Jack stepped forward. "We're grateful for your generosity. Of course we want to stay here. But I'm afraid that our finances are . . . limited at the moment, and we would be able to offer only a fraction of what it's worth."

"Did I hear correctly? That this house is for sale?"

We turned to see Marc, dark and elegant as always, approaching us.

"Because if it is, I'd like to make an offer."

I felt the hors d'oeuvres I'd already consumed threaten to return, and if they did I would make sure they ended up on Marc's brightly polished Italian shoes.

Irene and George turned to Marc, their collective gazes taking in his expensive tailoring and shiny shoes and both seeming to find him lacking.

"No," Irene said. "At least, not yet. Melanie has been living here and taking care of this house for a while now. And she and Jack have two babies and a teenager. Our own boys will be out of the house in just a few short years. I think that this old house would like to hear the sounds of little children again."

Marc smirked. "Almost as much as I'm sure you'd like to hear the *ching-ching* of money landing in your bank account. What sort of figure are you talking about here? Because poor Jackie-boy is out of work right now, and Melanie is in a sort of holding pattern. Last time I checked, the market value of this house was in the middle seven figures. I'm sure they're not lying, saying they couldn't afford it, even if they did want it." He sniffed. "Which, if you ask anybody, Melanie definitely does not. Not so long ago she'd tell just about anybody that she hated old houses."

Jack took a step toward him, his hand already in a fist. I tugged on his arm, pulling him back. Forcing a smile, I addressed the Gilberts. "You are very kind to make this offer. And if we could afford it, could some-how scrape together enough money, we would do everything we could to hold on to this house." My voice broke and Jack put his hand on my back, letting me know that he was there. "But the truth is, we can't."

"Great," Marc said, stepping forward to hand Irene a business card. "I'm in the middle of my rehearsal dinner right now, but call me in the morning and we can talk."

Nola, who I'd forgotten was still there, stepped forward and yanked the card from Irene's hand and shoved it back at Marc. I was too shocked to reprimand her for her manners, and even more surprised by what she said next.

"What would be fair market value?" she asked Irene.

Irene looked at Jack and me for approval, but we just shrugged, not knowing where Nola was heading with her question.

I was proud of Nola when she didn't blanch at the figure Irene gave her. Instead, she thought for a moment and turned to me. "And how much of your own money have you invested in the house?"

I told her, still too surprised to question her motives.

She looked up at the ceiling as if doing a mental calculation. "Okay. Great. We can do it. It won't be an all-cash offer, but I can do about seventy percent down and then get a loan for the rest. If you can wait a couple of days so I can get approved and find a good interest rate, then I think we might have a deal."

"Now, wait just a minute," Marc said, stepping forward.

Nola turned on him. Stabbing a finger in his direction, she shouted, "Back off! I know how to hurt a man where it counts. So either be quiet or suffer the consequences."

Marc stared at her, stunned, and very wisely kept quiet.

Jack spun Nola around and held her by her shoulders. "Nola, sweetie, what are you doing?"

She shrugged. "I've got the money. I just sold the new song to Jimmy Gordon, and Apple bought the rights to 'My Daughter's Eyes' for a new commercial. The money's not in my account yet, but it will be soon. I'm sure we could make it work."

I shook my head. "No, Nola. That's your money. For your college. For the rest of your life. This has nothing to do with you."

She looked as if she'd been struck. Pulling away from Jack, she stalked toward me. "Nothing to do with me? I haven't lived here for long, but it's the only home I've ever known. And I've got a baby brother and a baby sister now who deserve to grow up here. And you, Melanie. You took me in and have been a mom to me from the first moment you saw me, no questions asked. You never made fun of my clothes or my makeup. You accepted me as I am, and helped my real mom find peace. If I can do this for you, and for my dad, it will be only a tiny bit of thanks for all that you've done for me." With her fist, she angrily wiped away a tear. "I really want to do this. What use is money unless you can use it to help the ones you love most?"

That was the closest she'd ever come to saying that she loved us, and I thought my heart would expand until it burst. "Nola. I don't know what to say."

"Then say yes. Please. I don't want to live anywhere else but here. With you, and Dad, and JJ and Sarah. This is our home."

Jack cleared his throat, his voice thick when he spoke. "All right, Nola. If you're sure. But only as a loan. We won't accept your help any other way. We'll sit down with our lawyers tomorrow and work out terms. All right?"

She nodded, her arms crossed over her chest as if she were trying to hold in all of her emotions. Despite our knowledge of prickly teenagers, both Jack and I enveloped her in a hug, and she didn't even fight back.

Jack turned to the Gilberts. "Is that acceptable to you?"

Irene had tears in her own eyes. "Absolutely. We'll make it work, and our lawyers will make sure it's all legal." She smiled broadly. "I think this is how it's supposed to be."

I nodded, then hugged her tightly. "Thank you," I said, turning to George and hugging him, too. "Thank you both. I don't know what else to say."

George smiled. "Then we'll say good night and let you get back to your party. We'll see you tomorrow."

Feeling like a spirit with my feet barely touching the ground, I walked them to the front door. I opened the door and George stepped out onto the piazza, but Irene held back, giving me a quizzical look. "Do you believe in ghosts?" she asked.

I coughed. "Yes," I said. "I think I do. Why?"

"Because I think the house might be haunted—but by a nice ghost. A maternal ghost. Every time I come here, it's like someone's hugging me. But it still doesn't feel like *my* house. It feels like a house I like to visit, but not live in. I hope the ghost understands that."

"I'm sure she does," I said, smiling softly.

Irene raised an eyebrow at the word "she," and returned my smile. "I think this house was meant for you and your family, Melanie."

"Me, too." I said good night, then closed the door behind them. Turning around, I saw that Jack and Nola were practically beaming, while a very unhappy-looking Marc just turned on his heel and headed back toward the dining room.

"So," said Nola. "Are you totally happy now?"

I thought of my sweet, healthy babies, of my renewed relationship with my parents, my friendship with Sophie, my beautiful daughter Nola. The house—*our* house. I was about to give a resounding yes when I stopped, hearing Louisa's voice in my head. *Listen to your heart and remember that sometimes when you think you have lost everything, you have won your heart's desire.*

Maybe it was necessary to believe you'd lost everything before you found out how much you really had. I still had my pride, clung to it like a baby clings to his pacifier. Maybe I had to give it up to win the one thing I needed to make my life complete.

"No," I said, surprised at the word coming from my lips. I turned to Jack. "Jack, I love you. I think I've loved you from our first date, when you made me wear a bib and eat barbecued shrimp. I love you despite how crazy you make me, how much you laugh at my Mellie-isms, and because of how much you love all three of your children. I just need to know one thing. Do you love me, too?"

His eyes widened, his mouth opened wider—not the reaction I'd been hoping for—and I felt my expanded heart begin to stutter and shrink back to normal size.

Jack stretched out his hands toward me, palms up. "Are you really asking me that? Of course I love you. I've loved you since you slammed the door in my face on that same first date so you could mess up your hair and make yourself more casual after I told you where I was taking you for dinner."

He rubbed his hands through his hair as he did when he was agitated. "I love you despite your charts, and your spreadsheets, and your vanity about wearing reading glasses. For crying out loud, Mellie, I sold my Porsche and bought a minivan. If that doesn't say 'I love you,' then I don't know how else to say it."

We were facing each other now like two chess players in a tournament, each unsure whose turn it was.

"Dad, seriously? You've never actually *told* her that you love her?" Nola smacked herself in the forehead. "Just say it already so everybody can get back to dinner."

We both looked over her shoulder to see that a small crowd had gathered in the dining room doorway.

Jack stepped forward and took my head gently in his hands. "I love you, Melanie Middleton. And I always will." He pressed his forehead against mine. "Marry me, Mellie. Please tell me you'll marry me for real this time."

I looked into his eyes, and felt my heart do that squishy thing again, as I imagined it always would when Jack was near. "Yes, Jack. Yes."

He pressed his lips against mine, bending me backward, and I kissed him back, our arms wrapped around each other as if we were trying to become one.

"I think I'm going to hurl," Nola said, but if she did we couldn't tell, since all the members of the rehearsal dinner—except for two, I guessed—had exploded with applause.

CHAPTER 34

My mother finished adjusting the veil on my upswept hair, then stepped in front to admire her handiwork. Her eyes were moist as she inspected me, her own veil already affixed firmly in her thick, dark hair. "You look beautiful, Mellie. And incredibly happy."

"That's because I am. I have Jack, and the children. And this house. If you'd asked me three years ago what would make me happy, I don't think I would have thought a husband, three children, a dog, and a house would be anywhere in my answer."

"Yes, well, it comes with growing up. And I'm so proud of how you've turned out."

She picked up my grandmother Sarah's pearls and placed them around my neck. The pearls glowed in the light from the bedroom window, a gentle reminder of the strong Prioleau women who'd worn the necklace over the years.

"Are you sure you don't want to wear them, Mother?"

"No, dear. I've already worn them—the first time I married your father. It's your turn now. And then you keep them for Nola and for Sarah when it's their turn."

I smiled up at her reflection, then stood next to her as we studied ourselves in the mirror. We both wore knee-length, cream-colored dresses, with short Belgian lace veils. Sophie had found the veils in a vintage clothing store and seen the Susan Bivens name embroidered inside. It was her gift to us, a reminder of how the past touches the present in the most unexpected ways.

"You look beautiful, too, Mother. And happy." I swallowed, trying not to allow tears to wreck my eye makeup. "I'm so glad you and Dad are back in my life."

My mother faced me, smoothing the hair on my forehead. "We are, too. Does this mean I'm officially forgiven for all my past sins?"

"There's nothing to forgive. Everything you did was to help me. I should be asking *you* to forgive me for being such a jerk when you first returned. I was wrong, and I'm sorry."

She hugged me, the smell and feel of her bringing back to me the memory of her I'd carried with me all of my life but had tried to forget. I breathed her in now, creating a new memory of the day we both got married for the second time.

Holding her at arm's length, I said, "You once told me something that I don't think I appreciated at the time. You said, 'If you wait until everything's perfect, until all your differences have been settled and all the stars have aligned just right, then you miss your chance at happiness.' I didn't believe you then. Maybe I had to come close to losing everything first to find out you were right." I gave her a lopsided grin. "Why didn't you tell me I was being an idiot about Jack and so many other things?"

Her smile matched my own. "Because sometimes the hardest lessons are those we have to figure out for ourselves."

A brief tapping came at the door, and Sophie entered the bedroom. She still glowed like the moon, still looking like she was only three months pregnant, even though it was only a week before her due date. Despite previous threats to make her wear something outrageously formal and non-Sophie-like to my wedding, I'd instead told her to wear the togalike dress I'd worn to her wedding, telling her she'd be more comfortable. Birkenstocks peeked out from under the dress— white, of course—and I smiled to myself.

Two small black-and-white puppies—wedding gifts from Rebecca—scampered through the door with her, followed more sedately by General Lee. The puppies rolled to a halt at our feet while the older dog barked to show he was in charge.

"Your dad's wearing a hole in the Aubusson carpet, and everybody's been seated in the garden. Looks like it's showtime."

"Are the babies already with Chad?"

Sophie nodded. "Yes—JJ's sleeping in the pram and Nola's getting Sarah to sleep. She really has a special touch, doesn't she?"

"She's a pretty special girl," I said, not able to put into words exactly how special she was to me. "Did you make sure to sit Dr. Wise and Detective Riley together? I have a hunch about those two."

"I did," Sophie said. "Apparently Dr. Wise also comes from a huge family, with hundreds of nieces and nephews. Last time I saw them, they were comparing pictures."

"Perfect. Maybe if I stop seeing dead people, I can turn to matchmaking."

Sophie raised her brows. "Really, Mellie? It took you how long to figure out that you and Jack were made for each other?"

I laughed, then turned to my mother, taking her arm. "You ready?"

"Are you?"

"Yes," I said. "I really am."

Sophie placed the puppies in the crate at the foot of my bed, then followed behind us with General Lee in her arms. She'd insisted that he'd want to be at the wedding even if he couldn't be in it. I hadn't made him wear a bow tie. His new stature as a father held too much dignity for that kind of frivolity. "I'll see you out there. I need to make sure Chad is managing both babies okay. And I guess I should make sure Jack doesn't make a run for it." Sophie winked, then gave me an impulsive kiss on the cheek before heading down the stairs ahead of us.

My father waited at the bottom of the steps, his eyes alighting on my mother first. "You're even more beautiful today, Ginnette, than the day I married you the first time."

I stopped in the middle of the stairs and tried to block his view of my mother. "Daddy, the groom shouldn't see the bride before the wedding. It's supposed to be bad luck."

He waved his hand in the air, dismissing my comment. "I'm the luckiest man in the world. I get to give my beautiful daughter away in marriage to a man I actually like and admire, and then run back to the end of the aisle and return with the woman of my heart and get married again. I'm living the dream."

With an exaggerated sigh, I continued walking down the steps until I stood in front of my father. His eyes were damp as he looked at me. "I'm so proud of you, Melanie. I know I didn't give you the childhood you deserved, but you managed to become the woman and mother you are today. I couldn't be prouder."

I stood on my tiptoes and kissed his cheek. "Thanks, Dad." I turned toward the sound of the string quartet warming up. "Have you seen Nola? I can't walk down the aisle without my maid of honor."

"I'm here!" she shouted, racing from the kitchen. "I had to rinse the bottles out, because Mrs. Houlihan is crying too hard to see straight. I told her to go sit down and I'd take care of it." She gave us an exaggerated shudder. "Ew. I think a few drops touched my hand."

I bit my lip so I wouldn't laugh. I'd told her that as my maid of honor she could pick her own dress, and she had, although it was obvious that both my mother and Sophie had been heavy influences. The shift dress with the empire waist and cap sleeves was a beautiful pale blue eyelet that made her eyes look even bluer. But to make sure that nobody would think she didn't have her own sense of style, she wore it with purple stockings and matching purple high-top sneakers. I thought she looked amazing and so did Cooper, apparently. He'd been allowed a sneak peek at her ensemble long before I'd been trusted enough to see it.

My mother kissed me on my cheek, then left to be escorted down the aisle by one of Jack's cousins, a younger version of Jack, and seated across the aisle from Amelia and James. They would be seated directly in front of Yvonne, who had stopped by earlier to give her best wishes, looking lovely in a large yellow hat with matching netting, her reading glasses and chain noticeably absent from around her neck. I'd asked that she be placed with family because, in essence, she was.

Daniel, the wedding planner, hustled after Nola from the kitchen. "Your flowers! Don't forget your flowers!" We'd included Daniel in the wedding, but not Rebecca or Marc. I still couldn't forgive Marc for making an offer for my house. *Our* house, I corrected myself.

Daniel handed Nola a small basket filled with the petals of Louisa roses, then handed me my bouquet filled with the same fragrant blooms. The scent was so pungent I could almost believe that Louisa was still with us. The string quartet began playing the opening strains of Pachelbel's Canon in D Major, sending Daniel into a minor frenzy. "Hurry, hurry! You don't want to miss your big march."

Nola looked at me and rolled her eyes, then followed Daniel out onto the piazza and into the garden dotted with white chairs filled with friends and family. I stood with my father as Nola began her slow walk down the white runner that ran the width of the garden and ended at the old oak tree, where Jack waited, looking absolutely devastating in his black tuxedo. Our eyes met, and everything else seemed to disappear and it was just the two of us standing in the garden of the old house that had witnessed so much of life over the years. And there was still so much to come.

He winked, bringing me back to the sound of the violins and cellos and the people in the chairs watching Nola scatter the Louisa rose petals—acting as flower girl, too, since Nola said every wedding needed one—and then Sophie, my matron of honor, following sedately behind her in the toga that looked perfect on her.

Then my father was leaning toward me and asking me again whether I was ready. I nodded and we began the longest and shortest walk of my life. I forced myself to look at everyone except for Jack, afraid that I would trip because of suddenly rubbery knees. I smiled to myself, finally knowing that I had the same effect on him.

I saw Thomas Riley and Dr. Wise, who seemed very happy to be sitting together, and spotted a man who looked vaguely familiar until I realized it was my plumber/contractor, Rich Kobylt. He was actually wearing a suit and, I was relieved to see, a belt. He was with his wife, Claire, whom I'd met only once, but I could tell she was the one in charge. I saw Joyce Challis, the new receptionist, sitting next to my boss, Dave Henderson, and his wife, Robin, and beside them an empty chair. Nancy Flaherty had recently retired after it was revealed that she was one of Tiger Woods's flings that had ended his marriage. She had taken her golf obsession one step further and decided to move to Florida to be near him.

I almost stumbled when I spotted Suzy Dorf in the back row, wondering who had invited her, and then remembered that I had, at the suggestion of Detective Riley, in the hopes that she'd finish up her column on a positive note.

My father and I slowed our pace as we passed Chad, who, instead of leaving the babies in their pram, had a sleeping baby cradled in each arm like a natural. I couldn't wait until his and Sophie's daughter was born so we could watch our children grow up together and one day swing below the branches of the old tree. My chest ached at the sight of JJ and Sarah, surprising me again at how much love a mother's heart could hold.

It all seemed to go so fast, yet at the same time like I was in slow motion, watching a silent reel of an old film. And then I was at the end of the aisle and my father was telling the minister that he would be the one giving me away. With a final kiss to my cheek, he stepped back and sat down next to my mother, who was dabbing at her eyes with a handkerchief.

Then I was looking up at Jack, and he was looking at me as the sun sent dappled light through the branches of the oak tree like a gentle benediction. I was vaguely aware of the minister's voice, but I must have made the right responses, because when we were finished, he pronounced us man and wife. Again. Jack bent his head and kissed me slowly and sweetly, allowing for a cheer and clapping from the audience, and a groan and gagging sound from Nola.

The quartet began to play "Ode to Joy" and Jack reluctantly pulled away, his eyes sparkling. He crooked his arm and I took it; then we marched back down the aisle as Mr. and Mrs. Jack Trenholm.

He didn't stop at the end of the aisle, but pulled me into the back garden by the kitchen door, where we were partially obscured from the guests by the corner of the house.

"What are you doing, Jack? My parents are about to get married."

"I'm sure they understand that we need a few minutes."

"For what?"

The words were barely out of my mouth before Jack's lips were on mine again, but this kiss wasn't sweet or slow, but hungry and needy.

I opened my mouth to him, kissing him back with all the promise of what was to come.

He pulled away, his hands still around me, his eyes dark.

"I love you, Mellie. I promise to remember to tell you that often."

I smiled. "I love you, too, Jack. And I promise to remember to show you how much as often as I can."

"Together always, right?"

"Always."

I imagined I heard the sound of rope against bark, and looked back to where the old tree waited for us, its branches spread out over the people and the garden like a mother's arms. I moved my head, seeing Louisa and a young Nevin by the swing, and they were smiling.

They turned and walked toward the garden gate, vanishing as they passed through it, his small hand in hers, together for eternity.

"Did you see that?" Jack asked softly.

"Did you?" I asked with surprise.

He nodded. "Does that mean Louisa approves of my living here?"

"It must. That's what Mr. Vanderhorst said to me the first time I came here and I saw his mother in the garden."

"Good. Because I intend to live here with you forever. And maybe even longer than that."

He kissed me again as a strong breeze teased the brims of the ladies' hats, making the shawls of moss that hung from the tree shimmy their approval. Jack took my hand, then led me back toward the garden full of friends and family and memories, ready to start our lives together.

And above the sounds of conversation and the rustling of leaves in the breeze I thought I could hear the applause of a multitude of unseen hands, and my grandmother's voice. *Finally.*

EPILOGUE

Charleston Post and Courier

Could This Really Be the End of the Story?

Last weekend Melanie Middleton, owner of the Vanderhorst house that has been the subject of this column for several months, married bestselling local author Jack Trenholm in the garden at 55 Tradd Street.

For those following this story, it is unlikely that this was the anticipated outcome. DNA results confirmed the inheritance claims by New Yorkers George and Irene Gilbert, yet the house remains firmly in heiress Melanie Trenholm née Middleton's hands.

The Gilberts have refused comment, but one can only speculate what must have transpired for them to relinquish their claims. Perhaps help from beyond the grave? No one is talking, although an anonymous note was delivered to this newspaper claiming that there are more bodies to be found on the property (as if three weren't enough!) and that we haven't heard the last from the house on Tradd Street.

We will wait and see. Until then, we will redirect our attention to other houses and families in the Holy City, where the living, and the dead, seem to coexist in peaceful harmony. For now.

Suzy Dorf, staff writer

Photo by Marchet Butler

Karen White is the *New York Times* bestselling author of more than twenty novels, including the Tradd Street series, *Dreams of Falling*, *The Night the Lights Went Out*, *Flight Patterns*, *The Sound of Glass*, *A Long Time Gone*, and *The Time Between*. She is the coauthor of *The Forgotten Room* and *The Glass Ocean* with *New York Times* bestselling authors Beatriz Williams and Lauren Willig. She grew up in London but now lives with her husband near Atlanta, Georgia.

CONNECT ONLINE

karen-white.com
facebook.com/karenwhiteauthor
twitter.com/KarenWhiteWrite
instagram.com/karenwhitewrite